MURDER

IN THE

HEARSE DEGREE

Other books by
TIM COCKEY

The Hearse Case Scenario
Hearse of a Different Color
The Hearse You Came In On

MURDER

IN THE

HEARSE DEGREE

TIM COCKEY

HYPERION

NEW YORK

Library of Congress Cataloging-in-Publication Data

Cockey, Tim.
  Murder in the hearse degree / Tim Cockey.—1st ed.
    p. cm.
  ISBN: 0-7868-6712-4
  1. Sewell, Hitchcock (Fictitious character)—Fiction. 2. Funeral rites and ceremonies—Fiction. 3. Undertakers and Undertaking—Fiction. 4. Baltimore (Md.)—Fiction. I. Title.
PS3553.O277 M8 2003
813'.54—dc21

                                      2002027458

Hyperion books are available for special promotions and premiums. For details contact Hyperion Special Markets, 77 West 66th Street, 11th floor, New York, New York 10023-6298, or call 212-456-0133.

FIRST EDITION

10 9 8 7 6 5 4 3 2 1

To Rick and Ann

MURDER

IN THE

HEARSE DEGREE

Ray Ghost sidled up to me in the middle of a funeral to tell me that an old flame of mine had left her husband down in Annapolis and was back in Baltimore. He had an insanely huge grin on his Howdy Doody face when he told me the news, the kind of look a dog'll give you when he's dying for you to throw the stick.

"You're at a funeral," I reminded him. "You might want to hide your teeth."

"Huh?"

"That's better."

Ray drives the panel truck for the Church Home and Hospital Thrift Shop, picking up old furniture and clothes and books and whatever various knickknacks people want to unload in exchange for a little tax write-off. It's where Ray gets most of his clothes. The man is a sartorial miasma. Today he was sporting a chocolate-brown suit that rode on his lanky frame like a pair of pajamas. Either the sleeves of the suit coat were too short or the sleeves of his yellow dress shirt were too long; the cuffs came out over Ray's hands like bells. Ray planted his feet and put a heavy scowl on his face. He jammed his hands into his pockets then yanked them right out again and, mimicking me, clasped his hands at his crotch.

"Saw her yesterday, Hitchcock," Ray murmured tersely, his eyes fixed on a spot on the ground in front of him. "Bolton Hill. Didn't look so good. Asked about you."

I brought a finger to my lips and quietly shushed him. Ray reset his feet and coughed into his hand.

"Right."

I was keeping an eye on the widower. A backhoe operator from Dundalk. Young guy. Deeply tanned and looking uncomfortable in his suit. We were burying his wife. She had just stepped out of Finklesteins the previous Monday with an armload of new jeans for her boys when an ambulance racing down York Road had veered to avoid hitting a turtlebacked old dearie who was caning her way across the street in full oblivion—deaf, it turned out. The ambulance jumped the curb, taking out a wooden bench, a parking meter, two newspaper boxes (*The City Paper* and *The Towson Times*) and by far the saddest fact, the backhoe operator's wife. The couple had three boys, each one exactly a head taller (or shorter) than the next. They were standing with their father, staring holes into their mother's casket, which was suspended above the grave. I had come across the eldest of the boys earlier in the morning, outside the funeral home. He had one of those thermometer-style tire gauges with him and he was scrabbling around the hearse on his haunches, testing the tire pressures. The boy had insisted on wearing the new jeans his mother had purchased for him. He looked to be around twelve. That's the age I was when I lost my parents and my unborn baby sister to a charging beer truck at the intersection of Broadway and Eastern Avenue. Not the driver's fault, by the way. Just a case of really, really bad timing.

The widower summoned me over. I told Ray to hang tight and stepped over to the graveside to be of service.

"I've changed my mind," the man said to me. He indicated his three boys. "They don't want me to do it after all. Is that okay?"

The number-one laugh line in my profession is *It's your funeral.* May I go to my own grave having never uttered it.

"No problem," I said. "Whatever you want. We'll take care of it."

I glanced down at the boys. The twelve-year-old looked like he was ready to kick the next person that spoke to him. I decided not to be that person and stepped over to a nearby mausoleum where Pops and his crew were cooling their heels. Pops has been digging graves in Greenmount Cemetery since before they invented the shovel. I spent some time myself crewing with him in my strapping youth, during my growth spurt. It was the summer I was trying to grow sideburns. Pops had a pair of muttonchops back then that held me in awe; they came right to the edges of his mouth and were black and bushy and thick enough you could hide toothpicks in them. My painstakingly culti- vated crop of peach fuzz was dismal by comparison. I'd rub dirt on my cheeks to see if I could get some of it to cling to the silky down. Pops taught me how to chew tobacco that summer, which made up a bit for the nearly inert facial hair. I came out of the summer nearly a foot taller than when I'd entered it, with arms like steel, dirty cheeks, and firing off tobacco juice with machine-gun regularity. Come Labor Day my Aunt Billie put a stop to it. I washed my face, bought a bottle of mouthwash and shaved off my phantom sideburns.

Two of Pops's crew were playing checkers, kneeling on the grass with a faded checkerboard between them while the third, a fellow we all called Tommy Haircut, was leaning against the mausoleum James Dean style, chewing gum and blowing a gargantuan bubble.

"You're back on," I said to Pops. "He's changed his mind."

Pops sent a missile of brown juice into the clover. "Good. I didn't like it."

I knew that already. Pops had told me ten times that he didn't like it and I had patiently told him eleven times that he didn't have to like it, that it was what the customer was requesting.

"It was a bad idea," Pops said, running his thumb and forefinger along his white walrus mustache.

"It was a fine idea," I said. "The man just decided against it."

Pops smirked then turned to his crew. "We're on. Look alive."

Tommy Haircut popped his bubble and shoulder-shoved himself off the mausoleum wall. His blond pompadour wobbled on his head. The checker players folded their board. One of the two let out a sigh of relief.

I went back over to the canopy where the dozen folding chairs were set and gave a nod to the widower to let him know that everything was fine. He gave grim acknowledgment. His plan had been to climb up into the cemetery's John Deere at the conclusion of the service and begin the process of filling in his wife's grave himself. The thought had come to him the night before, during her wake. He discussed it with his sons, who had all gone along with the idea. Apparently something had changed. I suspected the twelve-year-old.

The service played out and each boy stepped forward to set a rose onto his mother's casket. White casket with silver handles. Very feminine. The twelve-year-old paused after placing his rose and worked something out of his rear pants pocket. It was a scrunched-up Orioles cap. He glanced at his father—who nodded—set the cap on top of the casket then stepped back over to his brothers, accepting a grim low-five from each of them. The widower gathered them in like a mother hen—or father hen—and that pretty much concluded the affair.

I gave a nod to Tony Marino. Tony had been standing in his full Scottish regalia some thirty feet off, as stock-still as a statue. Despite the unique air conditioning afforded by his kilt, Tony was sweating like a frozen beer mug under his furry headpiece. The widower had made a particular request and Tony—God love him—had stayed up half the night working out a passable arrangement on the bagpipes. Tony carries the gold medal for lovelorn; there's not a thing he wouldn't do in the service of a severed romance.

Tony puffed up his chest. He checked the position of his fingers, then commenced to squeeze and wheeze.

"If."

That's a song. It was recorded years ago by a group calling itself Bread. It has nothing to do with the Kipling poem. It's what the backhoe operator wanted. On bagpipes it was bloody god-awful. Sounded like a herd of little lambies being slaughtered. Tony worked it bravely, his face going as red as a blood-filled tomato.

The backhoe operator collapsed into tears.

Ray Ghost had drifted over to Pops's crew and was jawing quietly with Tommy Haircut, whose insane pompadour was wobbling on his head like Jell-O in an earthquake. I signaled to Ray and he shuffled over.

"Okay. So what's this about Libby?"

CHAPTER 2

Libby was fresh from the shower when she pulled open the door. Well, nearly fresh; she was clothed. Her black hair was plastered to her head in wet ringlets and she had a towel draped over one shoulder. Her cheeks were wet. There was a bead of water jiggling on the very tip of her nose and it dropped off when she saw who was standing at the door.

"Oh my God. It's an undertaker."

I removed an invisible hat and solemnly placed it over my heart. Libby's huge grin stretched across her moon-shaped face.

"Hitch."

If Libby had aged a dot in the past six years it must have been on the bottom of her feet where I couldn't see it. I didn't ask for a look. She was wearing a blue-and-white-striped scoop-neck T-shirt and white slacks. She looked like an awfully sexy gondolier. The last time I'd seen her she had looked like an awfully sexy bride. Her skin was still as Kabuki white as I remembered, offset by dark arching eyebrows, a small mouth and a pair of large and lovely Pacific-blue eyes.

Libby hailed from southern California but she was no big fan of the sun, rarely going outside without one of her army of large floppy hats. Libby was slim hipped; a trim girl-like frame. I had always felt she could have used an extra pound or two and she had always said she loved me for thinking so. Standing there in the doorway, we would have hugged, except that Libby had something balanced on her hip.

"What's that?" I asked.

Libby shifted her weight. "This is my little monkey."

I leaned forward for a better look. "You're a cute little monkey," I said. "You look like the kind of monkey they can teach to talk. Quick, what's the capital of Alaska?"

The little monkey burrowed her head into Libby's breasts.

"Her name is Lily," Libby said.

"She's cute. She's got your nose."

"She's got no such thing. I've got this little ski slope. Don't you be insulting my child."

I tapped Lily on her shoulder. "I think your mother is a wee bit sensitive. Don't you worry. Your proboscis becomes you."

The child burrowed deeper.

"She's shy around strangers," Libby said.

I took a beat. "And they don't get any stranger than me?"

Libby tossed her head and laughed. "I wasn't going to say anything."

Libby invited me inside. The entranceway floor was checked in large black and white tiles. There was an elaborate wooden piece of furniture right there by the door that you could sit on, store things in, hang things on and check out your own reflection in. About the only thing it didn't do was make omelets and sing lullabies.

"Whose digs?" I asked, following Libby down the narrow hallway. Lily had crawled up her mother's shoulder and was peering at me with the dull intensity that children can get away with. It didn't waver when I made a face at her. We paused at the end of the hallway where a set of stairs spiraled steeply upward.

"You remember my friend Shelly?"

"Crazy Shelly? The one who reads all those murder mysteries?"

"That's the one. This is her place."

"Are there any dead bodies in the basement?"

"She reads the books, Hitch, she doesn't reenact them."

I cupped my hands to my mouth and called up the stairs, "Mrs. Danvers? Is everything okay up there?"

Libby smirked. "Funny."

I'm glad she thought so.

Libby explained that her friend was away on vacation for several weeks and was letting Libby use the house. The place was pretty nicely done up; that is, if you go in for old stuff. There were several small rugs on the walls, which I've always thought was pretty classy. A painting of an ugly woman circa a long long time ago. Antique bric-a-brac collecting contemporary dust. The furniture in the room where Libby led me looked like what you'd expect at Versailles, just perfect for a megalomaniac little Sun King but nothing terribly Hitchcock-friendly. There were two floor-to-ceiling windows at the far end of the room, overlooking the street, bordered by long oyster-white curtains. The September sun was streaming through the windows like God himself had decided to join us.

Libby set her daughter down on the floor and I moved in for the hug. We screwed up the choreography. Our heads nearly clunked as we each bobbed in the same direction. Our arms didn't quite slink into place.

"Wow," Libby said. "That stank."

Once we got into the front room Lily overcame her shyness and decided that it was of the utmost importance that I not only meet her huge collection of inanimate bears and cats and frogs and dogs and tigers, but that I pay close attention to the conversations she was prompting them to have with one another. The little girl spoke in an animated murmur, so I crouched down next to her to hear better. The talk seemed to center on a character named Sydney who I gathered had misbehaved in some fashion and was being ostracized by the rest of the gang. The details were murky. Lily grabbed a giraffe by the neck—not terribly hard to do—and used it to knock over three animals with one swipe. She smiled proudly at her achievement. I stood back up and patted the girl on the head.

"Cute."

Libby winced a smile. "It's been a rough couple of days."

I sent an eyebrow running up the pole. "So what gives? Ray Ghost told me he was making a pickup next door and saw you out on the steps. Watering geraniums, I believe."

"Mums."

"See? My information is so doggone sketchy."

Libby was rubbing her thin arms, though I didn't think it was particularly cold in the place. "Let's go into the kitchen." She turned to her daughter. "Honey, before you go outside I want you to pick up all these toys. Do you understand me?"

Lily let off a world-class sigh. Correct me if I'm wrong, but is it not true that little girls learn exasperation way the hell before little boys do? I followed Libby through the dining room into the kitchen. It was a French-style kitchen, with a large ceiling rack on which hung nearly a dozen copper pots and pans that looked like they'd never been used. Libby offered me tea. I don't really like tea, but I told her tea would be just swell. I was raised to be accommodating. I took a seat at the kitchen table as Libby fetched me a teacup. She stuck a kettle under the spigot and ran some water into it. She put the kettle on the stove and kicked up the flame then leaned up against the counter and tucked her wet hair behind her ears.

"So how have you been, Hitch? Tell me what you've been up to."

"Me? Let's see . . . not much new, really," I said. "Of course I'm a lot handsomer now, as you can see."

"I was going to say thinner."

"We call that 'trim.' I work out once a month now."

"I see."

"My golf game has improved."

"Is that so? I didn't know you played golf."

"Putt putt. I've finally mastered that devilish old windmill."

Libby roped her arms over her breasts. "I happen to know that if I try really hard I can actually get a serious word out of you. How's Julia? Is she still in the picture?"

Julia is my ex-wife. One silly year of marriage. Ill-conceived, awkwardly executed, ended by mutual consent. We're still ungodly close. Julia is the loveliest libidinous creature you'd ever hope to stumble across. Also an acclaimed painter. Also a nut.

"Julia? Oh, she's fine. Still working the streets, you know."

"What a lovely thing to say."

"I've been rehearsing that line. How did it sound?"

Libby grabbed a basket from the counter and tossed it onto the table. It was filled with tea bags. The wicker on the handle had begun to unravel. I stirred through the basket and picked out a tea bag with the word "berry" on it. I don't know my flavored teas, but I'm pretty fond of berries.

"So what's up?" I asked. "Ray told me he asked you about Mike and you snapped shut like a clam."

Libby leveled a look at me. "You never liked Mike."

"That might be. But you can also anagram that sentence and it would be just as true."

"Don't I know."

Mike Gellman was Libby's husband, though when I first heard his name some six years previous, he had simply been the unlucky fellow from whom Libby had broken off her engagement. It was about a month after Libby pulled the plug that I met her. She was sitting across from me in a booth at Burke's Restaurant ignoring a plate of French fries with gravy, looking very grave and very pretty. I'm a fiend for French fries with gravy, so I had insinuated myself at her booth and remained there until I finally got a laugh out of her. Eventually I was able to convince her to go out dancing. I keep a list of women who have been able to resist the patented Hitch two-step, and even in my excessive humility I'm proud to say it's a very short list. One thing led to about a dozen others, and Libby and I ended up spending the next several months together making the world go away, which I strongly recommend trying if you haven't already done so. I was fresh off my goofball marriage with Julia, and Libby proved a vivacious panacea for that unfortunate episode. It turned out that Mike was still very much on the sidelines, lobbying hard to get Libby to come back to him, and his pull on her was more than even Libby had realized. Several months into our festive bacchanalia Libby abruptly called it to a halt. Despite her jitters, she did want to marry and start a family. I didn't. I bowed out with considerable grace and at Libby's request agreed to meet Mike. As far as summits go, ours was not a qualified success. I found Mike Gellman charming and tolerable, but also a little too patronizing. I like a humble man—even if it's cleverly disguised—and that certainly wasn't Mike Gellman. But then I didn't have to live with the guy; I only had to sweat through a couple of drinks and as much phony bonhomie as I could muster.

Libby's hair was drying out now, thickening before my very eyes. Like one of those flat sponges you drop into water. She shifted uncomfortably, crossing her arms. Her eyebrows collapsed in on each other.

"That was a strange time for all of us. I really behaved very badly with you. You were so kind not to hate me."

"I like to think so."

"Maybe I'm wrong. Maybe you did hate me." Her eyes narrowed. "Maybe you *do* hate me."

"I think we used each other in equal measure. In the end nobody seemed to get seriously hurt."

"I'm glad to hear you say that, Hitch. I've thought about you a lot the last six years. You showed a lot of style the way you handled all that. I wish I could say the same thing about Mike."

"Well, Mike and I had our differences, one of them being that I was a good loser and he was a sore winner."

Libby raked her fingers through her hair. She suddenly seemed uncomfortable.

"Mike has been . . . We've had our ups and downs in the marriage, Hitch. I know that's to be expected. Nothing's perfect. It's all looked pretty good from the outside, but I'm afraid it hasn't always been the greatest."

"No one said marriage is a walk in the park."

"Mike can be a little difficult sometimes."

"Now, for example?"

"Oh yes. Now is a good example. An excellent one, in fact." Libby set her hands on the counter as if she was going to perform an impossible gymnastic move. Her mouth drew a grim line. "Mike's in some sort of hot water down in Annapolis. I don't know the details, but I can tell it's bad. He's been under a lot of pressure lately."

"I'm sorry to hear that."

"Mike's an assistant in the D.A.'s office in Annapolis. He's been a big rising star there. There's been some talk recently of his maybe running for his boss's job in the next election. Mike would like nothing better. You wouldn't believe how ambitious he is. He's a maniac. The problem is, there's some sort of internal investigation that has started up. And Mike's the focus. I overheard him on a call with his uncle last week. He didn't know I was listening. It was scary. He was talking about possible disbarment. That would kill him, Hitch. He'd be crushed. I don't even want to imagine. Maybe you remember Mike has a little bit of an ego."

Nine parts ego and one part water, if I remember correctly. But I didn't say anything. The kettle began to whimper. Libby turned off the flame and poured water into my cup, then hers. I unwrapped my berry tea bag and commenced to dunking.

"So then why are you in Baltimore, Libby?" I asked. "Does it have to do with this trouble your husband's in?"

"No. It's not that." Libby was going with Earl Grey. She removed him from his packet and lowered him slowly into the boiling water. Not a sound.

"I'm here because the bastard hit me."

Libby and I went back into the front room. The room looked like the prelude to the Saint Valentine's Day Massacre. All of Lily's stuffed animals had been lined up facing the wall. Only Lily wasn't paying attention to the dolls. She was paying attention to a chubby little boy who was sitting in the middle of the floor. The boy was dressed in red pants and a blue shirt, like the baby Superman when he came down from Krypton. Lily was covering the boy with kisses. A fiftyish woman was seated on the couch, poking through her purse. She had thick ankles and a jowly face. Libby made the introductions.

"Hitch, this is Valerie. I'm borrowing Valerie from a neighbor of Shelly's. She's helping me look after the children. Valerie's a godsend."

The godsend looked up from her purse and smiled. She had large teeth and a mole to the left of her right eye. The eye was also a little lazy, but then some days, so am I.

"And this is Toby."

The force of a hundred kisses was finally too much for the baby Superman. He fell sideways and seemed content to stay there. I tilted my head to look at him.

"He's chubby."

"You're supposed to say he's cute."

"He's cute," I said. "And he's chubby. Is he yours, too?"

"Yes." She added, "And *he* has my nose."

Valerie was taking the kids out to a nearby park. She loaded Toby into a double stroller. Lily stepped over to the wall of stuffed animals and marched back and forth a few times like a junior field marshal. She finally picked up a tiger by the tail and climbed into the stroller. Valerie leaned into the stroller like Sisyphus into his rock and got it moving. Libby walked with them to the door and I stepped over to one of the large windows. Bolton Hill is one of Baltimore's handsome old neighborhoods. I believe the Cone sisters lived here for a while. And F. Scott Fitzgerald and his wacky Zelda. Gertrude Gertrude Stein Stein might have set a spell here, too, at least so I've been told.

A man across the street wearing several sweaters and shouldering two bulging garbage bags was peeing on a fire hydrant. Nothing handsome about that. Luckily, Valerie and the kids were headed the opposite direction. I turned around as Libby came back into the room.

"There's a man out there peeing on a fire hydrant," I said.

"Good for him," Libby grumbled.

I came away from the window and went over to the couch and sat down. Libby had moved to the fireplace, where she picked up a porcelain figurine from the mantelpiece and was fussing absently with it. The figurine was of a maid milking a cow. Libby ran her thumb absently over the cow's nose. Her mood had darkened. Libby set the figurine back on the mantelpiece and glanced in the mirror. Whether she was looking at herself or at me or at the tail end of Alice, I couldn't say. Finally she turned around.

"Ask," she said. "I know you want to."

"Why don't you just tell me?"

She held her gaze on me. "Okay. The answer is no. It is not the first time Mike has hit me. It has happened before. He has a temper."

"A person can have a temper and still not hit people."

"I'm not making excuses for him."

"I hope not. You'd find me hard to convince."

"It's a difficult relationship to explain. Mike and—"

I held my hand up to stop her. "I'm not asking you to explain it, Libby. I'm of the opinion that one strike and you're out, but it's not my marriage, it's yours."

"It might not be for long."

"Are you pulling the plug?"

"Something has happened. I mean besides Mike's hitting me."

She moved over to an armless chair and settled onto it. "Our nanny is missing."

"Your nanny?"

"Yes."

"What do you mean 'missing'?"

"Missing, Hitch. She's gone. She disappeared."

"When did this happen?"

"Just this past Friday night. Or Saturday morning. I guess it depends how you want to look at it. Her name is Sophie. She's very sweet. We've only had her a month or so. She's around twenty-two, twenty-three? Great with the children. She's from Hungary originally. Her father died and her mother remarried an American who brought them both over. She's very quiet. Pretty much keeps to herself. I'm worried."

"Have you spoken to her friends? Anything like that?"

"She doesn't have any. Or if she does she hasn't brought them around. For the most part, after the children go to bed, Sophie goes to her room and reads or watches videos. Though the thing is this last week she started going out. She didn't say where she was going and it's not really my business to pry. It did seem to me though that she was in a peculiar mood. Sort of preoccupied. But I didn't think anything particular about it."

"How about a boyfriend?" I asked.

"I suppose it's possible. She's shy. Maybe she wouldn't feel comfortable telling me."

"So what happened?"

"Like I said, it was this past Friday. Mike was working late. No surprise there. I wasn't feeling so great. I was coming off a cold I'd had most of the week and I was bushed, so after Sophie and I put the kids to bed I went to bed early. Sophie said she was going out. The next morning I got Toby and Lily up. Mike was up and out already, on his run. He jogs down to the river and across the bridge to the Naval

Academy campus every morning. I looked in Sophie's room and she wasn't there. Her bed was still made. She hadn't come home the night before."

"Has she ever done anything like that before?"

"Never. Our last nanny was a regular party girl, but not Sophie. She's just the opposite, in fact. Which has been fine by me."

"Did you call the police?"

"That's the thing, Hitch. We didn't. Not right away. And I could kick myself. At first we just waited for Sophie to come back. I wasn't real thrilled that she would stay out all night like that and not tell us, but maybe she'd suddenly gotten a life. I was still going to read her the riot act, of course. We waited all through Saturday. Nothing. I did want to call the police by late Saturday, but Mike overrode me. He insisted we hold off. Mike deals with the police practically every day. He said they don't respond to a missing persons call until the person has been missing for forty-eight hours. If they're an adult, that is. Which Sophie is. So what did I know? I argued with him a little bit, but he kept saying we didn't want to overreact. He said most of the calls the police get are people overreacting."

"What about her parents?" I asked. "Maybe she decided to go home for a visit."

"I've been trying that. Her mother and stepfather live up on Long Island. All I've gotten is a phone machine. I'm guessing they must be away on vacation or something. And I'm certainly not going to leave a message on their phone machine saying, 'Hi, your daughter is missing. Call me.'"

"Could Sophie have maybe gone on vacation with them?"

Libby shook her head. "I wish I could think so. But there's no way she'd just take off like that without saying anything. It just doesn't make sense. So anyway, on Sunday Mike finally did agree we should notify the police and they sent someone out to take a report. It was after the police left that I went into Sophie's room and started looking around. I hadn't felt right about it up to then. That's when it happened."

"It?"

"That's when he hit me. Mike came in and saw what I was doing and . . . well, he just went ballistic. He snapped. He started screaming at me that I had no right snooping around in Sophie's room and all sorts of garbage. I told you, he's been under a lot of pressure. He just blew. One minute we were standing there screaming at each other and the next thing I knew, I was down on Sophie's bed with blood coming out of my nose."

Libby put her fingers lightly against her cheek. "I thought he had broken my nose. It was horrible. Then Mike took off. He just turned around and stormed out of the house." Her eyes went flinty. "And goddamn it, Hitch, so did I. Maybe he knocked some sense into me. You're absolutely right. There is no excuse for that sort of thing. And I'm not about to make one for him. I called up Shelly, told her what had happened, and she said we could use the place as long as we needed. She wanted me to call the police but I said no. I just wanted to get the hell out of there. I threw some of the kids' stuff into the car and here I am. I have no idea what I'm going to do next."

"Has Mike contacted you?"

"You'd better believe it. I let him know where I was. I didn't want him filing a missing persons on *me*. He's called. He wants me to come back, of course. He apologized for hitting me, but every conversation has still ended in a yelling match. It's really no good, Hitch."

"And still no word from your nanny?"

"None. I feel responsible for her. I could shoot myself for letting the whole weekend go by without contacting the police. What the hell was I thinking?"

Tears suddenly sprang to her eyes. She looked up at the ceiling. "I'll be damned. I am *not* going to cry."

I got up from the couch and handed her a handkerchief. No self-respecting undertaker leaves the house without one. She took it and buried it in her lap.

"Look, Libby, maybe I can help with this. I can't promise you anything, but I know someone who has got some experience in tracking down missing persons. He's a private investigator. Maybe I can talk to him."

She shook her head. "That's very kind, Hitch. But there's no reason for you to get involved in this. I'm just being silly."

"It couldn't hurt just to ask."

Libby poked at her eyes with my handkerchief then wrapped her arms around herself and began to cry in earnest. She didn't say yes, she didn't say no.

I usually take that as a yes.

CHAPTER 3

I won't go so far as to say that the Fell's Point section of Baltimore is an area that time forgot, though I do think it's fair to say that time hasn't made nearly as much of an impression here as it has on other sections of town. Our buildings are on the small side and have been around long enough to settle at slight angles, giving the impression that they're leaning against each other in order to keep from falling. It's a posture that you can see somewhat mimicked—especially on weekends—by the hordes who descend on Fell's Point's poorly cobbled streets to negotiate the numerous dockside bars that proliferate in the neighborhood. Fell's Point used to be a sailors' haven and many of these bars have changed little from that time. The counters are scarred, the floors are uneven, the air is smoky and stale. They filmed a popular police show in this area for a number of years. The show got a lot of bang for its buck when it came to local color. Whenever there was a crowd scene to be filmed, the production crew let groups of locals bunch together in the background to gawk on cue. I come across the show in reruns sometimes when I drag my television out of the closet and fire her up. It's like having a little magic window onto the neighborhood, seeing my neighbors there on the tube, all of them working hard to get their crowd-scene-gawker Emmy. The show is gone now, but they did leave behind a false door down at the maritime building that has "Baltimore City Police" stenciled on it. You can yank on that thing all day if you'd like to—I've seen people do it—but if you're looking for the affirming balm of law enforcement, you're not going to get it there.

The funeral home that I run with my Aunt Billie is a couple of blocks in from the harbor. It's called Sewell and Sons Family Funeral Home, but don't let that fool you. There was never a son in the game; Aunt Billie and my ugly Uncle Stu never had any knee nibblers, they simply thought the name would be good for business. I moved in with the two of them when I was twelve, after the beer truck made its quick work of my parents and my sister. One thing led to another—which is, after all, the nature of things—and came a day that ugly Uncle Stu was dead and I was a licensed mortician all ready to take his place. I took a stab at convincing Billie to rename the place Harold & Maude's. To Billie's credit, she almost bought it.

Aunt Billie and Darryl Sandusky were sitting on the front steps of the funeral home smoking cigarettes as I came up the sidewalk.

"Hey, Sewell," I said to Billie. "What's with the runt?"

"I'm not a runt," Darryl said.

"How tall are you?" I asked.

"Five feet one and a quarter inches."

"That's a runt."

Darryl snorted. "Give me a break. I'm only twelve."

"I forgot. The cigarette makes you look older. Gee, I guess that's the point."

Aunt Billie shaded her eyes to look up at me. "Darryl and I are discussing the state of the world."

"It stinks," Darryl said. He took a humongous drag on his cigarette.

"Shouldn't you be off chasing cars with your friends?" I asked.

The kid squinted up at me. "What do you think I am, a dog?"

"Does your mother know you're sitting here with an old lady putting nails in your coffin?"

"Huh?"

"Skip it."

"Darryl wants to be a mortician," Billie said. "I've been explaining to him the vagaries of the profession."

"Are you trying to squeeze me out, kid?" I said.

"I'll be dead one day, Hitchcock," Billie said. "Perhaps Darryl could be your new partner."

"Sandusky and Hitch? I don't know. Sounds like a bad cop show." I considered Darryl again. "You look pretty scrawny to me."

"You were scrawny at his age," Billie remarked.

"Yeah," Darryl said.

"I'll tell you what, next body we get you can help me scrub it down."

Darryl flicked his cigarette into the street. He looked over at Billie. "Is he shittin' me, Mrs. Sewell?"

"No, Darryl. Hitchcock is a man of his word. I'm sure he's not 'shittin'' you."

"All right!"

"Don't go planning on any big busty blondes," I warned him. "You take what you get in this business."

Darryl pawed the air. "You're nuts."

Who told him?

Billie finished her cigarette and handed it to Darryl. The boy flicked it out into the middle of the street. Billie smiled up at me.

"My minion."

I went inside to my office and leafed through my mail. Big yawn there. I had a fax dangling out of the machine. A mortician in Columbus, Ohio, was being sued by the family of a customer who—there is no way to put this delicately—had blown up about a week after his interment in the family's mausoleum. It's rare, but it happens, and when it does it usually suggests a lousy embalming—or no embalming whatsoever. The explosion can be surprisingly powerful. In this case the door of the mausoleum had literally cracked when a piece of the concrete vault slammed into it at mach speed. The mortician was professing his innocence in the grisly event and was faxing newspaper articles concerning the trial to his colleagues all over the country. I wasn't quite sure how we were supposed to show our support. Were we expected to travel to Columbus in our hearses and ring the courthouse? As best I could tell the guy had simply botched the embalming and that was pretty much the end of it. Naturally, he was being sued for millions. Nobody sues for reasonable amounts anymore; it's all this bonanza seeking. Anyway, I set my feet up on my desk, skimmed the latest installment, then balled the fax and missed the three-point attempt into my doorstop spittoon.

About an hour later I popped down the street to my place and changed out of my suit, then swung down to the Cat's Eye Saloon to see if pretty Maria was playing. She wasn't. The Ferguson Brothers were playing. Neither of them is particularly pretty. I chewed on a mug of Guinness then angled over to John Steven's for a plate of mussels and an argument with Greasy Kevin about which member of the 1966 World Series–winning Orioles, Paul Blair or Frank Robinson, had almost drowned in a swimming pool during a team party about midway through the season. Kevin swore that it was Blair. My money went on Frank Robinson, who had been acquired that year from Cincinnati to help the Birds nab the pennant. Kevin could simply not stomach the idea that a man who was batting a season average of .316, a slugging average of .637 and who was well on his way to MVP and Triple Crown honors could not negotiate a backyard swimming pool. We both agreed, however, that it was the O's catcher, Andy Etchebarren, who had noticed the floundering ballplayer in the deep end and had dived into the pool to save him, but that was about all we could agree on. After that it was rankle, rankle, rankle.

Alcatraz was working on a quantum physics problem when I got back home, but he managed to shove all the papers into a folder and stow it away before I closed the front door behind me. He looked for all the world like a long-sleeping hound dog when I came in.

There were three messages on my phone machine. One was from my ex-wife, Julia. She was calling to tell me a joke she'd just heard but she couldn't remember how it went. "It was *very* funny," she said on the machine, and she laughed hysterically at the memory. The second message was a recorded voice telling me that I had a free hotel room waiting for me at a resort somewhere in Florida if I acted now. I didn't act. Neither then nor later.

The third message was from Libby. I was standing on one leg pulling off my shoes when her voice came on.

"Hitch? Hello, it's me. Listen, I appreciate your offer to help out this afternoon and everything, but . . . well, it looks like you don't have to. Sophie's been found."

I yanked the shoe off. The power of the pull sent me falling against the wall. I had to play back the message to be sure I'd heard the final part.

I had.

". . . she's dead."

CHAPTER

4

Sophie Potts's life ended in the Severn River. An account executive for a local radio station had gone down to the river to do his morning stretches out on his boat pier and had seen what appeared to be a human leg bobbing against the roots of an old hickory tree that stood half in and half out of the water. The account executive was enterprising enough to fetch a ten-foot pole from his neighbor's pool house and prodded around the vicinity of the leg until suddenly an entire body rose to the surface, but he wasn't strong enough to haul the body out of the water. In fact, he had been forced to slip the pole's net around the head and shoulders to keep the body from drifting from the shore and back into the current. He used his cell phone to call 911, and when the ambulance arrived the account executive was nearly epileptic from the strain of holding the body against the morning currents of the Severn.

I picked up this information from a woman named Judith, who was manning the front desk at the Annapolis police station. It turned out that Judith was a sister of the account executive and in her excitement over the single degree of separation from a real live corpse—so to speak—she was incapable of anything even approaching professional discretion. Mike Gellman had been called in late in the afternoon yesterday, Judith told me, to identify the body, after which the police had managed to track down Sophie's parents. They had been vacationing in Florida in the town of Rat Mouth (you'll see it translated on most maps as Boca Raton) and, according to my loquacious source, had flown in first thing this morning to claim the body.

Judith rapped a painted fingernail against her blotter and gave me a knowing nod.

"They're here."

Libby was taking a beating. She was standing in a dimly lit hallway that was lined with plaques. A tall woman was seated in a chair along the wall, her face buried in her hands. It was a stout man with small ears and a flat nose who was working Libby over. The sneer on his face was a cross between Edward G. Robinson's and Elvis A. Presley's, which is only to say it wasn't a pretty sight to behold. The man was mainly bald—a few errant wires poking out of his skull— with a narrow horseshoe of dyed black hair. There was a small egg stain on his tie. I picked up on the harangue as I stepped over to them. His voice was loud and instantly irritating.

". . . I just don't *understand*. The girl goes missing and what do you do? You *wait* for an entire *day* before you call the police? What the *hell* is that about?"

I could tell from the look on Libby's face that she'd been getting this treatment for some time now. She spotted me and threw out an S.O.S. The guy had started slapping the knuckles of one hand against the palm of the other.

". . . she lived in *your* house, for Christ's sake, under *your* roof—"

I stepped in. "Excuse me. I don't mean to interrupt." Libby's relief was so palpable I could have torn off a piece and taken a bite of it. The man gave me a nasty look.

"Who're you? You the husband?"

"I'm not." I introduced myself. The experience didn't seem to rock the stout man's world.

"Hitchcock is an old friend of mine, Mr. Potts," Libby said. "He was trying to help locate Sophie."

Potts studied my face. His eyes looked like little black raisins. "Well, I guess you can stop looking."

"I'm very sorry about Sophie, Mr. Potts," I said.

But Potts wasn't listening to me. "Where the hell's the husband?" he snarled. "That's what I want to know."

"Mike should be along any minute," Libby said. The strain in her voice matched the strain in her eyes. "I don't know what's keeping him."

"What are the police saying?" I asked.

"What I've heard so far is they don't have signs of anything criminal," Libby said. "They're thinking Sophie jumped from—"

"No!"

The word came out on a roar from the woman who was slumped in the chair. Her hands dropped from her face and she rose on wobbly knees. She was tall, much taller than Potts, with deeply set eyes, rimmed in red from crying. There was something quietly regal about her; maybe it was the way she roped her arms over her small breasts and straightened to her full height. The woman had high round cheekbones and a slender hooked nose. Frosted blonde hair caught up in a green scarf.

"No," she announced again. It was a husky voice, thick with accent. "Sophie did not jump."

Potts moved to put a hand on her shoulder. "Now Eva—"

"No!" The woman shrugged the hand away. "Sophie did not do this! I want this to stop. I do *not* want to hear it."

There was a slight smirk on Murray Potts's face as he turned back to me. *Women. They can be so emotional.*

His wife glowered at me. "You were looking for Sophie?"

"I have a friend who is a private investigator, Mrs. Potts," I explained. "I spoke about it with Mrs. Gellman. She was terribly concerned." I aimed this last line at Potts.

The woman played her deep eyes all about my face. It was a remorseful and heavy scrutiny.

"Sophie did not kill herself," she said again. "I know my daughter."

Potts aimed a stubby finger at Libby. "I want a goddamn accounting. Be sure of that."

"We can probably do without the pointing," I said to him. I made no friends with Potts in saying it, but somehow I had already sensed that the relationship was doomed.

Two policemen came into the hallway. The one with the cowboy swagger—the older of the two—had a brushy patch of rusty hair atop a creased ruddy face. The stale smell of tobacco arrived seconds before he did. The brass plate on his shirt said his name was Talbot and I didn't have any reason to believe it wasn't true. The younger cop was black. He had soft brown eyes and was essentially expressionless. His name was Croydon Floyd. Officer Floyd nodded solemnly at Libby.

"Ma'am."

"Hello again." Libby turned to me. "Officer Floyd was the one who came to the house to take the original missing persons report."

Talbot was the acting police chief. Apparently the regular police chief was in a nearby hospital hugging a teddy bear to his chest. Open-heart surgery. The teddy bear is one of the postoperative therapies they use these days. It helps to keep the staples together. Judith the receptionist had told me all about it.

Talbot rocked back on his heels as he addressed the parents. "Mr. and Mrs. Potts, Officer Floyd here was first on the scene yesterday at the . . . where your daughter was found. Croydon's a good man. He's in charge on this." The man had a folksy sort of delivery that could cut two ways, only one of them being genuine. "It's an awful thing that happened," he went on. "I know you both must be in shock. But I want you to know that Croydon here can answer any question you folks have. Anything you need, you check with him. We're here to help you in any way we can."

The acting police chief tipped his head toward Floyd and gave the officer a hard look. It seemed to me that Floyd made a point of not looking at his superior.

Eva Potts spoke up. "I want to see where it happened." Her voice was quavering. "Where was Sophie when this happened?"

"Officer Floyd can take you there. He's all yours. Croydon, you take the Pottses along now." Talbot reached out and patted the officer on the shoulder. It seemed a trifle patronizing to me. Floyd showed no reaction, but my guess was he didn't like it. Talbot turned to Libby. "Give my regards to your husband, will you, Mrs. Gellman?"

"I'll do that," Libby said. Talbot flashed an inappropriate smile all around as he took hold of his belt and gave it a tug. His hardware jangled. He turned and walked off. The sense that he had just palmed this whole thing off on the young officer was palpable. It was my bet that halfway back to his desk the acting police chief was already sorting out what he was going to have for lunch.

Murray Potts slapped his chubby hands together. He'd probably hoped to make a larger sound than he did.

"Okay then. Let's get rolling."

"No Mike," I noted as Libby and I got into her car.

Libby pulled a pair of sunglasses from the visor and put them on. One of her wide-brimmed hats was on the seat next to her. "You noticed that, too."

Eva Potts had requested that Libby accompany them to see where it was the police believed Sophie had entered the water. Eva had—she said—more questions for Libby. We watched as the Pottses got into their rental car. Croydon Floyd was leading in his police cruiser.

"So warm, so cuddly," I said. "What does he do, do you know?"

"Potts? Sophie told me that he owns a chain of dry-cleaning establishments on Long Island."

"In that case, he needs to take that tie of his into work."

The police had determined that Sophie Potts had entered the Severn River several miles north of where her body had been discovered, at the Naval Academy Bridge. Despite the condition of the body—I didn't see it, but I'm going to assume swollen and pearly blue and generally wretched—the initial observations lined up to the idea that Sophie had entered the water at a speed commensurate with that of a body of roughly 115 pounds falling from a height of approximately six hundred feet. Which is to say, she didn't slip quietly into the Severn River from its lapping banks. The girl slammed into it. Libby told me on the drive over to the bridge that the autopsy was being performed that morning.

We parked our cars at the foot of the Naval Academy Bridge and walked up onto it, to the middle. It was windy; Libby had to keep a hand on her hat to keep it from blowing off. Libby and Croydon Floyd and I kept back some twenty or thirty feet as Eva Potts stood gazing down into the water. Her husband stood by, twice checking his watch and once taking a short call on his cell phone.

"So what do you think?" I asked the officer.

Croydon Floyd was gazing off into the distance. For a moment I thought he hadn't heard me, but then he turned and looked over at me.

"About what?"

"What do you think? The lady swears her daughter didn't jump."

Floyd let his gaze rest on my face a few seconds. "It's a hard thing for a parent to accept," he said. His tone was affectless.

"But you're keeping open to other possibilities?"

"Such as?"

"There's more than one way to fall from a bridge," I said.

"What are you suggesting?"

"Nothing, Officer, except that it's possible the girl was tossed from the bridge. Those things happen. I was just wondering if the police were keeping that possibility in mind."

"We're doing our job," the officer said flatly. He didn't look too happy saying it. I indicated the couple at the guardrail.

"I'm sure they'd appreciate that. At least she would."

The officer returned his gaze to the horizon.

As we were waiting for the Pottses, a blue car pulled up at the base of the bridge and a man got out on the driver's side. Libby frowned.

"God. What's he doing here?"

The man came up onto the bridge. He was tall, nearly my height, and as he approached I saw that he was somewhere in his late fifties or early sixties. His hair was silver and he had a yachtsman's tan. He was wearing a light gray suit and a concerned expression. The face reminded me of Douglas Fairbanks, minus the mustache.

"Libby. I'm sorry I'm late."

Libby was still frowning. "What are you doing here, Owen?"

"I tried to get a message to you at the police station. Mike's been called in to a conference with the D.A. It's looking very bad, Libby." The man threw a glance at me.

"I'm sorry to hear that, of course," Libby said curtly. "I still don't understand why you're here."

"Mike can't get away just now. He planned to be here but he's putting out fires all over the place. I'm very worried for him, Libby. He told me you're still in Baltimore. This really isn't a good time, Libby. I think it would be good if you two could talk this out."

"Thank you very much for your opinion."

The man coughed into his hand. "Well, as I was saying, Mike told me he was supposed to meet with the young woman's parents this morning. He feels terrible, but—"

Libby cut him off. "Stop it, Owen. I really don't want to hear it. Mike's not coming. Is that the message?"

"He can't. He—"

"Don't. The answer is no, he's not coming. Fine. If Mike can't find the courtesy to meet with the Pottses in person, well, that's that. But sending you as his proxy? I know you mean well, Owen, but that's pathetic."

"You have to understand, Libby, Mike is under intense pressure right now."

Libby exploded. "And I'm not? For God's sake, Owen. Mike hit me. Did your cherished nephew tell you that? Has it occurred to either of you that I could be putting on a little pressure of my own? I could file a report on him. You want pressure, how about that?"

"Libby—" He reached for her arm.

"Don't." Libby pulled away from him. "Look, I've moved out of my own home with two small children. Do you know what that's like? And now this. This was our nanny, Owen. Sophie lived in *our* household, Mike's and mine. She looked after *our* children. Mike should be here. That's all there is to it. He's got a hell of a lot of nerve asking you to come down here in his place."

"Is that them?" the man said, indicating the Pottses. Eva was looking back in our direction.

Libby moved to place herself in front of the man. "Yes. And I refuse to have you speak with them. I know you mean well, Owen. You always do. But this is unacceptable. Mike should be here. He's not. It speaks volumes."

"I'm sorry you feel that way, Libby," the man said in a soft patrician tone.

"You can tell Mike that you tried. Tell him that bitchy Libby refused to let you run his errand."

"You're upset. You and Mike need to talk."

"Don't start, Owen. Not here. I'm sorry you had to come all the way down here for nothing. But please, I'd like you to leave."

The man paused then turned away. As he did he caught my eye. He smiled warmly at me.

"Hello. I'm Owen Cutler." He gave me his hand. It was a surprisingly firm grip.

"Hitchcock Sewell," I said.

"Are you with the police?"

Libby answered for me. "He's with me, Owen. He's a friend of mine. That's all you need to know."

I concurred. "I'm with her."

Owen Cutler's gaze rested on me an extra second then he pulled it in and headed back down to his car without another word. He opened the door and got in behind the wheel. Never once had he acknowledged Croydon Floyd.

Before I could ask, Libby said, "Owen is Mike's uncle. As you can tell, they're very close. Mike adores him like a father, he always has. The two are as thick as thieves. It's so typical of them."

"He seemed earnest."

"Absolutely, they don't get much more earnest than Owen. He's a sweet man, really. I hated to snap at him like that. Owen has helped Mike and me out quite a lot. He's a very influential person. Owen is in a big law firm in D.C. He's one of those people who knows everybody."

"Now he knows me."

Libby managed a smile. "Yes. And just wait until he tells Mike."

Eva and Murray Potts remained at the guardrail for about ten minutes. At one point Eva leaned so far over the railing that I was afraid she was going to lift her heels and plunge into the river herself. When they finally left the guardrail and made their way back to where we were waiting, Eva seemed to be making a special effort to keep her chin up. Her eyes were dry and clear.

"Was that your husband?" Potts asked Libby.

She shook her head. "It wasn't."

Before Potts could respond, a bird began chirping in his pocket. It was his cell phone. He pulled it out and answered it.

"Yeah. Hold on." He looked at his wife. "I'm going to take this." He headed down the bridge toward the cars. Eva turned to the police officer.

"You will find who killed my daughter?" Her tone was both imperious and imploring.

The officer gave her that flat look of his. "We have no reason at this time to assume that your daughter was murdered, ma'am."

"Sophie did not do this."

Floyd held her gaze. "I'm sorry, ma'am."

Libby turned to the officer. "All the woman is asking is that you find out what happened to her daughter. She'd like you to do your job."

Floyd looked a little uncomfortable. He took care of the problem by pulling a pair of aviator sunglasses from his shirt pocket and putting them on. Now he was unreadable.

"We're doing our job, ma'am. There's a protocol here."

Somebody let out a snicker. It was me. Officer Floyd turned his head in my direction. Two slightly concave reflections of my own pretty mug floated in front of me.

Eva was shaking her head. "This is how her father died. He fell. Do you understand? From a building. Sophie was only six. It was the ruin of our lives. She would not do this to me. I know this. A mother knows her daughter."

Floyd repeated, "Ma'am, I'm sorry. But—"

"No! This is something else. Somebody did this to Sophie." She turned to me. "My daughter was a quiet girl. She does not think this way. I know this. You have a friend? You said you have a friend who would help you look for Sophie? Will you find out who did this to my daughter? This is not how Sophie will leave the earth. It is not. I will pay."

I didn't respond immediately. I watched a ladybug crawling

slowly along the collar of the woman's blouse. I honestly didn't know what to say to her. Eva was searching my face with an urging that was damned close to ghastly. Her eyes darted down and she flicked the ladybug away. When she raised her eyes again, the urgency in them had been replaced by something else. It looked for a moment like fear, but it wasn't. I realized what it was. Loneliness.

"Please," she whispered. *"My daughter."*

We headed back to the cars. Eva Potts dropped sideways onto the passenger seat of the rental car, her feet out on the road. She began to cry. Libby sent me to fetch some tissues that were in her glove compartment. She knelt next to the distraught woman. Murray Potts was leaning up against the squad car. As Floyd reached him, I heard Potts say, "That thing's been squawking for you." The officer pulled open the door and leaned in. He took up his radio and spoke briefly. I was too far away to make any sense of the crackling that came back over the radio. But Potts wasn't.

"What!"

For a little man he moved fast. Potts shoved himself off the car and barreled toward Eva and Libby. I dropped the tissues and darted quickly to insert myself between him and the women. Potts was bellowing.

"The girl was *pregnant!* Under your goddamn stinking roof and she's goddamn pregnant?" The man's ears were beet red. "What the hell is going on here?"

From the passenger seat of the rental car, Eva Potts let out a low, horrid, spiraling moan.

Eva wanted to see where her daughter had been living. Croydon Floyd offered to accompany us to Libby and Mike's house but Eva said that she preferred he didn't. She and her husband traded a few sharp words, but Eva held her ground. The officer didn't look too crushed about being packed off. Libby and I climbed into her car and led the way.

"The police are ready to just write this off," I said as we started across the bridge. "You know her, Libby. Does it make sense to you? Do you think she jumped?"

Libby shook her head. "I don't know, Hitch. But I don't think so. Sophie was a hard girl to get a handle on, but . . . no. It doesn't make sense. It sounds wrong to me."

I twisted in my seat. The Pottses were directly behind us. Eva was staring out the window. Her husband was on the damn phone again.

"How the hell do some people get together?" I wondered out loud. Straightening in my seat I looked over at Libby. She was adjusting her mirror.

"You might want to ask someone else."

We took a right off the main road and wound through a series of wooded lanes. The houses were large and set back off the road. Libby and Mike's house sat at the bottom of a short driveway. It was a modern house with large windows and no single plane you could definitively call a roof. The general impression of the house was horizontal. It was built on the side of a gentle slope that spilled down into the woods. Eva and Murray Potts took a few seconds to survey the property. Potts was doing his best to appear unimpressed.

We entered on what was essentially the mezzanine level; upstairs to the main bedrooms or downstairs to the rest of the house. We went downstairs. A large living room greeted us. The far wall was nearly all glass and offered a striking view of the woods that bordered the property. There was a dining area and a large open kitchen. The décor was modern without being tacky. The walls were alternately yellow and a pale orange. In a far corner was a flat stone basin where a perpetual dribble of water burbled and splashed. On the opposite wall was an elevated stone fireplace.

"Some shack," I muttered to Libby. "How can you stand it?"

"Where is Sophie's room?" Eva asked.

"I'll show you," Libby said.

She led them down a hallway past the kitchen. I lingered. Best way I know to snoop. I stepped over to a set of sliding glass doors and looked out onto a redwood deck. It was a large deck, built out over the drop-off. At the far end I spotted something that was either a vat for squishing grapes into wine or a hot tub. The Sewell dollar went down on the latter.

I slid open the door and stepped out onto the deck. The trees bordering the property cut off any view of the neighbors on either side. The backyard down below held a sandbox and a plastic swing set for the kids. At the far corner of the property stood a small wooden tool shed. As I stood there, a yellow butterfly swooped in front of me, setting off floods in central China if you buy that sort of thing.

I stepped back into the house as Libby appeared from the hallway. She was pressing her palms against her temples like she was trying to keep her head from exploding.

"Aren't you going to join us, Hitch?" she asked, forcing a smile. "We're having so much fun."

As we headed back down the short hallway together, Libby muttered, "I can't take much more of that man."

Sophie was in love with Gary Cooper. That much was clear the instant I stepped into her room. The actor was all over the place. Without bothering to count I'd have to say there were easily two dozen pictures of the lanky actor plastered on the walls of the room. Two black-and-white posters dominated. One showed Coop in his cowboy getup looking off to his left with that perfectly placid disarming expression of his. The other poster was from his Capra movie, *Meet John Doe*, seated on a doorstep with his fedora pushed back on his head, aiming a moony bemused look at Barbara Stanwyck, who was standing in front of him in the midst of flamboyant chatter. The other pictures looked to be primarily pulled from magazines. Cooper with Marlene Dietrich. Cooper lighting a cigarette. A bare-chested Cooper swinging a sledgehammer. Cooper in the French Foreign Legion. Above the bed, an aging Cooper gazed longingly at the doe-eyed Audrey Hepburn. Eva Potts was standing there looking up at the poster.

"*Love in the Afternoon*," I said.

She turned. "Excuse me?"

"That's the name of the movie."

Eva placed a hand on the picture. "Sophie always loved Audrey Hepburn. This is who she wanted to be like."

Murray Potts was standing near the poster of Cooper sitting on the stoop. It occurred to me that Potts himself looked like the sort of portly character actor that might have had a small role in the film. He jerked a thumb at the poster.

"Well, she liked this guy, too," Potts said. "But he's dead so it wasn't him that knocked her up."

There are certain reptiles that have a poisonous spit. They can send it out some fifty feet or more. Eva Potts looked as if she'd have found that trait handy.

"You can talk nicer about Sophie?"

Potts avoided his wife's look. Instead he turned to Libby. "And you still claim to know nothing about who Sophie was hanging around with?"

Libby was looking terribly strained. "I told you, Mr. Potts, I'm not 'claiming' anything. Sophie pretty much kept to herself. You can see, she liked to read."

Indeed. Next to the bed were two stacks of books, each over a foot high. I picked up the top book from one of the stacks. *Raging Comfort*. There was a couple on the cover, swooning together against a maple tree. Or maybe it was an elm. The woman's raven hair tumbled down onto a pair of ridiculously heaving breasts. Her partner was none other than Fabio. He looked like a sated lion. His eyes appeared slightly crossed. The woman was either in an ecstatic throe or Fabio had just stomped on her foot.

I looked at a few of the other books. *Isle of Temptation. Passion Winds. Craven Heart.* Eva took this last one out of my hand and gave it a glance. The tiniest of smiles played over her face. She tossed the book onto the bed.

"This is not Tolstoy," she said.

She picked up a framed photograph that was on the bedside table. She looked at it a moment, then turned to me.

"Sophie's father was crazy for her. He loved his little girl," she said. "I could never see them together that Sophie was not up riding on Janos's shoulders. Janos built buildings. He was very powerful." She paused, allowing her eyes to drift in the direction of her husband. "Janos was very powerful," she said again. "But with Sophie he was gentle as a baby. She was his *angyalkam*, his little princess. When he fell . . . it was from a building. When he is in the hospital, Janos did not want Sophie to see him like that. His back was broken and he could not put her on his shoulders and ride her around. Janos was not even awake a lot because of the pain. It was two days before he died. But Sophie never saw him. Her memory of him is always . . ."

She trailed off. Tears came to her eyes but she blinked them back. "We were a happy family," she said, nearly in a whisper. "I don't know why this has happened." She handed me the photograph then moved next to me to look at it, her shoulder leaning ever so slightly against mine.

The photograph was in color but had faded. It showed a younger Eva laughing alongside a handsome dark-haired man wearing an open shirt. A pair of sunglasses had been pushed up on his head and from his expression he appeared to be singing a song. From Eva's expression in the photo he also appeared to be singing it badly, but entertainingly. In between the two, cradled in both their arms, was a baby. Itsy-bitsy Sophie. She looked like a little pug dog in a bonnet. There was a lake visible behind them. Eva was in a swimsuit. She had magnificent shoulders. The smile was vivacious. The pair of them—Eva and her husband—were pretty enough to be movie stars.

"Nice-looking family," I said.

Eva took the photograph back and looked at it again. Her face softened somewhat. A slight smile tugged at the corners of her mouth.

"Yes," she said. She slipped the photograph into her purse.

Eva and Murray continued poking around the small room for a few more minutes. Libby stood by silently, her hands clasped behind her. She looked nearly as forlorn as Eva. Eva slid open the closet door and stood looking at her daughter's clothes on hangers. She pulled one dress out and held it up. Her eyes welled with tears. She gazed at it then wordlessly put it back into the closet.

"I've got some extra suitcases if you'd like to pack any of this up," Libby offered.

Eva put her hands on her hips and surveyed the room. "No. Thank you. What's the point? What am I going to do with it all?"

Potts was stirring some papers on the room's small desk, over by the window. "What's this crap?"

Eva and I stepped over. Potts was holding a pamphlet of some sort. A brochure. On the front was a clean-cut all-American family, mom, dad, son, daughter. The daughter was holding a cat in her lap. A golden retriever was parked nearby. "The ARK" was printed up at the top of the pamphlet in bold black letters, and in smaller text beneath it, "The Alliance for Reason and Kindness." Potts grabbed up a handful of pamphlets. Each had the same pose as on the first one, but the races and ethnicities were different. An Asian family, a Hispanic family, a black family. Only the dog and the cat remained the same. I took a pamphlet and glanced through it. The pamphlet was a fairly straightforward tract promoting brotherhood, motherhood, core family values and regular church attendance. From the bright chipper smiles on the front, I suspected brushing and flossing were implied in there somewhere.

"What's up with this?" Potts asked. "Was Sophie some kind of Jesus freak?"

"You will not call Sophie names please?" Eva took one of the pamphlets and scanned it. She looked over at Libby. "My daughter was going to church, yes?"

"She did," Libby answered. "She went to church every Sunday."

"Do you know this? The A-R-K?" She spelled it out.

"It sounds familiar," Libby said. "The ARK. It's one of those religious coalition groups, isn't it?"

Eva had moved over to the dresser. There was a small green jewelry box. She opened it and began poking through.

"Maybe I will take these," she said sadly, pulling out several sets of earrings and a few bracelets. As I watched, the woman went pale. She turned slowly to Libby. She was mordant.

"What's this?" She was holding up a wedding band. Her voice wavered. "Murray?"

Potts went over to her and took the ring from her.

"Jesus Christ."

Eva's shoulders sagged. Gravity took hold of her face as well. "I don't understand. I want to leave. Murray, I just want to go."

Libby stepped over to the couple. "Can I see that?"

She took the wedding band from Potts and eyeballed it, then gave it back to Eva, who dropped it back into the jewelry box and flipped the lid closed. She glanced once more around the small room.

"My baby girl . . ."

She left the room. Potts started to say something, then thought better of it. He followed after his wife. I turned to Libby. The blood was gone from her face.

"The ring, Hitch. That wedding ring."

"What about it?"

It took her a moment to focus on my face.

"It's Mike's."

CHAPTER

5

I had a customer waiting for me when I got back. His name was Oliver Engelhart. Mr. Engelhart had run one of the antique shops on what is called Antique Row over on Howard Street. In its long-ago heyday, Howard Street was one of Baltimore's bustling boulevards, south Howard featuring some of the city's premiere theaters and vaudeville houses. Charm City's Broadway. I'm all of thirty-four last time I checked, so I can't exactly start waxing nostalgic about all this, but I've seen glossy black-and-white pictures and it looked awfully good to me. Fancy sedans. Furs. Top hats. Excitable marquee lights. By the time I had reached the age of sentience all of that was long long gone, of course, and the only big thing remaining on Howard Street was the large Hutzler Brothers Department Store building, scattered wig shops, and anemic-looking shoe stores. The city has now banned a portion of Howard Street to all traffic except for buses and the light rail. It's a pedestrian street now, though my imagination fails to come up with too many reasons why anyone would want to be strolling around the old boulevard anymore. That is, except for north Howard Street and its Antique Row. Which is where Mr. Engelhart worked. Which is where my digression began.

A fellow named Clifford was responsible for making the arrangements. Clifford was a compact little man with a Steve McQueen haircut and hands as freckled as a leopard. Clifford wanted a viewing, and he wanted to know if he would be allowed to include in the viewing a few of Mr. Engelhart's personal possessions.

"Oliver had a grandeur. I don't want him just . . . *lying* there in a casket," Clifford said to me. "That really wasn't Oliver."

Well, I hope that really isn't any of us, but of course I kept that observation to myself. I assured Clifford that he was free to bring along whatever knickknacks he wanted in order to personalize the event. It's a long story that perhaps I'll tell some other time, but we once had a live ostrich at a viewing, standing at the head of a casket. The Health Department had wanted us to put a muzzle on the bird, which can be known to take nasty bites out of people with lightning speed. Of course no one knew where to locate a muzzle that could be fitted for an ostrich, so we ended up tying its beak closed with a green satin ribbon. Some of our visitors complained about the ostrich, some complained about the ribbon. This is not a world in which one can expect to be able to please everyone.

Clifford left me with a black-and-white checked worsted suit ("Oliver's favorite") and of course a photograph of Mr. Engelhart, along with an adjective to work with.

"Oliver was the most insouciant man you've ever met."

As soon as Clifford left I popped downstairs and got to work on Mr. Engelhart. It wasn't until I was halfway through that I remembered my promise to Darryl that he could help out with the washdown. Oh well. So I had lied. Something told me that Darryl wouldn't be too upset.

Mr. Engelhart couldn't have been more cooperative. Just a delight to work with. After draining the man's blood and replacing it with my own special blend of herbs and spices, I popped upstairs to consult the dictionary.

Insouciant (French) Marked by blithe unconcern; nonchalant.

Well hell, you can't get more blithely unconcerned than being dead. *Sewell and Son's Parlor for the Newly Insouciant.* Works for me. I went back downstairs and wrestled Mr. Engelhart into the black-and-white-checked suit, then started in with the cotton balls and the face massage. Consulting Clifford's photograph, I worked one of Oliver Engelhart's eyebrows up into a quizzical arch (this wasn't easy, but it's why I get paid the big bucks), and then with my patented invisible Hitch stitch I closed his lips together in an expression that was probably more dour disregard than insouciance. But the cocked eyebrow counterbalanced sufficiently, I thought, and overall I'd say that the result was pretty damned insouciant. A little puff, a little powder, a stinkless spray to hold the hair in place, and the man was as ready as he would ever be.

Pete Munger was kneeling in the middle of the floor of Julia's art gallery with pieces of wood scattered all around him. A couple of nails were poking out of his mouth. Tough guy. Chews nails. I picked up a hammer by the head, flipped it, caught it niftily by the handle, and started toward him.

"Here, I can take care of those."

Pete spit the nails onto the floor. He intoned, "Step away from the carpenter."

I surveyed Pete's work. He was building a new sales counter for Julia. Julia had been seeing a guy lately she called Eric the Red, and a few days previous he had driven his motorcycle right through Julia's sales counter around three in the morning. Julia had been riding on the back. What the two of them were doing driving a motorcycle around inside Julia's gallery at three in the morning was something I was beg-

ging Julia not to tell me. At any rate, the counter was a goner and Pete
had offered to build her a new one. From what I could see, Pete didn't
appear to be in a hurry.

"Remind me, are you building or destroying?"

Pete gave me the one-eyed glare. "Exactly. You're looking at a
goddamn metaphor is what you're looking at."

"It's a sure thing I'm not looking at a spanking new sales counter."

Banished from the fiefdom of her sales counter, Julia's assistant,
Chinese Sue, was cooling her heels on one of the large windowsills,
taking in the sunshine like a lazy cat. She was reading *The Mill on the
Floss*, large-print edition. The thing was about the size of a phone book.
I called out to her, "Hey, Sue!" She looked over at me with her patented
opaque stare and said nothing, though she did manage to make a large
noise turning a page. I love that Chinese Sue. So bubbly. So engaging.

Pete was grumbling on the floor. "I can't get my damn corners to
fit."

"Not to worry. You're doing this for Julia," I said. "Her corners
never fit."

"I heard that."

My ex-wife's lovely upside-down head popped down from the
fireman's pole in the ceiling. I stepped over to the pole and looked up.

"Hello, sugar beet," I said. "Did you know you've got a man on
his knees down here?"

Julia batted her upside-down cows. "Sounds lovely."

Her head disappeared. A moment later she came down the pole in
a languid spiral. Her big bare feet hit the ground and she gave me a
smackeroo. Julia was wearing white bicycle pants with the words
"Charm City" running up one leg, an oversized black T-shirt with a
purple Ravens logo on it and an Orioles cap.

"What are you?" I asked. "The chamber of commerce?"

She performed a little spin, flipping the tail of her T-shirt as she
tick-tocked her astounding tush. I was married to that tush for just
over a year so I can handle it. I looked over at Pete. He didn't seem to

have suffered a coronary. Or if so, he wasn't making a spectacle of it. Julia stepped over to where Pete was still kneeling. She stood in a wide-legged Jolly Green Giant stance.

"Interesting."

"It's a metaphor," I explained.

Pete got up off the floor. Pete's fifty-year-old body is the opposite of a rubber band. It was not a pretty ascension. Pete announced that he needed a drink.

"I'm game," Julia said.

The three of us went next door to Bertha's. A guy named Larry was working the bar. Larry didn't like me. His mother had died several years back, leaving explicit instructions that she be cremated. When I had refused to let Larry talk me out of it Larry had been fit to spit. His anger with me was now a permanent addition to his craw.

Pete noted the waves of hostility that Larry hit me with as I ordered three beers. We took to our stools, Julia in the middle. She explained the story to Pete.

"Hitch cremated Larry's mother against his wishes."

Pete leaned forward on the bar to look at me. "You can be a real shit sometimes, can't you?"

While we waited for our beers, Julia entertained us with a story of a trip she had taken the previous winter to Norway. Julia is a big hit with the Scandinavians. They snatch up her work like it's chocolate. In fact, as often as they can, they snatch *her* up like she's chocolate as well. She junkets there at least once a year for some serious adoration and snatching up. Her story involved a captain in the Norwegian Air Force, a very rare albino moose and very loud sex along the crest of a glacier "beneath the flickering green lick of the Northern Lights." Julia muddied the details (precisely who—or what—was engaged in the high-volume carnality was never made clear), but she managed to make the story entertaining nonetheless.

Our beers came. Larry set mine down sharply.

I rolled my eyes. "Damn it, Larry, it's what she *requested*."

Julia chattered on a bit more about her Scandinavian junket until finally Pete landed his hand on top of hers and asked her to stop. Julia stuck her tongue out at him and picked up her glass. We fell silent for a bit. Halfway down our beers I asked Julia, "Do you remember Libby Parker?"

Julia rifled her mental Rolodex. "Libby Parker . . . Oh yes, of course I do. That's the girl you scampered off with right after our divorce."

"Hitch don't scamper," I reminded her. "Hitch lope. Hitch saunter. Hitch don't scamper."

"Hitch don't talk too well either."

"Neither."

"Certainly I remember," Julia said. "She dumped you and married someone else. As I recall you were simply more fun than the woman could handle. What about her?"

"She's in Baltimore."

"That's just fascinating, Hitch. Wow wee, what a wonderful story."

"Sarcasm causes wrinkles," I said. "Makes your hair fall out." Next to Julia, Pete grunted. I continued, "Libby has left her husband. For now anyway. She's staying at a friend's place in Bolton Hill."

"And I take it you've seen her?"

I told her I had and I gave the two of them a rundown on my visit to Annapolis with Libby. Pete appeared to be only half listening. He seemed to be more interested in the play of molecules on the rim of his glass. But he looked up when I explained how Libby's nanny had been fished out of the Severn River and was having the word "SUI-CIDE" stamped on her forehead.

"You sound like you've got a problem with that," he said.

"Fact is, Pete, I do." I explained how Eva Potts was convinced that her daughter wouldn't do such a thing.

"Of course that's what she thinks," Pete said. "You think a parent can swallow something like that easily?"

"Libby's not convinced either."

Munger asked, "But the police are?"

"I couldn't get a complete read on that. The cop on the scene was pretty tight-lipped."

Munger shrugged. "Some people are tight-lipped. If everyone talked as much as you do there'd be nobody left to listen."

"I don't like it. It turns out the girl was pregnant. No boyfriend that Libby knew of. I think it'd be interesting to at least find out who was responsible for getting the girl pregnant."

Pete finished off his beer. He signaled for another. "And we're going to assume that this guy killed her, is that it? You're a regular bloodhound."

"Derision is the last refuge of knaves," I said.

"So I'm a knave. Is that going to kill me?"

"I've got a feeling about this."

Pete pulled out a cigarette and lit it. "The last time you had a feeling about something like this it almost got you killed."

"But everything worked out."

"You've got too much time on your hands, son. What you need is a hobby."

"What I really need is for a trained professional to help me out."

Julia looked over at Munger. "I think he means you, big guy."

Pete sniffed. "I know he means me. And he knows I'm not interested."

"No he doesn't," I said.

"He does now." Pete's beer arrived and he had a brief chat with it.

"How's this then?" I said, and I told them about Mike Gellman's wedding ring showing up in Sophie Potts's jewelry box. Pete came out of his suds with a sneer.

"So okay, now *he* done it. Damn, Sewell, you're quick. What do you think you need me for?"

Julia took pity. "Did Libby have any explanation?"

"None at all. She has no idea how it got there. She said that Mike never wore it."

"Maybe the girl stole it," Pete said.

"Seems like a strange thing to steal."

Pete shrugged. "There are strange people out there. You know that."

"Come on, Pete," I cajoled. "I know you want to help me. I have faith in the true humanitarian beneath this crusty façade."

The true humanitarian didn't have much to say about that so I let the subject drop and ordered another beer. A few minutes later I asked Pete about Susan. Susan is Pete's wife. I don't really know why I asked the question. Unless it was just to piss him off. The Mungers' marriage was like one of those relentless monsters in the old movies, the ones that keep taking the bullets but refuse to stop. It just lurches onward. Ever since Pete turned fifty earlier in the summer he'd been try-ing to figure out why his life stank and what he could do to make it stop stinking. He'd done a bit of noodling around in the self-help universe but so far what he had essentially done in response to his crisis was to begin to dismantle his livelihood—which was private investigation—start drinking more, and fall in love with a woman who wasn't Susan. As best I could see his life was still in a shambles, but at least now he had more free time, was drunk more often and he had a bittersweet bruise he could push whenever he felt like feeling sorry for himself.

"She's fine," Pete said flatly.

I winked at Julia, who turned to Pete. "Okay then . . . So how is Lee?"

He grumbled. "How should I know?"

Julia answered in a singsong voice. "Oh . . . I don't know. Maybe Hitch said something."

Pete glared past her at me. "What did he say?"

I leaned forward on the bar to address him. "I said I thought you're goo-goo for Lee but that you're determined nonetheless to make your marriage work." I held up my glass in a salute. "I also said this was driving you insane, not to mention those who get within swatting distance of you."

"*I'm* insane?"

"In your slow, laconic way."

Pete ignored this. To Julia he said, "Last I heard Lee was singing at a club down in Annapolis. I don't know if she still is."

"Annapolis, huh? Seems to be in the news a lot these days. At least in this bar."

"Welcome to the small world," Pete said. He switched to whiskey after his beer. I went ahead and joined him. "Make mine a double," Pete said to Larry.

I held up two fingers. "Ditto, barkeep."

Julia called out, "And they're off!"

Julia told us that she had a date that evening with Eric the Red. She said he was taking her to a tractor pull down in Largo.

I commended her. "You're really digging your hands into the soil with this one, aren't you?"

"I don't really think it's going to last much longer," Julia said. "I'm not cut out to be a biker chick."

I licked my finger and drew an invisible hash mark in the air. "Onward."

Julia took off to get ready for her date and Pete and I kept the bar stools company a while longer. I had been practicing card tricks lately and I pulled a deck from my pocket and tried out a few on Pete. He picked-a-card-any-card and after a couple of goof-ups I was able to produce the card from my shoe. Pete was unimpressed. Tommy Haircut had come into the bar with pretty Maria and the two of them were sitting off at a table under the neon Guinness sign. I went over to chat with them, then came back to the bar and cajoled Pete into picking another card. He did and I shuffled the deck. I asked Larry for four shots of Jameson's, and when they arrived I called Tommy and Maria over.

"One, two, three, down the hatch."

We tossed back our shots, then I reached into Tommy's pompadour and produced a card. I held it up to Pete.

"Is that your card?"

Pete smirked. "Okay, so you've got a hobby."

As the place began to fill up with the predinner crowd Pete and I migrated to my outdoor office, the rotting pier at the west end of Thames Street. We had a quarter bottle of Maker's that I had confiscated from behind the bar when Larry wasn't looking. The sun was dipping below the horizon, pulling a soft blue sky behind it. Pete and I took turns sighting the Domino Sugar sign across the harbor, using the bottle as our telescope. The red neon was brown and murky for a while, but after numerous sightings it began to clear up . . . which is more than I can say for Munger and Sewell.

We talked mainly about girls. Despite his earlier balking, Pete talked mainly about Susan. He gave me his theory that marriage is like a brick wall that both partners must beat their heads against equally if it is going to succeed. I had to admit that I didn't find it to be a terribly hopeful theory, but when I said this to Pete he pooh-poohed me.

"I've been married for twenty-six years. It's no easy sprint to the finish, believe me. You've just got to grapple your way forward somehow."

"So marriage is about grappling and about beating your head against the wall," I said. "You're very inspiring, Pete."

Eventually I rolled our conversation back around to Sophie. When I brought up Mike's wedding ring for the second time Pete dropped a paw on my arm.

"Do you know what your problem is?"

"No."

"Well, that's your problem."

"Your insight is blinding."

"Okay, I'll tell you. You want to get the drop on this guy. That's it. You want to impress the old girlfriend."

"Listen. Pete. I asked Libby some questions. I got some names from her of a few people we could talk to. Just to get a better picture of things." Pete said nothing. "Oh, come on, Pete. You're the old pro at this. You can keep me from looking like an absolute idiot."

Pete tried to raise an eyebrow at this, but the mechanism wasn't quite working. He rubbed his hand over his jaw.

"I don't get you, Sewell."

"There's a dead girl, Pete. That's what it comes down to. She got in twenty-three years and then she dropped into a river. That's it. Her story has ended. And her mother wants to know why. It makes perfect sense to me. Her girl is gone and she wants to be able to make some sense out of it. Even if Sophie did jump, her mother at least deserves a reason. You can't argue with that."

"And you're the one who is going to give it to her?"

"Give me one honestly good reason why I shouldn't give it a try. A real one, Pete. An honest reason."

"Besides the fact that it's none of your business?"

"The woman asked me. She invited me to make it my business. You tell me what you would say if someone did that."

Pete lit a cigarette and aimed his first drag up at the sky. Our bottle of inspiration was empty. We took in the night. A few flickering stars were penetrating the depleted ozone. A sharp brackish breeze came off the water in waves. A car alarm somewhere off in Little Italy was running through its routine. I recalled a time when dinosaurs roamed the planet . . . then remembered that I hadn't been around at the time. I was glad the bottle was empty. Pete took a few hard drags on his cigarette then tossed it into the black water. The water sizzled its thanks.

Pete sighed heavily. "All right," he said. "Nine o'clock tomorrow morning. I'll swing by your place."

He stood up. Rather, he made it to as level a position as he was likely to make for the evening, then made his way back down the pier. He looked like a man walking on a water bed. Some twenty minutes later I took up the empty bottle and aimed it at the Domino sign. Missed it by about four thousand feet.

CHAPTER 6

We crossed into Annapolis on the Naval Academy Bridge. The Severn River was a deep blue and rippled with diamonds. My head was feeling a little rippled as well. Sailboats were out on the water. Also a pair of scullers, slicing cleanly through the water, trading the lead like the tips of cross-country skis.

When Pete picked me up earlier I had told him that my head felt like it was in two pieces. He requested that they be two silent pieces, so I crunched up against the passenger-side door and went back to sleep until we reached the bridge. Frank Sinatra was singing when I woke up, backed by the Tommy Dorsey Orchestra. "Street of Dreams." Munger was singing along. Or humming. Or muttering. Whatever he was doing I knew he wouldn't want me catching him doing it, so I came up stretching and yawning.

"Nice sleep?" Pete asked, turning down the Frank.

"I feel like a new man."

Pete looked me over. "You're not."

The Naval Academy chapel appeared to our left as we crossed the bridge. Pete asked me if I knew who was buried there. I didn't.

"Who?"

"John Paul Jones."

"John Paul Jones. Wait," I said. "I can get this."

Pete shook his head. "You'd think someone in your line of work would be up on where the famous people in the area are buried."

"I am. I know where Poe is buried. And Francis Scott Key. And John Wilkes Booth. Almost no one knows that one."

"Good for you."

"And Mencken," I went on. "And the lead singer for the Ashtrays."

"Who are the Ashtrays?"

"The Ashtrays. Great garage band. They used to play at the Marble Bar during my misspent youth."

"What happened?"

"I grew up. Got staid and boring."

Munger looked over at me. "I jerk this wheel, we take a bath."

"The lead singer of the Ashtrays fell off a wooden fence and broke his neck," I said. "No one could quite figure out how he did it. The band was nothing without him. They folded."

Pete raised a professorial finger. "'I have not yet begun to fight,'" he proclaimed. "John Paul Jones."

We were coming down off the bridge. A motorcycle raced through the intersection in front of us. A paper cup was skipping across the street. I raised *my* finger.

"'Don't spit on my heart.' Ashtrays."

Annapolis is the state capital of Maryland. The original city hugs a small and picturesque harbor and runs gently uphill from there on several narrow streets of small brick and clapboard houses along with the wide Main Street, with enough little shoppes to fill your little shoppe needs. At the crest of the hill sits the statehouse, a handsome colonial brick building with an elongated wooden dome, more of a cupola really. It is the oldest continual-use statehouse in the nifty fifties and it is where the Treaty of Paris was signed in 1783, officially calling an end to the Revolutionary War and declaring the pesky colonists winners and all-around champeens. What they were doing signing a Treaty of Paris in Annapolis is something I must have slept through during high school history class. The building is also where George Washington officially stepped down as generalissimo of the U.S. Army so that he could begin laying the groundwork to pose for the dollar bill.

I learned all this from reading a metal plaque that was planted on the statehouse grounds. Pete had double-parked in front of a deli to run in and buy a pack of cigarettes and I had wandered off to the state-house to drink in a little history. When Pete came back he leaned on the horn. When he did, a flock of seagulls took flight.

"For that," I told him as I was getting back into the car, "I'm not going to tell you what I learned."

Pete slid in behind the wheel. "For that, I'm grateful."

The Annapolis Visitors Center was only a few blocks away. We swung by and picked up a map. It turned out the place we were going was only a few blocks away, on Calvert Street. I had called ahead, first thing in the morning. Even so, the woman who met us at the door seemed a little uncertain. She remained behind the screen door while she checked us out.

"Mrs. Pierce? I'm Hitchcock Sewell. We spoke on the phone this morning?"

Pete had his wallet open and was pressing it against the screen. It identified him as a bona fide private investigator. I had a card, too, but all it did was prove that I buried people for a living. I decided to keep it in my wallet.

"We just want to ask you a few questions," Pete said.

The woman replied, "I said to you on the phone, I haven't heard from Sophie since the beginning of the summer."

"We understand that," Munger said. "We won't take long."

The woman considered the two of us a few seconds longer. She must have determined that we weren't in fact vacuum-cleaner salesmen employing an elaborate ruse in order to get ourselves inside and toss black dirt down on her carpet. She opened the door and let us in. We were led to a sun porch. It was so choked with a flower motif I half expected to see bees buzzing around the cushions.

Kathy Pierce was a skinny woman with a pinched nose and a nervous tic. She wore—naturally enough—a floral-print skirt along with a navy blue blouse.

"This is so tragic," she said. "That poor girl."

"How long did Miss Potts work for you?" Pete asked.

"Just under a year."

"And how many children do you have?"

"Two. Patrick and Patricia. They're twins."

"How was Miss Potts?" I asked. "I mean, as a nanny? Was she responsible? Were you happy with her?"

The woman bobbed her head vigorously. "Oh yes. Sophie was wonderful with the children. Paul used to say Sophie wasn't much more than a kid herself."

"Paul's your husband?"

"Yes."

"What exactly did your husband mean by that?" Pete asked. "Did he mean she was immature? Naïve?"

"Playful. That's really what he meant. Sophie just had a natural way with children. She was more comfortable with children than she was with adults. She could be very shy."

Pete asked, "Any boyfriends?"

"Certainly not while she was living with us."

"She was from New York, is that right?"

"Hungary originally. But grew up on Long Island."

"Did she talk about that?" Pete asked. "I mean, about her friends back home? Maybe a boyfriend up there?"

The woman shook her head. "When she talked at all about her life

Sophie spoke more about growing up in Hungary. She said she was there until she was eleven."

I asked, "That's when she came to America?"

"Yes. Do you know the story? She lost her father when she was only six. Then her mother remarried and they came over here. I could hear from the way she told it how horrible it all was for her."

"Did Sophie ever talk to you about her father?"

"She did talk about him a few times. Briefly. It was clear she still missed him. She told me once how sad she was that she only had a handful of memories of him. She had lots of stories from her mother, but her actual memories of her father, she said, were just of a few events. She said to me once that sometimes she pretended that he was still alive, that he was still living in Hungary and that this was the only reason she didn't see him. Because he's there and she's here."

"Do you know if she blamed her mother for bringing her over?"

Kathy Pierce frowned. "Why no, she certainly never implied anything like that."

"Just a thought."

Pete leaned forward in his chair. "Aren't you a little off subject here?"

I shrugged. "Just trying to put a picture together."

"The fact is, probably the most animated I'd see Sophie was right after she'd gotten off the phone with her mother. They'd speak in a mix of English and Hungarian. Sophie would be almost chatty after talking on the phone."

"How was her English?" Pete asked.

"Oh, it was fine. Perfect, really. There was a bit of an accent, very light."

"Do you know what she did for fun, Mrs. Pierce?" I asked. "I assume she had time off."

"She had a bicycle that she loved to ride around. She loved the water, even though she told me that she couldn't swim. But she was always riding to the river and down to the harbor. We had some friends over once who have a sailboat, and the subject came up. They offered to take Sophie out on the boat one Saturday. Sophie was so shy, she kept saying no, no, no, even though it was clear that she was dying to do it. I cajoled her and finally she said yes."

Pete shifted in his chair. "So she went?"

"Yes. She was practically bursting when she got back in the evening. You've never seen someone so happy. She began pulling pictures of sailboats out of my magazines before I recycled them. She put them up on her wall. Along with her movie posters. Sophie loved old American movies. She was always getting them from the video store."

Pete and I tossed a few more questions, but there didn't seem to be much more to ask. Pete stood up and thanked her for her time. She followed us to the front door, where Pete paused.

"One more thing," Pete said. "Can you tell us about the circumstances of your letting Sophie go?"

The woman's head flicked like a bird's, taking in both of us. "There were no 'circumstances.' The twins started first grade this year. Sophie knew that we wouldn't be needing her once they started school. It was understood."

"So you didn't fire her. She didn't quit. Nothing like that."

"No. Not at all."

A thought came to me. "Mrs. Pierce, do you have a picture of Sophie?"

"I certainly do. I have one on my refrigerator. Hold on."

While she was off fetching the snapshot, I asked Pete what he thought. He shrugged.

"Naïve girl. No friends. Likes kids. Loved the water. Read books. Rode a bike. Enjoyed old movies. Hadn't ever gotten over leaving Hungary. Missed her daddy."

"Damn. You're good at this."

Pete took hold of my earlobe and tugged on it. "Use it."

Kathy Pierce came back and handed Pete a photograph. He looked it over then handed it to me.

"It was taken at Christmas," Kathy Pierce said.

Chances are that the Douglas fir in the photograph festooned with decorations and colored lights would have tipped me off, but I knew the woman was only trying to be helpful. The photograph showed a young woman standing in front of the Christmas tree. The twins were on either side of her. Little Patricia was wincing an overlarge smile and on the other side of the nanny, darling Patrick was sticking out his tongue at the camera and bugging his eyes. The twins were dressed in matching red and green outfits. Like elves from hell.

For her part, Sophie seemed oblivious to the overposing going on around her. She stood erect, her hands down at her sides, wearing a dark blue dress that fell just below the knees. Her brown hair was an explosion of unkempt waves falling well past her shoulders. Sophie had a slender hooked nose, like her mother, and a small pointed chin. Her eyebrows were thick and quite dark, as were her eyes. Unlike her mother, however, the girl looked to be short. Maybe five four. She was slightly built, though not exactly waiflike. The look on her face was extremely earnest. Her smile was tiny, almost imperceptible.

"She's cute," I said. "She looks like a real nice kid."

Kathy Pierce took the picture back. "Yes, she . . . well, she was."

Pete handed her his card, along with his rap about giving him a call if she thought of anything that we might want to hear. We thanked her for her time and returned to Pete's car.

"Where next, Sherlock?" Pete asked me.

I opened up the Annapolis map on my lap. I ran my fingers along the paper.

"Go up here and take a right," I said. "Then a left. Then check back with me."

In about ten minutes we pulled up in front of a three-story brown clapboard house that sat back from the sidewalk on a nick of land that needed some watering and maybe just the slightest bit of thought. The windows had pale blue shutters with the design of a simple sailboat jig sawed into them. A pair of last-gasp bushes sat on either side of the front door, looking like lost tumbleweeds a long long way from home. Planted in the middle of the yard was a wooden duck, painted yellow and red. Its wings windmilled backward in the breeze, like it was trying to get the hell away from this place. The door knocker was a crab.

The woman who answered the crab had a head of hair not dissimilar to the dying bushes, only smaller, of course, and in her case sprayed orange. The parts that had missed the spray were a dull pewter. She was wearing a blouse of such electric fuchsia that it hurt my eyes to look at it, and a pair of lime-green slacks, the hips of which filled half the doorway. The woman was close to sixty. She looked like George Washington. I was awestruck.

She sang out, "Can I help you?"

"You're Mrs. Gibbons?" I asked.

"Stella Gibbons."

"I'm Hitchcock Sewell. I phoned this morning?"

"You most certainly did."

"Mrs. Gibbons, we'd like to talk to you about a boarder you had here a while back," Pete said.

"Yes, I know. Sophie Potts." The woman pursed her lips and took a hard look at Pete. "Are you her daddy?" She let out the sort of cackling laugh that would split ice. "I'm teasing with you, hon." She gave Pete a conspiratorial look. "Unless you *are*?"

"Unless I'm what?" Pete asked.

"Her daddy."

"We'd like to ask you a few questions about Sophie," I said. "You see, she—"

"Come in, come in, come in."

She swung the door wide open and ushered us in. She made a big fuss about inviting us into the parlor. That's what Stella Gibbons called it. She popped her *p* when she said it. "The *p*arlor." I might have called it a walk-in closet. It turned out to be a stuffy wood-paneled room that absolutely slaughtered what little natural light came in through the small windows. On one wall was a pair of carved wooden ducks frozen in flight. The wall opposite held wooden cutouts of a crab, a lighthouse and a ship's anchor. The couch that Pete and I took looked like it had a body stuffed into it. It was all about springs. Pete sat first and when I followed, Pete gently elevated.

Stella Gibbons turned out to be all about springs, too. At the slightest provocation she was up on her feet and fetching something for Pete and me to take a look at. A Chesapeake Bay retriever had nothing on this woman. There was a photograph we simply had to see, of her late husband, Randall, and herself, posing together with a twenty-pound bluefish that the two had hauled in during a fishing excursion in the bay. The photo must have been at least thirty years old as best I could tell. Stella Gibbons claimed to have fetched it so that we could see her late husband ("May he rest in his peas," she cackled), but it was my guess she was showing it to us more for the leggy charm that her younger self had been able to pull off. Randall Gibbons was wearing a large floppy hat that totally obscured his face. The woman fetched us cookies and lemonade. She fetched a book of photographs by A. Aubrey Bodine, turning to a dog-eared page that included a black-and-white picture of three naked boys diving into a river from a wooden bridge. Stella placed her finger directly on the skinny butt of one of the boys. "Jeremy Lynch. First boy I ever kissed. And not the last!" We got another sample of her laughter with that one.

"You caught me on pinochle day," Stella announced, flouncing down on the couch between Pete and me. We rose and fell like a cal- liope. "On Friday the witches all get together for pinochle and mint juleps." She winked at Pete. "You ought to catch me *after* pinochle."

We finally crowbarred the conversation around to the subject of Sophie.

"You rented a room to Miss Potts for several months this summer, isn't that right?" Pete asked.

"That's right. Bath down the hall. Kitchen privileges. Why? What's wrong? That little girl rob a bank?"

"That little girl is dead," I said.

Stella's face froze. "What do you mean, dead?"

"Miss Potts was pulled from the Severn day before yesterday," Pete said. He shot me a look before continuing. "It appears that she jumped off the Naval Academy Bridge. The police aren't sure when. It might have been as long as a week ago."

"That little scamp? I just can't believe it. Why in heaven's name would she want to do something like that?"

"That's exactly what we're trying to figure out," I said.

Stella shook her head slowly. "Isn't that the silliest thing in the world?"

"So the police haven't been by to ask you anything about Sophie?" I asked.

"The police? Not at all."

Pete asked, "What can you tell us about her?"

"About Sophie? Well, sweet little girl. Wouldn't know how to have fun if you wrote it on her forehead."

"What do you mean by that?"

"Just that. Cute little thing once you fixed her up, but as homely as a rug when she first got here. I'd tell her, get out there and have some fun while you're young. Get yourself a boyfriend. Not that it was any of my business, of course. But the girl would much rather hole up in her room and read her damn romance books. I'd tease her. I'd say, 'Sophie, while you were out Mr. Fabio himself was here to see you. He was right here in the parlor, honey, wearing that tattered shirt of his.'"

She cackled again, and slapped her hand down on Munger's knee.

"I fixed her up, though," Stella went on. "If I do say so myself."

Pete asked, "Fixed her up?"

"Did you ever meet her?" Stella asked us. "Do you know what she used to look like?"

"We just came from the home where she worked before she came here," I said. "We saw a picture of her."

"Was it one with all that hair of hers?"

"She had a good head of hair, yes," I said.

"Lopped it off," Stella said proudly. "I took her into town myself and sat her down in Elsbeth Finkle's chair and I told Elsbeth exactly what we wanted."

"Excuse me," Pete said, "what do you mean by that? What *we* wanted?"

Stella gave Pete a fierce look. "Girl looked like a little ragamuffin when she got here. I told her if I didn't know better she could have passed for a twelve-year-old. No sense of style in that child. None at all. I'm sorry, you might say it was none of my business, but I say a person only lives once. And I told her. I told her we were going to get her fixed up and I got Elsbeth to lop off that hopeless hair of hers and we got her nice and cute in a little bob cut. Now that, I told her, that's sophisticated. Give the boys something to look at. You could see her face, for goodness sake. With all that crazy hair she was like someone peeking out of a cave. Still had to pinch the silly little thing to get her to smile, but at least now you could see it. And for a little thing the girl had herself a nice little fig- ure." She grinned at Pete. The way a shark grins at a foot wagging off a raft. "And don't men like a good figure. Of course the problem was you wouldn't know Sophie was even a woman in those god-awful sacks she wore. So I got her to pick up a few nice-looking outfits."

I squinted at the woman's electric citrus wardrobe. Say it ain't so.

Stella lifted her bulbous nose into the air. "All the girl needed was a little guidance. I don't know how long she'd been living under a rock, but I'll tell you two this much, I dragged her out into the sun and I'm plenty proud of it. She looked good enough to eat by the time I was through with her. You could see it in her face, too. She felt a whole lot better about herself. You boys probably wouldn't under- stand. Men can go three days without shaving and girls'll still crawl over you, isn't that right?"

Neither Pete nor I responded quickly enough. Stella elbowed Pete in the ribs.

"Isn't that right?"

"If you say," Pete said. He was sounding pretty helpless.

"I do. And I'm just saying in this world it's the woman who's got to do all the prettying up. That's just how it is. Now myself I've never had a problem with that personally. But I told Sophie. I said girl, you've got to blossom. You've got to make it happen. There's too many other pretty flowers out there." Stella wagged her head. "I just cannot believe she's dead. Poor girl didn't get much out of this life then, did she?"

"We understand from Sophie's last employer that Sophie was working for a caterer when she was living here," Pete said. "Do you know anything about that?"

"That's right. She got a job helping serve food. She didn't cook it, she just walked around and handed it out. I'm not sure the girl could cook water. One time she brought home a whole bag of chicken on a stick. There was some sort of peanut goop all over them, but they weren't half bad after you washed them off. The chicken was fine."

I asked, "Would you know the name of the caterer?"

"The name? Nope. No idea. Food something something. Sophie wasn't exactly the world's biggest talker, you know. I had to hold up both ends when I'd get her to sit down for a talk. Practically had to crawl into the little girl's mouth sometimes just to grab a word out of her."

She cackled again. Deep within my soul, glass shattered.

"Poor little thing, though. She was foreign, you know. It's very sad. Her father dying like that. You know about that?"

"We do," Pete said.

Stella clucked. "Little girl comes all the way over here to the New World and ends up serving sticks of chicken to total strangers. What kind of life is that? I remember the first time she put on that little white catering dress of hers, though. It was right after Elsbeth and I got her all spruced up. She was as pretty as a lollipop. I told her in that dress of hers she looked just like one of the cadets at the academy. In fact, some of the parties Sophie worked were at the academy. I'd tell her to watch out, they might think she's an enlisted girl. I'd tell her feel free to bring home one of those enlisted men sometime and I'll take a look at him for her. Oh the girl could blush." She shook her head. "But all she ever did bring home were those goopy chicken pieces."

Just then a phone rang from elsewhere in the house. Stella excused herself—slapping her hand down on Pete's knee as she struggled to extract herself from the couch—and went off to answer the phone. The woman's absence critically darkened the already drab room.

"Hey, she's cute," I said to Pete.

Pete was looking around the room. "This is depressing."

I shrugged. "Nothing a new coat of paint and a hurricane couldn't fix."

I conjured the picture of Sophie and tried to imagine her with the bob cut Stella had described. It seemed her head would be three times smaller.

Stella came back into the room a minute later.

"That was one of the witches," she announced. "Her power went out last night and the ninny only just now noticed. All the mint juleps have thawed. I could spit."

Before she could flounce back down on the couch, Pete and I rose. We thanked Stella for her time. She looked at Pete like he was a great big cookie.

"No need to rush off," she said.

Pete seemed to feel differently. He was angling toward the front door as if drawn there by a magnet. Stella stood out on the front steps and posed for us in the doorway as we headed back to the car.

"Now wave," I said to Pete as he fired up the engine. Stella was wagging her large paw. Pete lifted his hand to the window. He pulled away from the curb and we were several blocks away when I reminded Pete that he hadn't given the woman his card.

"We could go back," I said.

"We could also shoot ourselves in the heads."

As we drove back through town I tried to convince Pete that we should stick around for dinner then catch Lee's early show at the George Washington Inn.

"I mean, since we happen to be in Annapolis anyway."

Pete refused.

"I'm sure she'd like to see you," I said.

"Don't do this, okay?"

"It was just a suggestion," I said.

Pete's jaw worked hard. "Well here's a suggestion. I'm screwing my life up just fine without any extra help from you."

"That's not a suggestion," I pointed out. "That's an observation."

I couldn't tell if it was the engine of Pete's car in need of a tune-up or whether Munger himself was responsible for the low growling sound. We continued up Main Street, right past the George Washington Inn. Pete didn't so much as glance at the building.

"Tough guy," I said.

"I don't even hear you." He grabbed a pack of cigarettes off the dashboard and shook it, then pulled one of the cigarettes out of the pack with his lips. He tossed the pack back onto the dashboard and pushed in his cigarette lighter with his thumb. "You're not even in this car."

The accoutrements provided by Clifford for Oliver Engelhart's wake included an ivory walking stick, a shiny antique gold pocket watch, a pair of white bifocals on a chain, a Meerschaum pipe, a purple velvet throw, a standing Tiffany lamp, a leather-bound omnibus volume of Kipling and a small Nepalese carpet. All he needed was a stuffed mongoose and a pith helmet. Sam and I brought Mr. Engelhart up from the basement and got him set up in Parlor One.

I slipped the bifocal chain around Mr. Engelhart's neck and rested the glasses on his chest, then wedged the Kipling into his right hand, tucking his index finger into the pages as if he were keeping his place. Clifford had set the gold pocket watch to 11:15, the time of Oliver Engelhart's arrival on the planet, according to the gentleman's birth certificate. I placed the watch in the dead man's left hand, the lid flipped open, then worked a white carnation into his buttonhole. Enough insouciance to choke a horse.

It was five o'clock by the time I had finished and I dragged Billie in to show off my work. She applauded like a guest at the opera. Clifford arrived in advance of the mourners and spent a few minutes arranging the purple throw along the open lid of the casket. We arranged the Nepalese carpet just so, then set up the Tiffany lamp off to the side of the casket and lowered the parlor lights. Clifford leaned the ivory walking stick up against the casket, then began to cry quietly.

"Your friend is looking very jaunty," I said, handing him a handkerchief.

For the most part, Mr. Engelhart's mourners were a chatty and joke-telling bunch. They were terrifically supportive of Clifford, who continued going in and out of sniffles all evening. They were all quite caught up in posing with their departed friend, both in single shots as well as several group shots. I was asked to take the group shots, and of course I obliged. Everyone gathered around the tableau and posed. I took several shots of the gang all looking appropriately hangdog and morose, as well as a few hammy shots, fake fainting spells and all the rest.

I went home and changed into my civvies then swung by the Oyster for a late dinner. Frank was on duty, so overall the atmosphere was about as hopping as my embalming room. I ordered a lousy hamburger from Frank and he obliged. It tasted nominally better with a Murphy's stout, more so with a Maker's chaser. I stared into the mirror behind the bar a good long time until I was able to conjure a reflection seated next to me. Sophie Potts. The girl didn't even look old enough for a legal drink, so I bought one for her. I drank it for her, too. Gentleman Hitch. I held the glass up under my chin. *What happened to you, kid? You look like a nice quiet girl. Why would someone have it in for you?*

Ether will not answer. And that's all she was.

I wound up playing some darts with a woman named Darlene Darling. I thought she was slurring her words when she first told me her name. Darlene *was* a darling, but halfway through our third game she told me her boyfriend was a stevedore. I have a strict rule against getting on the wrong side of stevedores so I let her win the game and then retired to the bar. Darlene Darling came over a few minutes later and pulled up a stool next to me. Right where Sophie had been sitting. I thought she'd look cute if she giggled so I told her what I did for a living. I was right. I ordered up a round and discovered soon after that my tongue had gotten loose. I found myself telling Darlene all about Sophie and the bridge and the speculation about whether Sophie had jumped to her death. Darlene had a sympathetic ear. She also had a funny laugh. And of course she also had the stevedore boyfriend, so I kept to my best behavior. At some point I heard myself telling Darlene about the beer truck that ran over my family. I wasn't sure how it was I had gotten around to that sprightly conversation, but I must have done a good job of telling the story, for Darlene was in tears before I finished. That was when her stevedore boyfriend showed up. Luckily, he turned out to be an easygoing character and he took Darlene under his wing and let me buy him a drink. Darlene blurted out to him that I was an undertaker and a gentleman. She also tried to tell him the story of Sophie and the bridge, but she didn't do a terribly good job of it.

I excused myself at that point and slipped off the stool. I swam over to the pay phone in the rear of the bar. It seemed an awfully long way away. I made a call. It was a short call. Maybe a little belligerent. The call was to Mike Gellman. I told him I was too tired for niceties and asked could we get together the next day.

"Why?" Mike said.

"Three guesses," I said. "And the first two don't count." At least I remembered something from grade school. I had a pistols-at-dawn tone to my voice . . . but we settled for lunch at one. Weapons unspecified.

Darlene was drinking coffee when I got back. Her boyfriend was nibbling on a pickled egg. Darlene looked up at me over the rim of her mug. Her eyes were tired and sad. Her boyfriend slapped me on the back and offered to buy me a drink. I slapped him back and said, "No, thanks." He fell into a pretend boxing crouch so we had to go through that. I joined him for a pickled egg, then I knocked back a cup of coffee of my own. It didn't really take. Back home I dropped into bed. At least I assume that's what happened, as that's where I woke up in the morning. I must have been asleep before I hit the mattress. I dreamed I was falling from a bridge. Slow motion. In the dream I was falling on my back, facing upward. I could see somebody up on the bridge. Whoever it was they were turning away. The last part of the dream I can remember was sensing that I was about to hit the water. I recall taking a very large breath, one that I knew would have to last me an eternity. I also remember my feeling about it all.

I was furious.

CHAPTER 8

My head was humming a Verdi tune when I woke up. *Il Travatore*. The so-called anvil chorus. Gotta be those sinister pickled eggs.

My reflection in the bathroom mirror mocked me, shadowboxing like a happy clown as I just stood there and took it. Dressing for death didn't exactly perk me up either. My tie slithered in my fingers like a well-oiled snake; it took me nearly ten passes to get the job done right. My shiny shoes took me out the door before I was really ready. As Sam and I rolled the Engelhart casket out of Parlor One he put an amused eyeball on me. He kept shifting it back and forth between me and the Engelhart casket.

"Which one of you are we burying?"

Aunt Billie was shuffling down the steps in a bathrobe she'd picked up a few centuries back. A cigarette was dangling out of her mouth. Her hair was a silver dust mop.

"You look like an old madam," I said to her as she approached me with an English muffin.

"Say ah."

I did and she poked the English muffin into my mouth.

"That'll have to keep you."

Sam and I got Oliver Engelhart loaded into the hearse, topped him off with a selection of flowers, and hit the road. I made Sam stop singing, then I made him stop tapping his hand against the steering wheel.

"What am I supposed to do," he asked. "I've got the music in me."

We delivered Oliver Engelhart into the cold cold ground without any catastrophes. At the grave site, Mr. Engelhart's cronies were a bit more somber than they had been at the wake. A tenor with the Lyric Opera Company chorus sang something Italian. Not the anvil chorus; it was quite beautiful, in fact. Oliver Engelhart's corgi—named Porgy—had been brought along. The dog was in a shoulder harness, with a little black band fitted onto his front left leg. Porgy was a bewildered-looking pup, one ear up, one ear down. He was suffering from a cold and kept sneezing in violent disproportion to his small body mass. Unfortunately, Porgy was a humper; he was all over Clifford's shin during the singing of the aria. But Clifford was in such a free flow of tears at that point that he didn't seem to notice.

I got to the Middleton Tavern sometime after one o'clock. Mike wasn't there. I was able to snag an outdoor table. I ordered a coffee. "Black, strong, dirty. . . ."

The couple at the table next to me were arguing. It was impossible not to listen in. She said he didn't pay enough attention to her needs and he said he didn't know what the hell she was talking about. It was a nearly perfect argument. They eventually left and were replaced by an elderly couple. She was wearing a straw hat and a string of pearls and a pair of sun goggles. He was in a plaid shirt and was gripping a transistor radio. A wire ran from the radio to a little earplug in his right ear. Once they were seated they proceeded to freeze in place like a pair of George Segal sculptures. They may still be there, for all I know.

The sun was high and hot. The restaurant was doing a brisk Sunday business. I rolled up my sleeves and ordered a second cup of coffee and then a third, and then decided I'd better have something to nibble on to take the edge off the jitters. I ordered a plate of calamari. I do love those briny rubber bands. I was ploinking on the salsa when Mike Gellman showed up. The sun was directly behind his head, sending out a brilliant corona. I had to shade my eyes with my hand to see him. Mike wore the sun well. He was one of those tall strapping blond types, a boyish mop on top and a smile that could seduce a nun. I've been told that I've got one of those, too, but I'd never use it so irresponsibly. Mike was wearing white slacks, a navy blue tennis shirt and sunglasses. He was smiling a smile that was patently false. I scuttled about in my bag of facial expressions and came up with one myself. Off to a false start. In track meets they make you go back and start again.

"Sorry I'm late. Things are a little nuts right now." Mike swung one leg over the chair and lowered into it as if he were riding a pneumatic. The old cowboy still had it. He reached across the table and tried to break my fingers. "How goes it, Sewell?"

"You know. This way, that way."

"Long time, huh? I take it you're still burying people for a living?"

"Yes, sir, I am. Planted one this very morning, in fact. Makes a man feel alive, you know what I mean?"

Of course he didn't. I was talking through my hat. He gave me another of his false smiles.

"I understand you're having a little trouble at work these days," I said. *Always hit them where it hurts.* I got those marching orders once in a fortune cookie.

Mike darkened for an instant. "It's all bullshit. Don't believe everything you hear. Accusations are the easy part. Someone's just trying to throw dirt on me. It's not going to stick."

"Hey, in my line of work throwing dirt's all a part of the game."

I don't think Mike even heard me. "I'll be fine," he said brusquely. Our waitress came over. She was blonde. She was cute. She was young. She was aware of all these things.

Mike asked me what I was drinking

I raised my mug. "Primordial sludge."

"Can I talk you into a drink?"

"You can't. But you go right ahead."

Mike ordered a Corona. "And a lime with that?" he added. He didn't need to ask. They always bring limes with Coronas. But it gave Gellman a chance to flash his piano keys at the waitress. She answered Mike's big grin with one of her own then skipped off to do his bidding. Mike was watching her as she left.

"The older we get the cuter they get," I sawed.

"Brother, you can say that again." Mike reached his arms over his head and stretched, as if to show me how long and lanky he was. "But hey, we're not dead yet."

I wasn't exactly sure what he meant by that but I didn't ask. Mike's arms were invading the space of the elderly couple, though they still didn't budge. It would have served him right if the woman in the sun goggles had suddenly taken a nip at his fingers.

Mike brought his arms down on the table. He leaned forward into my space and slid his sunglasses up onto his head. He looked tired. The eyes were somewhat glassy. Lack of sleep.

"Okay, Sewell, let's have it. You were a real crap head on the phone last night."

"I guess I was," I said. "I apologize for that. I was between a bad hamburger and a pickled egg. I really shouldn't pick up the phone when the bile is rising."

"I know what this is all about. You and I have only one thing in common."

"Is it our nascent charm?"

"It's my wife."

I corrected him. "She wasn't your wife when we had her in common, Mike. Gargantuan distinction."

"I mean now. I know you've been seeing Libby."

"I guess you got the report from Uncle Owen."

"Leave Owen out of this. I'm talking about Libby. She's probably been going on and on about what a schmuck I've been lately."

"She didn't use that precise word. But yeah, now that you mention it I guess it's fair to say she sullied your good name a little."

Mike's beer arrived. His face relaxed and he ran his little flirting game again with the waitress. She had brought two limes and a pot of coffee.

"My name is Hitchcock," I said as she topped me off. "I'm the single one at this table."

"I'd forgotten what a wise guy you are," Mike said after the waitress moved off. He was thumbing his limes into the bottle. The look he was giving me, it's possible that he'd have liked to have thumbed me into his bottle as well.

I pulled and fired. "Libby told me that you hit her."

Anger flared in Mike's eyes. He leaned forward on the table. "You want to keep your voice down?"

"Not particularly."

"I did not hit her. That's a lie."

"It's what she said."

"I might have pushed her."

"*Might* have?"

"Libby was upset. We were arguing. Hell, she was hitting *me*. She probably didn't mention that part. I shoved her down onto the bed. It wasn't very dramatic."

"You make it sound downright banal."

"I was there, Sewell. She's blowing the whole thing out of proportion. Can't you see she's using you?"

"Oh? I missed that part."

"For Christ's sake, Sewell, she did it six years ago and she's doing it again. She wants to get me angry. She's using you to make me jealous. I think that's pretty obvious."

"I guess I'm denser than I thought, Mike."

"I don't mean to be insulting here, Sewell, but there's a word for what Libby was doing with you back then."

"Is the word 'discerning'?"

"The word is slumming."

"You know what, Mike. I think you *do* mean to be insulting."

Mike folded his hands together on top of the table and took a long deep breath. "Look, I'm not here to refight an old battle. I've got nothing against you personally. I just want you to stay away from Libby. And from my kids."

"Libby's an old friend. My reading of the Constitution is that it affords me the right to spend time with an old friend. Do I have that wrong?"

"I don't need any more problems now, okay? Just do me a favor."

I picked up my coffee cup and blew on it. Some fifty feet off Mike's shoulder a Rollerblader had just slammed into a lamppost and was holding on to it like a Bourbon Street drunk.

"Let's try this. Did you know that Sophie was pregnant?"

"Sophie?"

"Yes. Sophie Potts. She was a nanny? She worked for you and—"

"I know who the hell she is."

"Did you know she was pregnant?" I asked again.

"Of course I know. It's in the coroner's report." He took a swig of his beer. "I think it's time you started minding your own business."

"Here's something that wasn't in the coroner's report. Did you know that your wedding ring was found in Sophie's jewelry box?"

Mike didn't respond immediately. He put a hard look on me, though it didn't exactly start my skull sizzling. Behind him the Rollerblader released the lamppost . . . and dropped out of sight.

"Who told you that?"

"I was there when Sophie's mother found it."

"I haven't seen my wedding ring in months. I guess she stole it.

Wouldn't be the first time a nanny stole something. I thought I lost it at the gym."

"What's your take on Sophie anyway, Mike? You knew her. What do you think happened to her?"

"It's like I told the police. She was depressed. You could tell that the moment you saw her. She got herself in trouble. Damn stupid kid jumped off a bridge, that's what happened to her."

I leaned forward and spoke in a loud whisper. "Uh . . . Mike, you might want to conserve some of that rampant sympathy of yours. It's almost too much. Really."

He picked up his bottle by the neck and pointed a finger at me. "I agreed to meet with you so that I could tell you to your face to stay away from my wife and my kids. I'm not discussing anything else with you."

"Fine. You did that. Let me ask you one more question. Nice and direct. Did you sleep with Sophie and get her pregnant and then kill her?"

I drummed my fingers on the table and sat back triumphantly. Damn, now *there* is a concise way to put a question. Mike's answer was a disappointment.

"You're fucking nuts."

"Come on, Mike, hombre to hombre. Were you niggling with the nanny?"

"I should fucking slug you."

"You do and I won't pay for that beer."

Mike leaned in close. He spoke in such a low tone that from more than a foot away I doubt you'd have even seen his lips moving.

"This is a small town, Sewell. Rumors travel fast. Have you got that? I've got a public profile here. If I find out that there's a goddamn whispering campaign going on about me, I'm going to know exactly who to blame. I don't need this kind of shit flying around in the papers, do you understand? Just back off of it."

Mike slid his sunglasses back down onto his face. He skidded his chair back and stood up. I braced but he didn't reach down and drag me up by the collar. The sun wasn't so much making a halo this time as it was setting his yellow hair ablaze. He pulled a few bills from his wallet and dropped them onto the table. I looked up at him sadly.

"Is this good-bye?"

Without a word Mike turned to leave. As he did he nearly collided with a man who had just stepped over to the table. The man was wearing one of those Australian cowboy hats, the cockeyed ones with the folded brim. He was also wearing a gigantic shit-eating grin.

"Hello, mate." He had whipped out a slender notebook and was fetching a pen from behind his ear. "Nick Fallon. *The Daily Cannon.* I'd like a quote from you concerning the Stanley Arena situation. I understand a grand jury is being considered to—"

"Fuck off."

Gellman pushed past the reporter and stormed off down the sidewalk. We watched him until he had disappeared around the corner at the end of the block, then the reporter turned to me, his pen still poised above the notebook.

"Not much of a quote then, was it?"

There was a festival of some sort taking place at the harbor. The *Pride of Baltimore II* was moored at one of the piers. A Coast Guard ship was tied up aft of it. Or maybe fore. I'm more nautically challenged than I care to admit. Tours were being given on both ships. On a small stage on the pier a bearded fellow with a mandolin was singing a song about mermaids to an audience of about a hundred folding chairs. I wandered over to a large white tent. Under the tent were displays about the Chesapeake Bay region, about crabbing and oystering, ecology, the history of the bay. I plunked down some money to save the bay and was given a bumper sticker to add to my collection. I don't put these on my car. I don't happen to think you should distract people while they're driving. I'm saving them up for my casket. God's truth.

I strolled along the piers. There was a little platform set up for people who wanted to try their hand at oyster tonging. A teenage girl was all giggles and elbows as she attempted to move a pile of oyster shells from Point A to Point B using the tongs. I passed a kid who was sitting lotus style against a pylon wearing a T-shirt that read Zen Bastard. He was plunking on a calimba. I gave him a dollar and he did a little run on the calimba. It sounded like the notes accompanying "Tah da!" Which in a way it was, for just then an idea struck me. I tossed in an extra buck. Soft-touch Sewell.

I found a pay phone. No one had yet been able to tell me which caterer Sophie had worked with before Libby and Mike hired her. I called information and got a list of local caterers and their phone numbers. The pay phone was kind of fritzy—a quarter doesn't buy what it used to—but I phoned the numbers anyway. I got no live bodies, just machines. I left messages, asking anyone who had worked with Sophie Potts over the summer to please give me a call. I left my home number.

I strolled over to the Naval Academy campus and up the street toward the officers' residences. The lawns were neat as a pin. What a surprise. I crossed into a large quad and stopped at a gazebo. A male and female cadet were standing in front of a camera on a tripod, reading from a cue card. My guess was that it was some sort of promotional video. *Do you just love crisp white uniforms? Does the term "shore leave" send tingles up your spine?* The Naval Academy chapel was right in front of me. I thought about going inside and maybe picking up a John Paul Jones souvenir for Pete, but a wedding was in the process of breaking up and the front stairs were clogged with guests. A professional photographer was going spastic with organization. Most of the guests were trailing off toward a large canopy tent that was set up at the far end of the quad.

I crossed the quad and looked out past the track-and-field facility to the river beyond. A portion of the Naval Academy Bridge was visible. Technically, I was standing at a spot where, with a full moon and a good pair of eyes, a person might have been able to see Sophie Potts going over the side of the bridge to her death. I peered over at the bridge. By some theories of relativity I've heard, every single moment of existence in the entire universe plays out all at once—one huge flash—forever and ever, simultaneously. By those workings, Sophie was pitching toward the water this very instant, over and over and over. But I couldn't see it. No falling body. No splash. Nobody hurrying away. There was nothing but cars crossing back and forth over the bridge.

I angled over to the field house and looked at the monument to Tecumseh. The monument was comprised of what had originally been a ship's figurehead of the Indian chief. The guy looked fierce and pissed off. Who can blame him? I asked a passing cadet what time it was simply to see if he'd give it to me in military time. He didn't. It was two fifty-five and he told me it was two fifty-five. However, he did add a snappy "sir!" to the end of it. He also pointed out a pay phone for me at the corner of the quad.

I dialed my home phone and retrieved my messages. There was only one. It was a woman's voice.

"Is this Dickie? It better be Dickie. Your message was garbled. Damn it, where are you? I'm going to kill you. Call me on my cell."

She left a phone number. I called it. The same voice answered.

"Hello?"

"Hi," I said.

"Is this Dickie?"

"Afraid not."

"Who is this?"

"You just called my number," I said.

"I . . . the Baltimore number?"

"Yes."

"It was all garbled. I was hoping you were Dickie."

"I'm not."

"I need Dickie now, damn it. If I get ahold of him I'm going to kill him. He is really screwing me over."

"I'm sorry to hear that."

"Who is this anyway?"

I told her my name. There was a pause. There often is.

"Look, I can't talk. I'm totally swamped here."

"I won't keep you," I said. "I was calling to see if you knew a person named Sophie Potts. She's—"

"Sophie? Sure, I know Sophie, why? Wait. Hold on." I heard her speaking with someone on her end of the line. *"No, Judy, the six-inch plates. If you use the eight-inch plates they're just going to load up on the food. We'll run out too soon."*

While she was talking the chapel bells began ringing. There was a peculiar echoing sensation in the receiver.

She came back on. "Look, I've got to go. I'm really screwed here."

"Hold on," I said. "This might sound strange, but could you wave your arm?"

"Excuse me?"

"Your arm. Just wave your arm over your head."

"What the—"

"Just do it."

"Okay. Okay, I'm waving."

I peered out across the quad, toward the white canopy at the far end.

"I'll be right there," I said.

CHAPTER 9

The bride was the first one to go into the water. She was an Irish-Catholic girl, large and boisterous. She kicked off her white shoes and lifted her bustling dress up to her knees and charged down one of the piers at the field house basin and launched herself into the river with a squeal of glee, folding up at the last instant to enter the water like a cannonball. The artillery barrage followed. Some bridesmaids. A couple of ushers. A cousin of the groom. Then the groom himself. He entered the water in a perfect frog dive, feet splayed Charlie Chaplin style, knees and elbows forming perfect diamonds. The wedding party splashed around in the water like they were fending off piranha. Apparently the best man was squeamish. He was half carried and half dragged by several cohorts to the end of the pier. A bouncy thing in a peach-colored dress hippety-hopped behind them, protesting. The best man was taken by the arms and legs and given a one-two-*three*, and tossed into the drink. Miss Hippety-Hop bounced up and down on the end of the pier. One of the cohorts gave her a hip check and in she went.

"Ah, to be young and drunk."

This came from Stephanie. Stephanie was the caterer I'd spoken to on the phone. She stood about five five. Bristle of straw-colored hair, shoulders of a fullback. She was built low to the ground. I'd seen her yanking cases of beer and booze like they were paper goods. I fully believed that if she got hold of this Dickie character she could put a serious hurt on him.

Her instructions to me had been to pour a good drink.

"The quicker they fall, the quicker we get out of here."

And they were falling now. Into the Severn. Climbing back onto the pier and launching themselves back into the water. The only wet blanket was Miss Hippety-Hop, who had climbed out of the water and barked at her boyfriend, who had then scrambled out of the water and disappeared into the field house, emerging a few minutes later with a snappy white cadet's jacket, which he draped over the shoulders of his dearly beloved. The couple came over to the tables where I was tending bar and Miss Hippety-Hop ordered a whiskey, straight. Her lips were blue and her eyes were furious. She threw back the whiskey, gave a raspy cough and asked me for another. She kept one of the furious eyes on me as she took a sip from the second drink. Her boyfriend was looking feeble and uncertain. Unbidden, I poured him a whiskey.

"Keep up," I whispered to him as I handed him the glass. His date glared angrily over her shoulder at me as they moved off.

"You ever think about bartending full-time?" Stephanie asked me.

"I'd have to say, it's certainly different from this side."

"I can't thank you enough," Stephanie said, pouring herself a ginger ale. She took a seat on one of the ice chests. "You saved my ass."

"It's one of the ways into heaven."

"You can punch out now, Hitch. The crunch is over."

The white jacket Stephanie had conjured for me to work the bar was built for a lesser man. The sleeves gave up well back on my arms and my shoulders had been trussed all afternoon. I peeled the jacket off and folded it atop a box of chardonnay.

"So you're really an undertaker, eh?" Stephanie asked.

"Yes, ma'am. Where I come from, 'business is dead' is a good thing."

"Must be creepy."

"Not really. For one thing, our customers never complain."

She laughed. "I never thought of that."

A man in an orange sports coat came over to the table and asked for a gin and tonic. I put one together for him. He looked off at the water revelers and wagged his head slowly, then drifted off. I returned to my perch.

"So what can you tell me about Sophie?"

Stephanie pulled in her lower lip. "There's not much to tell, really. She answered an ad that I ran in the paper. She didn't have any catering experience but she could put one foot in front of the other and she could carry a tray." A grin grew across her face. "Plus she was cute in her little white dress."

"Something about a gal in a uniform?"

She grinned again.

"Stephanie, please don't tell me you corrupted the morals of a shy little Hungarian girl."

"Not a chance. For one thing, I don't do that sort of thing. I'm happily partnered. But there was no sway in that girl anyway. That was obvious. You said you never met her, right?"

"That's right."

"Let me tell you something, she would have melted for someone like you. Sophie was like a kid in a candy shop when it came to tall good-looking guys."

I thought of Gary Cooper. I also thought of Mike Gellman.

"Could you elaborate?"

"What's to elaborate? The eyes go wide. The lips begin to tremble. . . ."

I said, "I've been given the definite impression that Sophie was a shy girl."

"Oh, she was. Terrifically shy. But you know sometimes that can be pretty appealing. And guys love to flirt with the shy ones. You must know that. Sophie was a pretty little thing. You get a girl like that to blush . . . well, it was cute, watching her get all flustered. In fact it was probably . . . yes, it would have been one of the last times she worked with us. Right here again on campus. We were working some sort of orientation party. All these snappy cadets all over the place. Sophie's eyes were practically popping out of her head. There was a particular group of them. Four or five. For whatever reason they decided to goof on her. I'm sure it was because she was so easy to ruffle. They got a little game going. Every time Sophie came out with a new tray of hors d'oeuvres they descended on her. They surrounded her and teased her, pretending that she had cooked the food herself and telling her how fantastic it was and all the rest. Their little game was to empty the tray before she had a chance to take a step. It was all just silly. They were having fun."

"How did she react to that?"

"Oh, she blushed like crazy. But I'm sure she loved it. All these good-looking middies? I finally had to step in and tell them to cool it, though. The nice thing about military boys, they're all 'ten-hut' and 'yes, ma'am.' They don't give you any bullshit. One of them even came up to Faith later on to make sure she knew it was all their doing, that Sophie hadn't been egging them on or anything. It was sweet."

"Who's Faith?"

"She's my business partner. She works at one of the restaurants in town. She ought to be along soon to help break down. She can't always make it to the jobs."

We had a return visit just then from Miss Hippety-Hop. Her hair had dried into twisting blonde snakes. She was still wearing the white cadet's jacket, holding it closed at the neck with one hand. Her eyes were red. She had been crying.

"I hate goddamn weddings," she said. "Another whiskey, please."

I told her the bar was closed.

"Closed? As of when?"

"As of one drink ago. I'm sorry."

She tried to kill me with a look. It didn't even strafe me. She turned and weaved back along her rocky road to her boyfriend.

I helped Stephanie and her workers load up the van. Stephanie ran a tight ship. Her workers clearly respected her. Partway into it Stephanie's partner showed up. Faith was a willowy item, a long-waisted corn-silk blonde with iris-blue eyes and a deep deep tan. Her hair fell down over her ropelike arms like yellow lace and she had a tattoo of a mermaid on her inside right thigh. Not that I was looking, of course.

Stephanie said, introducing us, "Hitch saved our ass. Dastardly Dickie never showed. Hitch worked the bar like he was born to it."

"Dickie is fired," Faith said.

"Drawn and quartered if I get ahold of him," Stephanie said.

Faith cocked her head and eyed me. "So how did we find you?"

"I popped up out of a hole."

She gave me a long slow look-over. "Must've been a very large hole."

Stephanie explained that I had been looking for information about Sophie Potts.

"You remember Sophie, don't you?"

"Of course I do," Faith said. "I promised her I'd have her over to the inn to sample my Hungarian goulash one of these days."

"Too late now," I said.

"What do you mean?"

Stephanie ran her finger along her neck. "Deadskies."

Faith's eyes and mouth turned to zeroes. "Sophie's *dead*? What happened?"

I gave her the lowdown. Faith was in disbelief.

"Oh, that's horrible. Poor girl. And she was pregnant? How in the world did that happen?"

Stephanie grinned. "Well, you know that part that comes after kissing?"

Faith slapped her lightly on the arm, then turned back to me. The top of her head came up just about to my nose. The part in her hair was as perfectly straight as a runway.

"Have we met before?"

"I don't believe so," I said. "In fact, I'm sure of it. I'd have remembered."

"You look familiar to me."

"Maybe you're thinking of Cary Grant," I said.

"You don't look like Cary Grant."

"You should see me in a tux. Changes everything."

Faith studied my face a few more seconds. It didn't bother me a bit. Gave me the chance to study hers. There were yellow starbursts in her eyes. Seven freckles on her nose. A slightly chipped tooth. All this on a neck like the proverbial swan's.

"Hmmm," she said. "Maybe I'm wrong."

I grinned. "But thanks for shopping."

Faith excused herself to go talk turkey with the parents of the bride. She moved with a slow-motion bounce; her hair went this way and her dress went that way. I turned to Stephanie.

"She likes boys, am I right?"

Stephanie nodded. "Gee, how did you guess?"

I tapped my finger against the side of my head. "Hitch Sewell, boy genius."

Stephanie and I folded up the bar tables and slid them into the van. Stephanie pulled a fistful of money from her pocket and handed me a hundred dollars. Then she dug in and handed me another fifty.

"Ass-saving bonus."

A few minutes later Faith rejoined us. She mentioned something to Stephanie about the George Washington Inn. Turns out that's where she worked. I told her that I had a friend who was singing there.

"No kidding," Faith said. "Is that Lee Cromwell?"

"Yes."

She said she hadn't had a chance to catch the show yet, but she had heard it was good.

"You know, I just thought of something about Sophie," Faith said. "She called me a couple of weeks ago."

"Is that right? What about?"

Faith turned to Stephanie. "I guess I never bothered mentioning it to you. It was about Tom."

"Who's Tom?" I asked.

Stephanie answered. "Tom Cushman. He works for us off and on. He's an aspiring actor." She floated her hands in the direction of the other workers. "They're all aspiring somethings. Tom hasn't been able to commit much lately. He got a job at one of the local theaters. I can't remember the show." She turned to Faith. "Do you know?"

Faith shook her head. "I don't remember. Something old."

"So what was this call?" I asked.

Faith tapped a fingernail against one of her front teeth. "Sophie called me up and said she wanted to get ahold of Tom. She wanted to know if I had his number."

"Did Tom and Sophie work together?"

"A little bit this summer, yes."

"Did she say what the call was about?"

"No. And I didn't ask. I just gave her the number."

"He's not in the phone book?"

"Tom has a roommate," Faith said. "The phone's under the roommate's name."

"Give me a thumbnail on Tom," I said.

Stephanie and Faith shared another look. "That one's yours," Stephanie said.

Faith took her fingers to her chin and gave me an appraising look. "Well, let's see. Tom Cushman. Tall, but not quite as tall as you. Good-looking." She smiled. "But not as good-looking as you."

Stephanie chimed in. "He's no Cary Grant."

"Any idea why she'd be wanting to call him?" When neither Stephanie nor Faith could come up with a reason, I asked, "Well, how's this? What are the chances that the two of them were mixing it up while they were working together?"

Faith was shaking her head. "Not a chance."

"You say that with conviction."

"That's because I know," she said. "It didn't happen."

"How can you be so sure?" I asked.

Faith checked me out one eye at a time. An amused vapor was whipping about her face. "Trust me. I know."

I looked over at Stephanie, who was trying to keep a leash on her laughter.

"I see."

Even with the tan, the blush came up in Faith's cheeks. The blue in her eyes deepened. They looked like a pair of deep watering holes into which someone had thrown a couple of rocks. I could almost feel their splash.

I went ahead and popped into the Naval Academy chapel before I left the campus. I have to say they do like their blue. John Paul Jones is ensconced in the basement level. As we say so hilariously in the trade, he was still dead. The chapel was crawling with visitors. The stained-glass windows were dominated—no surprise—by nautical imagery. Near the altar a young mother and father were trying in vain to placate their baby, whose wailings were offering an impressive display of the chapel's acoustics.

I left the chapel and meandered the narrow streets until I found a pay phone. I made a few calls. One was to the local theater. They were running *The Seagull* by Chekov. I asked the box-office person to run down the cast list for me, and when he read out the name Tom Cushman I told him I wanted a ticket for the evening's performance. No problem. Curtain at eight, don't be late.

I caught up with Lee Cromwell for an early dinner. The club where she worked, downstairs at the George Washington Inn, was called the Wine Cellar. We ate upstairs in the bar. Lee looked great. At forty-seven Lee was in the midst of a new blooming. She had dumped the two-timing husband, dumped the booze, put the statuesque body back into great shape and was up onstage behind the microphone after a twenty-year detour. Lee still smoked. She handled cigarettes like the sex objects they once were. Full head of auburn hair. A laugh like Rita Hayworth's. Her dinner was a spinach salad. Every few bites she would grimace at me so I could tell her whether she had spinach in her teeth.

"How's Peter?" she finally asked.

I shrugged. "You know Pete. There are a dozen answers to that question."

"He's a shit."

"I guess that's one of them."

"I miss him," Lee said. "Would it kill him to pick up the phone?"

"Lee, you know he's completely hell-bent on trying to work things out with Susan."

"I know that. I'm not trying to interfere, believe me. Peter has to work all that out. But am I a pariah? The man can't talk to me?"

"Maybe he can't, Lee. It's not easy for him. Maybe that's the problem."

Lee stirred her salad absently with her fork. "He's just an irascible old bear, anyway." She looked up from her plate. Her eyes were glistening. "Well, say hi for me."

CHAPTER

10

The Seagull. **It goes** like this:

A half-talent young playwright spends too much time in a tree house writing tortured melodramas that nobody in their right mind wants to screw their fannies down in a chair and actually sit through. He is smitten by a pretty young thing—an actress named Nina—who hasn't a clue in her pretty little head that this fellow—his name is Constantin—is completely ga-ga for her, even though his plays are all written with her in mind. Constantin's mother is a celebrated stage actress who is approaching the apex of her beauty and celebrity. The mother's amour du jour is a famous writer of whom Constantin, naturally enough, is envious. The first big scene of the play is when Constantin comes down from his tree house and puts on one of his plays—featuring Nina—and it is met with howls. And no, it is not a comedy. Constantin bitches and fumes and condemns everyone else as crass and incapable of recognizing "true art" when they see it. Which of course they haven't seen from Constantin. Eventually the famous writer leaves Constantin's mother and runs off with Nina, who becomes a star herself while Constantin and Mother remain home and lick their wounds. Nina eventually ditches the guy, who comes bounding back to Constantin's mother. Nina returns as well, no longer the unsoiled crystal that once stirred Constantin's loins and poetry, but now a part of the crass world that Constantin cannot abide. And so he shoots himself.

The End.

Tom Cushman played the role of Constantin, the anguished half-talent playwright. It would be too easy for me to state that Tom Cushman was a half-talent actor, so I won't. Maybe it was an off night. Or maybe he was doing such a convincing job of portraying the half talent of Constantin that the overall glow of half talent simply encased him. That is, if "glow" can encase. Or for that matter, if half talent can glow. Whatever the case, I really don't think that what Chekov had in mind was for the audience to applaud when Constantin shoots himself at the end of the play.

As it happened I played this role once myself. I'm a Gypsy Player, which doesn't mean that I wear dye-running scarves and travel about on donkey carts, but that I throw my hand in now and again with the local amateur theater troupe in my neighborhood who mount extravagant fiascos and the occasional gem at the Gypsy Playhouse, a few doors down from Julia's place. In fact, Julia appeared in the Gypsy's *Seagull* as well. She found Nina to be an insufferably clueless child and so she finagled the role of Constantin's mother. We played beautifully opposite each other (we always do), even with the idiotic conceit that we were mother and son.

I asked at the box office how I could get backstage after the show and was told to go outside and around to the back of the building, down a short flight of stairs, along a hallway, through a couple of doors and to watch out for the low-hanging pipes. Being an amateur ham myself, the atmosphere backstage was all too familiar to me. Clusters of people stood waiting for their thespian friends to emerge from their dressing areas. Members of the stage crew crisscrossed swiftly, carrying props and pieces of costumes along with an urgency to wrap it up quick and get the hell home or off to the nearest bar. There was a large bulletin board with schedules pinned to it, notes, cartoons, a few reviews, a comic collage made up from magazine pages, the usual backstage flotsam. The green room was a pale blue. I shared it with several people who stood there gazing at the ceiling.

The first actor to emerge was the one who had played Nina. Onstage she had seemed to have it in her head that Nina should move about like a ballerina. In my view, Nina is ditsy enough already without giving to her character the additional weightlessness of someone who does all their emoting while up on the balls of their feet. But then who paid me to judge? In her role as a human being, the actress was a lot more solidly attached to the ground. She appeared from her dressing room in a sleeveless T-shirt, baggy capri pants and a sweatband snapped tight around her head, her hair pulled back into a bronze ponytail. On her shoulder she carried a black bag large enough to contain a small automobile. She was slender, but her biceps betrayed—perhaps "ballyhooed" would be a better way of putting it—hours spent in the gym carving away with weights and machines. Her name was Shannon. The couple who were there for Shannon let out a little cry. The woman was holding a bouquet of flowers, and as Shannon widened her arms and came forward for the hugs and kudos, the woman handed the flowers over to her boyfriend or husband or whatever he was, who stuck his nose into the flowers while he stood waiting his turn for the hug.

The rest of the cast was emerging. I had seen in the program where the fellow who portrayed the famous writer had been doing plays at this theater since before the lightbulb was invented. The actor emerged from the hallway, a fedora pulled down low over his nose and trailing a scarf that might nearly have tripped him. He was followed by Constantin's mother, who in my view had been the best actor of the lot. She was pulling on a cigarette and making a beeline for the door. Tom Cushman appeared next. Shannon called him over and introduced him to her friends, who heaped all sorts of praise on the actor, to his obvious delight.

I stepped over.

"Excuse me. Tom?"

The actor turned my way with the expectant smile of a happy puppy.

"Nice work," I said. "Very nice."

"Oh, thank you!"

The eyes of Shannon were upon me. "You, too," I said to her.

The actress took a beat to see if I had anything more to add. My praise hadn't exactly knocked the thespian on her rear end. Seeing that I was only handing out scraps, she turned to her friends.

Tom had a bag not unlike Shannon's. He was rifling through it. He found what he was looking for. Lip balm. He uncapped it and ran an invisible smear over his lips.

"I was wondering if I could talk to you," I said to him.

"Sure. Are you a critic?"

Well, I am. But not the kind he meant. I lowered my voice. "It's about Sophie Potts."

Even at my reduced volume, the name caught Shannon's ear. She skipped only half a beat, shooting a sharp look at Tom, which she then attempted to cover with a flourish of the bouquet and a controlled laugh. Tom wasn't quite as skilled. His eyebrows collapsed in a frown, and for a moment he looked as if I'd tossed him a calculus question. He feigned an indifference that he clearly didn't feel.

"Sophie? Um. Yeah. What about her?"

"Can we talk someplace else?" I asked, adding, "You probably want to get out of here."

"Yeah. Uh . . ." He looked over at Shannon. "McGarvey's?"

The voice said "Yes." The look was considerably less positive. We left the theater and trudged up the street to McGarvey's. A few of the stagehands were already there and had commandeered a booth. Shannon and her friends joined them. Tom and I settled in at the bar and ordered a couple of beers. Tom was fidgety so I sought to settle him down first. While we waited for our beers I complimented him again on his performance.

"You really found Constanin's heart," I told him, which was effectively saying nothing, but I suspected the actor wouldn't notice.

"Oh God, though," he said. "What about those hiccups? I couldn't believe that. I thought I was going to die."

In the early scene where Constantin is railing against the others for their insensitivity to his artistic efforts, Tom had suffered a walloping case of hiccups. Personally, I felt that they underscored the excitable nature of this tragic boob who holes up in a tree house and I told Tom so. He got that calculus-question look again.

"You think Constantin is a boob?" He sounded crestfallen. "You don't think he's Chekov's stand-in? The true artist?"

"I think Constantin's a boob," I repeated.

"But that would take the importance out of everything he does in the play."

"There is no importance in what Constantin does," I said. "He is a dreamer and a fruitcake and he needs to get a life. I blame his mother. She should have slapped him years ago and told him to get on with it."

Tom was fascinated. "You think so?"

"Absolutely. She has made her way in the theater world because she is brassy and she knows what the public wants. Constantin hasn't got a clue. I think Chekov is laughing at him. Look at it. He put him in a *tree house*."

The actor looked perplexed. Our beers arrived and he picked his up by the neck.

"So you don't think the tree house was to signify purity and innocence?"

"Pathetic immaturity," I said. "The guy couldn't cut it in the real world."

"But that's purity and innocence."

"That's being a baby well past the diaper stage."

Tom took a thoughtful sip of his beer. "I think I hate you," he said despondently. "I think you just ruined the play for me."

I shrugged. "Hey, it's just my opinion. But for what it's worth, I think you did a great job. Constantin really came across."

The actor was happy to hear that. They're always happy to hear that. He took a long pull from his bottle then set it on the bar and began picking at the label.

"Okay," he said, after running a tear halfway down the label. "So what's up with Sophie?"

I told him. "What's up is that she's dead."

It's possible that he looked as if he'd just been hit in the head with a sack of cow manure. I've never actually seen this happen to anyone and of course I had only known Tom Cushman for a matter of minutes, so who am I to judge how he'd react to such a blow? But his head literally jerked and his face opened up in a mixture of disbelief and unquestioned queasiness. So sure . . . sack of manure.

"You're kidding."

"I make jokes," I said. "But not like that. No. She's dead. She was pulled out of the Severn River a few days ago. So I take it you hadn't heard?"

He said he hadn't and I tended to believe him. I knew for a fact he wasn't a good enough actor to fake it. His face had gone slack.

"Jesus, what happened?"

"That's the question of the hour, Tom. I was hoping maybe you'd be able to shed some light."

"Are you a cop or something?"

"I'm looking into Sophie's death," I said in all honesty. I didn't elaborate and he didn't ask.

"Well, what are you asking me for? I don't know anything. I barely even knew her."

"What were you doing the night of September fifth?"

The question came out of me so quickly I didn't even have the chance to give it the noir spin it deserved.

"That's not funny," Tom said. As a matter of fact, he was right.

"So it's not funny," I said. "But that's the last time Sophie Potts was seen alive. How about you answer the question anyway?"

"Hey, you know. I don't think I like your tone."

"Sorry. But a girl's dead."

Tom was making quick work of the beer label. I've heard somewhere that this is a sign of schizophrenia, but in this case I was willing to keep my prognosis toned down to simple nervousness.

"Was Sophie murdered?" he asked. "Is that what this is?"

"Well, there's a certain stench around the cesspool," I said. "I'm talking to people to see if I can get the air a little clear."

"God. I can't believe it." He took a sip of his beer. "So the fifth? You say that's when it happened?"

"No one is exactly sure. That's when she disappeared. She wasn't found for about a week."

The actor gave it some thought, tugging on his chin and staring a hole into the bar. I could tell he'd be a wobbly Hamlet.

"Well, unless it was a Monday night I was at the theater. I mean, if you're looking for an alibi."

A burst of laughter came from the booth where Nina and the others were sitting. I glanced over. Nina was entertaining the others with a mimed cigar. She appeared to be doing Groucho. Tom glanced over as well. I decided to wind up and let loose with the hard stuff. Right down the middle. I'd gotten such a rise from Mike Gellman with this approach earlier in the day I thought I'd take it out for another trot.

"Tom, did you sleep with Sophie?"

"Did I *what*?"

"Sleep with her, Tom. Did you sleep with Sophie Potts and get her pregnant? That's the question."

"Jesus Christ, are you kidding?"

"I'm not. I'm completely serious."

"No!"

"Did she call you up a few weeks ago and tell you that she was pregnant?"

"No."

"Are you sure?"

"Of course I'm sure. That's ridiculous."

"But did she call you up?"

He hesitated. "Why? Did someone say she did?"

I leaned in. "A little advice, Tom. If you're going to lie, just lie. Don't fudge. So okay, she called you up. What did she call you for?"

"It's possible that that's none of your business," he said snottily.

I could have given him additional advice about not being snotty, but I didn't really have the inclination.

"That's entirely possible," I said. "It's also entirely possible that it's something that the police might consider to be *their* business."

I was bluffing, of course. As far as I could tell the police were already finished with the death of Sophie Potts. I was just curious to see how much dodging this guy was up to. When he didn't respond, I pressed.

"Did she call you up and tell you that she was pregnant, Tom? If she did, you might as well tell me now and get it over with."

"I told you, I never slept with that girl. You're way off."

"Uh-huh."

"I didn't."

"I said 'uh-huh.' "

"You said it like you didn't believe me."

I took up my drink. "Uh-huh."

Tom glanced over at the booth again. Shannon caught his eye. She smiled at him like a python.

"She's pretty," I said. "Your little Nina."

"Shannon? Yeah."

"Are you sleeping with her?" I asked.

Tom made a melodrama of rotating his head back to me. "Is this what you do? Keep asking people who they're sleeping with until you get it right?"

"Did I get it right?"

"I don't think I have to answer you."

"You don't. Why don't I just mosey over there and see if Shannon feels like answering me?" I started to slide off the stool and Tom stopped me. He did a little hemming and hawing, but as I say, he was not really much of an actor.

"Yeah," he said. "We're sleeping together. So what?"

"Is it because of Shannon that you don't want to talk about Sophie?" I asked.

"I didn't sleep with Sophie, okay? We worked together a little this summer. I'm telling you the truth. I barely knew her."

"That's curious. If she barely knew you then why would she call you up? What was that about?" When he didn't respond, I pressed. "Somebody slept with her, Tom. And I've got to tell you, there aren't really a whole lot of candidates at this point."

"What does it matter who slept with her?" he asked testily. "I missed the part where that was a crime."

"No one said it is. But pushing someone off a bridge, last time I looked, that's a crime. Especially if it kills them."

"I didn't push anyone off a bridge," he said.

"The phone call, Tom. Sophie Potts called you up about a month after she quit the catering gig. Convince me she wasn't calling to tell you she'd gotten pregnant."

"How many times do I have to tell you? I didn't sleep with the girl."

"Why did Shannon spit daggers at you back at the theater when I mentioned Sophie's name?"

"She doesn't like Sophie." He corrected himself. "Didn't like Sophie."

"Jealousy?"

"Sophie had a little crush on me, okay? Shannon wasn't real thrilled about it."

"What kind of crush?"

"What do you mean?"

"Schoolgirl crush? Stalker crush? They come in all flavors."

"Nothing crazy like that. Schoolgirl crush."

"Did it start when you two were catering?"

"If it did I didn't know it. I swear."

"So what happened?"

"She called me up. You're right about that. A couple of weeks ago. Three maybe? A month? I'm not sure. I wasn't there. My roommate took the call and he told her I was doing this play. She came to the theater that night. I spotted her halfway through the first act. You were there tonight. You saw how small it is. She came backstage and told me how much she liked the show and all that. The usual stuff. She told me she had a job as a nanny. She said she liked it. We really didn't have a whole lot to talk about. But then she came back to the show the next night, front row center. You couldn't miss her. Shannon couldn't miss her either. She came back the next night, too, and the next and the next."

"Did she come backstage again?"

"Not at first, no. It was kind of weird. Then she finally did again. She was real jumpy. I could see she was uncomfortable. She sort of stammered a little bit, and then when Shannon came out of the dressing room Sophie practically flew out the door. I felt sorry for her. I always thought she was a nice girl."

He went back to his beer label and completed its decimation. I slid my bottle over to him.

"You want to start on mine?"

He wagged his head. "I can't believe she's *dead*. That's just crazy."

"Crazy and true."

Tom stared a hole into the counter. I waited. He couldn't keep his hands still. His fingers were knotting and unknotting. The bartender started toward us but I waved him off. Off in the booth Shannon let out a whooping laugh. Tom glanced over his shoulder, then turned a wretched expression to me.

"She made me promise not to tell anyone," he said softly. "Not a soul."

"Who did? Sophie?"

"Yeah."

"Well, Sophie's dead, Tom. I think the promise probably dies with her."

Tom fidgeted. "I guess it really doesn't matter as much. I mean you're right. Now that she's dead. It's kind of a weird story."

"Do you want another beer?"

"Good idea."

I signaled the bartender. Tom shifted on his stool.

"There's this thing called the ARK," Tom said. "Do you know what that is?"

"I've heard of it."

"It's this religious thing. And this guy who runs it . . . Look, don't tell Shannon any of this, okay? What I did was pretty weird."

"It's between us," I said.

Our beers came. Tom took a long pull.

"Sophie wanted to know if I could do her a favor," he said. "It was weird."

"That's what I'm hearing."

Tom let out a half laugh. "I mean seriously. Just listen."

I slept in the next morning. Monday. My morning dream featured an amalgam of Sophie and the actress named Shannon, smoking a cigar and stepping off the edge of a tree house. The Sophie/Shannon didn't drop, but floated like a sheet caught in an updraft. I was down below, at my catering table, handing out gin and tonics to an endless line of naval cadets, each of whom saluted smartly when he received his glass, then went down on one knee like Al Jolson. Libby and Mike made an appearance in the dream. They were standing together under the tree house, holding a large umbrella over their heads. Mike looked like he was about to cry. Libby looked coldly at him. The empathy I felt for Mike was palpable. I think that's what woke me up.

There was a head on the pillow next to me. It had eight-inch ears and a cold black nose.

I was out of dog food so I gave Alcatraz the last of the Grape-Nuts. I showered and shaved and pushed my hair around until it told me to stop. After the Grape-Nuts I was out of people food, too, so dog and I went over to Jimmy's, where I ordered a double omelet, sausage and home fries. I felt like flipping my skull open on a hinge and having Edna pour coffee directly onto my brain, but I refrained.

The little bells above the door jangled and Ray Ghost walked in. He was wearing a glen plaid suit, red tennis shoes and a dingy baseball cap with the ESSKAY logo on it. He looked like a Harry Dean Stanton character on his wedding day. Ray's real name isn't Ray Ghost, by the way. It's Ray Stone. He picked the nickname up a number of years ago when he was strolling across the grass at Greenmount Cemetery in the mustard-colored suit of a recently deceased butcher from Randallstown on the same afternoon that the butcher's widow happened to be out at the grave site doing a little weeding. When she looked up and saw Ray in her husband's suit—a suit she had always despised—she had fainted dead away, convinced that she had seen a ghost. On her way out of the cemetery she spotted Ray again; this time he was sitting on a gravestone with Greasy Kevin, sharing a box of Cracker Jack. She cried out, "Ghost!" and fainted again. Greasy Kevin told the story so many times that the name stuck.

Ray took a seat at my table and ordered a cup of tea. Edna tilted her coffeepot toward the table and I slid my mug under it.

"Coffee's bad for you, Hitch," Ray said as Edna shuffled off. "It dehydrates your brain. That's why so many people these days can't remember anything. You notice that? People are saying it all the time. 'I just can't remember.' That's because their brains are drying out."

"I'll try to remember that," I said. I made a loud sipping noise on my coffee then looked back up at Ray. "When did you get here?"

Ray said he wasn't hungry, then proceeded to pick from my plate. I offered him a fork but he preferred to use his fingers. Ray was about to head over to Read Street for a pickup. Billie had hosted a funeral the day before for a retired suit salesman. The widow had asked her about the dispensing of her husband's clothes and Billie had steered her toward the Church Home and Hospital Thrift Shop. Ray was expecting a gold mine.

"He worked for Stewarts for *fifteen years*," he said, wide-eyed. "And then Joseph Banks after that."

Ray asked if I didn't want a little pepper on my home fries.

"Sure," I said.

As he gave the shaker a vigorous workout he asked me about Libby.

"Are you going to marry her now, Hitch?"

"She's married, Ray."

"But she's leaving him, right? Isn't that right?"

"I can't say for sure. It's possible."

"So are you going to marry her?" he asked again.

"I'm not in love with her, Ray."

Ray set the shaker back down and considered this. "When I saw her the other day, I thought maybe you two could pick up where you left off."

I reminded him that where we left off, Libby was leaving me to go back to Mike. Ray scratched his head. Actually, he scratched his ESSKAY cap.

"She's still real pretty."

"Well then maybe you ought to marry her," I said.

He blushed. "Hey. C'mon. You said she's still married."

"You see how it works?"

I paid for my breakfast and for Ray's tea, then Alcatraz and I zig-zagged over to the funeral home. Aunt Billie was upstairs in her apartment, watching a rerun of *Love Story*.

"She dies, you know," I said, tipping my chin at Ali MacGraw on the screen.

Billie sniffed. "Not soon enough."

"How did your funeral go yesterday?"

Billie smoothed her dress with her palms. "It was fine. A sister read a poem that I couldn't for the life of me see how it might relate. A lot of barnyard imagery. A cow kissing a chicken. A little goat digging holes. It didn't make any sense to me, but then I didn't know the man. But they did bring a very nice suit to bury him in. And a lovely green tie. I thought it would look good on you."

"You didn't snitch it for me, did you?"

"I took a Polaroid."

She pushed herself out of her chair and went over to her desk, where she stirred through loose papers, muttering and humming to herself. On the television, Ryan O'Neal was making mincemeat of his lower lip as his eyes welled up with tears. Such a baby.

Billie stepped back over and handed me a Polaroid snapshot. A silver-haired gentleman lying in a casket. Large ears. Downturned mouth. Snappy green tie. Very dead.

"I thought I'd keep it in my purse. See if I don't run across it when I'm out shopping."

"You're going to go around town flashing this picture?"

Billie took the photograph back from me and gazed at it. "It's a lovely tie."

Alcatraz curled up at Billie's feet and set his muzzle on the floor. I stayed another few minutes but I couldn't take any more of Ali MacGraw's trash talking, so I went downstairs to my office. I picked up the phone and started to dial Libby's number in Bolton Hill, then I hung the phone back up. I really had no reason to speak with her. Instead I phoned Jay Adams, a fellow I knew at the Sunpapers. Jay and I had fought over the same woman the winter previous. Eventually we both lost her. No stronger form of male bonding if you ask me. I got Jay on the line and asked him if he had the time to be nosy for me. I wasn't asking for any heavy lifting. I gave him a name. It was the name Tom Cushman had given me the night before.

"I'm trying to get the story on a guy named Crawford Larue," I told him.

"Crawford Larue? You mean as in the ARK?"

"That's the one."

"Interesting fellow, Larue," Jay said. "What's your interest?"

"I'm not exactly sure. A friend of a friend apparently met with him a few weeks ago."

"Please, Hitch, I hate it when you bury me with specifics."

"Sorry."

"Why don't you just ask your friend's friend?"

"She's dead," I said.

"Ah . . . now you're setting the hook. What gives?"

"I'm not sure yet," I said. "I want to give this Larue character a call. I thought a little background first would be good. Can you just get me a general sketch?"

"I can tell you that he's an ex-con."

"That's a good start. What was he in for?"

"We have a thing in this country called taxes?"

"I've heard of them."

"And that would be why Mr. Larue went to jail and you didn't."

"He didn't pay them?"

"In his own way."

"I see."

"And before that he was the governor of Kentucky."

"Is that a joke?"

"I'm sure it wasn't to the citizens of Kentucky."

"Mr. Larue sounds like a well-rounded character."

"You could say that."

"What brings him to our neck of the woods?"

"Power. Prestige. Influence."

"Oh. That stuff."

"Listen. How about I call you back in fifteen?" Jay said. "I can dig up specific dates and all that kind of sexy stuff."

"Sounds good."

While I waited for Jay to call me back, I leafed through casket brochures. Talk about sexy stuff. I picked up the phone and dialed

Munger's number. Pete wasn't there. Susan answered. I didn't think I should give Susan a message for Pete about Lee Cromwell's having said hi. The two had never met, but conceptually at least, Susan knew that Lee was out there somewhere. I told her to tell Pete I'd called. I half suspected she'd pocket the message. Susan Munger and I are never going to be old drinking buddies.

Jay called back. I took a few notes as he gave me the lowdown and I thanked him for his time.

"Is this an interesting corpse?" Jay wanted to know. "This friend of a friend?"

"It's getting more so."

"What does Crawford Larue have to do with it?"

"I'm not sure," I said. "That's what I'm going to try to find out."

"He's a well-connected guy, Hitch. You want to keep your eye out."

"It's out," I said. "Thanks."

We hung up. I called Washington information and got a number. I called it. A woman with a southern accent answered the phone.

"Welcome to the ARK. How may I direct your call?"

I told her that I wanted to speak with Crawford Larue. She asked me my name and then put me on hold. I nearly hung up on an all-strings version of "Up, Up and Away," but I dug in and toughed it out. The receptionist came back on to say that Mr. Larue was unavailable. I asked her if she would please pass along the name Sophie Potts. I was put back on hold and a few minutes later a man came on the phone. He had a thick accent. Kentucky, I knew, checking my notes.

"This is Crawford Larue."

"Howdy. Hitchcock Sewell here."

"I understand you would like to speak with me."

"Yes, sir. It's about Sophie Potts."

"Miss Potts." He pronounced the name with an air of resignation. "Yes. Miss Potts. Enterprising young lady, Mr. Sewell. It *is* Mr. Sewell? That's your name?"

"My . . . Well, yes. Sewell. Two *l*s, two *e*s."

"Mr. Sewell, this is a delicate matter, as you know. You should hardly expect me to conduct this sort of business over the phone. Believe me, I would like to expedite this matter. But face-to-face, Mr. Sewell. And without games this time?"

"Games?"

"We need to talk."

"Fine," I said. I was now as intrigued as I was confused. "No time like the present. What say I pop on down?"

There was a brief coughing fit. When Larue came back on his syrupy voice had darkened a grade or two.

"That would be awkward. My wife and I are hosting a rather large party at the house this afternoon. Perhaps this evening. We can arrange a neutral location."

"Neutral location?"

"Yes."

"How about I think about this and get back to you?" I said.

"No." He fairly barked into the phone. "Please. Mr. Sewell. We have to talk. Don't hang up."

First rule of negotiation: Show 'em who's boss.

I hung up.

A minute later I picked up the phone and dialed an old familiar number. An old familiar number answered.

"Julia," I said. "I just heard the word 'party' and who do you think I thought of?"

Bells of delight chimed in her voice. "Me."

CHAPTER

12

Julia had her bare feet up on the dashboard. She was painting her toenails in an elaborate rainbow motif. My music of choice—*The Art of the Bawdy Song* by the Baltimore Consort— was no longer playing. Julia had ejected the tape and tossed it into the backseat. She had a tape of her own. Rosie Flores. "Rosie kicks buttskies," Julia announced. And so it was; Rosie was kicking buttskies as we tooled down the Baltimore-Washington Parkway.

Julia was dressed like a genie. Her near-transparent harem pants flapped in the wind, and I wasn't quite sure what it was holding her tiny silk vest together over her breasts . . . unless it was simply the breasts themselves. She was wearing a bright red scarf around her head, tiny gold bells on her ears and too much makeup. She flipped down the visor to admire herself.

"We're not going to visit a sultan," I said.

"Haven't you ever just woken up in a Turkish state of mind?"

We zipped past the exit for Greenbelt. NASA has a place there.

Somewhere beyond the trees lurked hundreds and hundreds of real-life rocket scientists.

"So who did you say is this big daddy we're going off to see?" Julia asked.

"His name is Crawford Larue. He used to be a horse breeder in Kentucky."

"I flew over Kentucky once."

"After that he was elected governor, though the governor thing didn't last long. He got caught up in a tax scandal before the end of his first year and got sent to the pokey."

"Can't govern from the pokey," Julia said. "Even I know that."

A rusted van with its rear bumper being held on by wire was in the slow lane. I drifted left to pass it. The driver looked like a member of ZZ Top. As we passed, Julia looked over at him and wiggled her fingers in a hello. The guy's jaw dropped so far I thought his beard might get tangled in the pedals.

"According to Jay Adams, the guvnah found the Lord while he was in stir."

"Is that where he's been hiding?"

"Larue got out after nine months of a two-year term. No doubt some strings were pulled. He came to Washington after that and landed the top spot at the ARK."

"That's the Association of Righteous Kooks?"

I glanced over at her. "We're just full of beans today, aren't we?"

The Turkish gumdrop was quite happy with herself. "We are."

"The Alliance for Reason and Kindness," I said.

"I see. And what do they do exactly?"

I shrugged. "Pretty much what you'd think. Preach the gospel of squeaky-clean living and family picnics. They support people who believe the way they do and spend money to squash the ones that don't. They take senators to lunch. That kind of thing. Jay says they're a pretty staunch crowd."

"Staunch?"

"Rigid. Righteous. I'm sure you're going to fit right in."

"And we give a hoot and a half about all this because *why*?"

"I told you. The nanny. Tom Cushman accompanied Sophie down here a few weeks ago to meet with Crawford Larue. It had to do with her baby. According to Tom, Larue and his wife are looking to adopt."

"Bully for them."

"When I dropped Sophie's name to Larue on the phone this morning, he didn't sound so bully. He sounded tense."

"Is that why we're going down there, Hitch? So that you can ease his mind?"

"It's awfully good of me, isn't it?"

"Oh yes. You're an awfully good man."

Julia moved her right foot up into the open window. Her harem pants ballooned like a sausage. She entangled a loose curl of hair on her finger and twisted it mercilessly. Her little ear bells tinkled in the wind.

Crawford Larue lived in a stately Georgian mansion smack in the middle of Georgetown. It's an area generally chockablock with elegant little Federal-style houses squeezed so close together you can borrow a cup of sugar from your neighbor by reaching out of your kitchen window and directly into theirs. Not so Larue's. Crawford Larue's house sat atop a small hill. A low stone wall surrounding the property reminded me of a moat. There was a circular driveway that encompassed a small stone fountain in which there was a sculpture of a pudgy little cherub having sex with a couple of swans. At least that's how it looked to me. Maybe it was simply a complex game of Twister.

An expressionless black man in a green jumpsuit and matching cap slid behind the wheel as I got out of my car. God knows where in the car-clogged streets of Georgetown the cars were being parked. You always hear stories in Washington about secret underground tunnels and bunkers where the top bananas would ride out the obliteration of the world should the global situation ever deteriorate to such an unsavory point. Maybe Larue had cadged one of these for his party. I watched the valet's expression as he searched for the transmission.

"Push-button," I told him, pointing out the buttons to the left side of the steering wheel. He hit the D button like he expected the car to explode.

Not too many of the women of D.C. were running around in harem pants and bejeweled peek-a-boo vests; Julia pretty much had that look all to herself. She was a regular eye magnet as we made our way through the crowd over to the makeshift bar. Several women gave me a sideways glance as well and I very politely returned them all. I recognized a drunk senator as well as a sober one and I pointed them out to Julia; also a steel-haired congresswoman most famous for having a voice that sounds exactly like Walter Cronkite. Most avuncular. I won't say the scene was outright dull, but I didn't see anyone swinging on the chandeliers. I did see chandeliers.

Julia and I had come unbidden through the open door. I cadged a couple of drinks for Miss Finney and myself and we stood scanning the crowd.

"Which one is our felonious host?" Julia asked.

"Can't rightly say. Though I'll recognize the voice when I hear it."

As we stood sipping our corn a man surfaced in front of us. He seemed familiar, but I couldn't immediately place him. He was wearing a brown sports coat and a faded jean shirt with a tie pulled loose. Tousled blond hair, a two-day stubble on his jaw and something mischievous in his blue eyes. He looked like a Hollywood bad boy, except that he was nearing forty. He had a cigarette tucked behind his ear and a martini glass in his hand. He took a few unapologetic seconds to track Miss Julia stem to stern. Julia went ahead and did the same to him, which seemed to amuse him to no end. He raised his glass in a small salute.

"You must be the Ostrows," he said. He had a down-under accent.

I saluted back. "No, we mustn't."

He frowned. "You didn't produce *The Bells of Titan?*"

I looked at Julia. "Did you produce *The Bells of Titan?*"

"I've never heard of *The Bells of Titan.*"

"Then you're the only ones in this room who haven't," the man said. "Where've you been, under a rock?"

Julia batted her lashes. "We're from Baltimore."

The man pointed at her with his glass. "Don't you go picking on Baltimore. My second wife came from Baltimore. We had some wild times there."

"I know you," I said. "You're a reporter. I was having drinks with Mike Gellman in Annapolis yesterday when you tried to sandbag him."

"Man of few words, our Gellman. Yes, I'm Nick Fallon. *Daily Cannon.*"

I quoted, " 'We Blow 'Em Out of the Water.' "

Fallon raised his glass. "By God we try."

"I'm Hitchcock Sewell," I said. "And this superficial bauble is Miss Julia Finney."

Julia handed him her fingers. Fallon wasn't exactly sure what to do with them. He looked like he might want to put them in his pocket but Julia slid them free and took a two-hander on her glass.

"I'm sorry we're not the Ostrows," she said.

Fallon made a face. "Ah, screw the Ostrows. This *Bells of Titan* is a load of tin trash anyway, be glad you haven't seen it. How the hell they roped the ARK into sinking so much money into that dog I don't know. I guess it's the ridiculous ending. Everyone's calling it redemptive. All I know is that if redemption is as tedious and maudlin as that then go ahead and make my bed in hell and I'll be happy."

Julia asked, "Are you drunk, Mr. Fallon? Or are you just a teensy bit insane?"

Fallon let off a huge laugh. "I like that!" He jerked a thumb at her. "She's something else."

I agreed. "She is."

"Is she yours?"

"I take her out for a walk once a week."

"That must be fun." Fallon took a long pull on his drink. "I'll tell you, I like the two of you more than the Ostrows already. I was supposed to get a quote from them but you know what, I'll just make one up. Hollywood people never read anyway."

He finished off his drink just as a young black woman was coming by with a tray collecting empties. Fallon set his glass on the tray.

"Are they paying you enough?" he asked gruffly. The girl smiled awkwardly. Fallon produced a ten-dollar bill and set it on the tray. "Of course they're not. You deserve to drive out of here in a gold Cadillac." He winked at her. "That's a vodka martini. Dry as a boot."

The girl moved off.

"I think they only collect empties," I said. "They don't deliver."

Fallon polished his tie with his knuckles. "They deliver."

Fallon latched on to us as we meandered the room. I asked him if he would point out Crawford Larue for me.

"I think Crawford must be in the living room," Fallon said. "It's about time for his speech. You might want to find a blanket and pillow."

"What speech is that?"

"What speech do you think?"

"I have no idea."

"Come on then. Follow me."

As we crossed to the next room we were met in the doorway by a young blonde woman in a black pants suit. She couldn't have been much more than twenty or so and she was very pretty, with a wide red mouth and Cherokee cheekbones. She came through the doorway like she was negotiating the deck of a ship.

"Mrs. Jenks!" Fallon cried. The young woman's head turned in our direction and her eyes settled like those little globe compasses people have on their dashboards. They were as black as the bottom of a well. Her hair was cut short and angular, with too much of it on one side. I suspect it was stylish. Her neck was the width of my wrist.

"Mrs. Jenks," Fallon said again. "Nick Fallon. *Daily Cannon*. How are you doing?"

The young woman peered at Nick like a raccoon from a hole. When she spoke her voice was nearly a whisper.

"I am . . . fine. Thank you." The voice was faint, but the accent was huge. It twanged like a banjo. Her gaze drifted to Julia and me. If she noticed that the woman in front of her was wearing harem pants and a teeny tiny silk vest, she didn't let on. If she noticed that I was trying out my best smile, she didn't let on about that either. Her gaze seemed to settle on my left earlobe.

"Hi," I said.

"Hello," she whispered.

"We're looking for your father," Nick said. The young woman's compass globes traveled back to Nick's vicinity.

"Daddy is in there."

She winced a smile, though it looked more as if someone had just landed a whip on her back, then she moved on into the room we'd just left.

"That was an odd one," I said. "Has she been on our planet long?"

Fallon tugged on his ear. "That's Crawford's daughter. The former Sugar Larue."

Sugar Larue. I couldn't be certain, but I believe I once met a stripper with a name like that. Or maybe I just dreamed about her.

"Is she sleepwalking or is that her usual party demeanor?"

Fallon shrugged. "She's a wacko kid, isn't she? I couldn't tell you. Did you see those eyes? Long ago and far away."

We moved into the living room. It was packed tighter than the room we'd just left except for a spot near the fireplace that had been cleared out. A lone figure was sitting there, in a wheelchair. His face was gaunt and pasty, splotched with an ash-gray beard. His shoulders were hunched and his large head hung forward like a vulture's. He was dressed in a seersucker suit and had a transparent tube running from his nose to a small red tank next to the wheelchair, strapped to a luggage caddy.

"Is *that* Crawford Larue?"

I had spoken too soon. The crowd was just quieting down and a little man shaped like an egg stepped over next to the wheelchair and turned to address the gathering. I recognized the rich mellifluous syrup immediately. *This* was Crawford Larue.

"Mah friends, mah honored guests. Ah'm indebted to the Lord for the gift He has made to us *all* of the great man you see seated before you. . . ."

Fallon let out a low groan. "Ah need mah mahtini."

Crawford Larue was all of five feet two if he were standing on a bucket. He was decked out in a three-piece cream-colored suit, shiny brown-and-white saddle shoes and a dark blue bowtie. A transparent frosting of sugar-white hair thinly covered a terrifically pink scalp. The face was also pink and somewhat elfin. On the phone with Larue I had pictured a larger, Noah-like figure. In the flesh he was a Weebles toy.

The egg rested a small pink hand on the old man's shoulder.

"Jack Barton was the agent of mah salvation in mah hour of need. We would not be here today . . . *Ah* would not be here . . . and possibly the ARK itself would not be here today, if not for the blessing of this magnificent man. . . ."

Larue blew on in this fashion a while longer. The man in the wheelchair glared out into the room as if he were trying to ignite the guests through the power of his watery eyeballs. It wasn't working. The girl collecting empties had tracked us down and she delivered Fallon his drink.

"Is that old guy going to live to the end of the speech?" I muttered. "He looks awful. Who is he?"

Fallon purred as he took a sip of his drink. "Big Jack? He's an old horse trader, like Crawford. The Virginia version. I'll tell you, it's a crime seeing him like this. That was one powerful man in his day, believe me. Jack Barton had more politicians in his pocket than most people have change. The poor old pisser stroked out a couple of years ago. It's been downhill ever since."

As Larue was wrapping up his tribute, the crowd parted and a tray came wheeling forward. There was a large rectangular cake on the tray with somewhere in the neighborhood of a thousand candles planted in it. Pushing the tray was an attractive redhead. She was packed into a conservative blue dress, and packed rather nicely, as I see these things. Larue concluded his speech, and the redhead turned to the room and pumped her arms in the air, getting the Happy Birthday song going. As it often does, it came out sounding more like a dirge. The woman bent down and planted a kiss on Jack Barton's forehead. The old man's hand raised, as if on pulleys, and swung out in the direction of the woman's sumptuous fanny. She slapped the hand away with a high laugh.

"That's Jack." Fallon chuckled. "Ain't dead yet."

The cake was rolled in front of Barton, and there was a bit of awkwardness at the realization that the old guy didn't have the wheeze to even begin working on the candles. Crawford Larue and the redhead bent over the cake and blew out the candles for him.

As the cake was being cut and pieces placed onto plates, Fallon led Julia and me over to Larue, who had moved off to the side of the fireplace and was engaged in conversation with an angular man wearing horn-rimmed glasses. He was around my age, with a narrow isthmus of curly black hair, the last holdout on a prematurely receding hairline. He jabbed his glasses up onto his nose as we approached and showed the world what a good solid sneer really looks like. Larue's eyes snagged on Julia and he stopped talking mid-sentence. A large smile crossed the oink face. Nick began the introductions.

"Mr. Larue, this is Julia Finney. Miss Finney, Crawford Larue."

Julia pinched her harem pants and curtsied. Larue nodded solemnly. "It's a pleasure to meet you, dear."

I stepped forward. "We spoke on the phone this morning, Mr. Larue. I'm Hitchcock Sewell."

The smile froze on his face. "*You're* Mr. Sewell?"

"That's right."

He studied my face a few seconds. "Well, aren't we full of surprises?"

"I wanted to apologize for hanging up on you this morning."

"And you came all the way down here to do it in person. How thoughtful of you." He took hold of the points of his vest and gave them a sharp tug. "I believe then that we have some business to discuss, Mr. Sewell. If the rest of you all will excuse us. Russell, why don't you circulate this exotic creature?"

Larue's companion aimed an uncertain look at Julia.

"Watch out, Russell," Fallon said. "I think she bites."

Julia slid her arm through the man's elbow. "Not true. Maybe a nibble now and then."

"Be sure to introduce her to Virginia," Larue instructed.

They moved on and Larue led me into his office, which was down a small hallway. The room was wood paneled, book lined, and stank of money. It also stank of leather. There was a large leather-appointed mahogany desk at one end—clutter free—a brown leather couch and matching armchair, puckered with leather buttons. On the far wall a wooden gun rack was mounted behind glass doors. I don't know my guns terribly well—I'd flunk the NRA quiz in a heartbeat—but the half dozen guns in the rack appeared to be shotguns. I wondered if the kick from one of those fellows wouldn't knock little Crawford Larue right onto his roly-poly. The wall by the door was dominated by a series of five leather-framed black-and-white photographs that showed from left to right a racehorse pulling away from the pack. In the first photograph the horses were clustered, but with each succeeding photograph, fewer and fewer horses appeared, until finally in the fifth shot the lead horse was all alone, straining for the finish line, its closest competition being the jockey on its back, who was himself straining forward, his chin down near the animal's ears.

"Damascus." Larue pronounced the name with a mixture of reverence and deep melancholy.

"The Derby?"

"Belmont. His Triple Crown."

"He's a beautiful horse," I said. The truth is, I don't really know one glue factory from another. But you say it about babies who in reality pretty much look like Eisenhower, and you say it to a man who has just said his Triple Crown winner's name the way Crawford Larue had just said it.

Larue directed me to take a seat on the leather couch. I did. The leather squeaked. Larue took the armchair. Even though the furniture was cleverly scaled down—my knees felt suspiciously close to my ears—Larue's shoes still didn't quite reach the floor without his having to tip the toes downward, which he did.

"Mr. Sewell, I would appreciate our getting directly to business. I do not want to be absent long from my party."

"That's fine with me."

A silence fell. Apparently we each felt that it was the other's to fill. Larue stepped in first.

"You said on the phone that you had business to discuss with me concerning Miss Potts?"

I corrected him. "In fact, you're the one who said there was business to discuss. I simply want to ask a few questions."

Larue balled his hands into a single fist and leaned forward in his chair. "How is the young lady? Is she well?"

"I'd say not. She's dead."

"She's dead?" Gravity took hold of the man's face. "Bless her soul. Young thing. What horrible news. Grievous. If I may ask, what happened?"

"She drowned. She went off a bridge."

"That's horrible." Larue sat back in his chair. As he did his feet rose from the floor. "Ah pray for her soul."

And by God he meant it. He folded his hands and bowed his head, nearly touching his forehead to his fingers. My hands felt suddenly like two large dripping fish. I pressed them together. Larue remained still for nearly a minute.

"Amen," he said presently. "Praise the Lord." He lowered his hands and raised his head. I detected the hint of something smug on his mug. The small eyes twinkled.

"You have me at something of a disadvantage, sir," he said.

"I'm sorry. How so?"

"I was expecting someone else."

"I don't understand."

"Your friend Miss Potts was accompanied by a young man when she visited. I expected you were he."

"I gave you my name on the phone. Two *l*s? Two *e*s?"

"The young man also gave me a name when he was here. He was very studied about it and I have to say, not terribly convincing. To be blunt, I believed very little of what came out of the young man's mouth. I was not born yesterday. There was an obvious deception going on. The young man was a bad actor."

I laughed. "That's a very good observation, Mr. Larue," I said. "The fact is, he's a terrible actor. I mean onstage."

"I am afraid I do not follow you."

"His name is Tom Cushman. He's in a community theater production of *The Seagull* right now, down in Annapolis. I caught it the other night."

"Tom Cushman?"

"What name did he give you?"

"He called himself Stan."

"Stan?" I rolled the name around in my head until it bumped into a wall. "Constantin."

"Excuse me?"

"Constantin. That's the name of the character he's playing in *The Seagull*. Con-*stan*-tin."

"I'm sorry, I don't understand."

"Forget it. Yes, he was posing. I met Tom just the other night, Mr. Larue. He told me that you met with him and Sophie concerning her baby. That's why I called you."

Larue made a temple of his fingers and brought it to his chin. "We did. My wife and I are in the market, so to speak, for a child. We're offering to pay all medical and related expenses."

"Tom was posing as the father."

"I'm not certain *what* your friend was posing as. Yes, he said he was the father of the child. He also said that he was married to someone else and that he was not in a position to help the young woman in any substantial way, which was why they had come to me. It all sounded off to me. Miss Potts said she was a good Christian. She would not be murdering the child."

"You mean having an abortion?"

"That is what I said, sir. The poor girl was quite upset. It is a horrible predicament when young women allow themselves to get into this position. My heart goes out to them. They who cast aside the armor of the Lord shall invite incursion from the devil."

I shifted in my chair. "I guess they shall. Um . . . look, Mr. Larue, I'm just trying to piece together Sophie's story here. Was this the first time you'd met her?"

Larue was studying me closely. He seemed almost to have missed my question. Certainly he ignored it.

"What is your agenda here?" he asked bluntly.

"My agenda?"

"Yes, yes. Let's move this along. Your agenda. Why are you here?"

"I'm . . . I just told you. I'm trying to piece together—"

"*Why?*" The pink in his face was deepening. "Were you terribly close to Miss Potts, Mr. Sewell?" He leaned forward in his chair and locked a hard look onto me. He lowered his voice into the accusatory range. "Was this your child, son? Is that what this is all about? Are you among the sinners here?"

I didn't respond immediately. I wasn't sure if I'd ever again field such a juicy question as his last one and I wanted to savor it.

"I never even met the woman," I said.

Larue blinked. Not simply a run-of-the-mill keep-the-eyes-moist sort of a blink. This one was Olympian. His eyes practically gulped. The muscles in his jaw seemed to relax.

"You never *met* her?"

"No, sir."

"Never spoke with her?"

"No, sir. Never."

"You had no contact with her either directly or indirectly?"

"That's right."

His lips pursed and suddenly he looked extremely pleased with himself. "I am going to ask you one more time, sir. What is your agenda? What are you seeking from me?"

I gave my noodle a scratch. "Well, for one thing, I'd be interested to know how it was Sophie got in touch with you in the first place."

"With all due respect, I believe that is a private matter, sir." He slid down off the chair. Our interview was apparently over. He ran a pink hand down the lapel of his jacket. "Mr. Sewell, I apologize, sir. There has apparently been a misunderstanding. I interviewed Miss Potts and . . . this other fellow."

"Cushman."

"Mr. Cushman. And nothing came of it. It appears that our paths, Mr. Sewell, have crossed by mere accident. I need to be getting back to my guests. By all means, I hope that you and Miss Finney will remain and enjoy my and my wife's hospitality."

I unpeeled myself from the leather couch and followed Larue back out of the room, where he quickly insinuated himself back among his guests. I scanned the room for Julia and found her holding court over by a punch bowl. The redhead who had brought out the cake was listening to Julia with a frozen smile on her face. The fellow with the horn-rimmed glasses was also with them. Julia was telling her Greek belly-dancer story. I waited until the punch line, which drew more laughter from Julia than from her audience, then came forward.

"It's time we hit the road, dear. They'll be sending out the dogs soon."

"We haven't met," the redhead said. "I'm Virginia Larue. Crawford's wife."

I'll be damned if the dapper little egg hadn't gone into the trophy room and pulled one down off the shelf. My guess was that she was in her late thirties and determined to remain there. The eyes were crocodile green. The smile was warm but the fingers were cold. I tested their temperature when she handed them to me.

"Mr. Sewell, I have been having the most intriguing talk with your friend here," Virginia Larue said. "She certainly seems to lead an . . . interesting life. Should I be believing everything she has been telling us?"

"Oh, why not? I do," I said. "It's so entertaining."

She introduced me to the fellow with the horn-rimmed glasses. His name was Russell Jenks.

"Russell is executive director of the ARK. He is Crawford's right-hand man," Virginia Larue said proudly, placing a hand lightly on the man's arm. "The ARK would be sunk without Russell." I wondered if she had intended to make a joke. Her expression indicated not.

Jenks gave me a vigorous handshake and a disarming smile. He blushed slightly. "Ginny is extravagant with her praise. I am a soldier. Plain and simple."

"The Lord has reserved a special place for his soldiers," Virginia Larue said. Julia moved her foot and gently pressed it onto my shoe.

"Jenks," I said. "I believe I met your wife."

"Sugar."

"That's the one."

Julia chimed in. "She has lovely eyes." She smiled sweetly at the man then averted her gaze as her own eyes crossed.

"We're off," I announced. I bid the soldier and the redhead a good afternoon and took hold of Julia's elbow.

"Lord save me," Julia muttered as I steered her toward the door.

As we reached the front door Nick Fallon appeared. He produced a business card and handed it to Julia.

"When you ditch this bloke why don't you give me a call?"

Julia didn't even glance at the card. She reached into Fallon's inside pocket and pulled out a pen. Smooth move. She scribbled something on the back of Fallon's card then tucked it into his breast pocket, giving it an extra little pat.

"I don't call, Mr. Fallon," she said. "I answer."

Mae West herself could not have said it so well.

CHAPTER

13

I took Libby and the kids for a picnic lunch in Patterson Park. We opted for the all-grease menu, a bucket of Popeye's fried chicken and a couple of bags of gloriously oily Utz potato chips. We set up near the Chinese pagoda. If you want to know why they stuck a Chinese pagoda in the middle of Patterson Park you're going to have to consult a guidebook; I've never sussed it out. Every Fourth of July the oriental structure is draped in patriotic bunting and a municipal band sets up for a program of John Philip Sousa. As far as anomalies go, the Patterson Park pagoda is an attractive one.

Libby and I sat on the pagoda's wooden steps and watched as Toby and Lily attempted to work out a tumbling routine on the grass nearby. We had Alcatraz along with us; he was keeping busy trying to pick up a slinky redhead named Polly. Polly was an Irish setter, skittish and swift. She was having none of my hound dog's moony moves. Libby looked beat. She had mentioned on the way over that she wasn't sleeping awfully well.

"Look at the bags under my eyes. I'm a wreck. I must get up at least three or four times a night and check in on the children. I've never done that before. It's exhausting."

There was something peculiar about the Irish setter. It was the way she ran. Her tail end moved faster than her front end—or nearly so—so that she practically ended up scampering sideways. Alcatraz was having a hell of a time figuring out which way the dog was actually going. I pointed it out to Libby.

"I've had a few relationships like that before."

Libby wasn't really watching. She planted her chin in her hands and gazed off past the romping curs.

"Mike called last night."

"Oh?"

"Yes, that's the other reason I'm so ragged. It must have been three in the morning. He'd been drinking, there was no question. He was pretty belligerent. He'd heard from my lawyer. I've started proceedings for a legal separation and I guess it really set him off. He yelled over the phone for a while until I finally hung up on him. He called back maybe an hour later. He was in tears."

"Full range of emotions. I guess that's sort of a healthy sign."

She sighed. "I really don't know what's going on with him, Hitch. Mike has so much going for him. He's smart, he's good-looking, he works hard, he's good at what he does. But he's one of those people who never seems satisfied. Do you know what I mean? He's always grabbing for more. This whole mess he's in now at work. I think he's really stepped in it this time. It's so damn ridiculous of him. Why would he risk everything like that? We could still be having a good life together, him and me and the kids. Just a normal regular life. That's all I ever wanted. For God's sake, I left you and went back to Mike because that's what he represented. You know that."

"That's the picture I got."

"So what is his damn problem? He swears he loves me, but some-times he's got a hell of a strange way of showing it."

"Like clipping you."

"Yes. Like clipping me."

Out on the grass, Lily was trying to teach her brother how to do somersaults. The concept clearly escaped the boy, who seemed content to squat down on his pudgy legs and set the crown of his head on the ground and just remain there. "Roll!" Lily implored, but her brother wouldn't budge.

"Maybe it's me, Hitch," Libby went on. "Maybe I'm a fool for thinking there's such a thing as a perfect domestic life. Mike and I looked good from the outside. But it was never near perfect. And you know the damn thing about it? On some level I knew what I was getting into. I think down deep I knew all along that Mike was a handful. I think that's why I freaked out originally, that's why I broke off the engagement. But I really wanted to start a family, Hitch. And so did Mike."

"And this was not a card I was playing."

"No, it wasn't." Libby looked down at her hands. "Mike is scared. There was a piece in the paper about the trouble he's in."

"I didn't catch it."

"Mike's being accused of looking the other way on a construction scheme. That half-built sports arena off I-50? It's public-works stuff, I don't understand it all. Apparently there's been some questionable fees"—she made a pair of quotation marks in the air—"solicited from certain law firms to help grease the rails on getting the thing passed through the legislature. Some sort of extortion. Or bribery. They're saying Mike has been working from the inside to keep the D.A.'s office from looking into it. He's being accused of blocking the investigation."

"Why would he do something like that?"

"You tell me. He swore to me on the phone last night that he's done nothing wrong. But do you make drunken phone calls at three in the morning if your conscience is clear? He was going on about his career being ruined. It was scary, Hitch."

"I saw him yesterday."

"I know. He mentioned that early on. He wasn't real thrilled that I've been in touch with you."

"That was the impression I got, too. He tried to warn me that you were up to your old tricks."

"Is that right? And what tricks are those?"

"Using me to get him jealous."

"Oh, for Christ's sake. As if I want to make him jealous. That's ridiculous. Mike just doesn't like you, Hitch. Plain and simple."

"Oh, I know that. He used the word 'slumming.'"

Libby looked up toward the roof of the pagoda. "God, yes, I've heard that one before. Mike thinks he's so damned lofty. Mr. Big Shot. Just ignore him when he talks that way, Hitch."

We fell silent for a moment. Lily's attempts to get her little brother to complete the somersault were fruitless. When she pushed him he simply fell over sideways. When she took hold of his ankles and attempted to swing his legs over his head, she ended up with a pudgy little wheelbarrow.

"I have something to tell you," I said to Libby. "It's about Sophie's pregnancy. Did Sophie ever mention a fellow named Tom?"

Libby turned the name around in her head. "No. I don't believe so."

I told Libby what I had learned about Sophie's ruse, about Sophie getting Tom Cushman to agree to pose as her husband for her meeting with the Larues.

"You're kidding. Oh, Hitch, that's horrible."

"You remember those pamphlets? The ARK?"

"In Sophie's room. Yes."

"And you're sure Sophie never mentioned anything to you about someone named Tom?"

Libby shook her head. "Never."

"That's where Sophie had been going every night. You told me she was going out that last week and not telling you where she went? She was going off to the theater in town to see Tom in his play. Apparently she developed a crush on the guy."

"Then it could have been him, right?" Libby said. "Why couldn't it have been this Tom guy who got Sophie pregnant? After all, that's what you say he told Larue."

"He also gave him a fake name and a fake story. It doesn't add up for me. I think Tom's telling me the truth."

Libby looked off toward the horizon. "I just can't believe Sophie went through all that. It's so sad."

"I tried to get Larue to tell me how Sophie got in contact with him in the first place but he didn't feel the need to cooperate. He seemed to lose his patience with me."

"What about this Tom? Does he know?"

"Could be. I didn't even think to ask him. I'm going to go back down to Annapolis tonight and look him up. I also want to ask him about Mike's ring."

"Oh, God. The ring."

"I'm thinking Sophie used it to help make her case that she had gotten in trouble with a married man."

"I guess Sophie could have stolen Mike's ring easily enough if she wanted it. It's true he never wore the damn thing."

Alcatraz had exhausted all his efforts with the Irish setter. He joined the children. Lily's somersault tutorial was a bust and she moved on to leap frog. Or in this case, leap dog. Alcatraz was the hurdle. Toby wasn't much interested in grasping this concept either. He preferred to fall against the dog and push his face into Alcatraz's fur. Lily had all the moves for exasperation down pat. I left the pagoda steps and joined them. I held Toby upside down and let Alcatraz lick his face, which seemed to please the both of them. Lily informed me that my new name was Underpants and she bounced around like a jumping bean crying out, "Underpants! Underpants!"

Some minutes later Libby got up and began spreading out the sheet for the picnic lunch. I left Toby teething happily on Alcatraz's tail and Lily and I helped her mother unpack the food. When we were set, Lily insisted on feeding her brother. With a ferociously determined expression she wielded her drumstick like a paintbrush and soon had Toby's face liberally smeared with grease.

"I wonder if this is how Julia got her start," I said. "If it is, you'd better put a stop to it. Surely you don't want your daughter following in those footsteps."

"You know, I don't understand why the two of you didn't stay together," Libby said.

"What's not to understand? Marriage turned out not to be our métier."

Libby gave me a look. "Don't go thinking you can squirm out of it with a little French."

"I'm not. It's a fact, Libby. Marriage nearly ruined a beautiful friendship. It was a bad fit for the two of us."

"But you love her, Hitch. That was always so obvious."

"Of course I do. And she still thinks I'm a pretty sweet pickle as well. Look, I've known Julia since we were in diapers together. We shared side-by-side bassinets up on the bar at the Screaming Oyster. We took baths together. She's like a very very sexy sister to me. I know her better than I know anyone. And yes, I love her to death. But none of that is a reason why we should climb into a box together and do each other irreparable damage. We're lucky we figured it out as quickly as we did." I ripped open a new bag of Utzes and held it out to her. "Besides, that woman is nuts. Don't forget that. A man has to protect himself."

"I still think it's sad."

I wasn't sure what to say to that, so I said nothing. I've had these conversations about Julia before. It's nothing that words really succeed in explaining. I have a whole pocketful of metaphors for my friendship with Julia, but I've never found one that satisfies the situation. There was a time there when it obsessed me somewhat, trying to get a handle on the nutty thing. Big waste of energy. It was like trying to stuff a sperm whale into a popcorn bag. One day I simply decided that *Julia* was a nutty thing—granted, a drop-dead nutty thing of absolute maximum vivacity—and that there was simply no getting a handle on *her*. She wouldn't fit into the bag.

"I'll bet she's still gorgeous," Libby said.

"Julia? Still makes strong men weep."

Libby shook her head slowly. "Hitchcock, can I go on record that I think you are an absolute fool?"

"Noted."

We fell into a silence and watched the kids a while longer. Alcatraz had seen all that he could take and was licking the mess off of Toby's face. The boy got such a case of the giggles that he erupted into hiccups. This set Alcatraz barking. Made for an interesting chorus.

Lily came over to us and I handed her a plum. She had a little pink plastic pocketbook with her—about the size of a change purse. She opened it up with much ceremony and dropped the plum into it.

"Is that for later?" I asked.

"'S for Cindy."

"Cindy? Is that your goldfish?"

Lily rolled her eyes. "Noooo."

"Who's Cindy?"

Libby ran a napkin over her daughter's face then bapped her on the fanny.

"Scoot."

Lily shouldered her little purse and made her way up the steps onto the pagoda. She was talking to herself. Libby watched her for a few seconds then turned back to me.

"Cindy was our other nanny," she said. "The one we had before Sophie. Lily's been bringing her name up a lot the last couple of days. I think she's beginning to combine the two in her mind."

"What happened with that one anyway?" I asked. "I don't think I know about that."

Libby rolled her eyes. "There's one I'd as soon forget."

"How so?"

Libby hesitated. She glanced up again at her daughter.

"It just didn't work out. The thing is, Mike grew up having a live-in nanny, but that's not really the world I come from. I was happy to raise Lily without help. After Toby was born, though, my hands were full and Mike really pushed the idea of going the nanny route. I didn't argue. I needed the help. And we had the space. But Cindy just didn't turn out to be such a great choice. She was fine at first. No real complaints about how she dealt with the kids or anything like that. But she liked to go out a lot and she wasn't always—"

There was a noise behind us and Libby spun around.

"Lily!"

Lily had clambered up onto the railing, on her stomach, and was seesawing precariously over the ground some twenty feet below. Libby leapt up.

"Lily! Get down from there. Right now!"

Lily continued to seesaw. I jumped up and scrambled up the steps just as the strap from Lily's little purse slipped from her shoulder. Instinctively she reached to catch the falling purse. I lunged for her. Libby screamed. I got hold of the girl's right ankle just as she was tipping off and raised her up high enough into the air that she wouldn't hit the railing as she swung back like a pendulum. I prayed that the little ankle wouldn't snap.

"Gotcha."

I brought her safely back over the railing and Libby rushed over to help me set her back down. Lily sat a moment looking at the two of us, blinking like a canary, then her face suffered a minor implosion and she began to cry. Libby dropped to the ground and took the girl into her arms. I stood by in thumb-twiddling mode, which is what heroes have to do sometimes. Goes with the territory.

Libby sat rocking her daughter until the girl began to settle down. She looked up at me with a harried expression.

"The gray hair. It's coming any day. I just know it."

After a few minutes Lily turned off the spigots. The well was dry. The crisis was a thousand miles away. She announced that she wanted to go home.

"Okay, honey," Libby said. "I think we're about ready to go anyway. Why don't you go get your brother ready."

Lily gave her mother a first-rate scowl. I'm telling you, the kid really had it.

"I want to go *home*."

Libby looked over at me. I mouthed, "Annapolis?" She nodded.

"Go get Toby ready, honey," Libby said. Lily crawled down the steps backward, on her hands and knees, then went over to retrieve Toby, who was once more squatting down with the top of his head resting on the ground.

"She's reverting," Libby said, standing up and brushing off her pants. She ran a hand through her hair. "Every day she's acting more and more like a baby. It's a stress reaction."

"Could be worse," I said. "She could be hitting the sauce."

"Much more of this and that's what *I'll* be doing," Libby said.

We packed up and headed out of the park. Lily decided that the place she wanted to be was up on my shoulders, and I'm such a sucker for what women want, that's exactly where she landed.

Sam was outside hosing down the hearse as we rounded the corner off Aliceanna Street. We stopped and I introduced him to everyone. Lily's eyes went wide. I'm not sure she'd ever seen such a large person before. At least not up close. She asked Sam why he was black.

Sam gave her a large grin. "Because black is beautiful," he said to her.

Lily turned to her mother. "I want to be black."

"It takes more than just wishing," Sam said to her.

"I want to be black," Lily announced again.

Sam patted her on the head. "Keep wishing."

Libby and the kids took off. I popped inside and found Billie in the display room, vacuuming. I stood in the doorway and watched her running the Hoover in and around our half dozen display coffins. Her head was down and her focus was fierce; she didn't even see me.

I crossed the lobby and entered my office. Alcatraz trotted behind me. A midget was seated at my desk, leaning back in my chair, his feet up on my blotter. It was Darryl Sandusky.

"Hey, Goldilocks," I said, "that's my chair."

"I know. I'm trying it out."

"Why don't you go in there and help my aunt?"

Darryl smirked. "I like *your* job. Cleaning, that's women's work."

"You're swimming in politically incorrect waters, young fellow," I said, stepping over to the desk. Darryl was wearing scuffed black shoes. The sole of the left one had an elliptical worn spot. It was worn in gradations, like on a topographical map. Darryl had his fingers laced behind his head. I had to admit, the kid looked like he was born to kick back in a chair like that.

"When do I get to see a dead body?" he asked.

"I think I need a note from your mother before we start down that path," I said.

"That's not what you said before."

"Doesn't matter, it's what I'm saying now. No cadavers without a note from Mommy."

"You're no fun."

"Maybe you should try playing with someone your own age," I said.

"They're no fun, either."

"Sorry about that, sport. Come on now, scoot."

Darryl brought his feet down off my desk and stood up. He clomped over to the door. "I'm just trying to learn a trade."

"I understand that. And I'm just trying to get in your way."

Darryl sneered at me. "Well, you're doing a good job."

Darryl left. I got *my* feet up on my desk and I ran through my mail. Nothing to sing arias about. Billie had left the *Sun* on my desk. I checked to see what the world was up to—it seemed to be doing its usual skipping-along-with-a-club-foot routine—then I ran through the obituaries to see how the competition was doing. Seemed there were enough dead folk to keep food on everyone's table for at least one more day. I checked my watch. Oh, gee, quitting time. Billie was still vacuuming—Parlor One—when I left. I poked my head into the room and yelled, "Good-bye!" but she was a million miles away and didn't hear me. Alcatraz tried unsuccessfully to trip me several times in the half-block walk back to my place but I danced as deftly as Gene Kelly each time and remained upright.

After dropping Alcatraz off at home I headed over to Julia's gallery and found Pete there, putting the finishing touches on Julia's new counter. Chinese Sue was already ensconced behind it. She was nearly finished with *The Mill on the Floss*. Only because I'm a glutton for Chinese Sue's particular brand of disdain, I asked her how she was enjoying it. She looked up from the pages and puckered her lips, then simply outstared me.

Munger was in a foul mood. I ambled around the gallery and looked at Julia's stuff while Pete finished up. When he was done, he was in no mood for compliments. I gave him one anyway.

"Nice work, Pete," I said.

Chinese Sue set her book down carefully and leaned as far as she could over the counter to appraise it upside down. She looked up at Pete and granted him not much, but still a damned sight warmer look than she's ever given me.

"Only took me an entire week," Munger grumbled.

"Took God just as long," I said. "And a lot of the stuff he did ended up breaking."

Pete said he wanted a drink. Turned out he wanted several. We went to the Oyster and I sat on the bar stool next to him while he put a couple of dents into a bottle of Jim Beam. I stuck with coffee. When Pete asked me why he was drinking alone I told him I was the designated listener.

"If you've got anything to talk about, Pete, I'm ready."

He replied with a low threatening sound from his primal arsenal.

"That's good, Pete. That's a start. Just get the flow going."

Which in fact he did. For the next forty minutes he didn't shut up. He and Susan had had a fight. A real howler. Pete sought to put it in a historical perspective by taking a trip down memory lane to some of his and Susan's previous altercations. I give Pete points here; he wasn't condemning his wife. He didn't cast Susan as the villain, but showed equanimity in dispensing the blame. His most recent tangle, he said, had featured his throwing a bowl of cereal across the kitchen in the morning room and Susan heaving a half gallon of milk right after it.

"Same thing happened at lunch," Pete grumbled. "I threw my grilled cheese sandwich out the window. Plate and everything."

"You might have some kind of eating disorder," I said.

"Funny."

"Who made the sandwich?"

"Susan did."

"That was mean of you."

"I guess that was the idea."

"So what did Susan do?"

"She threw the frying pan."

"The one she'd just cooked the sandwich in?"

"Yes."

"Did she throw it at you?"

He shook his heavy head. "Out the window. I was egging her on. Married as long as we've been, you know how to push the buttons."

"Why do you figure you're doing it?" I asked.

"Because I'm an idiot."

I told the idiot to drink up. "We're heading down to Annapolis," I said, reaching for my wallet.

Pete balked. "Like hell. I'm staying right here."

"No, you're not. You're coming down to Annapolis with me. There's someone I want you to talk to."

"I'm not talking to Lee," Munger said sullenly.

"In fact, Pete, that's not who I meant. It's a guy I ran across last time I was down there. He was mixed up with Sophie just before she died. I want to ask him a few more questions and I thought a surly lunk like you might be of assistance." I signaled for the check. "But sure. Hey. While we're at it, why not pop in on Lee's show and catch a few tunes?"

"Last thing I need right now is to see Lee," Pete grumbled.

"Wrong, bosco. She's the elephant in the corner. You can't just pretend she's not there."

Pete finished off his drink. He tested the empty glass in his hand.

"You don't give a damn about my marriage, do you?"

"Your marriage sounds to me like a Warner Brothers cartoon, Pete. I'm picturing this house with all sorts of stuff flying out the window."

"That's how things go, sometimes."

I slid off the stool. "Come on."

Pete looked at me cross-eyed. "You're not hearing me."

"I hear you. And I'm ignoring you. Listen, if you really want to work on your marriage you're going to have to settle up with Lee one way or another. You kicked open that door. You're not going to be able to square with Susan if you leave it hanging open. It doesn't work."

"The expert."

"I'm glad you're finally starting to see reason. I'll bring my car around."

Pete murmured, "I can drive."

"I know you can. You can also run your car into a telephone pole or maybe off a bridge. It's amazing all the things you can do."

I made Sally promise to pour at least one cup of coffee down Mr. Munger's throat while I was off fetching my car. Even a gruff bear like Pete knows better than to argue with Sally. He was standing outside the Oyster when I pulled up. He was holding a paper cup.

CHAPTER 14

The Wine Cellar is a low-ceilinged brick sarcophagus in the basement of the George Washington Inn that feels very much like an underground bunker. The room used to serve as one of the inn's two wine cellars until sometime in the seventies when management determined that they could get by with just one wine cellar. They converted the other cellar into a jazz and blues club. There was room for about fifteen tables. Twice as many had been shoehorned into the space, perfect for accidentally picking up the drinks of people at neighboring tables or going to scratch your ear and ending up in a fight.

Pete and I descended the steep stairs to the Wine Cellar and worked out the engineering plan for getting ourselves safely to a table. Even before Lee appeared we were a captive audience. Our waiter lowered on ropes—so it seemed—and took our drinks order. He pooh-poohed Pete's cigarette before it even got to Pete's mouth. Pete eyed the guy. "Okay if I just chew on it?"

While we waited for our drinks I filled him in on the latest. He listened without interrupting, without so much as nodding his head, without giving any indication that he wasn't daydreaming of a Gauguin-like existence on the faraway isle of Tahiti. I described for Pete how I had gotten nothing from my conversation with Mike Gellman beyond confirming that the two of us didn't particularly care for each other. I told him about Stephanie and Faith and their leading me to Tom Cushman. I didn't go into detail on *The Seagull* production, but I told him Tom Cushman's story of his and Sophie's visit to the home of Crawford and Virginia Larue and then of my visit to see Larue. The Sphinx across the table showed no reaction. I leaned across the table and waved my hand in front of his face.

"I'm here," Pete grumbled.

"There was something strange going on," I said. "It was clear to me on the phone that he was anxious to talk to me. But when I got down there and we talked, I don't know, Pete. Nothing seemed to really come of it."

"So he was anxious when you talked to him on the phone but he wasn't anxious at the end of your meeting."

"He didn't seem it."

"Then you must have said something to ease his mind."

"But I didn't really say anything," I said.

Pete picked up his drink and looked at it a moment. "That must be what eased his mind."

I mentioned Mike Gellman's other problems and Pete said he had read about them in the paper.

"It sounds like your friend's husband really stepped in it. They're saying a buddy of his in the state legislature was a silent partner in a bogus law firm that was extorting money from the people putting together that arena deal. This so-called law firm was nothing more than a big black briefcase just sitting open on the floor. It didn't really *do* anything except collect some big fat fees that found their way into the legislator's pocket. In return he twists a few arms, calls in a few favors, does what it takes to get this arena deal through. Good old-fashioned influence peddling. You drop in the money and good things will happen. The D.A.'s office should have been all over this. It was apparently a very crude operation."

"And Mike's being accused of stonewalling the investigation."

"I think the word they use is 'obstruction.' Your friend Gellman could be facing some deep deep doo."

"I think the word they use is 'shit.'"

The house lights dimmed, then a soft blue light came up on the low stage. A shadow stepped up onto the stage and into the blue light. Lee Cromwell was in a sleek black dress that fit her tall body like a mermaid's skin. The dress was ablaze with silver sparkles that threw back the blue light like a disco ball. I glanced at Pete. I've probably never seen a sadder look on a face.

There was a smattering of applause. Lee placed her hand on the standing mike and with her other hand chased a stray wisp of hair from her face.

"Thank you," she said in a somewhat husky voice. "My name is Lee. I'll be your singer tonight."

"She looks good," I hissed at Pete across the table.

Pete didn't respond. I wasn't there. Neither were the several dozen tables nor the people seated at them. I'm not sure if Lee's bass player and the pianist even made the cut. Lee swung her arm back toward her bassist and counted off a languid, "One . . . two . . ." She lowered her lips to the microphone.

Can't believe, you want to quit
Just when the sun's gone down.
I can't conceive, that this is it
Thought you were coming 'round.

I started to say something to Pete, but he hushed me.

Am I the fool who didn't hear
The words you fought to say?

Or are you the fool, who won't believe
Where there's a will, there is a way.

I picked up my drink and leaned back in my chair. An image came to mind. It was an image of Susan Munger, seated at a table not unlike this one. Expressionless. She was placing a hand of cards facedown on the table and skidding back her chair.

Lee ran her show with scant patter between songs. At one point, maybe five or six tunes in, she did shield her eyes from the stage lights and look over in our direction. She consulted briefly with her musicians, then launched into "Don't Come Around Much Anymore."

"Subtle girl," I remarked.

I was also keeping my eye on the time. The theater where *The Seagull* was playing was just down the street. I didn't want to miss Tom Cushman.

At around ten, Lee took a break. The exaggerated hip moves required for her to make her way to our table are probably illegal in some countries. As she approached I stood up and told Pete I was popping upstairs to the bathroom. He tried to murder me with his look, but I turned and let it bounce off my back. As I did, Lee gave me a little wink.

Upstairs, a willowy blonde bumped into me as I exited the men's room. Her hair was pulled back and tied off in a skinny ponytail and there was a smudge of flour on her cheek. She was wrapped in a well-soiled apron.

"I know you," she said.

"I know you," I answered back. "You're Hope. Or is it Trust?"

"Faith."

"I was getting there."

"Hitchcock Sewell. Did I get it right?"

"Every syllable. So do you always run around in public in a dirty apron or do I assume you're working tonight?"

Faith asked me if I had time for a drink. I told her I could probably rearrange my schedule. I followed her to the bar. Her skinny pony-tail whipped and danced. So did my second chakra.

After we ordered our drinks, Faith said, "I never thanked you properly for helping out the other day."

"It was no problem. I had fun."

"Stephanie tells me you're an undertaker. Is that for real?"

"My customers think so."

"Well, that must be interesting."

"Good days, bad days. Like everything else."

Our drinks arrived and I tossed out a few of my stories on the trade. Faith was drinking a seltzer water with lemon. The bartender had given her a red stir straw with her drink. She stuck it in her mouth like it was an oversized toothpick and grinned at my stories. Every time she laughed that damned straw bobbed about in her mouth like she was conducting a symphony orchestra. We chatted on a bit until our drinks ran dry, then Faith said she had to get back to the kitchen. I thanked her for the drink. She set her fingers on my hand and left them there.

"No problem."

I reached out with my free hand and plucked the straw from her mouth.

"Sorry. It was driving me crazy."

"It's a nervous habit," Faith said. We slid off our stools at the same time. Same side. This left roughly a centimeter between us.

"You should come back sometime and try the food," Faith said. "If I do say so myself, it's very good."

"I'll do that."

"I get off in a couple of hours. Are you staying for the next show?"

"Actually, I'm popping out right now. But I'm coming back."

"Good. Why don't you find me?"

"That sounds like a good idea."

Faith slid away from our close proximity. She picked up the straw from the bar and popped it back between her teeth.

"It is."

She headed off for the kitchen and I headed out the front door.

Five minutes later I was nearly killed.

I had left the inn and trotted down Main Street toward the harbor. My chat with Faith had eaten up more time than I realized and I was afraid I was going to miss Tom. I paused on the corner just across the street from the theater. The tail end of the audience was coming out the front of the theater. As I stood there, the rear door of the theater opened and out came Shannon, followed by Tom Cushman. They started off in the opposite direction from me. I called out.

"Tom!"

They stopped. Tom spotted me.

"Hold on!" he called out. He said something to Shannon and then came trotting across the street. "It was *great* tonight!" he said as he neared the curb. He was beaming. "Constantin got some real respect. He—"

I never heard the rest of the sentence. The actor never got the chance to finish it. Or if he did his words were swallowed up by a loud squeal as a dark blue car came barreling through the intersection. I jumped, and landed hard on my front on the sidewalk. It was not squeezably soft. I heard a large sound, sort of like a sack of dough being dropped onto the floor—rather, *thrown* onto the floor—and something dark flew past me. It rocketed into the plate-glass window of an ice cream parlor on the corner. I heard an explosion and then glass was raining down on me. I ducked my head just as a large wedge of glass landed on me. I felt a kick in my hand.

And then there was silence.

And then there was screaming.

CHAPTER

15

PVA910. PVA910. PVA910. . . .

A Korean War veteran from Lansing, Michigan, got to me first. I raised my head to a pair of skinny legs with doorknob knees, a pair of Bermuda shorts and a T-shirt that read Erin Go Bra-less. The shirt included a cartoon of a perky colleen, barebacked, raising a mug of beer and winking over her shoulder.

PVA910. PVA910. PVA910.

"Don't move," the Korean War veteran instructed. "You've been hit."

PVA910. PVA910.

The Samaritan had a face like a beaten biscuit. Funny, because that's exactly how I felt. The man stripped off his T-shirt, revealing a Buddha-like torso tufted with wiry gray hair. He got down on his knees next to me and gingerly wrapped the shirt around my left wrist. The tip of his tongue peeked from the corner of his mouth as he went about it. He was wearing glasses, which were sliding down his nose. He kept knocking them back into place like those prizefighters who jab themselves as they dance around the ring.

"What's your name, son?"

I muttered, "PVA910."

He frowned and shoved his glasses again. "You're in shock."

He finished wrapping his T-shirt around my arm and asked me if I thought I could stand. He helped me to my feet. I was woozy, so he slid his shoulder under mine for support.

"We'll get you a medic."

Shattered glass was everywhere. I picked a few pieces out of my hair. People were darting every which way. Tom Cushman, however, wasn't. He was laid out on one of the ice cream parlor's cast-iron tables, which is where he had landed after going through the window. He was as still as the center of a glacier. There had been a couple seated at the table. The girl was the one who had started screaming. Her face was pinpricked with blood and a thick strand of her hair was dark and matted. It looked like a piece of pull taffy. She was standing next to the table where Tom Cushman lay. One of the actor's tennis shoes had come off. There was no sock. I stared at the motionless foot and my heart sank. The big toe just seemed to be begging for a tag.

Opposite the girl stood . . . I don't know. Her boyfriend? Her date? Her brother? Her guru? Whoever he was he was contending with a shirtfront covered with ice cream and chocolate syrup. He seemed quite focused on it.

I was still muttering, "PVA910. PVA910. PVA910."

"We need to get you to sit down, son," my good Samaritan said to me.

"Paper," I said. "Write it down."

"What?"

"Write it down."

He dug into his pants pocket and pulled out his wallet. He extracted a business card. He turned to a woman who was of an astonishingly similar body type and asked her if she had something to write with.

"Peg," he said to me as she stirred through her purse. "We're from Lansing."

Peg delivered a pencil. She snapped her purse closed and waited for further instructions.

"PVA910," I said. "Could you write that down?" He did and he handed me the card.

"Thank you." I held up the arm with the bloody T-shirt. "And thank you."

An ambulance arrived, burping and whining. Two police cars pulled up. The EMS workers waded through the glass and began working on Tom right there on the table. They stabilized his head and neck with a thick collar and a gargantuan emery board then brought in a gurney and transferred him to it.

"This man needs attention!" my hero called out, indicating me. People were looking at him oddly—or not at all—primarily I suppose because of his great exposed belly and chest. One of the EMS workers came over.

"Man took some glass in his wrist. We've got some bleeding."

A second ambulance arrived in another minute and I was escorted over to it and told to lie down in the back. Just before I got into the ambulance I handed one of the policemen the business card. Before I did I glanced at it. Walter Minnick. Authorized Ford and Chevy dealer. Lansing, Michigan. Korean War veteran. It said so right on the card.

"What's this?" the policeman asked.

"PVA910. Maryland tags," I said.

"The car?"

"The car," I said. "Dark blue. Midsize. I missed the make."

I was loaded into the ambulance and the doors were closed. I heard two sharp raps on the doors and I looked up to see Walter Minnick through the rear windows. He was giving me the thumbs-up. I responded by half.

The fellow who stitched me up held several patents. It seemed to be something of a hobby. He ran his needle and thread over my wrist like

Grandma working on the family quilt and told me about several of his inventions.

"Picture a tent, okay? You're camping. You've got all that gear you've got to tote along. So the ground is rocky and bumpy, okay? Now let's say you forgot to bring along your sleep mattress, okay? Well how about this? The actual floor of your tent *is* a sleep mattress. Okay? You've got a foot pump with you and you just inflate the entire floor of the tent. Okay? You get it?"

"What if you forget the foot pump?"

"You've got the option to blow it up the old-fashioned way."

He had another one.

"The soap bag. You know when you've used up most of your soap in the shower and it gets where it's all thin and hard?"

"Soap chip."

"Right. Okay? So there's this little baggie, right? It's porous. It's got a Velcro strip to seal it. And what you do, you stick your soap chips in the baggie, right? There's still soap in them. And it's like—"

"The soap bag," I said.

"Exactly! You get it."

He also had an idea for a hairbrush that had a safety razor in the handle and a small alarm clock embedded in the back of the brush.

I asked, "Perfect for travel?"

"Yeah! It's great, isn't it?"

Thomas Edison was putting in eight stitches to close the gash on the back of my wrist.

"You're lucky," he said as he finished up. "If this was the other side of your wrist you'd be in the morgue now."

"That's a pleasant thought."

"Yeah, man. You're lucky."

Tom Cushman hadn't been so lucky. He was still in surgery. The unofficial assessment of his injuries was that he was Battered to Hell and Back.

A policeman was waiting for me after I emerged from the emergency room. He was the officer I had handed Walter Minnick's business card to. He asked me a few questions about the car that had plowed over Tom Cushman. I repeated what I'd seen. A dark blue sedan racing out of nowhere.

"That was heads-up thinking," the officer said. "Getting the tag number."

"I have my heads-up moments."

I also have my play-dumb moments, and I trotted some of them out as the policeman asked me a few more questions. I really wasn't in the mood to explain precisely how it was that I knew Tom Cushman or to give the officer the sort of information that might make him want to expand his questioning of me. I suppose it was wrong of me, holding back like that, but I wrestled my conscience to the mat without too much trouble. What I wanted was a Garbo moment. I just wanted to be alone.

The officer let me go after not too very long and I made my way into the waiting area hallway. Shannon was sitting quietly in one of the molded plastic chairs. She was holding something in her lap, and as I approached I realized it was Tom's tennis shoe. It looked like a little shuttlecraft resting on her lap.

Shannon looked up at me with a decidedly unpleasant expression on her face.

"Well?"

The possibilities of her question were innumerable, but my energies were too depleted to do anything but give her the only warranted response. Who was the injured party here, after all?

"Well what?"

"He might die."

"And he might live," I said wearily.

"But he might die."

Apparently she was going to insist on this possibility's dominance.

"I guess we'll have to see," I said.

"It's your fault," she snapped.

I eased myself down into a chair opposite her. We spoke across the wide hallway.

"My fault? How do you see that?"

"Tom was so damned impressed with himself tonight," Shannon said. "He totally changed the way he was playing Constantin. He said you told him the other night at McGarvey's that everything he was doing was wrong."

"It was."

"Well, he was horrible tonight. He stank."

I leaned my head back until it rested on the wall. It's amazing how almost getting run down by a car and losing a lot of blood will take it out of you.

"Shannon, no offense, but he stank before. His Constantin was a wimp. Admit it."

The actress didn't make any defense. "Well, tonight his Constantin was macho and it was ridiculous. It didn't make any sense. All my scenes with him were idiotic."

I sighed heavily. "I'm sorry."

"Then he saw you on the corner and he got all excited and he went running off across the street like . . ." She searched for a good metaphor but came up empty. "Like an idiot."

My head was pounding. My wrist was pounding. And Shannon was irritating me. I closed my eyes. I had no idea what time it was but I knew it must be past closing time for the George Washington Inn and the Wine Cellar. My rendezvous with Faith had evaporated. And Munger was probably ready to throttle me. My guess was that he would have gotten a ride home with Lee. Oh, to be a fly on *that* steering wheel. Who knows, though? Maybe things had worked out with Pete and Lee and Pete was thrilled that I had disappeared. In which case it would be Susan Munger who would want to throttle me, if word somehow ever got to her. I made a mental note that in my next life I'd have to see about not meddling in other people's infidelities.

I opened my eyes. I was still there. So was the magnificent Shannon. "Do you want anything from the cafeteria?" I asked her. "I'm going to get some coffee."

"I don't drink coffee," she said with a petulant sniff.

I gave her a wink as I pushed myself out of the chair. "You're welcome."

There was no cafeteria, just a row of machines dispensing burned coffee, lifeless sandwiches and cardboard pies. I found the actress who was playing Constantin's mother seated at a table with a cup of coffee. She had a hard, weary look to her. Her hair was banged around the way Judy Garland's used to be.

"Mind if I have a seat?"

"By all means. Any word?"

"None that I've heard." I dropped into the chair opposite her. "Hi. My name is Hitch."

"Jean Rose. Looks like you got yourself a little banged up."

I held up my bandaged wrist. "Doctor says my clavichord-playing days are behind me."

"You're a friend of Tom's, aren't you? I saw you two leaving the theater together the other night. Tom mentioned you. You're the undertaker."

I gave her my weary smile. "Got any dead people I should know about?"

"That's not funny."

"I lost a lot of blood. I think it took the common sense out of me. I'm feeling a little light-headed." I rubbed my face with my good hand. "Hey, you want to get married and move to Guam?"

"You're cute."

"I liked you in the play, by the way. You're the best thing in it."

Jean set her chin in her hand. "I'm afraid that's not saying much."

"Still, you were good."

"Well, thank you." The woman gave a little punch to a stray bit of her hair. "Tom told me about that little girl. It's so sad."

"You mean Sophie?"

"It's a horrible thing."

I leaned forward on the table. "Tom told me that Sophie had been showing up at the theater every night."

"That's right. Glued to her seat. Front row center."

"He said she had a crush on him."

"I suppose she could've. Tom's a good-looking man."

"Any idea how Shannon took to that? She doesn't strike me as the magnanimous type."

"Shannon's a little bitch."

"So that's it. I couldn't put my finger on it."

Jean laughed. "I played Nina once. Back in the horse-and-buggy days. Now I'm Arcada. It's a shame Chekov didn't put an old crone in this one, I could be riding *The Seagull* right up to the bitter end. Our director dug through the archives and pulled out the reviews for my Nina. May I tell you that I was spectacular?"

"I'm convinced."

"May I tell you how gracious Shannon was?"

"I can guess."

"Snotty. Nasty. Take your pick."

I blew on my coffee. "What did Shannon think about Sophie's fawning over her boyfriend?"

"Not much, I would think."

"Do you think there might have been something going on between Tom and Sophie?"

Jean Rose pursed her lips. She looked like she was ready to blow a bubble. "I wouldn't know for certain, of course. But I doubt it. The girl didn't strike me as Tom's type." She laughed. "Nowhere near mean enough."

I bought her a second cup of coffee and she told me several theater stories. They were caustic and largely irreverent and they gave the woman the chance to show off her big smoky laugh.

"We're all children," she said. "That's what it really boils down to."

As we were talking, Shannon appeared from around the corner.

She was still holding Tom's shoe. She stopped at the concession machines.

"No more show," Shannon said. "Tonight was it."

"I think we knew that," Jean said.

"Well, now it's official," Shannon said. She glared at me. "Tom's dead."

She dropped his shoe into the trash can.

Jean Rose gave me a ride back to town from the hospital. I wondered if Munger might have left a note on my windshield, but he hadn't. The windshield was bare. I thanked Jean for the ride and she drove off. I got into my car and sat stock-still for at least five full minutes, then I cranked her up and drove out of town. On the Naval Academy Bridge I checked my rearview mirror, and seeing no cars I pulled over as far as I could to the side of the roadway and got out. I stepped over to the guardrail. The sky was black. The water was black. There was no distinguishing where the one let off and the other began. I tried to conjure some significance in that, but I couldn't. I guess there was none. I looked around and saw a soft-drink can on the side of the road. I picked it up and leaned out over the side of the bridge and dropped it. I counted, one . . . two . . . three . . . four . . . five. . . . The can took a turn under the bridge and out of my sight.

Six . . . seven . . . eight . . . nine . . .

I never saw it land. Never heard it. It simply vanished.

I got back into my car and continued on down the bridge. A half mile up the road I took a right and drove along a wooded road until I reached the driveway of Libby and Mike's house. I parked on the road and got out of my car and started down the driveway. There were no lights on in the house. A red sports car was parked by the front door. Another car was in the carport.

I could hear voices. They seemed to be coming from the trees. I continued down to the end of the driveway and high-stepped over the bushes there. My night vision was coming on and I detected a glow coming from the back of the house. I made my way along the side of the house, and slipping carefully from tree to tree (as Hollywood has taught us), I reached the backyard. Some twenty feet above me was the deck. The glow was coming from there. So were the voices.

I made my way cautiously along the perimeter of the lawn out to the far edge of the property, where the grass met the woods. Though partially obscured by tree branches, I had a better view of the deck from here. I could make out two people sitting in the hot tub. The blue-green glow was coming from a light—or lights—that were in the tub itself. The glow danced and wobbled, throwing off liquid shadows across the deck and onto the high branches above the deck.

One of the people in the tub stood up. It was Mike Gellman, dressed just as he had been on the day he was born. He grabbed a towel and crossed the deck, passing into the shadows. I heard the sound of the sliding glass door open. Soon after, the other person rose up from the tub. It was a woman. Her back was to me. Can't say I recognized the back. It wasn't Libby's, I could tell that much. Steam from the tub rose up with her. She stepped out of the tub and across the deck into the house. Swiftly, I made my ever-so-stealthy path back to the driveway where, not sure what to do next, I stood behind the shrubs like an uncertain lawn ornament. I waited less than ten minutes. The front door opened and Mike and the woman emerged. Mike was positioned so that I couldn't get a clear view of the woman as she slid into the driver's seat. Mike bent down. Unless Mike and the woman were biting down on the same piece of taffy I'm going to assume they were kissing. Mike pulled back from the car. The headlights went on—along with the engine—and the car pulled away.

I had to wait until Mike got back inside the house and had closed the door, then I moved as quickly as I could up to my car and took off down the road. I picked up the taillights of the red sports car before we had hit the main road. I kept my distance. The car went right. Twenty seconds later, so did I.

I was able to remain fairly far back. The red sports car was easy to keep in sight. We headed west and then slightly south. I tapped the cassette tape hanging out of the machine. The tape disappeared, and a second later, Rosie Flores appeared. Julia's tape. I remembered it like it was yesterday. Which, in fact, it had been.

Forty minutes later the red sports car took a left turn into a driveway. I was a block behind. I watched as the car's headlights swept briefly over a small stone fountain. Maybe one day I'd have to get a closer look. But to my eyes, the chubby cherub was still screwing the two swans.

And Mike Gellman was screwing Ginny Larue.

And presumably, vice versa.

CHAPTER 16

My alarm clock licked my face every hour on the hour, starting at one of the ungodly ones. I resisted the rousing call until finally I feared my dashing good looks would be slobbered entirely from my skull. Can't have that. On feet of lead I made my way to the shower, then afterward lowered my head into a bucket of caffeine. I pride myself on being in pretty good shape (I do a push-up on Tuesdays, on Thursdays I jog down the steps to the sidewalk, and on an average of once a month I pull my old Dunlop racquet from the closet and plunk on its strings banjo-style while jogging in place), but I suppose the gymnastic of diving out of the path of an oncoming car isn't the sort of thing for which even a hale and hearty carcass like mine stands at the ready. I sat at my kitchen table with that old hit-by-a-freight-train feeling and contemplated the dull life of the undertaker. Not for the first time in my life I reflected warmly on the idea of curling up inside a soft, quiet casket and pulling the lid closed.

I pulled on a pair of jeans and a Terrapins sweatshirt. I skipped shaving and took my mug of coffee down to the front step, where I sat and watched Alcatraz distributing While You Were Out notes up and down the block.

I tried to focus on the events of the previous evening, but unfortunately my brain was working like a loosely screwed in bulb. On a frayed wire. Dangling in the wind. I could flicker, but that was about it. The image of Ginny Larue rising naked from the steaming water of Mike Gellman's hot tub . . . that image flickered a fair number of times. In slow motion. In stop action. Zoom in, zoom out. The dancing blue light from within the tub. The steam swirling about Ginny Larue's hips. What it all told me beyond the fact that Mike Gellman was indeed a dog, I couldn't say, but as far as images go, it wasn't a bad one. Far better than the image of Tom Cushman lying motionless atop a faux-antique wrought-iron ice cream parlor table bathed in a chopping red light. With each flicker of this particular image—the girl standing next to the table in a horrified scream—a queasy feeling came over me, along with a stab of guilt and an unsettling spasm of anger. As I sat there, a trio of Jehovah's Witnesses came down the street and calmly discussed Armageddon with me until I finally cried uncle. I was told that God would welcome me into His Kingdom and that all who had not joined in the righteous battle would be destroyed.

"But what about my dog?" I asked. "Who will feed him?"

No one seemed willing to answer that one for me, at least not in the five seconds I gave them before pulling open my screen door and heading back inside. The dog in question bounded past the Witnesses and stumbled excitedly back up the stairs. I plodded behind him. I scooped some mush into his bowl, poured myself another mug of coffee and was asleep before it was quite half done. I woke up in my easy chair nearly an hour later with a neck that refused to swivel to the left.

"Get a gun," I said to Alcatraz. "Shoot me."

Maryland license tag number PVA910 was registered to a Howard Small of Severna Park, which is just outside of Annapolis. Howard Small was six feet five and fifty-three years old and I have to figure that if he hasn't heard every single riff on his name commensurate with his height then he simply isn't listening. Mr. Small runs a pest-control business in the Annapolis area called BUG OFF! He employs three field-workers and a secretary named Florentine. When the police had arrived in mid-morning to question Mr. Small as to the where-abouts of his car the night before, the pest-control man pulled out a checkbook and said, "All right, I knew this was coming. Just give me a figure." One of the two officers had exploded, "A check? You want to give us a damn *check*?" at which point Mr. Small had reached into a desk drawer and pulled a handful of cash from a metal box. The same officer spotted a pistol in the metal box. He immediately drew on the tall man and ordered him to raise his hands and to step away from the desk. When Florentine saw this, she went into a fit. Appar-ently Florentine could throw a world-class fit. Ten minutes later the police car pulled away from BUG OFF! with Howard Small *and* Flo-rentine in the backseat. Small was bellowing for his lawyer and Flo-rentine was simply bellowing. Matters got straightened out at the police station. It turned out that Howard Small had amassed unpaid traffic fines totaling three hundred and forty-five dollars and he had assumed when the police showed up that they had come to BUG OFF! to collect. The gun was found to be legally registered. Small was furi-ous. Fortunately for the two police officers, Florentine turned out to be an acquaintance of one Croydon Floyd, and the officer had been able to talk Florentine into persuading her boss to let the matter drop. In return for the favor, Croydon Floyd had a date with Florentine for the following weekend.

My information came from Croydon Floyd himself. After I woke up a second time I phoned the Annapolis police station and asked to be put through to Floyd if he happened to be there. He was. I asked him if he remembered me and he said he sure did. He said he had noticed my name in connection with the hit-and-run last night. He sounded a lot friendlier on the phone than he had been in person the other day.

"That Florentine has got a mouth on her," he said. "You've never heard a person screech so loud."

"It sounds like you saved the day," I said.

"Yeah, saved the day and messed up my Saturday night. Florentine wants me to take her dancing."

"What's wrong with that?"

"You've never seen Florentine dance. There'll be about a dozen medical emergencies before the night's over, I can tell you."

I steered the officer back to the original issue.

"So what about the hit-and-run?" I asked. "What about Small's car?"

"Describe the car again. The one that hit you."

"It didn't hit me."

"Describe it."

"Dark. I'm pretty sure it was blue. A midsize. Nondescript. Cars like that all look alike these days."

"Honda? Toyota? Saturn? Saab?"

"Yes," I said. "All of those. Any of them. I didn't see the name of the car. I was focusing on the tag. PVA910. I'm sick of it. It's like a bad song I can't get out of my head."

Floyd said, "Howard Small drives a Land Cruiser."

"A Land Cruiser."

"They're pretty big," Floyd said. "More like a truck. Definitely not a midsize."

"I see."

"His Land Cruiser is white."

"White."

"That's right," Floyd said. "And not on the dark side of white. Just regular old white. We're running the other combinations. Maybe it was PUA. Or maybe you inverted the numbers. Maybe it was 019."

"PVA910," I said. "It's tattooed on my brain. Maybe someone stole the plates."

"Stole the plates? And then what? Returned them later?"

"Right."

"Why would someone do that?" Floyd asked.

"I'm not sure. Maybe that way, if anyone spots the tags, which they did, you trace them and they go nowhere. Which they haven't. It's a regular old hit-and-run."

"Same question. Why would anyone do that?"

"Well, that's my point. It's *not* a regular old hit-and-run. The fellow who was killed last night? Tom Cushman? He knew Sophie Potts." Floyd didn't respond. "Did you hear what I said?"

"I heard you."

"Interesting, isn't it? Girl dies under mysterious circumstances and a few days later an acquaintance of hers is mowed down by a car."

Floyd cleared his throat. "I guess you could call that interesting."

"Is there anything new on the Sophie Potts investigation?" I asked.

"We have no new information."

"Except now. This is new information."

"What is? The fact that an acquaintance of the deceased got hit by a car? People get hit by cars every day."

"So you think this is just a coincidence?"

"I can't say either way, can I? I appreciate you passing on the information."

"Let me ask you something. Why is it that you're so convinced that this girl killed herself?"

"I could ask you why you're so sure she didn't."

"But I asked first."

The officer was losing patience. "Look. We have the report from her employer that the deceased was behaving erratically prior to her disappearance. She was then—"

"Wait. What are you talking about? Mrs. Gellman mentioned to me that Sophie kept to herself. That's hardly 'erratic.' "

"I interviewed Mr. and Mrs. Gellman when I took the original missing persons report," Floyd said flatly. "We followed up, of course, after the body was found."

"Followed up with who?"

The officer paused. "Who do you think?"

"I don't think anything. I'm asking."

"We followed up with the Gellmans, of course."

"Both of them?"

"I don't really have the time for all of this. Yes. Both of them. Mr. and Mrs. Gellman. What do you think we are down here, the Hardy Boys? We know how to do our job."

"And the Gellmans told you that Sophie Potts was . . . what did you say, unsteady? Erratic?"

"I assure you we are doing everything necessary to determine what happened." He sounded as if he were reciting from a script.

"Don't assure me, Officer. Assure the mother."

"Are you through giving me orders?"

"That hit-and-run last night was no accident. That's all I'm say-ing. I was there. That car veered right toward us."

"Maybe you should consider yourself lucky then," Floyd said. "Sounds like that could've been you in the morgue instead of the other guy."

He hung up. I looked at the receiver as if maybe I expected it to sing "Swannee River." It didn't. I hung up and dialed Pete's number. He answered on the third ring.

"Hi," I said.

"Who is this?"

"It's Mr. Lucky."

There was a pause. "Not when I get through with you."

Following Pete's instructions, I parked my car on Sulgrave Avenue and walked around the corner to the next block and tried to look incon-spicuous as I strolled down the street to near the middle of the block, where Pete's white Impala was parked. I got in the passenger side.

"Afternoon, Chief," I said.

"Don't call me Chief."

Pete was sitting behind the wheel with a cup of coffee in one hand and a glazed doughnut in the other. A box from Dunkin' Donuts was on the seat next to him, along with a pack of cigarettes.

"You really do this by the book, don't you?" I said. "I suppose you've got binoculars, too."

He shoved the box of doughnuts. Sure enough. A small pair of Minolta binoculars was on the seat.

Pete was on a stakeout. Even though he had disbanded his private detection company in the spring, Pete still needed to put the old flank steak on the table now and then, so until he discovered what he wanted to be when he got to the other side of his crisis, he accepted the odd snooping job. He was keeping an eye on a house near the far corner of the street. A mid-level executive for a local home-heating-oil firm was out on workman's compensation for injuries allegedly suffered on the job. Pete didn't know all the details. In addition to the compensation claim, the man had filed a lawsuit. The home-heating-oil company, along with the insurance carrier, smelled a rat. That's where Pete came in.

"What happened to your arm?" Pete asked.

I had picked up the binoculars and was scanning the second-floor windows along the block. In the movies you can bet you'll come across something nibbly in lingerie. The best I managed was a fat lady and her cat.

"Things turned a little interesting last night," I said. "Why don't I tell you later?"

"You're assuming I'm giving you that much time to live."

I lowered the binoculars. "Can I tell you something, Pete?"

He sighed heavily. "Can I stop you?"

"You think you're angry with me. But the fact is you're angry with yourself and you're taking it out on me."

He stared blindly at the windshield a moment before responding. He took a loud sip of his coffee.

"That's bullshit," he said.

I dropped the binoculars back onto the seat and took a doughnut from the box. Coconut. "Listen, I was planning to come right back to the table after the bathroom." I took a bite of the doughnut. Coconut bits rained onto my lap. "I knew you were scared down to your toes to be alone with Lee, but see, I ran into this girl outside the bathroom."

"You're so predictable."

"No. Just hold on. She's the chef at the restaurant there. And she also happens to be one of the caterers who hired Sophie this summer. Her name is Faith."

"Faith. Okay. I'm listening."

"Faith's the one who told me about Sophie calling up to track down Tom Cushman's number. So what I—"

Pete interrupted me. "There he is."

Down the street a man had emerged from the house. He was wearing a neck brace collar. Pete reached into the backseat and fetched a camera with a lens half the length of my arm. He winked at me.

"Size matters."

Pete clicked off a series of shots then set the camera down and started up the car. The man in the neck brace had gotten into a maroon car and was pulling away from the curb.

"I tailed my first car last night," I said to Pete as we pulled slowly down the street.

"Is that so?"

"Yes." As we followed the maroon car up onto the Kelly Avenue Bridge I described for Pete my going off to meet up with Tom Cushman and the blue car that thwarted my plans. When I described Tom flying through the plate-glass window of the ice cream parlor, Pete nodded his head sagely.

"Man is not designed to fly."

"Not like that."

"Sounds ugly," Pete said.

"It doesn't get much uglier. He's dead."

The maroon car had gone right on Northern Parkway and was remaining in the right lane. It appeared to be headed for the expressway. It was. It eased onto the ramp just as another car veered suddenly into the lane in front of us. The maroon car headed to the northbound ramp and we followed, slowed down by the pokey in front of us.

I started to continue my story but Pete held up his hand.

"Wait."

At the bottom of the ramp the car finally sped up just as an SUV was coming up on the left lane, forcing Pete to remain where he was.

"Move," he grumbled and he leaned on the horn. There was a woman behind the wheel of the SUV and to Pete's and my surprise, she gave Pete the finger.

"What the . . . ?"

We were running out of lane, but the SUV was squarely in our way, keeping us from merging onto the highway.

"Fall back," I said to Pete.

"My ass."

Pete sped up. The guardrail was creeping closer to my side of the car.

"Uh . . . Pete?"

The SUV was speeding up as well. The two vehicles were in a little race. Except Pete and I were the ones about to run out of roadway. As the gravel of the shoulder was just beginning to slip under Pete's right front fender, Pete hit the accelerator. The car surged forward. Pete whipped the wheel to the left, skidding his car in front of the SUV. I turned around to see that it was right on our tail. The woman gave *me* the finger.

"She's a monster," I said to Pete.

Pete reached for the light switch and pulled the knob. At the same time he stomped all the way down on the accelerator. I turned around again and saw the SUV swerving. It had dropped well back. Another car had to swerve to avoid hitting it. One—or maybe both—of the drivers was honking their horn.

I settled back in my seat. The maroon car was well ahead, but easily in view.

"What was that bit with the lights?" I asked.

"You put on the lights and it looks like your brake lights have gone on. They hit their brakes. Meanwhile you floor it."

I finished off my doughnut. "Okay, just so that I know. When tailing a car that you don't want the driver to know you're tailing, you skid all over the road, honk your horn, flash your lights and almost cause an accident. Am I missing anything?"

Pete was glancing with some satisfaction in the rearview mirror. "No, that about covers it."

"Good. I just want to make sure I've got it straight."

"Did you do any of that when you tailed your car last night?" Munger asked.

"Nah. I just kept back a few hundred feet and kept quiet."

Pete chuckled. "Amateurs."

The maroon car headed past the Beltway exits and took the expressway to where it spills back onto the regular roads. We were in the country now. The car took a right onto Seminary Avenue. I had a feeling I knew where the car was headed and I was right. A few minutes after the turn onto Seminary we followed the car onto the grounds of the Baltimore Country Club. We parked in the lower lot, next to the woods. The maroon car parked up by the tennis courts. We waited until the man got out of his car and disappeared into the clubhouse, then we got out of Pete's car and plunged into the woods. Pete had his camera with him, on a strap around his neck. The woods weren't particularly thick. We made our way about fifty feet or so straight in, then Pete angled off to his right.

"Have you been here before?" I asked.

Pete was high-stepping over a tangle of dead branches. "I've been everywhere."

Ten minutes later we were crouched behind a large rotting tree. Pete was squinting through the viewfinder of his camera, muttering.

"Yeah, baby. Do it. That's right. Work it. Go for it, baby. . . ."

It was my simple assumption that he'd gone mad. So sad.

The home-heating-oil executive was on the first green of the golf course, visible through the woods. He was no longer wearing his neck brace. He was warming up for his tee off, taking huge slicing practice swings. I know as much about golf as I do the diet of a fifteenth-century Azerbaijani teenager. Still, it looked like a pretty good swing. Fluid. A nice corkscrew twist of the torso. Clean follow-through. The man finished with his practice swings and placed the ball on the tee. Pete was clicking away like crazy as the man set his feet, drew back the club and let her fly. The little ball rocketed out of sight.

"All done," Pete said, getting stiffly to his feet. "Now comes the fun part."

I followed as Pete stomped through the underbrush and emerged from the woods some thirty feet from where the man was standing admiring his shot.

"Nice shot," Pete called out.

We approached. The man's shoulders dropped as he spotted the camera with the huge lens dangling from Pete's neck.

"What's this about?" he snorted. "This is private property."

"So is this," Pete said, patting the camera, and then he mentioned the names of the home-heating-oil company and its insurance carrier. "It belongs to them. At least the film does."

"What's going on here?"

"Listen," Pete said. "You might want to consider holding your backswing a fraction longer. I think the way you're doing it gives your swing too much chop."

The man obviously wasn't listening to Pete. He put no pause whatsoever on his backswing, but brought the club around suddenly and caught the lens of Pete's camera. He knocked it right off. Quite emasculating. The lens rolled to a stop on the grass, a noticeable dent along the rim.

"Assault," Pete said calmly. "And the list keeps growing."

The man swung again, but Pete was surprisingly quick. He ducked. The club sailed harmlessly over him, and from his crouched position Pete lunged forward, plowing his head into the man's rib cage. Already off balance from the force of his swing, the guy flew backward, literally leaving his feet, and he landed hard against the front wheel of the golf cart, his head smacking against the hard rubber. His golf club clattered against the side of the cart. I watched as the two men simultaneously reached for their necks. Pete was slow to straighten back up. A baffled expression came to his face.

"Hurt yourself, Pete?" I asked.

"Damn. That's not supposed to happen." He held on to his neck and twisted his head gingerly left and right.

I stepped over to the golf cart. The man was making it to a sitting position. A wince of pain came to his face as he attempted to swivel his head.

"Ouchy?" I said. He responded with vituperative relish.

I nodded sagely. "I see. And touchy."

He growled.

"And grouchy." I turned. "Hey, Pete, this guy's reminding me of you."

Pete dropped me off at my car and suggested we stop for a beer. Rain clouds had rolled in as we were heading back in from the country. We went to the Mount Washington Tavern. The skies opened up while we were sitting in the bar. The bartender had a goatee and was wearing a Duke baseball cap. He wanted to be friendly, but Pete put the whammy on him.

"I need this kid to pretend he's my chum?"

"God forbid, Pete."

We got a couple of beers. Pete took up his bottle, sliding the empty mug down along the bar away from him. Pete's gaze wandered about the bar. It had a high ceiling, an open area upstairs for eating, as well as a covered area outside. Blond wood. Behind the liquor were large plate-glass windows that reached all the way up to the ceiling.

"There used to be a place called Sparwasser's here," Pete told me. "Nice old place. Big horseshoe bar. Pool table. And the best French fries and gravy you've ever had. There used to be a school or something up the road. Maybe it's still there. These kids with something wrong with their heads. They'd come streaming into Sparwasser's and get Cokes. Whole bar full of these poor nutty kids. Add that to your standard daytime drunks. . . . Hell of a place."

Pete's neck was still sore. He was palming it every so often and testing its turning radius.

"Christ, I should have taken that guy's neck brace."

I picked up my story. I told Pete about the lovely Shannon and how she blamed me for Tom Cushman's being run over and killed.

Pete asked, "This actor guy was screwing her, right?"

"Yes."

"And he was chummy with the pregnant nanny?" I nodded. "Friendly guy," Pete said.

"According to Tom he was just doing Sophie a favor."

"Some favor." Pete looked up at the long windows. The rain was slapping against them as if it wanted to be let inside. "Looks to me like your actor friend did Sophie a little favor he just didn't want to tell you about."

"You think he's the father?"

"I sure as hell don't buy that story of his. Just helping the girl out? Why would he bother?"

"He probably saw it as an acting challenge."

Pete thought a minute. "From the sound of it his little actress girl-friend wasn't too keen on the nanny either."

"Well, then maybe Shannon killed Sophie," I said.

Pete waved his hand. "Sure, sure. Why not?"

"I think Tom was telling the truth. He didn't have to tell me about his and Sophie's going down to see Larue. If he wanted to keep the whole thing under wraps, why tell me that story?"

Pete shrugged. "Well, we've got the age-old problem now. Thems that knows is thems that's dead. That's a tough one to get around."

I went on and told Pete about the license tag number on the car that killed Tom Cushman and about my talk with Croydon Floyd.

"I'm positive about the license tag number. All I can figure is that somebody stole those tags so that their car couldn't be identified and then returned them afterward so that the police would figure it for a routine hit-and-run. Which is exactly what they do think."

"You're not convinced, I take it."

"It was no accident. That car had Tom in its sights."

"And you didn't get a look at the driver?"

"It all happened too quick. I was on the sidewalk before I knew it."

"Well, what do you expect from the police? You gave them a tag number and they ran it down."

"I can't quite get a read on Floyd. That's the cop I talked with on the phone this morning. I tried to press him on why they're so ready to pass Sophie off as a suicide and he told me both Libby and Mike reported to the police that Sophie was kind of unstable. Libby mentioned to me that the girl was acting a little peculiar, but she definitely didn't suggest the girl seemed like she was on the edge."

"Maybe the cops just remember wrong. Maybe it wasn't Libby. Maybe it was just Gellman who said it."

"But based on what? The girl was quiet and she kept to herself. Do you see the bridges of America lined with introverts all waiting their turn to jump?" I picked up my beer. "What if you went down and talked to the police, Pete? You habla the language. Maybe you can get a better take on this than I can."

Pete shrugged. "I'll have to check my date book."

We finished our beers and called for another round. The bartender ignored Pete's grumpiness and was as chipper as he damn well wanted to be. He asked us if we had seen the Maryland game. Apparently Maryland had been awesome. I told him that we hadn't seen the game.

"Awesome," he said.

I gestured to his baseball cap and asked him if he went to Duke. He flipped his bar rag onto his shoulder. "Nah. That's just my nickname. I went to Maryland."

"I went to Frostburg," I told him.

Pete spoke up. "They call him Frosty."

"Excuse my friend. I take him out for little walks on occasion, but I don't think it really does much good."

"Hey, no problem," Duke said. "My dad's the same way. But he's cool. It's just a thing."

"There you go," I said to Pete after Duke had moved down the bar. "It's just a thing."

Pete took up his beer. "I'm so relieved."

"Let me throw the final piece at you," I said. "This is the sexy part of the show."

"I don't like the sound of that."

I went on and told Pete about my driving over to Mike and Libby's house after leaving the hospital and about peeking in on Mike's little hot-tub party.

"A shame I didn't have your binoculars with me."

"A shame you didn't have the camera."

"True. Except I couldn't make out the woman's face. That was my tailing job. When she took off I followed the car back to Georgetown."

"So your friend's husband is mixing it up with Virginia Larue."

"Right. What's the scrabble with that? One day Mike's nanny is asking the Larues to adopt her baby, a week later she's dead. And now it turns out Mike is screwing around with Larue's wife?"

"Stinks, don't it?"

Gusts of wind were kicking up. The rain slapped even harder against the windows. A tree branch, bent by the wind, was scraping against the top of one of the tavern's high windows. Down at the far end of the bar, Duke was flirting with a pair of women who were drinking fruity drinks. I heard him saying, "That's my nickname. I went to Maryland."

"I have a theory," I said. "About the hit-and-run. Actually, it's only half a theory."

"Let's hear it," Pete said.

"Mike Gellman and Ginny Larue."

"What about them?"

"You don't see it? The day before yesterday I identified this guy Tom for Crawford Larue. Tom used a different name when he and Sophie went down to D.C. When *I* went down to Larue's place, he was expecting Tom, not me. Tom was the one he was anxious to talk with. I don't think Larue was necessarily fishing for Tom's name, but I ended up giving it to him anyway. I told him that Tom was an actor in a production of *The Seagull* over in Annapolis."

"So?"

"So let's say Crawford mentions it to his wife. 'Hey, honey, do you remember that young man and that young woman I told you about?' Ginny gets the name out of him, and the fact that he's in Annapolis doing the *The Seagull*. She runs off and tells Gellman. The very next night Tom is plowed down by a car with a stolen plate—"

"You say."

"I say. He's plowed down and then several hours later the love-birds are whooping it up in a hot tub."

Pete took a moment to finish off his beer. He studied the label as if it were . . . well, as if it were more fascinating than it was.

"So Mike Gellman and Ginny Larue killed the actor," he said.

"That's right."

"I see. And do we know why?"

"I'm recharging my batteries, Pete. You'll have to give me some time."

"And so I guess they probably also killed the nanny? Is that where this is going?"

"Yes."

Pete thought about it a moment. His thumbnail ran a tear through the label on his bottle. He ran the tear the complete length of the label with the precision of a glass cutter, then looked over at me.

"Why does it have to be both Gellman and Larue's wife?" Pete asked. "Why couldn't it simply be Virginia Larue who's doing all this?"

"Why would she kill Sophie?" I asked. "Jealousy?"

"It wouldn't be the first time. But why would either of them want to kill this actor? From the way you put it he was just an innocent bystander. You haven't sold me."

"Well, I told you it was only half a theory."

"And who got the nanny pregnant?"

"You're expecting a lot of me, Pete."

Munger gave me his lopsided grin. "That's how it works. Don't forget, I used to be a lawyer. If you dropped this kind of thing into my lap I'd hand it right back to you."

"Okay then. It could be Mike who got her pregnant," I said. "It works for me. Mike can be a real charmer when he wants to be. I'm willing to bet a kid like Sophie would be more than susceptible to a snake like Gellman. And then when he found out about the baby he panicked."

Pete was shaking his head. It was obvious that he was not terribly convinced by my sketchy scenarios. Not that I could blame him. The pieces weren't fitting terribly smoothly for me either. Every so-called answer spawned a new pair of questions. An exponential experience.

Pete called Duke over and ordered a whiskey.

"Yes, sir," Duke said. "Will Jack Daniel's do?"

"Jack's fine." Pete asked me, "You want?" I passed. Duke brought up a tumbler and a bottle of Jack Daniel's. He poured the whiskey with an unnecessary flourish, then returned to the two women.

"So what happened with you and Lee last night?" I asked, changing the subject. "I assume she gave you a ride home."

"She did," Pete said.

"Did you two straighten anything out?"

He took a dip into his glass. "About what?"

"Come on, Pete. You've got one foot in and one foot out. Lee doesn't want to get in the middle of things with you and Susan, but otherwise she's all over you. You're her kind of bear. She told me so. So don't get coy with me, Munger. It's a long drive from Annapolis to Lutherville. You must have talked."

"We talked."

"See?"

"Then she dropped me off at the house."

"Okay."

"Then we made out in the car like a couple of teenagers."

The wind slapped furiously against the windows. A noisy group came bursting through the front door, drenched and laughing.

"Duke!" I called out. "Get back over here. Another whiskey. Pronto."

Pete was rubbing his sore neck. "I don't know, Hitch. I really don't know. . . ."

CHAPTER 17

The rain was still falling with verve and spunk and the sort of focused intensity that not a few people on this planet could stand to learn something from. The slightly tipsy mortician stood outside the town house à la wet rat. His shoes were filled with water. Rain ran unimpeded down into his eyes; no little windshield washers to keep things clear. He rapped a snappy shave-and-a-haircut, but held off on the two bits. A few seconds later the door opened.

"Hello, ma'am. Me and Mrs. Noah were wondering if you were up for a little sea cruise."

"Jesus, Hitch," Libby said. "Come in." I stepped into the vestibule. "Did you walk here?"

Fighting off the urge to shake myself dry like a dog, I attempted to squeegee myself in the entranceway. "The closest parking spot was two blocks away. I forded."

I peeled off my soaked sweatshirt, rolling it the way you crank the lid off a sardine can.

"What happened to your arm?"

The bandage on my wrist was soaked through and pretty much at the end of its usefulness. The adhesive was barely clinging. The puffy red edges of my wound were showing through.

"Oh," I said. "Look at that."

Libby directed me to take off my shoes and leave them by the front door.

"Give me your socks and your sweatshirt. I'll throw them in the dryer. You might as well give me your T-shirt as well."

I peeled off the wet T-shirt and handed it to her. "Do you want my pants, too?"

Libby smirked. "Keep your pants on."

I followed her downstairs to the basement, where she tossed my stuff into the dryer. She pulled a clean T-shirt from a pile of folded clothes and tossed it to me.

"This will probably fit. I use it as a nightshirt."

I held it up. The T-shirt had Nancy and Sluggo on the front. Handsome devils, as always.

"I'll bet you look sexy in this," I said.

"I do. Especially when I've got rollers in my hair."

"I go wild for that look."

We went back upstairs and I waited in the kitchen while Libby went off to fetch something to replace my dead bandage. While I was waiting, Libby's daughter stepped tentatively into the kitchen. She stopped just inside the door. Her little brother followed a second behind. Toby was wearing a pair of plastic pants as big as his head. He stood motionless on his chubby legs, wavering slightly.

"I want a hot dog," Lily said.

"Hot dogs are nice."

"I'm four."

"Four." I nodded approvingly. "How about that?"

"Toby hit me."

"I see."

"You're wet," Lily said.

"Yes. It's raining outside."

"I have a go-fish."

"Goldfish?"

"I can take a bath."

"That's right," I said. "And then you'd be wet, too. Just like me."

She stood a moment, absently picking her nose. I couldn't imagine a comb ever getting through all those dark curls. Toby was staring at me with large baleful eyes. He looked stupefied. But then I suppose I was a stupefying sight.

"Daddy is mad at me," Lily blurted. "My go-fish is Debbie. She doesn't have a mommy. She can swim."

"And she's wet," I pointed out.

The little girl's face crunched up. "She's a *fish*."

Libby came in to rescue me. She had a package of gauze as well as some adhesive tape. Lily was still making her troll face.

"Have you two been talking?"

"I want a hot dog," Lily said again. Then she performed a ballerina move.

Libby pulled a chair up next to mine. Lily's eyes went wide as her mother peeled the soaked bandages off my wrist. My stitches were black and ugly. Toby wobbled and dropped to the floor, his plastic pants arriving well in advance of the rest of him. Libby tore a strip of gauze with her teeth.

"So tell me what happened."

"It's a long story," I said. "Just an accident."

Libby paused. "Isn't it either one or the other? Accidents are generally quick."

"But getting to it," I said. "That's a little involved."

Libby made quick work of putting fresh gauze on my wrist and wrapping it with adhesive tape. She leaned down close to bite the tape clear.

"That should hold you."

Lily was fascinated with the operation. She held her arm out to her mother.

"Me."

"Not you, honey," Libby said. "You don't have an injury."

The girl persisted until her mother went ahead and bit off a length of adhesive tape and wrapped it around Lily's wrist. From the floor, Toby made a noise.

"Nrgmm."

He was holding out his pudgy arm.

"I detect a trend," I said. Libby wrapped the boy's arm in tape. "You're next."

"Sorry. I'm not going to play." Libby stood up and marshaled the children into a small room just down the hall and parked them in front of a television.

"Electronic baby-sitter. A mother's dream."

We went into the front room and settled on the couch. The large windows were nearly black, the rain slapped invisibly against them.

Libby turned to me. "So, Sluggo, to what do I owe the pleasure of your drenched visit?"

I had determined on the drive over that I wouldn't tell Libby what I had seen out on her deck the night before. The name Larue had drawn no reaction when I had mentioned it in the park the day before and I saw no need to toss a new log onto the fire. Even if Libby had her suspicions about Mike, it seemed she was in the dark about the specifics.

"There's something I'm not clear about, Libby. When the police came out to your house to take the missing persons report . . . isn't that a little unusual? I mean, why didn't you and Mike go down to the station to file your report?"

"I guess that's the way it's normally done. But Mike has pull. He knows those people. He got on the phone and arranged with Captain Talbot to send someone out."

"That's convenient."

"Why are you asking? What's so strange about that?"

"Nothing, I guess. I spoke with Officer Floyd on the phone this morning. He indicated to me that you and Mike painted a fairly dire picture of Sophie. I wanted to know why it is they've leaned so quickly to her having killed herself, and he said that from what he had gathered it seemed Sophie was pretty unstable."

"I never said anything of the kind. He told you that?"

"Mike was the one who identified the body. That's right, isn't it?"

"Yes. Mike got the call. I was up here. In Baltimore."

"It's possible Mike said something to the police at that point. I mean, maybe he steered them toward the idea that Sophie committed suicide. That's possible."

"But why would he do that?"

Even as the question left her lips, Libby's expression darkened. From down the hallway came the sound of canned laughter from the television. Libby's laughter sounded along with it.

I asked, "Has Mike ever cheated on you, Libby? That you know of?"

"That's what you think, isn't it? You think Mike slept with Sophie."

"I don't think you should be naïve, Libby. Mike is not dealing straight here. I think that's obvious." I realized that I might have no choice but to tell her what I had seen the night before. Libby had dropped her head and was lacing her fingers over and over. A long low rumble of thunder sounded from outside. I waited.

"Yes." Libby spoke to her hands. "He did cheat on me. He had an affair." I started to speak but she silenced me. "No. Let me just tell you. It was a little over a year into our marriage. There was a woman in the D.A.'s office. Maggie Mason. Technically she was Mike's superior. I found out about it. Actually, a friend of mine saw them having drinks together at a bar outside town and she called me up. It wasn't just drinks. My friend said they were all over each other. Don't ask me how a couple of prosecutors can be so reckless, but there it was. We already had Lily at the time, I couldn't just hop in the car and rush off to confront them. My friend's description was very specific. I knew who it was. She called me back up when the two of them left the bar together. I looked up Maggie Mason's number in the phone book and kept calling the number and hanging up when the phone machine answered. Finally the woman answered and I asked very calmly if I could speak to my husband. She tried to bluff, but I told her to save her breath. 'He's right there,' I said. 'I know it.' And I named the bar where they had been earlier. Mike was home in fifteen minutes. It was not a pretty scene, Hitch. He was furious. *I* was furious. He said I could cost him his job. He tried to convince me that I was wrong, that my friend had been mistaken about what she had seen, but I wasn't born yesterday. I could tell he was lying. Then he tried to blame her. Maggie Mason. He said they were working on a case together. She was putting the pressure on him. It was a mess, Hitch. I nearly left him. I was that close. And Mike saw that I meant it. He begged me to forgive him. He swore he'd never do anything so stupid again."

"And you believed him?"

"Here's what happened. About a week after this whole thing I discovered I was pregnant with Toby."

"Nice timing."

"Tell me. But that's really what held us together. You have no idea. It was like being slapped sober. We made a clean start. It was like a miracle. It was made a lot easier when Maggie Mason took a new job in San Diego."

"Nothing like putting an entire country between the two of them."

"Toby came along and everything was great. Of course Mike is a workaholic, I've always had to put up with that. He's so incredibly driven, it can get scary. And there's no way you ever forget someone doing that to you. It damaged things between us, no question about it. I told him that if he ever did something like that again I would kill him."

My thoughts settled on an image of Ginny Larue and Mike in the dancing light of the Gellman family hot tub. In the image, they were both draped over the tub. Not moving. My ears were hot with guilt. I

should tell her. It was her right to know. Why in the world was I protecting Mike Gellman of all people?

Libby was crying. Her eyes welled up and a tear traveled uncer-
tainly down her cheek.

"He did it again," she said, nearly in a whisper. "After all that, the
bastard did it again." She attempted a smile. She failed. "And I didn't
kill him. I didn't even confront him."

"When was this?"

"This summer. Just . . . oh my God. I've been trying to put it out
of my head, but it was just this summer. I started to say something
about it to you yesterday in the park."

"I don't remember."

"Cindy."

"Cindy?"

"Our other nanny. The one before Sophie."

This time the long low rumbling wasn't thunder; it was coming
from my own stomach.

"Mike was sleeping with your *other* nanny? What is wrong with
this guy?"

"The thing is, Hitch, I don't know for absolute certain. I could be
paranoid. I guess I could be making the whole thing up. I never had
the smoking gun on the two of them. But there was definitely something strange going on. You just had to see them together."

"What kind of strange?"

Libby fell back on the couch and took hold of her scalp. There's a
yoga move where you do this and you vigorously move your scalp all
around as if you're trying to yank it clear off your head. That's not
what Libby was doing. Almost the opposite, in fact. She looked as if
she was trying to keep her head from blasting off.

"I hate this."

"Tell me."

"I don't know what there is to tell, that's the problem. Cindy was definitely a party girl. She wasn't like Sophie. You'd never catch her sitting around reading books in her free time. It was always off to the bars. Off dancing. Off whatever. I couldn't begrudge her going out, of course. But still. I had to give her the lecture a couple of times. It wasn't so much her coming home late like she sometimes did, but in the morning, that's when I really needed her. What I didn't need was someone I had to drag out of bed. A hungover nanny is not exactly part of the bargain. Cindy's one of those tall and slinky types. She's pretty. She's vain. And of course Mike can be such a flirt. That's a dangerous combination right there."

"Why didn't you let her go?"

"Fire her? Believe me, I wanted to. But I just kept putting it off. Giving her another chance. The children really did get along wonderfully with her. I guess I was just avoiding the confrontation. And all the hassle of locating a replacement. And then this thing with Mike started up. Like I said, it wasn't something I could specifically put my finger on. It was just . . . sometime during the summer the vibrations between the two of them just started to get very strange."

"Strange. In what way?"

"It just began to feel creepy when the two of them were in the same room together. As if they were making an extra effort to appear normal. It just felt very much like they were putting on an act in front of me. Like they were trying too hard. That sort of thing. Of course that set off the alarm bells right away."

"And you didn't say anything?"

"I know it sounds lame but the truth is I really tried to push it away. I just wasn't ready to go through it all with Mike again. That whole thing with Maggie Mason . . . it was all still a bad taste in my mouth. I tried to tell myself that maybe I was just a little bit envious of Cindy and that was it. Young and pretty and running around all the time. It's kind of embarrassing to admit."

"So then what was the end of it? Why did Cindy stop working for you?"

"She quit. It was all very sudden. I came home one day and Cindy was packing up her stuff. She said she was quitting and going back to her old waitressing job. No explanation. She just said she wanted a change. It was incredibly unprofessional, of course, but frankly I didn't care. I couldn't believe I hadn't canned her earlier. Fine. Go. Get the hell out. I was tired of baby-sitting the baby-sitter. When Mike got home that night and I told him that Cindy had quit, he tried to look surprised. But he couldn't pull it off."

"He knew?"

"He knew. And that's when *I* knew. Or figured I did. Either she had told him in advance or they had talked sometime during the day after she left."

"Why didn't you put it to him at that point? Confront him."

"I know, I know. But where's my proof? He could simply deny it and tell me that I was being paranoid. I was just happy to have her gone. Turns out the little sweetie stole some of our silver on her way out. Just a real class act all around."

"You're kidding. Did you contact the police?"

"Mike did. Or maybe he didn't, who knows? He told me he had. It was stuff from his side of the family. Frankly I didn't even care at that point. I just wanted that girl out of my life."

Libby stood up suddenly and stepped down the hallway to check on the kids. I watched her as she stood at the door and spoke to them, though I couldn't make out what she was saying. She came back down the hallway and stopped just inside the entrance. Her arms were coiled tightly against her chest. She looked either like she was hugging herself or like she was wearing a straitjacket. Both, I suppose.

"I hate this," she said.

Aunt Billie had been an embalming machine.

"Where have you been, nephew?" she asked me when I came through the door. "They've been dropping left and right."

Two new customers had come in. Billie had handled them both.

They were in the basement, chock-full of formaldehyde, glycerin, phenol, borax, alcohol, and water. Billie mixes a mean cocktail. She took me downstairs to introduce me to our customers.

"Woman named Brenda. Tripped over her cat at the top of the stairs and fell all the way to the first floor. She broke three ribs, her collarbone, ankle, and dislocated her shoulder."

"She should be in a hospital," I said. "Not a funeral home."

"Well," Billie said, "there was also the neck."

Brenda was a hairdresser from Woodlawn. As bald as a billiard cue. Billie told me that some of the women from the shop were due by any minute to work on her.

"They asked if they could do the makeup. They're bringing some wigs."

Our other customer was named Lenny. Lenny was a butcher at the Eddie's in Charles Village. His heart gave out while loading a pound of pastrami onto the scales. Billie and I flipped a coin. Billie won the bald hairdresser. Lenny was mine. I was in my office flipping through trade journals when the hairdresser's colleagues arrived. There were three of them, each in a primary color. Red. Blue. Yellow. Each was holding a wig. Blonde. Brunette. Redhead. Each had a little square purse that matched one of the others' dresses. Billie met them at the front door and brought them into my office. I guess she thought the place could use a little color. They were all three speaking at once, a sort of barnyard chatter, and I couldn't quite make out which words were coming from which woman. My inability didn't seem to be of much consequence. Two of the three women were giving me the whammy, I just couldn't latch on for sure to which two it was. I smiled at whatever was being said. They were all three holding on to their wigs like muffs. Billie ushered them out after a minute or so. A deathly silence fell over my office. The place suddenly looked so . . . pale.

Lenny's son and daughter showed up soon after. They brought along a dark suit and a request.

"There's a song Daddy loved," the daughter said. "It's from the seventies."

Her brother chimed in. "It's called 'Spirit in the Sky.'"

"Norman Greenbaum," I said.

"Yeah. Wow. How do you know that?"

I tapped the side of my head. "Stuff flies in, doesn't fly out."

They wanted to know if they would be able to bring along a boom box and play "Spirit in the Sky" at their father's graveside. I told them they could.

"Really?"

"Just as loud as you want."

"Daddy would love that," the butcher's daughter said.

"Then by all means, Daddy should have it."

After my satisfied customers left I swung by Julia's gallery to see if she wanted to join me for an early dinner. Chinese Sue was seated behind her new counter. She was finished with George Eliot and was on to something new.

"What'cha reading?" She tilted the book so that I could read the title. *Peptides of Passion*. "Are you enjoying it?"

She nodded.

"What's it about?"

She opened and closed her mouth. "Peptides."

"Where does the passion come in?"

She lowered the book slightly and focused on the wall directly behind me. Chinese Sue answers a lot of questions with this blank stare. It has crossed my mind more than once that perhaps she is deeply committed to some sort of spiritual discipline that places a severe restriction on verbiage. Or possibly she is just hopelessly dense. Either way, I didn't feel like lollygagging the next hour or so until Chinese Sue emitted her next sound, so I snaked my way up the spiral staircase to Julia's studio.

Julia was standing at her easel. She was wearing a pair of bright yellow gym shorts and a Batman T-shirt snipped off just below the breasts. Her hair was in a half dozen cigar-plug pigtails that on anyone else would have looked ridiculous.

"How far did you have to chase Batman to get that shirt?" I asked.

"Ha ha."

I stepped over to have a look at her canvas. It was a still life. A glass bowl on a table. In the bowl was an orange, some grapes, two apples and several naked figures balled up, hugging their knees to their chests. There was a wineglass next to the bowl, three-quarters filled with red wine. Hands and part of a face were pressing against the inside of the glass, submerged in the wine.

"I'll never figure out you artsy types," I said.

"No," she said, smiling. "You never will."

"I like your funny-looking hair."

"Thank you, Hitch."

I dropped into Julia's hammock.

"Don't go making yourself comfortable," Julia said. "I'm about to go out."

"Say it ain't so, Joe. I was going to ask you to join me for dinner."

"Sorry. I've got a date. You want to guess with who?"

"Rosemary Clooney."

"That would qualify as a . . . wrong answer. It's Nick Fallon."

"Fallon? No kidding? Our intrepid reporter?"

"Yes. He left four messages on my machine. And he sent me those."

She pointed with her paintbrush at a huge bouquet of flowers in a vase on the floor next to the hammock.

"There's a very charming note. Read it."

I swung myself on the hammock and plucked the note from the flowers.

We must mate. Nick

"Sweet," I said. "And so subtle. Well, then, I'd better push off. You need to get dressed."

"Oh, I'm dressed," Julia said.

"Of course you are. Silly me."

Julia stepped over as I got out of the hammock. I kissed her on the cheek.

"Be gentle," I said.

She was still laughing as I slid down the fireman's pole.

I grabbed a quick bite at the Wharf Rat. Bill was working the bar. Bill used to work at the steel plants until he lost both of his legs there in an accident. Bill mans the bar from a series of padded stools. His upper-body strength is so massive he can whip himself from one stool to the other faster than a person with legs. He can also twist around and grab a bottle off the back counter and land it on the bar in around half a second. Incredibly limber.

I asked Bill if he could make me a Hairy Dog. I don't know exactly what goes into one of Bill's dogs, but they do the trick if you've been tipping too many afternoon glasses. I was right as rain and pleased as punch by the time I left the Rat. I swung by my place to get into my somber suit. I had a phone message on my machine. The message was intriguing on several counts. I called back and also got a machine, so I left a message of my own.

We held the wake for the bald hairdresser that evening. Billie wasn't feeling too hot-n-tot, so I stood in for her. The hairdresser's colleagues had settled on the redheaded wig. They had applied enough makeup to shame a drag queen. The wake went off without incident. When it was finished I went back home and changed into comfort clothes and drove down to Annapolis. I had a lovely meal at the George Washington Inn. Sea bass stuffed with crab imperial and a clever little pyramid of stringed vegetables with some sort of raspberry vinaigrette. The plate was dabbed with mystery sauce in a sort of Jackson Pollock mélange. The food was quite good. So was the dessert.

Then I went home with the chef.

CHAPTER

18

Faith served me breakfast in bed. She whipped up a Spanish omelet along with some extremely tasty little scones and a bowl of fresh fruit. She made some mimosas into which she plunked a pair of plump strawberries, then sat cross-legged at the foot of the bed and watched me eat.

"Aren't you going to join me?" I asked.

"I'm a voyeur," she said. "I just like to watch."

I was propped up on the pillows with the breakfast tray tucked up to my waist. Faith's bedroom had sheer curtains that lifted in the soft breeze much in the manner of Faith's silky blonde hair. The omelet was fluffy. The scone fell into crumbs with a glance. There was a general weightlessness to the entire room.

Faith sat in a short white robe watching me with a simple Mother Earth expression as I gobbled up the goodies. When I was done I announced, "That was superb." Faith crawled forward and I twisted to my left to place the breakfast tray down on the floor. The beatific expression never left her face. I glimpsed it a few times through the veil of her golden hair as I again gobbled up the goodies. When we were done I announced, "No, *that* was superb." She smiled and slid out of bed, trailing her robe behind her and letting it drop as she stepped across the floor and out of the room. A moment later I heard a shower running. I found my mimosa glass on the floor and picked it up. One sip left. There was a mirror on the wall above the dresser directly across from the bed. The figure in the reflection looked disheveled and blissed out. I saluted him with my glass.

"I know exactly how you feel."

After Faith got out of the shower I rolled in and watered down the old carcass. Good pressure. Plenty of hot water. Faith was hanging up the phone as I emerged from the bathroom. She gave me a thumbs-up.

"We're all set," she said.

As we left Faith's apartment I thanked her for the breakfast. "And all that other stuff, too. You're a top-rate hostess."

I followed Faith in my car. The Fates gave us a pair of parking spots, one behind the other, and we headed down to the harbor. The day was crisp and clear and so was I. Faith floated along next to me.

"There he is."

We had arrived at a place called Pusser's Landing, a bar and restaurant with tables right on the water. A midshipman was sitting by himself at one of the tables. He was spiffy in his bright whites. He rose as Faith and I approached. I guessed he was around twenty. With the buzz cut and the sailor suit, there was an overgrown-boy look to him. He looked earnest and nervous.

Faith spoke first. "Bradley, this is the man I told you about. This is Hitchcock Sewell."

The middy had a hold of my hand before I knew what was coming. His arm jerked with a piston move.

"Bradley Hansen, sir!" It's actually a low-volume shout, the way they snap this off.

I shouted back, "Nice to meet you, Bradley! And you can skip the 'sir' business."

"Yes . . . okay."

Faith placed a hand on my back and leaned into me. "I'm going to go. I'll see you later?"

"Roger," I said. Her arm trailed down my back. She headed off down the docks, in that floating style of hers. I turned to Bradley.

"Hell of a tan on that woman, eh?"

Bradley looked confused. "Sir?"

"Tan. Woman. Very nice."

"Oh . . . yes."

I took a seat and signaled for him to do the same. A waiter popped up out of a hole and I ordered coffee. Bradley was fine with his water. Navy man.

"Faith tells me she ran into you on the street yesterday," I said.

The cadet swallowed hard. "Yes."

"She recognized you from one of the parties that she catered."

"That's right. She did."

"You were the one who came up to her and her partner and apologized for teasing one of their workers. The little Polish girl."

"It was Hungarian, sir."

"Of course. Hungarian. I knew that. Just checking you. Faith tells me you asked about her yesterday. About Sophie."

"Yes, that's right. I did."

"Bradley, are you nervous?"

It wasn't just his clipped delivery—this was part of his training, after all—but for all that it was a beautiful morning, probably somewhere in the upper sixties, and the boy was sweating like crazy.

He stammered. "I just . . . she told me Sophie was dead."

"And you hadn't known that."

"No, sir. No. Absolutely not."

My coffee came. For some reason (probably omelets, mimosas and an audacious dose of Faith) I was feeling extraordinarily calm and mellow. The breeze was perfect. The boats in the harbor were swaying gently. Seagulls were hovering in the air as if suspended on filaments.

I picked up the little pitcher of milk. "Bradley, did you sleep with Sophie?"

He answered without hesitation. "Yes, sir."

I poured some milk into my coffee. I picked up the spoon and stirred slowly, then placed the spoon back on the table, just so. I took a teensy sip. The midshipman was sitting ramrod straight. He was suffering nobly as I went through the motions of being a jerk.

"You got her pregnant," I finally said.

"Yes, sir."

"She told you that she was pregnant?"

"Yes, sir."

"And what did you say to her?"

He finally unfroze. He blinked hard and his head swiveled, as if he was afraid someone might be listening in on our conversation. His skin looked pale against his crisp white uniform.

"I can't be a father," he said. His voice had gone hoarse. He could barely get the words out.

"Is that what you told her?"

He nodded. He took a sip of his water.

"And what did she say, Bradley?"

"She said she couldn't have a baby on her own. I . . . I told her, I just can't. My father went to the Naval Academy. My uncle went here. And my grandfather. I can't get booted out. I just can't."

His face had gone from white to red. The pleading was in his eyes. Along with the fear.

"I can't," he said again, nearly in a whisper.

"And you weren't about to just leave the academy on your own and take up with this girl you didn't even know."

He shook his head. More of a tremble, as if his chair was being jostled.

"I guess you didn't think of all this when you slept with her, did you?" I said. I said it a little more sharply than I had intended. Having just rolled out of the rack with the ethereal but essentially unknown Faith myself, I have to say it was hardly my place to be lecturing this kid on the responsibilities of the morally upright. But I allow for a little fraudulence when making a point. A strict adherence to the avoidance of hypocrisy would paralyze a person. The issue here was Bradley, not me.

"It just happened," Bradley said.

"You mean sleeping with Sophie. It just happened."

"That's right. I asked her for her phone number at the end of the party. She gave it to me. I met her a couple nights later. We went to a movie."

"Good movie?"

"I guess. She liked it. There wasn't a lot of action. She said she didn't like action movies."

"It was one of those relationship movies?"

"I guess so. It was pretty sappy."

"And then one thing led to another?"

"Well . . . yes."

"It's a story as old as the hills," I said.

"She said she would take care of it. I offered to help. That's the truth. Then I didn't hear from her again."

"I guess now you know why."

"I can't believe she's *dead*."

"Did you have any contact with Sophie after she told you she'd 'take care of it'?"

He took a moment to sip on his water. His eyes flitted about again. "No, sir."

"What did you think she was going to do?"

He lowered his head. He was running his finger absently around the rim of his glass. "I didn't ask."

"Did you kill her, Bradley?"

His head snapped up. For just an instant, the sad, doughy face was replaced with a look of anger. It was gone as quickly as it had arrived.

"That's not funny," he said.

"Not a whole lot about this whole mess is." I skidded my chair back from the table. "Everyone I've talked to tells me she was a sweet kid," I said.

Bradley swallowed hard. "I liked her laugh. She had a really cute laugh. When we . . . after we, you know, did it, she was laughing. It was weird, because she was also crying. But she was happy. I mean, she couldn't stop smiling."

I stood up. I took a few dollars from my pocket and dropped them on the table. Bradley was looking at his water glass again. That crystal-ball gaze. I squinted at the boats out in the harbor. The crew of the *Pride of Baltimore II* was readying the ship to set sail. They sail this ship all over the world, as what they call a goodwill ambassador. When I was younger I used to imagine that every port the *Pride* came into, the docks were loaded with locals who had come out to greet it. All very colorful. Waving handkerchiefs. Cheering. Smiling. I looked back down at Bradley. There was nothing I could think to say.

CHAPTER 19

I stopped off at Faith's apartment but the angel wasn't home. I pulled out one of my cards and wrote a short note on the back. I decided it was too silly so I pocketed it and wrote out a second one. This one was silly too, but it would have to do. At the bottom I added, *I'll call you.* With all due respect, it's a known fact among the caveman set that women go nuts for that line.

Before heading back to Baltimore I swung by the police station. I was curious to see if there had been any shimmy or shake about the car that had plowed into Tom Cushman. The woman at the front desk remembered me. I remembered her. Judith. Judith told me that Croydon Floyd was out on patrol. Judith also told me that Croydon Floyd's allergies were acting up today. She told me about her husband's bowling league. She told me about her laser surgery, about her son's science project, about a trip the family took recently to the Shenandoah Caverns, about the funny smell she couldn't get out of her cat's fur, about getting a pretzel stuck in her ear. . . . I was leaning toward the door like a man in a hurricane but I couldn't . . . quite . . . get there. I was rescued by acting chief Talbot, who rounded the corner just then. He recognized me from before.

"You can tell him later, Judith," he muttered to the receptionist. He motioned for me to step outside.

"Thank you."

We stopped just outside the glass door. Talbot thumbed his belt loop and hitched up his pants. He indicated my bandaged arm.

"Understand you clipped yourself the other night."

I held up the arm. "It's nothing, really. Small price to pay for still being alive."

"I can see your point." Talbot squinted up at the Maryland state flag snapping smartly atop a flagpole out on the grass. A metal grommet somewhere along the anchor rope was making a pinging sound as it bounced against the pole. Talbot addressed himself to the flag . . . but I could tell who he was talking to.

"Croydon told me he spoke with you the other day. He said you were questioning the way we're doing our job. Is that right?"

"I was calling to ask Officer Floyd for some information as well as to give some information. An exchange of information, if you will."

"Croydon says you're nosing around in the death of that Hungarian girl. We got a call from a Mrs. Pierce who told us that you and a friend of yours went by her house the other day asking a lot of questions."

"Is there a crime in that?"

Talbot broke away from the flag and turned his squint to me. "Fact, there is. Interfering with police business."

"I guess I wasn't aware that there was much police business to interfere with on this one. My impression is that the Annapolis police have laid this case to rest. So to speak."

"Lots of people want to play detective, Mr. Sewell," Talbot said. "I'm going to ask you to stop now. If you have information relevant to the investigation, of course we want to hear it."

I suppose a perfectly upstanding citizen would have offered up Bradley Hansen at that point as the father of Sophie's unborn baby. I didn't. So much for my upstanding standing. The police didn't seem to be shaking the bushes and breaking down doors trying to learn a whole lot about Sophie Potts; I kept the information in my pocket.

"Sophie Potts wasn't suicidal," I said. "I think that's relevant information."

Talbot seemed disappointed in me. Not to mention increasingly impatient.

"I wasn't aware that you knew the young lady," he said.

"I didn't. Never had the pleasure."

"Girl got herself in trouble. Some people aren't so good at handling trouble."

"You mean she was pregnant. But the police didn't find that out until after she was pulled from the river. Until the autopsy, right? I'm just wondering how come she was marked as a suicide from the very beginning. I'm just curious what you were going on."

Talbot worked up a good-old-boy's smile and tried it out on me. "I thought I just asked you a moment ago to stop playing detective."

"I'm playing citizen," I said, and I gave his fake smile right back to him.

"Well, then, I'd like you to play citizen back in Baltimore."

"Did you know that Sophie Potts was pregnant before the coroner's report came out?"

"Mr. Sewell, I believe we've spent enough time on this topic."

"Fine. Then how about Tom Cushman. The guy who got run over the other night. He was an acquaintance of Sophie Potts."

"Croydon passed that information along to me. We appreciate your sharing it with us."

"I'm not sure I should have bothered," I said.

A pair of policemen were approaching the building. Talbot and I stepped aside to let them pass. They nodded tersely at their boss. Talbot caught the glass door before it swung shut.

"It's been nice talking with you, Mr. Sewell." A patent lie, but I let it slide. "You have a good day now," Talbot said, then turned and followed the officers inside the building.

Billie was sitting out on the stoop when I returned to the funeral home.

"Hitchcock, there's a man inside to see you. He wanted to know if he could lie down in one of the caskets."

"What did you tell him?"

"I said if he took off his shoes."

It was Nick Fallon. He was in our display room, stretched out in an Ambassador model. His arms were crossed behind his head like he was lounging on a chaise. His eyes were closed.

"Comfortable?" I asked as I came into the room.

Fallon's eyes opened slowly. "I feel dead."

"You've got the moves down."

Fallon scooted up in his casket. "There's some nice padding in this. Real snug. It's a damn shame you've got to waste these things on corpses."

"I'm glad you like it. You'd be surprised how many people have one in their homes."

"No kidding. Their own personal coffins?"

I named a well-known actress.

"No shit," Fallon said.

I named a local sports figure.

"Him?"

I named a popular writer of self-help books and his rock-star wife. "Matching caskets," I said. "His-and-hers." I was making it all up, of course, but I saw no reason to spoil Fallon's fun.

Fallon clambered out of the coffin.

"You've got to give me the whole scoop here, padre. I could pull a story out of this." Fallon leaned up against the wall and started to put his shoes on. He didn't appear to be too steady on his feet. Rather, his foot.

"You look beat," I said. "What brings you here?"

The answer walked into the room. "I do."

It was Julia. She floated forward on an invisible cloud. Her smile was the size of Wisconsin. Fallon had one shoe on, one shoe off. He waved the loose shoe in Julia's direction.

"That woman isn't human."

"She's a national treasure, isn't she?"

Fallon met his foot halfway and worked on the shoe. "Jesus. You have no idea."

Julia came over to me and tipped her head onto my shoulder.

"Oh, he does."

All three of us were starving. Billie had come back inside and she offered to whip up a lunch for us. Julia said she would help. I gave Fallon the nickel tour. The highlight of the nickel tour is our embalming room, downstairs in the basement. Nick studied the table with a jaundiced eye as I explained the process. Some people find it fascinating, others go as green as a Granny Smith. Fallon was leaning toward the Granny, so I kept the explanations tame.

"What's with the posters?" Fallon asked.

He was referring to a pair of posters on one wall of the room. One of them showed Groucho Marx in a pith helmet down on one knee, arms spread. Directly next to it was a poster of Sophia Loren in a tight peasant dress.

"Stand here." I positioned Fallon at the opposite side of the embalming table. "Now, picture a corpse laid out in front of you. You're going to be down here with it for at least an hour. Maybe longer. Just you and silent Joe. And let's face it, you'll be doing some pretty strange stuff when you stop and think about it. Okay? You got all that?"

"Got it."

"Now, look up."

He looked up from the table at Groucho and Sophia. His eyes flitted from one to the other.

"I got it."

"Let's go eat."

Billie and Julia had put together a platter of BLTs and Billie was still whipping up a large bowl of potato salad. We gathered around Billie's kitchen table and started in on the sandwiches. Fallon ate like a feral child having his very first indoor meal.

"I've got news," I announced.

"So does Nick," Julia said.

"Mine's about the nanny," I said.

Fallon had a mouthful of sandwich. He bobbed his head madly and waved a thumbs-up. Julia translated.

"So is his. I told Nick last night why you and I were at Crawford Larue's party. I told him all about Sophie Potts."

"Well, I know who got her pregnant."

They listened as I told about Faith's running into the midshipman the day before and how she had immediately inferred something having transpired between Bradley and Sophie. I told how Faith had arranged for Bradley to be at Pusser's Landing so that I could meet him, and I described how guileless the young man had been, how cooperative and readily truthful.

"So did you get the feeling that the guy was getting it off his chest?" Fallon asked.

"That was definitely part of it."

"He knocks her up and leaves her out to dry. Maybe the girl threatened to make a stink. His future is on the line. He's feeling the pressure."

"I don't think so."

"Take a look at it," Nick said. "That bridge. It's awfully damn close to the academy. Watery grave? What do you think? I can see the navy angle on this one."

"Nick, you're thinking like a cheesy tabloid writer."

The cheesy tabloid writer made a face. It had "duh?" written all over it.

I went on. "I figured that finding the guy who slept with Sophie would clear things up," I said. "But that was when I figured it would turn out to be Gellman or even Tom Cushman. Frankly, the navy boy was something of a wild card."

Billie brought a large serving bowl of potato salad to the table. Fallon was downright Pavlovian as he heaped his plate full.

"Tell Hitch about your phone call, Nick," Julia said. She looked over at me. "I think you're going to like this."

Fallon shoveled a huge forkful of potato salad into his mouth and masticated with a steady deliberateness. He looked as happy as that clam we always hear about. He held up a finger, indicating for us to hold on. He continued chewing. The earth hurtled around the next corner.

"Got a call," Fallon said at last. "A couple of weeks ago. Maybe more, I'd have to check. It was at the paper. A girl. Woman. Whatever the hell I'm supposed to call them these days. She didn't identify herself. I've got caller ID, but it turned out she wasn't calling from a private phone. The call was from a phone booth."

"Tell him where," Julia said.

"Call came from Annapolis."

"What did she want?" I asked.

"She wanted money. For a story. Now you've got to remember, we get these calls all the time. A couple of high-profile stories over the years that *The Cannon* has paid big bucks for and everyone thinks we're just sitting by the phone with a big bag of dough just waiting to give it away. I told her it didn't work that way. She said I should listen to her, that she had a nice juicy scandal."

"Can you believe that?" Julia said. "In *The Daily Cannon*? I'm mortified."

"Well, here was the thing. She told me that it had to do with the ARK."

My little ears perked up. "The ARK? My old buddy Larue?"

"That's right. Crawford and company. Now you've got to remember what they're all about, okay? It's the Alliance for Reason and Kindness, for Christ's sake. They're do-gooders. I mean there's nothing wrong with that as far as it goes. They tell people to make their beds in the morning and be good to one another. But I think you see what I'm saying. They're straight shooters. Family values. Upright and uptight. No hanky, no panky."

"Where do you suppose adultery would fit into that?" I asked.

"The scarlet letter?"

I gave them the lowdown on my backyard snooping down at the Gellman ranch. Fallon continued shoveling the potato salad into his maw as I told the tale.

"Do you think it could have been Sophie who called?" Julia said. "Do you think she saw something similar and tried to cash in on it?"

"I can buy that," I said. "Mrs. Larue was not exactly behaving like the ARK poster child."

Fallon was shaking his head. "Let me tell you what the people in Washington say is stenciled on that woman's undies. 'Virginia Larue's Home for Wayward Boys.' Ginny Larue is a regular one-woman men's club. That's common knowledge inside the Beltway, but if that's all this call was about, there's no scandal there. I mean, there *is*. The ARK is all about being preachy and morally upright and here you've got the wife of the damn joint running around town spreading a hell of a lot more than the gospel. But as a story, it's a fizzle. It's all accuse and deny. It's just never been worth going after. It's Washington, after all. There's a hell of a lot of dirty laundry that you just don't even bother with. We need a little more zing to our sex scandals."

"What about Crawford Larue?" I asked. "Is he in the dark about all this?"

"Does Crawford know that his wife is a public popsicle? Who can say? She sure as hell didn't marry him for his looks. Look, here's the thing. Virginia Hallowell had been bouncing around the D.C. party circuit for a number of years. She was one of those gals who just loved the smell of power in the morning, you know? You can't run a political city without them, just check your history books. Anyway, a couple of years ago she fell pretty hard for a low-level something or other at the White House. He was married. There was a bit of a mess there and then suddenly up she popped on the arm of little Crawford. Mr. Purity and Light himself. His first wife had died a few years back. Talk was that Miss Hallowell was mending her salacious ways, but of course that turned out to be a crock. Old dog old tricks. She married the guy. You've seen the house. Crawford's doing all right for himself with his little dynasty. I guess Virginia just decided she needed to get herself a harbor. Nobody gets any younger."

I jerked a thumb at Julia. "This one does."

Fallon said, "I already told you, this one ain't human."

"This one could stand for a better compliment than that," Julia said.

I pressed. "So this scandal your girl was trying to peddle. You don't think it had to do with the indiscretions of Lady Larue?"

Fallon shook his head. "I was getting a bigger pitch than that. The thing is, she refused to go into details unless I promised her a cut of cash, but what she did tell me was that she had the dope on the ARK being involved in all sorts of anti-ARK things. Abortions, for one thing. And you *know* the ARK lobbies long and hard to the right on that one. Even creepier, though, she said they were involved in forced sterilizations. Of minors, no less. Of course if any of that were true, that's the stuff that topples empires. But like I said, I tried to get her to fill in the details and she wouldn't really give me anything I could work with. She wanted money first and I told her I'd have to take that up with the publisher. I tried to wrangle a number from her where I could reach her but she wouldn't bite. Said she'd call me back."

"And when was this again?" I asked.

"I'd have to check to be sure, but it was at least a few weeks back." He shrugged. "I figured it was probably a load of crap, but I went ahead and rang up the ARK and put it to them for comment. You can guess what they told me. They wouldn't dignify this filth with a comment. I was also told that if the *Cannon* even trotted out so much as a teaser article on garbage like this, the ARK would drag our asses into court faster than we could blink. It was Russell Jenks I spoke with. You met him, right?"

"Briefly."

"He labored long and hard not to look at my breasts," Julia said. "With limited success."

"Mrs. Larue described him as her husband's loyal soldier," I said. "Or maybe it was the Lord's loyal soldier. I can't remember."

Fallon smirked. "Jenks is high up there on the ARK food chain. Of course nabbing the boss's daughter doesn't hurt. You remember her, don't you? The girl with kaleidoscope eyes?"

"Odd fish," I said.

"I'll say. Girl's in la-la land. Bird like that you can park in the corner and not even have to worry about her."

"Anybody tries to park me in a corner," Julia said, "I'd throw it in reverse."

"So did you hear back from your mystery caller?" I asked Fallon.

"No. I waited, but she never called. Ninety percent of the time that's how it goes. People fish for money then they disappear. Turns out there's no story, of course. It's either a fruitcake who just gets off on making these kinds of calls or it's a disgruntled employee or a pissed-off spouse or who knows. I considered poking around a little more to see if the ARK had recently dumped anybody who might want to be getting back at them. But then I just forgot about it."

"If it was Sophie she'd have a damn good reason for not calling you back," I said. "That old 'being dead' thing."

"Who do you see killing her?" Fallon asked.

"How about Virginia Larue? Maybe she got tipped off somehow that Sophie was stirring up the mud."

Fallon waved his fork in the air. "Hold on. That's another thing. Julia told me about that whole 'adopt my baby' routine. I don't buy that. There's no way for me to know for sure, of course, but I don't see Crawford and Virginia Larue suddenly deciding to become parents.

Ginny Larue couldn't care less for kids. That woman's just not the mommy type, if you ask me. And Crawford? Maybe, I guess. Old guys do get that immortality thing going sometimes. Though that's usually about fathering the child themselves, to show the world that they've still got the stuff."

"But if Sophie wasn't really meeting with the Larues so that they could adopt her baby, then what was it?"

"Let me try to get this straight," Nick said. "This girl calls me up and blathers on about all sorts of nefarious bullshit going on at the ARK. At the same time she's meeting with Crawford Larue personally, allegedly about his and Ginny's adopting her kid? Do we know for a fact that she was actually pregnant?"

"We know that," I said. "Coroner's report."

"Right. Okay. So then what? Next thing we know she ends up in the river. That's what we've got?"

"And there's also Tom Cushman," I said.

"Tom who?"

"Cushman. He's the actor who posed as the father of Sophie's child when she went to talk with the Larues."

"But you just told me that the navy boy was the daddy."

"Bradley sliced it off with Sophie the minute she got pregnant. There's no way he would have gone with her to meet Larue. Tom took it on as an acting gig. From the sound of it he failed the audition."

"And where is he now in all this?"

"He's dead in all this," I said. "A car ran him over a few nights ago down in Annapolis. The police have it as an accident, a hit-and-run."

"And you definitely believe the navy boy?"

"I hardly think he'd go out of his way to lie about something like that," I said. "He wants to stay out of trouble. Why in the world would he say he was the father if he wasn't?"

Billie piped up. "To protect the real father?"

I shook my head. "I don't buy it. This kid wasn't falling on his sword for anyone."

"What if this Tom character knew navy boy," Fallon said. "Then he . . . Christ, we're just running around in circles. I'm more interested in knowing why this girl really went to Larue in the first place. Something's not kosher there."

"She was living in Mike Gellman's home," I said. "Maybe she found out about Gellman and Ginny Larue."

"Yeah, but I just told you, that's a small potato."

"Sophie wouldn't necessarily know that," I said.

"No, it's something else." Fallon linked his hands behind his head and sat back in his chair, closing his eyes. "I don't know what the hell it is. But it's something else. Give me a minute."

We did. And he took complete advantage. By the time it arrived Fallon was fast asleep.

CHAPTER

20

The next day I got into my car and headed south. The day was warm and I rolled my windows down. On 95 South I passed an exit that read FUTURE. I was sorely tempted, but I resisted. Several years earlier on a visit to New York I'd taken the bait of a sign that read UTOPIA PARKWAY and had surely not found my bliss there. These signs can be misleading.

Two exits past the FUTURE I found myself ingloriously stuck in the present for nearly a half hour. A jackknifed tractor trailer was hogging the road, leaving only half a lane and a narrow shoulder for the rubberneckers to squeeze by. The truck looked like a large animal that had decided to roll over on its side and take a nap. A half dozen policemen and an ambulance crew were standing around scratching their heads when I crawled past, so things didn't appear to be too dire.

A minute longer in traffic and I would have missed Virginia Larue altogether. As it was she was just coming out of her driveway in her little red sports car as I pulled up. She met me going in the opposite direction and stopped, her window gliding smoothly from sight.

"Good morning," I said. "Or good afternoon."

She answered with a wary, "Hello."

"Do you remember me?"

"I do. Mr. Sewell." I can't say that the woman looked me up and down—for of course I was sitting in a car—but she took in the car. "Is this a coincidental meeting? Were you just passing this way?"

"In fact I was coming by to see you," I said.

"Oh?" The word didn't come out exactly like a purr. But close.

"I probably should have called."

"That would have been wise. I'm leaving, as you can see. I have an appointment."

"It wouldn't happen to be with a certain assistant D.A. from Annapolis, would it?"

In less time than it takes to blink, Virginia Larue went all hard around the edges. I basked in her icy stare.

"I'm running late. What do you want?"

"I'm not really sure," I said, glancing in my rearview mirror. A car was coming up on me. "A little chitchat, I suppose."

Virginia Larue looked as if she had eaten something distasteful. "Two o'clock. The Commodore Hotel. It's near Union Station."

"Hotel?"

"They have a restaurant," she said flatly. "You can buy me lunch."

She drove off before I could respond, leaving me a little puff of oily smoke to chew on. The car behind me honked. On an impulse I turned the wheel and pulled into the Larue driveway. I decided that the swans and the cherub weren't having sex; they were merely getting to know each other. A squirrel ran along the gravel up to my door, twitched his whiskers at me then bounded off to the lawn and spiraled up a tree. A flash of white off near the rear of the house caught my eye. There was a small lattice structure set back against a pair of large boxwoods. A wooden swing—like a porch swing—hung from a pair of chains. Someone in bare legs was sitting on the swing. The flash of white was from the legs, which appeared and disappeared behind the boxwoods as the swing moved backward and forward.

I got out of the car and stepped across the grass. The legs continued to appear and disappear, and as I approached I could hear the faint creaking of wood from the swinging chains. A pale blue baseball cap was visible on the back swing. I rounded the boxwoods. It was a young woman, head down, reading a book that was open on her lap. She was in cutoff jeans and what looked like a cotton pajama top, loose and formless and patterned with pink angels. Her feet were bare and one of them—the left one—was pushing off the grass each time the swing came forward, to keep it rocking. I cleared my throat. She was very slender. Long neck, no waist, trim pale legs.

"Hello."

She looked up. For a moment I didn't recognize her; the baseball cap was pulled low on her head, shading her eyes.

"Hello." The word didn't come out much louder than the creaking wood. But I recognized the twang. It was Sugar Jenks. Crawford Larue's daughter. She pulled the open book up to her chest and hugged it.

"I didn't mean to disturb you," I said. "I just . . . ah, I just ran into your mother." I ticked my head to indicate the street and Sugar gazed off in that direction as if she expected to see something. She stopped kicking against the grass. "I'm Hitchcock Sewell. We met the other day. At the party. Very briefly."

"I remember." She seemed uncomfortable holding eye contact for more than a few seconds. She gazed down at her knees.

"What are you reading?" I asked. She mumbled her answer. "Sorry," I said, "I missed that."

"Trash." She made it into a two-syllable word. She looked back up. "I'm just reading trash. It's about a woman who is an international spy and men fall in love with her."

"Are you enjoying it?"

"Yes, I am."

"Then it's not trash. It's entertainment."

"Daddy thinks it's trash."

"Well then Daddy shouldn't read it," I said.

The swing had come to a halt. "I'm not dressed," Sugar said in a husky whisper.

"Of course you are."

"No, I'm not. I didn't expect any visitors."

"Do you live here?"

She cocked her head. "This is my home."

"You and your husband?"

"Russell and I live in the east wing. Daddy and . . . my stepmother have the rest of the house. Are you here to see Daddy?"

"Not exactly. I was driving by and I spotted your stepmother as she was leaving. I was just turning around in your driveway and I saw you over here and thought I'd come say hi."

"Are you friends with Virginia?"

I thought I detected a slight urgency in her question. She pushed the cap farther back on her head and her eyes appeared. Large, dark, and anxious.

"I only met her the other day," I said. "Same day as I met you."

"At the party?"

"That's right."

"It was a nice party, wasn't it? There were a lot of people there."

She was speaking like a child. Or like a child might speak to her stuffed toys. If I'd happened to have a lollipop in my pocket I would have offered it to her. From the far side of the house came the sound of a lawn mower starting up. Sugar's head flicked again in the direction of the noise.

"Sugar?"

Crawford Larue was stepping from the back of the house. He was wearing slacks and a pink dress shirt, unbuttoned at the neck. He did a lousy job of hiding his frown as he made his way over to us.

"Sugar, honey, what's going on?"

"Manuel's mowing the lawn," she said dreamily.

Larue aimed a pudgy finger at me. "What are you doing here?" He was also doing a lousy job of sounding friendly.

"At the moment I'm enjoying a conversation with your lovely daughter," I said as unctuously as I could. "Nice to see you again, Mr. Larue. Though I'm surprised. I'd have thought you'd be off at work."

"I conduct much of my business from home," Larue said. He turned to his daughter. "Is everything all right?"

Sugar nodded her head. "Yes, Daddy."

"To what do we owe the pleasure of this visit?" Larue asked me. I repeated my lie about having been passing by. It wasn't a very good lie, which Larue seemed to sense. He turned back to his daughter.

"Why don't you give me a kiss then go inside and get dressed. You're half naked."

Sugar rose from the swing, her arms still wrapped around her book. I shot her a smile but it didn't seem to penetrate. Larue presented his chubby cheek and Sugar leaned forward and dutifully kissed it.

"That's a good girl." Larue pulled the cap from Sugar's head and tucked it between Sugar and her book. "You want to take a shower, honey. Say good-bye to Mr. Sewell."

The peep of a bird would have been louder. The woman's eyes traveled well past me. Sugar stepped heavily across the grass and disappeared into the house.

"She's a pretty girl," I said.

Larue made an indifferent face. "Nowhere near as pretty as her mother."

Larue escorted me back to my car. Before I got in I asked him, "Mr. Larue, are you aware that the man who was here the other week posing as Sophie Potts's lover was hit by a car a few nights ago?"

Larue took a beat before he answered. "I don't know how such information would have come my way."

"He was killed."

"I am sorry to hear that."

I slid in behind the wheel and closed the door. "I just thought you might find that interesting."

Larue placed his hands on the open window. "What I find interesting, Mr. Sewell, is that it appears to be your habit to show up at my door with stories of persons who have recently died." He smiled and added, "I have to say, sir, I am becoming a little concerned myself about being of your acquaintance."

I had some time before my lunch date with Virginia Larue, so I killed it at Union Station, nosing around the shops there and pestering the clerks with my collection of bad foreign accents. I picked this habit up from my father, who, I have to say, was much better at it than I am. He was especially adept with his Russian accent and in my more gullible pipsqueak years I actually believed he was a spy for the Russians and that he had another family just like ours stashed over in Russia. I pictured a little Russian Hitchcock in a huge fur hat goose-stepping back and forth in front of the onion-domed Kremlin and I would draw pictures of myself and my mother and of the neighborhood, sticking them into my father's jacket pocket so that he could take them over to Russia with him when he left "for work" in the morning. (My geographic skills were slow in percolating.) I would write on the drawings, *For Hitchcock, From Hitchcock,* and upon my father's return from work in the evening he would pull the drawings out of his pocket and announce, "Well, look at this. I've got something here for someone named Hitchcock," and he'd hand them to me. Naturally, I hoped for a drawing from my Russian brother, but of course I never did get one.

Virginia Larue was already seated when I arrived, at one of the tables next to a window off near the rear. I spotted her when I entered and I waved. She did not wave back.

The restaurant was nearly empty. It was the tail end of the lunch crunch. Virginia Larue sat stone-still as the hostess walked me over to the table. She was wearing a ruffled blouse under a burgundy blazer. The blouse was two buttons open, revealing a small gold cross on a thin chain around her neck. She looked like she was practicing her posture. Her eyes followed me as I settled into the chair opposite her, but the book did not fall off her head.

"Who the hell do you think you are?"

I could swear that the woman's lips had not even moved. It was as if she snapped this off to me through telepathy.

I saw that she was drinking a white wine and I asked the waiter who had sashayed over if I could have the same. The waiter suggested a carafe. I gave my lunch partner an inquiring look, but it bounced right off her.

"A carafe sounds fine," I said to the waiter. His nameplate said his name was Andrew. He wore a burgundy vest and a black bowtie.

"I should have worn something burgundy," I said after Andrew had vamoosed. "Seems to be the theme."

I broke no ice with that nonsense.

"You seem a little uptight," I said, snapping my napkin and setting it onto my lap. The fact is, Virginia Larue's full frontal venom was unsettling, but I wasn't about to let it show.

This time the lips moved. "You haven't answered my question."

The hand moved, too. It took hold of the wineglass and brought it to the lips. I feared she was going to take a bite out of it, but she only sipped. A pudge of lipstick remained on the rim of the glass. Her eyes were on me like a laser beam. If they blinked, I didn't notice.

"That's a nice blouse," I said, killing her with kindness.

"What do you want?"

I set my elbows on the table. "Well, first I want to compliment you on your nice blouse. I'll probably take a few more stabs at trying to get you to cool off, but I won't make a whole production out of it. Then I want to look at the menu and choose something yummy. I'm starving. I take it you've been here before. Maybe you'll be able to recommend something."

"The bullshit sandwich is very nice."

I smiled. She didn't. "Well okay, I'll take that into consideration."

She began tapping a fingernail against the base of her wineglass. As things were going, this had to qualify as a full-fledged thaw. I hummed a nonsense tune as I pretended to look over the menu.

"Do we need to be pleasant here?" Ginny Larue asked. "I really do not like to play games. I have no idea what you and that tramp were doing in my home the other day, but it was clear you had no business being there. Crawford simply dismissed it when I asked him. And now you come around slinging insinuations at me. So why don't you tell me what this is all about and let's be done with it."

The waiter arrived with our carafe. He filled my glass and aimed for Ginny Larue's. She waved him off. He set the carafe down and asked if we wanted to hear the specials.

"Give me your fanciest burger, Andrew," I said.

Ginny Larue opened and closed her mouth. "Spinach salad."

Andrew started to say more, but I gave him the cut-and-run look. He obeyed. I turned to the iron maiden across the table.

"For starters," I said sweetly, "she's not a tramp. Julia dresses provocatively on occasion because why the hell not? She's got the goods. Some people blend in with the woodwork and some don't. Julia don't. And the fact is the majority of people are entranced, intrigued or in some way quite taken with her, whether they're willing to admit it or not." I took a sip of my chardonnay. "Besides, Julia is an unmarried woman and she only sees unmarried men."

Ginny Larue picked up the carafe and topped off her glass. The ice was still burning in her eyes, but I sensed that the posterior stick had been removed. There was movement in the shoulders. The head seemed willing to swivel.

"You're a good-looking man," she said.

The awesome power of her transition threatened to ruffle my hair but I went with it. "Well thank you," I said. "Allow me to return the compliment. You're a dandy-looking number yourself, Mrs. Larue. Mr. Larue must clap his pudgy little hands with glee every time you walk into the room."

Her glass froze halfway to her lips. "What in hell are you about? I am about three seconds from throwing this chardonnay in your face."

"May I be blunt?" I asked.

"I seriously doubt that I could stop you."

"It's possible you could. But I'll take that as a yes. Does your husband know that you screw around as much as you do?"

She had been a little off in her calculations. It was more like ten seconds, not three. I was glad we hadn't been drinking red. As I dabbed at my face I watched the smoke coming out of Ginny Larue's ears. The color came up in her pale face. Her once-rigid posture was downright loosey-goosey.

She hissed, "You son of a bitch."

"I deserved that."

"You damn well did."

I folded my napkin and set it down, then reached across the table and calmly retrieved the woman's silverware. I also retrieved her empty wineglass and the carafe and brought them to my side of the table. Safety first.

"I'll rephrase the question. Does your husband know that you're screwing around specifically with Mike Gellman?"

She began to protest. I held up a hand to cut her off.

"We can save a lot of time if you'd forgo the protesting. I saw the two of you in Gellman's hot tub the other night."

"You're a shit."

I nodded. "I'm a shit. I guess that's something I'll have to live with. But you're worse, Mrs. Larue." I took a high kick and sent it right down the middle. "You're a killer."

Wise old me, I had left her nothing to throw at me. However, it didn't seem to matter. She used a weapon I would not have expected.

She laughed.

Hysterically.

"I'm a *killer*? Oh my Lord, that is *rich*. That is really . . . what kind of imagination do you have? Oh my goodness." She held her wrists out to me across the table. "Arrest me. Please."

Virginia Larue fell back in her chair and split her sides. Right there in a public restaurant. Color rushed to her skin and she guffawed like an old horse.

The girl had a fine old time with that one. She had to dab at her pretty makeup to make sure she didn't suffer a little mudslide. Andrew arrived just then with our food and I silently cleaned the space in front of me for my burger. The waiter set our plates down. Ginny Larue was still yucking it up. Andrew and I swapped a glance. His was bemused.

"Good-bye, Andrew." I refilled the woman's wineglass and returned it to her. "You behave. I'm trusting you."

She was getting over her laughing fit. Quite fully thawed now as far as I could tell. Her eyes flashed a wholly different temperature at me across the table.

"Don't let your hamburger get cold." She hiccupped a laugh. "Or I might have to kill you."

I retreated behind the burger. Retrenched behind it.

"Who exactly am I supposed to have killed?" she asked, poking her fork about in her large bowl.

"Skip it," I said. "I was just making conversation."

"Well then maybe you'll tell me what you were doing spying on me?" she asked.

"I wasn't spying on you. At least, that's not what I was intending to do. I only drove out to Gellman's house that night to do a little thinking."

"Funny place to think."

"If I may ask again, does your husband know about you and Gellman?"

She lowered her fork and looked at me across the table. She smiled. It was such a lovely smile. Two rows of tiny piano keys, the very slightest crinkling of crow's-feet. "Are you insane or just insanely stupid?"

"I'm curious about something, Mrs. Larue. How do you know Mike Gellman?"

She threw some extra syrup into her voice. "I assume you mean besides biblically?"

"This entire ARK thing is really a complete crock for you, isn't it?"

"We are all sinners on the road to salvation. The Lord has room for the imperfect."

"Gellman," I said again.

She shrugged. "People meet people. What interest could that be of yours?"

"Let me ask you about someone else. Sophie Potts."

She picked up her wineglass. "Sophie Potts."

"Does the name mean anything to you?"

"Should it?"

"She came over to the house to see your husband several weeks ago."

"Crawford sees a lot of people."

"He was seeing this one because he was thinking of adopting her baby."

"Oh. The adoption."

"You don't sound terribly excited."

"I'm sorry. I hope you won't hold that against me."

"It just seems peculiar, that's all."

"I'd really prefer not to talk about it."

I pressed. "It just seems strange. I mean, if your husband is interviewing people who are the potential parents of your child? Isn't this something you would discuss?"

"You do have a bad habit of minding other people's business, don't you?"

"I guess I'm just a people person."

She looked at me a moment over the rim of her glass. "Okay, yes. I suppose I do recall something about this woman. What I recall is that Crawford was not terribly impressed with her. There wasn't really much to discuss."

"Sophie Potts is dead," I said.

If I was expecting a big reaction, I was disappointed.

"I am sorry to hear that," the woman said. "What did she die of?"

"She tried to drink a river. It turned out to be too much for her. Especially after a long drop from a bridge."

"May I say that our conversation is not making a lot of sense to me?"

"I admit, I'm not the most linear dog in the park," I said. "Sophie drowned. She may or may not have been pushed off a bridge."

"Is this the person I am supposed to have murdered?"

"The fact is I'm a little frustrated here, Ginny. I assume I may call you Ginny. I feel so much closer to you after the wine in the face."

"You may."

"Ginny. You see, I'm having a real problem. I'm trying to get a clear picture of things. I was hoping to muscle you into giving me some information."

"I don't suppose it crossed your nonlinear brain simply to ask?"

"Well, I did. I asked you how it is that you know Mike Gellman."

"That's simple. Mike's uncle introduced us."

"His uncle?"

"Owen Cutler. Owen is a dear friend of Crawford's. He has known him for years. His firm represents the ARK in legal matters. Do you know Owen? He is an exquisite gentleman."

"I've met him." I thought about this for a few seconds. Owen Cutler. I pictured the distinguished gentleman coming up onto the Naval Academy Bridge to represent Mike to Sophie's parents. "Gellman sent him along as an errand boy a few days ago."

"Mike is devoted to that man."

"Let me ask you something else. Do you know how it is that your husband heard of Sophie Potts in the first place?" I already knew the answer.

"I seem to recall that that was Owen as well. Owen is aware that Crawford has been . . . looking into adoption. He came to Crawford and told him that he knew of a young girl who was in a 'difficult position.' "

"Did Cutler also tell your husband that Sophie was Mike Gellman's nanny? For that matter, did Mike tell you?"

Ginny Larue looked authentically surprised. "Mike's nanny?"

"Yes."

"You're sure?"

"Absolutely. He didn't tell you?"

"I would hardly expect Crawford to think I might find that information the slightest bit interesting."

"*I* find it interesting."

She smiled. "Of course you do. It's other people's business."

"Okay, I can understand your husband not bringing it up. But Mike?"

"Perhaps he wasn't aware."

"That his uncle had ushered his own nanny off to see your husband? Sorry. He must have known. But he didn't mention it to you. Seems odd to me."

She thought a moment. She also made a gesture to the waiter. She wanted the bill. "It does. I agree. The fact is, Mike and I don't really spend a lot of time talking about things like that."

"Things like what?"

"Our lives." Ginny Larue finished off her wine. I started to pour her some more, but she reached out and stopped me. Her fingers rode mine as I lowered the carafe, then she withdrew her hand and touched a finger to the side of her mouth.

"It's my turn to ask a question," she said.

"Fine. Shoot."

"Room sixty-five has a superb view of the Capitol." She took her napkin from her lap and set it in her salad bowl. "Would you like to see it?"

I had an uneventful drive back to Balti-more. I got caught up in a little early rush-hour traffic. But then I'm so blessed to have a thirty-foot commute between my place and the funeral home that I don't think I've much place to crab about being caught up in traffic when it happens. I searched around the radio dial and found an interview show with a man in England who had managed to breed a type of rabbit that glows in the dark. Phosphorescent green. The man was giggling so much I never did discover what the purpose of this was.

All things considered, Ginny Larue had taken my polite refusal to check out the view in room sixty-five pretty much like an adult. She had told me that she was not going to ask me a second time, that this was a once-in-a-lifetime offer.

"It's a spectacular view," she said. "Like no other you'll ever get."

I expressed my gratitude and explained that it was nothing at all personal. She apologized for her earlier hostility.

"I don't like it when a man thinks he can boss me around. I won't put up with it. I never have."

"Equal rights for equal fights," I had responded, wondering where the hell that had come from, let alone what the hell it really meant.

I swung by Bolton Hill on the off chance that I'd catch Libby. She wasn't in, but the baby-sitter from up the street was. Lily appeared at the woman's side and screwed her face up when she saw me.

"I can pee in the bathtub," she announced.

I was noting a definite water theme with the child.

"Good for you," I said.

"I ate a pumpkin."

"I swallowed a restaurant," I told her, and she made another screwed-up face and ran back into the house, laughing.

Darryl Sandusky was sitting on the front steps of the funeral home when I got back, enjoying a cigarette. So was Pete.

"What are you up to," I asked Darryl, "corrupting the morals of all my adult friends?"

"Huh?"

I turned to Munger. "Pete, why don't you go inside and make yourself useful? Darryl and I are going down to the Oyster to hoist a few."

"I don't drink," Darryl said. "It's bad for you."

"You think you're puffing on oxygen there?" I asked him.

"Leave the kid alone," Pete said.

"Hey, he's my future business partner," I said. "I want to make sure he lives that long."

Darryl squinted up at me. "Cigarettes only kill adults."

Pete and I shared a look. I said it. "Interesting perspective."

I noticed a duffel bag on the sidewalk.

"Somebody doing laundry?"

"Susan asked that I vacate the premises," Pete answered.

"I don't suppose she's bombing for termites?"

"I told her about Lee."

"I see."

Darryl piped up. "She sounds cool."

"Who does?" I asked.

"Lee. She sounds cool."

"Pete, are you spilling your guts to this runt?"

"I'm not a runt," Darryl said.

Pete shrugged. "Kid gave me a cigarette. I was all out."

Pete needed a place to stay. He said he could have called on some of his other friends, but he felt uncomfortable doing so, most of them also being acquaintances of his wife.

"Besides, this is all your fault anyway," he said.

"My fault?"

"If I don't know you I don't know Lee."

"Right. So then what you've got is a miserable marriage without even a glimmer of hope out there for a different life. There are some who would be giving me credit, not blame."

"Maybe if he didn't like Lee so much he could figure out his stupid marriage," Darryl said.

The boy had a square head and a single eyebrow. He was built like a box. His shorts came down past his knees. I cocked my head at him.

"Does your mother know you talk this way?"

He snorted and flicked his cigarette into the street.

"You can sleep on my couch if you want," I said to Pete. "Or you can have my old room here. I'm sure Billie wouldn't mind."

"It's only a couple of days," Pete said, looking everywhere but at me.

"Does Lee know?"

"No."

"Are you going to tell her?"

Pete jerked a thumb at Darryl. "He thinks I shouldn't."

I took a beat. A siren sounded in the distance. Darryl gave me his ugly smile.

"Pete. He's twelve."

I had been hoping to pop down to Annapolis that night and catch the tail end of Lee's show and then the tail end of Faith. But with a mopey Munger on my hands it didn't seem like such a good idea. I phoned Faith at the inn and told her I was a good-for-nothing thus-and-so. She said she'd find a way to get over it.

Pete had determined to swear off drinking until he had straightened out his life. That seemed to me like a sensible equation. He picked up his duffel bag and followed me down the street to my place. I offered to whip up a plate of hot dog supreme but for some reason the idea didn't appeal to him. Pete roamed my living room floor like a dog in a pen. We couldn't stay in, that was clear. I put a call in to Julia.

"I was just about to call you," she said.

"Don't trouble your pretty little fingers. Look, Jules, I've got Pete over here. Long story, but he's going to climb my walls if we don't get out and do something. I thought I'd see what you're up to."

"Nick and I are going out to Chubby Checkers," she said.

I called out to Pete. "You feel like putting on your twisting shoes?" His grunt didn't indicate a swell of enthusiasm. "I think we're going to pass," I said into the phone.

"I've got an idea for you. It's the reason I was about to call. How would you and Pete like to go see *The Bells of Titan*?"

"Isn't that the movie Nick told us to run from as fast as we could?"

"Yes. There's a special screening at the Senator tonight. I thought you might be interested. It's a fund-raiser for one of your favorite organizations."

"The League of Single Young Undertakers?"

"The Alliance for Reason and Kindness. Nick has a couple of passes. He says he wants to see that movie again about as much as he wants to jump off the Washington Monument."

"Ours or the one in D.C.?"

"Either one, I think."

I cupped the phone. "What do you think, Pete? You want to see a flick?"

He was standing in front of my music collection.

"Is this the crap you listen to?"

"We'll take them," I said to Julia. She said she'd leave the passes with Chinese Sue.

"Don't forget, it's a fund-raiser. No jeans and T-shirts, big boy."

I hung up the phone. "Have you got any good clothes in that bag?" I asked Pete.

"What do you mean 'good'?"

"Suit. Tie. Nice shirt?"

"What're you planning to do, bury me?"

I snapped my fingers. "Perfect."

It's an old saw that dead men can't tell tales, so there wasn't much chance that Lenny the butcher would tattle on us for borrowing his suit. He didn't need it until his wake, so as long as Pete was careful not to spill anything on it, what did it really matter? It fit Pete perfectly.

Pete looked at himself in the mirror. "I feel creepy."

"You look fine."

"Yes, but I *feel* creepy."

"You'll get over it."

Pete took a couple of swats at his hair.

"I can give you a dead man's trim," I volunteered.

"What's that?"

"The front only."

Pete found me in the mirror. "I'll pass."

The Senator Theater looked fine, too. It always does, with its huge wraparound marquee and its deco façade of illuminated glass bricks, red and green and yellow. The threat of destruction hangs over the old movie palace year in and year out. It is on the list of endangered landmarks. Grand as the theater is, it's hard for the place to turn a nickel against the eminently more flexible multiplexes.

The wide sidewalk outside the theater was packed when Pete and I arrived. Julia was correct. No jeans, no T-shirts. We handed over our passes and shuffle-stepped inside and found halfway decent seats midway down and off to the left.

Pete wanted popcorn and headed off to fetch it. While he was gone a woman with top-heavy hair stepped up to a microphone located to the side of the screen and welcomed us all there, thanked us for coming and proceeded to rattle off a list of names of "very special people" who she said were responsible for tonight's event. I perked up at the very last name.

". . . and of course Crawford Larue, who so much wanted to be with us tonight to thank you personally for all your support. Unfortunately Mr. Larue has been called away on urgent business."

I can't quite report a collective groan coming from the crowd. It appeared they would survive their disappointment. The woman continued.

"In Mr. Larue's place, however, we are honored to have the executive director of the ARK with us tonight, who would like . . ."

A man in a tuxedo seated near the front stood up and made his way toward the aisle. I recognized him from Larue's party.

". . . Mr. Russell Jenks."

Jenks stepped up to the microphone. He tapped it, then stood by as a techie darted over to adjust it to his height. Jenks balled his hands behind his back and leaned into the microphone. He thanked the woman who had introduced him and he thanked God. In that order. Pete was coming back with his popcorn. He squeezed his way past a sea of knees and dropped down next to me.

"What'd I miss?"

"Same thing we all did. Crawford Larue was supposed to be here tonight. You'd have had a chance to see the egg himself."

Pete sunk his fist into his popcorn. "My dumb luck."

Jenks kept his comments brief. He tossed up the word "redemption" a few times and batted it lightly around the room. Easy pop flies. He had a smooth delivery and he concluded with a solemn Amen and a broad smile. The audience applauded politely as Jenks headed back to his seat. I spotted another face I recognized. The lights were beginning to dim. I jabbed Pete with my elbow and pointed.

"There's Sugar Jenks."

"Where?"

"Right over—" Too late. I was pointing at blackness. "Forget it," I said. "Just sit back. Relax. Enjoy the show."

Easier said than done. Nick Fallon was right. *The Bells of Titan* was a derivative tedium. The movie told the story of an independent coffee-bean grower in Bolivia who fights off a multinational corporation intent on buying him out. The point man for the multinational corporation turns out to be involved in running drugs and weapons and is angling to use the coffee plantation as a platform for his operations. The coffee-bean grower figures this out, nearly gets killed a half dozen times in his efforts to thwart the scheme, and in the end emerges victorious. Along the way—added bonus—he inspires the bad guy's bottle-blonde girlfriend to ditch the guy and join in with him, even to the point of taking a sexy shower with him during the movie's big hit song, "Touch Don't Look." There is a subplot about the man's sister, a nun in the village, and her efforts to involve the townspeople in a production of *Man of La Mancha*. Munger told me afterward that he wished the nun had been the one to take the sexy shower. I chastised him for his blasphemy, but I had to agree he had a point. The same actress who played the nun had popped up in one of the previews, playing an uptight-but-beautiful nuclear scientist with a secret passion for cha-cha.

After the film was over there was a grapes-and-cheese-ball reception in the lobby. It was difficult to get a sense of what the crowd thought of the movie. I loaded up on cheese balls and took a ginger ale as a chaser. I spotted Sugar Jenks again. She was standing next to a display window that held a vintage poster from *How Green Was My Valley*. That's a black-and-white movie about a coal-mining town. If you ask me, the title poses a damn good question.

Pete had gone outside to smoke a cigarette. I made my way over to the vintage poster and the young woman standing in front of it.

"Hi." You might have thought I'd nipped her with a cattle prod; she practically jumped out of her skin. "It's me again. Hitchcock Sewell." She looked at me as if I had just spoken in olde Welsh. "What did you think of the movie?"

"I thought . . . the movie was good."

"It has a redemptive quality, doesn't it?" I said, smiling broadly.

She returned roughly a quarter of my smile. "It does. It has a redemptive quality."

"I thought the nun was good."

"Yes . . . the nun was good."

I never attended dental school, there's only so much teeth pulling I'm capable of doing. We went on in this excruciating fashion for a few more exchanges. Sugar looked like she'd gladly dive into the nearest hole if one would only open up. The girl was rescued—*I* was rescued—by Russell Jenks, who materialized next to her. He took hold of her elbow and spoke softly to her.

"Sugar, there are some people I think you should meet." He looked at me. "I hope you don't mind if I—" He cut himself off. "We've met."

Sugar spoke up. "Russell, this is Mr. Sewell."

"I was at the party the other day," I said.

"Of course. I remember."

"Bang-up movie," I lied. "I was just saying to your wife. Redemptive, no? It's too bad Mr. Larue couldn't make it tonight."

Jenks smiled pleasantly. "What we need are four or five Crawfords. Maybe that way we could meet all the demands that are on his plate."

"Four or five Crawfords." I nodded gallantly at Sugar. "If four or five Crawfords yielded four or five Miss Larues, how fortunate for us all."

Not to disparage the young woman, but I know a line of hooey when I hear one . . . especially when I'm the one saying it. Sugar blushed. If I'm not mistaken, I blushed as well. Sugar Jenks was wearing a silk shawl over her bare shoulders. She clutched it tightly and winced a smile at me. It seemed to require all the energy she could muster.

"Thank you for coming," Jenks said again, and he steered Crawford's daughter off into the crowd. I went outside and found Pete on the sidewalk looking up at the moon.

"Looks full," I said.

"It is," he said. "I'm not. Let's go get something to eat."

We grabbed a couple of cheese-steak subs at Maria's just north of Coldspring, then made our way down to the Inner Harbor. A street performer who looked like he had just stepped off the stage of a *Godspell* production was wowing a small crowd of onlookers with his juggling and banter. The night was uncommonly warm, and the Harborplace promenade was brimming with humanity in all its assorted shapes and sizes. We moseyed to a bench and had a seat.

"I remember when this area was nothing but derelicts," Pete said. "None of this stuff was here. Not even the *Constellation*. It was half sunk and pretty much forgotten in one of those piers over there." He jerked his thumb to the east. "This area was nothing but a big patch of grass and dirt. It was bums and drug pushers. The idea of coming down to the harbor didn't even exist. People steered clear of it altogether. Now look at it. It's like Disneyland."

I wasn't quite ready to equate Harborplace with the Magic Kingdom, but I understood his point.

Pete was frowning.

"What's wrong?" I asked. "Do you miss the bums and drug pushers?"

Pete didn't answer right away. He was watching a teenaged couple feeding pizza to each other. Several feet away from the couple, a middle-aged couple with impressive middle-age spread were working on a pair of ice cream cones. A shirtless skateboarder came slicing by, his cap on backward and his large pants fluttering like flags.

"Susan got mugged down here once," Pete said. His voice was flat. His eyes held steady toward the water. "Broad daylight. The McCormick Spice factory used to be over there, where that brick crap is now."

I remembered. The air used to smell like a combination of cinammon and pepper. It used to make my mother sneeze.

Pete went on. "Susan was a schoolteacher back then. Fresh out of college. Same year that we got married. A couple of the classes were on a field trip and the McCormick Spice factory was one of their stops. I think they also went over to the Holsum Bakery and the Lexington Market."

I asked, "Was it a field trip or a shopping run?"

Pete ignored me. "Everyone was on the bus and one of the kids said that she'd left a sweater behind. Susan went back for it. They jumped her right outside the building. They smacked her around. It was three of them. She got a black eye out of it."

A rueful grin came to Pete's face.

"Damn fool woman fought back. One of them had her purse and she was playing tug-of-war with him. Another one knocked her down and they kicked her a couple times. The girl was one big bruise when she got home. But you know what? They didn't get her purse. She put a death grip on the damn thing and Charlie Atlas couldn't have pried it loose. The muggers finally left. Susan went on to McCormick's and fetched the sweater then went back to the bus. The kids didn't really get it. They thought the muggers had wanted the sweater. They thought that Susan had gotten beaten up because she refused to hand it over. She was a real hero."

Pete fell silent. He peered out over the black water. After a minute he said, "No, I don't miss the damn bums and pushers. I say bulldoze the whole damn place."

———

A bull moose stormed into my office the next day. I had been busying myself putting papers into neat stacks. I like neat stacks and I find that if I leave them unattended for too long, they get un-neat all on their own. Either that or Billie sneaks into my office and musses them. By the time the bull moose showed up I had actually finished with my paperwork and was on the phone with Pete, who was camped out on the couch back at my place. I was reading to him from one of my trade journals, about a fellow mortician in the town of Blue Nose, Canada—that's in the Saskatchewan province—and the frenzy of activity he has each spring burying the folks who have been held in cold storage through the long bitter winter when the ground is simply too frozen for digging graves. The article was titled "Spring Planting." Pete was finding it somewhat less amusing than I was.

"Hang on," I said, glancing out the window. "I've got company." I hit the speaker-phone button and dropped the receiver back onto the cradle. The bull moose stormed in.

"Where the *hell* do you get off interfering with my personal life?"

You'll know the bull moose by his more familiar name. Mike Gellman. Mike looked to me as if he hadn't gotten a terribly good night's sleep. Sometimes all that's required is that you flip the mattress, though I don't believe in Mike's case his bleary eyes and disgruntled demeanor were stemming from that sort of comfort issue. He planted his hands on my desk and bellowed at me like . . . well, in fact, like a bull moose.

"I want you off my back, Sewell! You have no fucking idea what you're screwing around with!"

I was tempted to reply that I had a very precise idea what *he* was . . . but why wave a red flag?

"Would you like a nice cup of tea, Mike?" I asked.

He grumbled, "Are you listening to me?"

"I'm sure as hell *hearing* you. And so is half the block, I'd imagine. Why don't you put it in reverse, Mike. Take a seat. Count to ten."

I have a novelty pen and pencil set on my desk. One of my sales reps gave it to me a few years back. The pen and pencil are shaped like two femur bones and they sit inside a little tin casket. Mike swept his hand across my desk. He sent the little metal casket flying across the room. It sailed right out the open window.

"Nice shot," I remarked.

Mike dropped into a chair. "I want this stopped. Do you understand me?"

Of course I understood him. He was speaking in simple clear sentences. No big words.

"I capiche."

"I don't want any of your bullshit, Sewell. This is the wrong time for you to be snooping around in my private affairs."

"I have to say, Mike, you turn a phrase with uncanny precision."

"This is no joke, Sewell."

I steepled my fingers. "I agree with you, Mike. It's not a joke. If *I* may be precise here. A young woman you employed is dead under suspicious circumstances, whether your buddies in the local police force want to think so or not, and not a week later you're frolicking in a hot tub with a woman who is not only not your wife but who had some rather peculiar dealings with your nanny fairly soon before her death. You're right, Mike. Not a laugh riot by a long shot."

"My private life is none of your business. And where the hell do you get off snooping around on my property in the middle of the night?"

It seemed to me that of the two indiscretions—trespassing and adultery—the better question was where did Gellman get off asking me where *I* got off. But it was too convoluted a question to ask.

The sun was angling in the window in a narrow beam that landed directly on Mike Gellman's lap. He crossed his legs and the sunlight settled on his knee.

"Look. I'm not an angel, okay? I'm human. I make mistakes. Is that what you want to hear?"

"Not to push a point, Mike, but I don't need to hear it. And, I gather, neither does Libby."

He shifted in his chair. "What do you mean? Have you told her?"

"About Ginny Larue? As it happens, I haven't. Not yet anyway. But Libby has been giving me the rundown on some of your past affairs."

"What are you talking about?"

"I have to tell *you*?"

"You mean Maggie Mason? Oh for Christ's sake, that was years ago. Ancient history. I slept with the woman exactly twice. That's hardly 'an affair.' It's a pair of one-night stands. I ate so much goddamn humble pie over Maggie Mason it's not even funny."

"What about Cindy, Mike? You can't call that one ancient history."

"Cindy?" A frown creased his face. "Our nanny? What the hell does Cindy have to do with anything?"

"You were sleeping with her," I said.

"Oh really." Mike crossed his arms and sat back in the chair. "How interesting. Is this someone else you spied me with in my hot tub?"

"Libby told me."

"Well let me tell you something. Libby doesn't know what the hell she's talking about. I never slept with Cindy. That's absurd."

"Libby says you did."

"Did *she* see me?"

"She sussed it out."

"She sussed it out wrong. I never slept with that girl. Though I wouldn't put it past her to plant the idea in Libby's head. That damn girl. If I ever got ahold of her . . ." He trailed off.

"What, Mike? If you got ahold of her, what? You'd throw her from a bridge?"

He leaned forward in his chair. "I'm telling you, Sewell, I didn't touch Sophie. You have no idea what you're talking about."

"Fine. Do you want to convince me? Libby says you were working late that night that Sophie went out. Maybe you were, maybe you weren't. I sure as hell notice that the local police haven't pressed you to explain yourself to them."

"Do you want to know where I was? I'll tell you." He fell back in the chair. "But if you tell Libby I swear I'll take your head off. I was with Ginny Larue, okay? We were at the Commodore Hotel. I can have that confirmed, but obviously I'd rather not if I can avoid it. I was nowhere near that girl. Bud Talbot has a statement from me concerning my whereabouts. I came clean with the authorities on that. They're doing me the courtesy of keeping it confidential. It's nothing Libby needs to know."

"And when did 'Bud' get this statement from you?"

"When I came in to identify Sophie. Naturally with a death on his hands and not just a missing persons, he wanted to get as broad a picture of things as he could, starting with the night Sophie disappeared."

"Was that also when you told Talbot that you thought Sophie must have killed herself?"

Mike frowned. "What are you talking about? Who said I said anything like that?"

"Officer Floyd recalls that it was you or Libby or both of you who told the police that Sophie was unstable. But it wasn't Libby."

"He's mistaken."

"But you knew she was pregnant. You didn't have to wait for the coroner's report. Which probably means that Talbot knew, too. You told him, right? You told him the girl was unsteady, she found out she was pregnant, she threw herself off the bridge."

"Now I knew she was pregnant? Where are you coming up with this, Sewell?"

"Virginia Larue. She told me yesterday who set up the meeting between the Larues and Sophie. It was Owen Cutler. And you're the logical link between him and Sophie. If Uncle Owen knew that Sophie was pregnant, something tells me you weren't in the dark."

Mike got out of the chair and stepped over to the window. He dropped into that famous JFK pose, hands on the windowsill, weight of the world on the back of his neck.

"This is all fucked up," he muttered, which is probably pretty close to what Kennedy had to say at the time as well. Mike stood there a while staring at his knuckles, then turned to face me.

"How much of this have you told Libby?"

"She knows that Sophie went to see the Larues. She doesn't know who set it up."

"Look, you've got to do me a favor. You've got to drop all of this right now. I don't want you telling Libby a thing. I don't want you telling the police a thing."

"How about the newspapers?"

"Jesus, Sewell, you have no idea what you're getting into. No. Not the fucking newspapers. I'm about to be indicted in this goddamn arena mess. I can't have this other stuff coming up. Do you understand what I'm saying? I'm fighting for my life here. I'll pay you, Sewell. I swear. I had nothing to do with Sophie's death. I didn't kill her, if that's what you're thinking."

"Or Tom Cushman?"

"I had nothing to do with that, either."

"But you know who Tom Cushman is. You know that he was the person who went with Sophie to see Crawford Larue."

"I never met the guy. I couldn't tell you what he looks like."

"But Virginia Larue knew what he looked like. And where to find him."

"Fine. So what?"

"So she could tug on your sleeve and tell you, 'There he is. Go get him.'"

Mike was exasperated. "Yes. Fine. I killed him. And I killed Sophie. For Christ's sake, anybody else? Have you got any bodies lying around this place you can't account for? I killed them, too. I killed everybody. I'm a maniac. Someone should kill *me*."

He stepped away from the window and dropped back into the chair. He tried but failed to wipe his features off his face. "How the hell did everything get so fucked up? I can't believe what's happening."

"What I want to know is what the hell you and Owen Cutler were doing sending Sophie off to Crawford Larue. Unless my information is way off, I happen to know that it wasn't either of you who got her pregnant."

"Don't go there, Sewell. Seriously. Why can't I get through to you?"

I shrugged. "Titanium plate in my head. Deflects everything. I'm also B-vitamin deficient and I don't eat enough seafood. Rotten retention. It's not your fault, Mike. I know you're trying."

Mike grimaced. "No, Sewell, *you're* trying."

"I'll tell you what, Mike. I'll make you a deal. I haven't told Libby about the little hot-tub scene I witnessed the other night. I'm sure she'd be intrigued to hear all about it. You put the Sophie-Larue picture together for me and I'll keep that scene to myself. How's that?"

"And I'm supposed to trust you?"

"Trust this. If you don't tell me I'll pick up the phone and call her right now. You can sit there and listen to me tell her all about it. My powers of description might dazzle you."

Mike glared at me. "You're going to be disappointed."

"Go ahead, Mike. Disappoint me."

He shifted in the chair. "Here's the thing. I was actually being a nice guy. That's what it really comes down to. It was a fluke of timing. I was having lunch at a place called Griffin's. It was a Saturday. Libby was off with the kids on some sort of play date. I was heading up to where I'd parked my car, and I ran right into Sophie. She was sitting on a bench on the sidewalk. She was crying. She tried to pretend that she wasn't, but the moment she opened her mouth to speak, she exploded into tears. She was a real wreck. I sat down and she blurted it out. The whole pregnancy thing. She said she had found out that she was pregnant a couple days before and had just come from seeing the guy who was responsible. Basically, the guy was giving her the cut-and-run. I tried to get from her who he was, but she clamped shut. She wasn't going to tell me. She wasn't even blaming him. Not really. She was putting it all on herself. I'm telling you, she was a real mess. I did what I could to calm her down. She said she was afraid we'd fire her. Eventually I got her to calm down. We went to a café and had some coffee. And that's when I suggested she go see Larue."

"Stop. You knew that Larue was looking to adopt?"

"I did. Owen had mentioned it to me. Larue doesn't want a lot of publicity about this. He wants to handle it privately. I thought maybe this could work out for everyone so I put Sophie in contact with Owen."

"And what about Libby? Why was she kept in the dark about all this?"

The sunlight had tracked down to Mike's thigh. He brushed at something on his leg. Lint perhaps. It looked as if he were trying to brush the sunlight away.

"That was Sophie's call. She swore she didn't know she was pregnant when we hired her. We'd only had her about a month. She begged me not to tell Libby. Of course it was inevitable that it would come out, but she just wanted to hold off. The truth is I had a hell of a lot on my mind already at that point. I was just as happy not to add any more troubles to my plate."

"You lent Sophie your wedding ring, didn't you?"

"That was stupid. But yes. I did. Larue wanted to see the father as well as the mother. He's an old horse breeder. He wanted to check out the 'stock.' Sophie was working up some cockamamie story and she thought the ring would help. Frankly, I didn't care, just so long as my name didn't come up. I wasn't going to send her up there saying that she worked for me. Maybe you can understand I didn't want my name being bounced around Crawford Larue's house."

"And you didn't tell Virginia Larue any of this."

Mike leaned forward and put a hard look on me. "Let me tell you something. I've been living one day at a time here. I don't know how everything's gotten so unraveled. No. I didn't tell Ginny a damn thing. She's here, Libby's there, my job is over there. I compartmentalize. That's how I operate. I keep things separated."

"It looks to me like they want to all come crashing together."

Mike said nothing. He gazed at the edge of my desk a few more seconds, finally shook his head slowly and left. I lifted the phone receiver. The red light indicating speaker phone clicked off.

"You catch all that?" I asked.

Munger answered, "Yep."

"What do you think?"

He paused. I glanced out the window and saw Gellman out on the sidewalk. He bent down and picked up my pen and pencil set.

Pete answered, "Generally? I was unimpressed."

CHAPTER 22

Pete dropped into the chair where Mike Gellman had been sitting. He was showered and looked curiously refreshed. Nothing like a night on somebody's couch, I guess. He pulled out a cigarette and I threw a chair at him. Well, in fact I didn't. But I put as much energy into the scowl that I sent across my desk. Munger stuck the cigarette behind his ear.

"I think your friend's husband speaks with forked tongue," he said.

"Could be he's a liar, too."

"All that crap about keeping the news from his wife because the girl asked him to?"

"Exactly. I thought that was odd, too. Since when does loyalty to a nanny outrun loyalty to a wife?"

"Could be when you're nailing the nanny behind your wife's back."

"I don't think Mike was sleeping with Sophie," I said.

"You're still sold on the midshipman?"

"Call me crazy."

"Maybe you don't really have the full story there," Pete said. "I've noticed that about you. You trust people too much."

"You're not suggesting that Bradley's trying to cover for Gellman, are you? That's a stretch, Pete."

"I'm just thinking out loud," he said.

"There's something else going on here that we're missing," I said. I was unable to finish the thought. The phone rang. It was Julia.

"Waffles?"

I responded, "Yes, my lovely little bacon. It's me, your very own waffles."

"Funny."

"That wasn't a term of endearment?"

"It was an invitation to breakfast."

I noted that it was almost noon.

Julia said, "Fine. If you want lunch, put a waffle between two pieces of bread. Whatever works for you."

"Jules, should I remind you that you don't cook?"

I detected a giggle. "I have my own personal chef."

"I see."

"So can you come over?"

"I've got Pete with me," I said.

"Well, he has certainly become your little shadow these days."

"He's in between lives right now," I said, glancing over to see Pete sneering at me.

"Bring him along," Julia said. "There's something here that might interest the both of you."

"Well of course there is. That goes without saying."

"Don't be flirting with me, Hitch. There's a naked man running around my place."

"Waffles and a naked man. Is this going to be a regular breakfast, Jules, or am I in for something salacious and off-color? I just want to know if I should change."

"I guess you'll have to come over and see for yourself," she said.

We were about to hang up when she asked, "Oh, Hitch. One other thing. Could you bring over your waffle iron?"

She uses me. Isn't that perfectly clear? The woman uses me.

Nick Fallon was ravishing in a silk mandarin kimono with turquoise piping and an embroidered dragon on the back. He was standing in Julia's kitchenette, stirring batter in a ceramic bowl with a wooden spoon. He greeted me cheerfully. "Hey there, mate."

"Nice duds," I said, setting my waffle iron down on the counter.

"What's with the waffle thing?" Nick asked. "She was insistent."

"They're Julia's postcoital breakfast of choice." I turned to my ex-wife, who was pouring out mimosas. "What happened to your waffle iron?"

She plopped a strawberry into a glass and handed me the drink. "Burned out."

I settled into Julia's hammock as Fallon got to work on scorching the first several batches of waffles. Pete drifted to the window and gazed out in the direction of the harbor. His body language suggested that he would not at all have minded suddenly spreading a pair of wings and drifting out over the bricks. Julia positioned herself in front of me and did a yoga move that by all logic should have crippled her for life. She didn't even spill her mimosa. Her grin went from Maryland to California.

"You're a happy clam," I noted.

She rested the heel of one of her feet just inside the opposite ear and chanted, "I am, I am, I am, I am. . . ."

Fallon finally came through with the waffles. Golden brown. As square as a windowpane. The regulation thirty-six dimples per waffle. We ate on the floor, seated on pillows, except for Pete, who dropped into one of Julia's butterfly chairs and ate off his lap. Julia propped up canvases behind each of us as a sort of backdrop. This is how the woman decorates a place. Each of the canvases behind Fallon and Julia was from a recent series of her paintings that she was calling inverses. Fallon's showed a guitar seated on the edge of a fountain, strumming a human. Julia's canvas depicted a family of forks, knives and spoons enjoying a hearty dinner, using human cutlery. I recognized myself as one of the knives.

I told Fallon that Pete and I had gone to see *The Bells of Titan* the night before. He pinched his nose.

"Stinkpot, isn't it?"

"Merely imbecilic," I said. "I ran into Sugar Jenks. She really is an awfully peculiar bird, isn't she? I didn't know they made them that shy anymore."

"Was Crawford there?"

"He was supposed to be but he had to cancel."

Fallon leered. "How about that shower scene?"

As we finished our waffles Fallon set his plate down and got up off his pillow. "I've got something I want you to listen to." He indicated Pete. "How much does he know?"

"Pete's a pretty smart banana," I said. "Go ahead and try him out on a topic. I think geography is one of his strong suits."

"How much does he know about this nanny thing?"

"Everything."

Nick padded off to the rear of Julia's studio, where a wooden screen cordons off her bed and dresser.

"I hope he's going to change out of that bathrobe," Pete muttered.

"Too disturbing for you, Pete?"

"He looks like a fruit."

Fallon returned—still a fruit. He was holding up a cassette tape.

I rubbed my hands together. "Oh boy. *Zeppelin One*?"

Fallon stepped over to Julia's stereo. "After we talked the other day I went back to the office and dug this up. Actually, this is a copy. I record every call that comes into me at the paper. Job like mine, you never know."

"Is this your call from Annapolis?" I asked. "Sex, lies and Crawford Larue?"

"After what you told me I thought I should give it another listen, just to see."

He popped the tape into the machine and hit the Play button, then retreated to the hammock. The quality of the recording was lousy. At first there was only a crackle of static. Fallon shrugged.

"We got a low-tech thing going on at the paper. Just hang on."

He reached a foot down to the floor to nudge the hammock into a gentle rocking. Eventually the static abated somewhat and Fallon's voice sounded from the tape player.

Fallon. Cannon.

More crackle, then a female voice responded.

Are you the reporter?

The voice was dim. Competing against the static. Not terribly easy to make out. Nick's voice sounded again.

This is Nicholas Fallon. Who's this?

I've got a story. Do you want to buy a story? It's big.

What kind of big?

You know ARK, that religious group? You know them? I've got some dirt on them.

Is that so? Why don't you tell me about it?

I want to sell you a story. How much can you pay me for a story? These people are hypocrites. They're liars. They're really sick. They say they're antiabortion and all that? It's not true. These people arrange abortions all the time. For teenagers. And not just that. They're also sterilizing girls so they won't get pregnant at all. It's sick.

All around the room, eyebrows rose. On the tape, Fallon cleared his throat.

Why don't you give me your name? Why don't we start there?

There was silence on the tape. Well . . . there was static. Fallon was swinging gently on the hammock. He held up a hand. "Hold on."

After several more seconds of silence, the caller spoke again.

Never mind. Do you want this or not? It's a story, you can't tell

me that it's not. If you don't want to buy it, just say so. I can go some-
where else.

Fallon's voice on the tape was clearly sounding exasperated.

Look, you've got the sex, you've got the religious thing. That's all
great. But I'm not going to do this on the phone, okay? If you've got
something for real to tell me . . . and I mean real. Actual evidence.
Something I can trust. I'll listen to you. That's fair, right?

I want money.

Hey, don't we all?

I'm serious! I mean this. I thought you liked good stories. These
people are perverted sex maniacs and they're pretending they're bet-
ter than everybody. This is a good story.

Listen, right now you're just a voice on the phone. I can't go to my
boss with that. If you want—

The static abruptly stopped. There were a few seconds of dial
tone, and then the recording stopped altogether. Fallon got up from
the hammock and hit the Stop button. He ejected the tape and turned
to us.

"Like I said before, we get a dozen of these things a week sometimes. You can tell this one wasn't really much to go on. It just
sounded like someone disgruntled. Or a wacko. When there's really
something good you can usually tell. It'll have just the right stink to it.
If I chased down this kind of crap every single time it came in I'd never
get any real work done. I dated the tape and tossed it in the files."

"So what are you thinking now?" I asked.

"Well, now we've got a dead girl. And you've got her linked with
Crawford Larue."

"So now you're thinking this one stinks the way you like it?"

"It's getting ripe, yeah."

I downed my mimosa and got up off the floor.

"Can I borrow that?"

Fallon tossed the tape to me. It was a bad toss—wide—and I

missed it. I turned in time to see Pete catch it. He held it up to his nose and sniffed.

"He's right. It stinks."

Mike Gellman was emerging from the front door as we pulled up. I identified him for Pete. Pete grabbed his camera from the backseat and snapped off a few pictures.

"What's that for?" I asked.

"Habit."

We waited until Mike had rounded the corner, then we got out of the car and went up to the door. Libby appeared seconds after our knock. She was pale. She looked as if she had just passed the cocktail hour with a vampire.

"Mike was here," she said. "You just missed him."

"Are you okay?"

"I'm fine. I don't know about Mike, though. He's a mess."

"Can we come in?"

Libby pulled the door open wider. "Sure. Why not? It's visiting hour."

A few minutes later we were in the kitchen. Libby was seated at the table, listening to the cassette tape of Fallon's phone call. The tape ended and I hit the Stop button. Pete was leaning up against the kitchen counter, gazing up at the copper bowls. I was seated across from Libby. I'd been gazing at her face as she listened to the tape.

"Well, what do you think?" I asked.

"About that tape?"

"Yes."

"What am I supposed to think?"

"Sophie had an accent, didn't she?"

"Not a thick one. But yes. She had one."

"There's no accent in the voice on that tape," I said.

"Well, no," Libby said. "It's not Sophie. Is that who you thought it was?"

"When Fallon told me about the tape yesterday, yeah, I did. Fallon said he had been able to trace the call back to a pay phone in Annapolis. I just figured it was her. But it's not Sophie. It wasn't Sophie who called Nick Fallon with dirt on the ARK."

Libby was drumming her fingers on top of the cassette player.

"I guess you'd like me to tell you who it is then?"

Pete pushed off of the counter and grabbed a chair. Swinging it around backward he lowered himself into it.

"If you know that, Mrs. Gellman, it would be helpful."

CHAPTER

23

I recall a summer back when I was only a few feet tall when I was shipped off each morning to a day camp out in Catonsville. At the time I felt that I had been thoroughly abandoned by my parents, banished to this place from dawn to dusk for what felt like months on end, though I've since come to realize that these day camps customarily take up roughly half a day and extend for all of a few short weeks. For the parents they are little more than a brief respite, but for pipsqueaks time has a peculiar inter-minability. Weeks can seem to last several years, the minutes and hours of the days themselves forever cleaving in half and then in half again to the point where you simply rip up the calendar and gaze hopelessly out the window as the entire galactic dance seems to grind to a complete halt. At any rate this is how *I* felt during my tortuous several weeks of summer camp, which happened to fall that year during a period of uncustomary rainy weather, day after day of rain and drear, forcing the day campers to remain inside and go slowly nuts with arts and crafts. Popsicle-stick houses were the rage. Our counselors had us building entire subdevelopments of the damn things.

There was a particular day camper named Henry Aranow who stood out for his unique architectural madness. Henry was a chubby and mildly demonic boy who responded to the mass incarceration by rejecting the conventional glued-together Popsicle-stick structures of his peers for more elaborate creations. Henry had vision. His motif was the splinter, the shard, the remnant. Disorder was order in Henry's world, and in his Popsicle-stick creations this proclivity was manifested by constructions that looked by all rights as if they should crumble immediately, as if in fact they had no physical logic in even standing in the first place. Henry gleefully split his wooden sticks into pieces before even beginning to build his creations; he then worked wonders with glue—lots of glue—to bring forth peculiar little houses and towers and bridges that for all of their weird jutting angles and shredded woodlike appearance were nonetheless structurally sound. While the rest of us were toiling away at right angles and level planes, Henry was out there following his oddly angled Muse. The boy had vision; that was all there was to it.

Another thing about Henry, he was the very first skirt chaser I'd ever met. Certainly the youngest.

I prattle on about all of this by means of explanation as to why it was that when Pete and I pulled into the gravel parking area of the restaurant to which Libby had directed us, my jaw practically dropped into my lap. The building was a Henry Aranow creation. And I don't mean that figuratively. It *was* a Henry Aranow creation. Henry owned the place, and quite clearly had had a hand as well in its construction . . . or deconstruction, if you prefer.

CAP'N HENRY'S CRAB SHACK

"Good Christ," Pete muttered.

It was all there, just like the Popsicle-stick monstrosities that little Henry used to build as a tot. The place was constructed of unpainted wood, weathered gray and grainy, and it loomed out over a narrow tributary of the Severn River as if it was ready to tumble right in. I was reminded a little of Libby and Mike's house in that the restaurant itself—a good three-quarters of it—was an open deck. This was the part that actually loomed over the water. The deck was of a vastly irregular shape, as if a blind man had taken a jigsaw to an already amorphous rectangle. But it was the ragged collection of splintery-looking pieces serving to support the thing that really showed the Aranow touch. The large deck was essentially on stilts that went down into the water. The stilts looked like toothpicks. Or long skinny legs.

Henry was no longer the chubby sort but had blossomed into a downright large man with a barrel chest, a big broad face and a proud golden mustache the size of a small propeller. He had an easygoing look to him. His robust smile revealed a gold cap on one of the top teeth and his small blue eyes sparkled with mirth. He was wearing a tattered Greek fisherman's cap, dirty khakis and a loud Hawaiian shirt.

"This is a hell of a crab shack you've got here, Henry," I said to him after Pete and I had been shown to our seats. Henry had given us a table along the railing, one of the zigzag offshoots seemingly held in the air by nothing other than a prearrangement with gravity. Pete was looking warily over the edge at the river below. His grip on the metal arms of his chair seemed especially secure.

"I think big," Henry said, rapping his ham hands against his belly for emphasis. He tugged on his cap. "This 'cap'n' stuff is pure horse, you know. It's a good look though. Truth is I'm a landlubber. Can't stand the water."

Henry's wife, Joan, was our waitress. Henry directed Joan to load us up with a couple of platters of oysters and a pitcher of beer. I asked after the crab cakes and Henry told me they were as big as my fist and no filler.

"Bring 'em on, Cap'n."

It being a Saturday, the joint was jumping. And so was Joan. She was working the tables with a demon energy. When she delivered our pitcher of beer it sloshed over the rim and onto a few of our oysters.

"Sorry. I'll get you some more." She grabbed up the several splashed oysters, shoving them into her apron pocket, and hurried off.

"And so laid back," I said, forking a little snot of oyster into my dish of cocktail sauce. Henry had moved on to work his cap'n shtick on his other customers and Pete and I decided to wait until after our lunch before waving him back over. As we finished up our mollusks, I caught Henry's eye across the deck. His gold tooth glistened and he made his way back over to our table.

"How was everything?" he asked.

I told him it was supreme. "Can you spare a couple minutes, Henry?" I asked. "We wanted to ask you a few questions."

"Questions? Sure. What's up?"

"It's about one of your employees," I said.

"Pull up a chair," Pete said.

Henry sat down between us. "I hope it's not Joan. I've told her she works too fast. It can get the customer jumpy."

"It's not Joan," I said.

Joan was flying by just then at supersonic speed. She banked hard left and pulled up at our table with a nearly audible squeak of her rubber shoes.

"Is everything all right? Anything wrong?"

"Everything's fine, Joan," Henry said soothingly. "How about some apple pie for my friends?"

"Pie." As if she had uttered an incantation, Joan vanished.

Henry smoothed his walrus mustache. "She's something, isn't she?"

"We want to ask you about Cindy Lehigh," I said.

Henry's mustache drooped, along with the rest of his face.

"That one. What about her?"

"Is she working here today, Mr. Aranow?" Pete asked.

"Henry."

"Is she here?"

Henry wagged his head. "Not today and not any other day either. Not anymore she isn't. And this time I don't care if she comes crawling back on all fours. Fool me twice, but that's it."

Pete and I swapped a glance.

"Do you mind explaining that, Henry?" I asked.

"What's to explain? Cindy worked for me early in the year. Right before the summer hit she went and quit on me. Crappy timing for me, but that's how the business goes. She told me she got some other job. She wanted her nights free. So she left."

"She got a job as a nanny," I said.

"Yeah. That's what I heard. Something like that."

"But she came back recently, isn't that right?" I asked.

"About a month or so ago, yeah. I guess I'm a pushover. I let her talk me into taking her back on."

"It didn't work out?" Pete asked. "Is that what you're saying?"

"That's right."

"Did she quit again or did you fire her?"

Henry showed us his gold tooth. "Afraid I didn't get the pleasure. I should have while I had the chance."

"So then she quit."

"I suppose you could call it that. The girl didn't stand on ceremony. What happened is that she just stopped showing up for work one day. I guess you could call that quitting."

"She didn't give you a reason?" I asked.

"You mean show common courtesy? Let me take a stab here. You two have never had dealings with the girl. Am I right?"

"You're right," I said. "We never had the pleasure."

"Well, it's not as much of a pleasure as it seems, trust me. She's a looker, I'll give her that. And I guess that carries more weight than it ought to, but there it is."

"Is that why you hired her back?" Pete asked. "Because she's a looker?"

"What do you mean by that?"

"Was Cindy at least a decent waitress?" Pete asked.

Joan materialized just then. She heard Pete's question. She skidded a pair of plates in front of Pete and myself—two large slices of apple pie—then dropped a pair of forks noisily onto the table. She shot a look at Henry.

"Thank you, Joan," Henry said.

She vaporized.

I picked up my fork and took two stabs. One of them was into my pie. "Let me guess. Those two didn't get on, did they?"

Henry nodded slowly. "You could say that. You can see, Joannie works like the devil. Our little Cindy had . . . well, she had a different style. You'd look up and see her gabbing with customers over here while customers over there are waiting for service. She wasn't always real punctual either. And she got in a couple of fights with the cooks."

"Sounds like a model employee," Pete noted.

Henry grunted. "Model for disaster."

"So then why did you hire her back?" Pete asked again.

"We were short," Henry said. "One of my girls had just quit and I happened to run into Cindy in town. She asked if we needed help out here. At least she was already trained. She could hit the ground running."

"I wouldn't think it would be that hard to locate good waitresses," Pete said.

"You're right. I guess I made a mistake. And I guess I paid for it. The day after she stopped showing up we realized we were short in the till."

"She stole money from you?"

"Can't prove it, of course. But I'd say it fits the profile. The girl's a little goldbricker."

"We're trying to locate her, Henry," I said. "Any idea how we can get ahold of her?"

Henry stroked his mustache thoughtfully. "I can't help you there.

All I know is that she was living with a friend of hers somewhere in town."

"In Annapolis?"

"Yes. But I don't have an address."

"What about Joan?" Pete asked. "Maybe your wife knows how we can get ahold of Cindy."

"I don't think so."

"Wouldn't hurt to ask though." Pete started to rise from his chair. Henry placed a hand on his arm.

"Whoa. Slow down there."

Pete glanced over at me, then back at Henry. "Problem there, Cap'n? I just want to ask your wife a question."

"I told you, she doesn't know anything." Joan was dumping a tray of crabs onto a table across the deck from us. Her eyes weren't on the job. They were on her husband. "Look, I'd as soon you not bring Cindy up to Joan, okay?"

Pete smiled ruefully as he pushed his chair back. "I'll be right back." He got up and headed across the deck.

"That was the precisely wrong thing to say," I said to Henry. Henry let out a low groan. "What's the problem, Henry?" I asked.

"Aw, shit, Hitch, the girl was a looker, what can I say? She's a little manipulator is what she is."

"Did Cindy lure you over to the Dark Side, Henry?" I asked.

"Easy for you to make a joke." Across the deck, Pete and Joan were chattering away. Henry tugged on his mustache again. "Good thing I've got a comfortable couch in my office."

"Did Cindy really walk, Henry, or did your wife fire her?"

"No. She vanished, that's the truth."

Pete was headed back to our table.

"Nothing personal, Hitch, but I wish you and your friend just hadn't showed up. I've been cooling Joan off for a month now."

"She seems like a nice lady," I said.

"She is. I'm just a shit."

Pete arrived at the table.

"Let's go."

He pulled some bills from his wallet and dropped them onto the table.

"No, no," Henry said. "It's on the house."

"It's for our waitress."

Henry looked at the bills. "That's a big tip."

Pete smiled. "Tit for tat."

Joan had given Pete the name of a bar where she thought we might have some luck locating Cindy. The Swan. She told him that Cindy frequented the Swan.

"Sounds like Cap'n Henry frequented the Swan, too," Pete said as we made our way into town. He stared glumly out the window. A minute later he muttered, "I guess I shouldn't talk."

The Swan was located a few blocks west of the statehouse, not terribly far from the home of Kathy Pierce, Sophie's employer for a year. It was a wood-sided colonial affair painted black with white trim. The sign outside heralded local brews. There was outdoor seating. The several people taking in the late-afternoon sun were only a couple of decades past diapers.

"This is going to be your crowd," Pete said to me. "An old fart like me goes in there and starts asking questions it's going to look strange. This one's all yours, cowboy."

It seemed to me that it was too early to be nosing around the bar. Pete agreed.

"You want to wait until the place fills up a little. Right now it's just the bartender and a couple of customers. That's no good."

We decided to give it a few hours.

"Do you want to go see what Stella Gibbons is up to?" I asked. If Pete thought this was funny he did a bang-up job hiding it. We parked the car near the bar and walked the several blocks back up toward the George Washington Inn.

"It's ironic, isn't it?" I said as we rounded the corner by the state-house. "Of all the gin joints in all the cities in the world, what are the odds that we'd each have a girl working in the same damn place?"

Pete stopped to pull out a cigarette. He lit it, holding the lit match a few seconds and giving me a hard look.

"For one thing," he said, "this isn't a gin joint."

"I know that. I just never pass up a chance to quote Bogie."

"For another thing, this isn't irony. People are always using the word 'irony' the wrong way."

"I know," I said. "Isn't that ironic?" Munger looked like he wanted to put his cigarette out on my cerebral cortex. "And another thing?" I asked.

Pete pawed the air. "Forget it."

"No. Go on. There's something else."

Pete gazed up at the dome of the statehouse—or possibly right through it, on out into deep deep space. Something was clearly on his mind. He finally brought his gaze back down and put it on me.

"I was never like you are," he said.

"I'm sure you weren't," I responded. "But what exactly does that mean?"

"I mean about women, okay? I got married straight out of college. That's where I met Susan. Sophomore year we started dating and then when we graduated we got married right off the bat and started a family. Of course we had our rough patches. That's inevitable. When I quit being a lawyer, all the crap around that. That was rough. That was very rough for both of us. We had some real problems back around then."

He looked up at the statehouse dome again. "But I've always been faithful to Susan. Right up to now. You can call me old-fashioned if you want, but that's how it is."

He took a hard drag on his cigarette. I didn't say anything. I sensed that he wasn't finished and I was right. He pointed at me with the cigarette.

"You're a cocky son of a bitch sometimes," he said.

"I've taken that rap," I admitted.

"And your whole thing with women . . ." He trailed off.

I protested. "What whole thing?"

Munger waved his hand off in the direction of the inn, which was just up at the end of the block.

"That's just another of your fly-by-night girls in there. I'm not criticizing, I'm just saying. You've got this whole come-and-go attitude, you know? That's fine. That's none of my business. But I'm not you, okay? *I'm* not on a goddamn lark here. I'm on the verge of busting up a twenty-nine-year-old marriage. Whole damn relationship's nearly as old as you are."

"Fine, Pete. I realize all that. So what are you saying?"

"What I'm saying is that Lee is not just some girl. That's not how I operate. Truth is, I don't know what the hell is going on. But this is not just a lark. You and I don't 'each have a girl working in the same damn place.' That's not what's going on here."

"Is that your message?" I asked.

He dropped his cigarette and ground it out under his heel. "Yeah. I guess." He didn't look up from the ground.

"Well, I respect it, Pete," I said. "I didn't mean to make light. I apologize."

"Forget it."

"No. I mean it. You're absolutely right. I withdraw my comment. You know I'm fond of Lee, Pete. I think she's great. And you're right. There's nothing fly-by-night about her. Or about you, either. That's not what I meant. I apologize."

Pete looked me square in the face. He was a hard book to read. But then his lopsided grin—or at least part of it—slotted into place.

"You do have your fun though, Sewell, don't you?" he said.

"Yes, sir," I answered. "I keep my eyes on the prize."

We continued on up the street to the inn. Lee hadn't arrived yet. Pete parked himself at the bar and asked for a cup of coffee. It was clear that he didn't want company. I pushed through the kitchen door and found Faith chopping up onions. Her eyes were moist with tears. She looked up as I came in and gave me a wet smile.

"It just rips you up, doesn't it?" I said.

"Well, if it's not my little undertaker friend."

I got a slightly bigger kiss than I had expected. A couple bits of onion on the back of my neck. I came out of our wild clutch and licked my lips.

"Mmmm, you taste like a pumpkin, pumpkin," I said.

"Pumpkin soup," Faith said. "Do you want to help me? I need all those carrots cut up."

She handed me a Jack-the-Ripper knife. "You want these cut up or slaughtered without mercy?"

We worked side by side, she on her onions, me on my carrots. Faith noted that we worked well together. I told her maybe she could come up to Baltimore sometime and we could embalm together.

"I'd like that," she said.

"I pray God that you're kidding."

Faith wanted to know if her steering me toward Bradley Hansen the other day had cleared things up for me concerning Sophie.

"It helped," I said, and then I gave her a brief rundown of the lay of the land. Her ears pricked up when I mentioned the Swan.

"That's a pretty popular place. I go there sometimes myself."

"Well, according to Joan, Cindy went there a lot. She says it's a pickup joint."

"That's a silly term. It's just a bar. So how do you think this Cindy is involved with Sophie? You don't think that *she* killed her, do you?"

"At this point it wouldn't surprise me to discover that *I* killed her. I have no idea where Cindy fits in or whether she even fits in at all. But she must. She made the call to Fallon about hanky-panky at the ARK. Sophie and Tom went to Crawford Larue's house and met with him. That can't just be a coincidence."

"Maybe Sophie and Cindy knew each other," Faith said. "They both worked for the same family, after all."

Faith's assistants had arrived. Faith introduced me to them.

"You have to go sit on that stool now," she said to me. "You're now officially in the way."

I sat and watched the team for a while. Faith threw me a look now and again. She had a dusting of flour on her cheek. Drives a man wild, that flour. After a bit, Stephanie showed up. She was pitching in for the night. We hugged like old pals.

"So what brings you here?" she asked, then she looked over at Faith. "Oh . . . you breeders," she cracked. "You're something else."

Stephanie tied on an apron and plunged in. I finally decided that I was becoming a piece of furniture. I got off the stool and came up behind Faith while she was gutting a butternut squash. I gave her ponytail a tug.

"Me leave now," I said.

She turned her head. "Go bar?"

"Go bar."

"Later. Come back?"

I gave a peck to her flour patch.

"Come back."

I agree; it's disgusting the way people talk sometimes. Stephanie thought so, too. She made great big goo-goo eyes at me as I left the kitchen.

Pete was in a heavy powwow at the bar with Lee when I came out of the kitchen. He was facing away from me. Lee glanced up and saw me but didn't acknowledge me. It was clear from her expression that Munger wasn't telling her any jokes. At least not any good ones.

The sun was gone. The moon was a sliver. A faint serpentine cloud scribbled a sloppy Z in the coal-dust sky. I walked in the opposite direction from the Swan, swinging down to the harbor and to the theater where *The Seagull* had been playing. A red banner— CLOSED—ran diagonally across the production poster. I crossed to the corner where the dark sedan had clipped Tom Cushman. The glass had already been replaced in the ice cream parlor window. There were several customers inside. A couple was seated at the same table where Tom had landed after crashing through the window. They were giggling about something, which for some reason began to get me angry.

I headed off for the Swan.

The place was packed. A pair of TVs in opposite corners over the bar were broadcasting a couple of college football games, though nobody in the bar seemed particularly wrapped up in them. The ceiling was stamped tin, painted black. A historical marker at the door suggested that colonists used to get schnookered on this very spot back in the early days of the Republic. It's nice to see some continuity in this great nation of ours.

In honor of our forefathers I took a frothy mug of stout from the bartender, nearly slipping my shoulder out of its socket maneuvering around the crowd to reach my drink on the bar. It dawned on me— awfully damn late, I think we can all agree—that I didn't even know what Cindy Lehigh looked like. It was entirely possible that she was no more than five feet from me in any direction. Was she the blonde with the large teeth? Was she the brunette with the snorting laugh? Maybe the pale Morticia Addams–like creature erect and disdainful seated dead center at the bar? I contemplated the question while I worked on my beer. Pete had warned me earlier against asking direct questions when you're trying to locate someone who might be nearby. "When you're looking for someone, you don't necessarily want them to know that you're looking for them. If they don't want to be found you might just scare them away." Well, great. What was I supposed to do, stand here and pray that Cindy Lehigh was a) present and b) would get it in her head to simply come over to me and identify herself?

I consulted my beer and together we chewed the issue over. The population of the bar seemed to be spread fairly evenly between clusters of one sex checking out clusters of the other. I spotted a sign taped to the bar mirror: BEER. GETTING PEOPLE LAID SINCE 1886. I guess that about tells the story.

I finished my beer and called for another, at the same time sticking my thumb in my ear, placing my pinky at the edge of my mouth and sending my eyebrows up the pole. The bartender pointed. I took my beer to the rear and found the pay phone. A few minutes later I emerged looking for a tall thin young woman with straight brown hair down to the middle of her back, small breasted and likely wearing leather pants, black, brown or dark green. According to Libby, Cindy's standard prowling garb nearly always included the leather pants.

I took a tour of the bar but didn't see anyone fitting the description. The pale creature seated by herself showed a little promise; her hair was closer to black than brown but it was long and straight, as was the woman herself, the way Libby had described. The crowd was in a little too tight for me to make out her pants at a distance. I worked my way forward, and when I was close saw a pair of legs—no leather pants—that I have to say were well worth the effort. She caught me looking and she tried to shame me with a heavy-lidded stare and a curled lip. Minimal movement seemed to be her oeuvre.

"I'm looking for someone named Cindy," I blurted, ignoring Pete's advice. I could practically feel the swirl of wind as the suave, sly Hitchcock flew out the door at gale-force speeds.

"I'm not her," the leggy one replied.

"My name is Hitchcock," I said, niftily completing the blowing of a cover that I suppose never really stood a chance anyway.

"What do you want with Cindy?"

She knew her. At least it sounded as if she did. I took a slug of beer as I tried to arrange my thoughts. The woman on the stool looked monumentally bored. I was reminded of the Sphinx.

"I ran into her here a couple of weeks ago," I lied. "I've been out of town. I thought maybe I could catch her."

The woman simply blinked. Slowly. "The person you want to talk to is Paula."

I gave a scratch behind my ear. "Well, no. The person I want to talk to is Cindy."

"Paula's her roommate."

"Oh. Well, then you're right. I'm sorry. The person I want to talk to is Paula. Is she here?"

"She will be."

"What about Cindy? Doesn't she usually come in? It's Saturday night, after all."

"I haven't seen Cindy in a couple weeks. I think I heard she was gone."

"Gone? Gone where?"

Blink . . . "You'd have to ask Paula."

"Right." I gave a shrug of indifference. "It's no big deal, but if you happen to see her, Paula, maybe you could let me know."

"I can do that," she said.

Okay, I thought, but don't strain yourself. I left the lady and her legs to fend for themselves and worked my way to a spot near the door. Despite the crush of people, my Sphinx lady remained easy to spot, a tall implacable lighthouse in a sea of bobbing faces. I tried to get interested in the football game under way just over my head, but neither team seemed capable of moving the ball down the field. I chewed on what the Sphinx had just said. If I could believe her, Cindy had not been coming around for several weeks now. That was about how long it had been since Cindy had suddenly stopped working at the restaurant. It was also, I realized, somewhere around the same time that Sophie Potts had taken a header off the Naval Academy Bridge.

I watched an interception turn into a fumble. Two helmets collided violently above the wobbling ball. Each player dropped to the ground and the ball squibbed out of bounds. The two players got up off the ground, each a little unsteady, and gave each other a congenial fist tap. No hard feelings here on the collegiate gridiron.

Nearly an hour passed. A guy next to me was trying to make some progress on a pair of women with a display of his aptitude with lyrics and tunes to old television shows. Exactly how far along he thought he might get with a display of such trivia I couldn't say, though it appeared in fact that one of the women was beginning to nibble at the bait. I was nursing my third beer and it was down to its final inch when I picked up the signal from my beaconess. She caught my eye and then pointed with her chin as a woman passed directly in front of her. She was a frosted blonde in jeans and a sheer blue top. She squeezed her way to the bar and a minute later was sucking on a pink drink in a martini glass. A minute later I was squeezing in next to her, ordering another beer.

"What you got there?" I asked, indicating her drink.

She was tapping a purple fingernail against her glass. Her hair was teased up as if one of her toes was stuck into an electrical outlet.

"Cosmopolitan," she said.

"Can I buy you another?"

She had heavily made-up eyes and she trained them on me with a mixture of curiosity and mistrust.

"I just got this one."

"I know," I said. "It's just a stupid line I use. My name's Hitch-cock."

"Like the director?" she asked.

"Exactly like. Except in my case it's my first name."

"Is your last name Alfred?" she asked.

"No," I said. Something akin to a lightbulb flickered above my head. "It's Lehigh."

"Really?" Her eyes played about my face. "I know someone with that name."

"First or last?" I asked.

"Last."

"Well, it's a pretty common name."

"I guess."

"Who's your Lehigh?" I asked.

She took a sip of her cosmopolitan. She left a big red lip print on the glass. She shrugged. "No one really. Someone I know."

I wasn't sure what to do with the little corner I had backed myself into but I decided to take a plunge.

"It wouldn't be Cindy Lehigh by any chance, would it?"

Paula set her glass down. A faint frost came into the air.

"Who are you?" she asked.

"I told you."

"You told me your name. But who *are* you?"

"I'm Cindy's cousin," I said. When she didn't respond immediately, I added, "From Boston." I flattened the *o* just a touch. I was too far in to suddenly bring out a full-blown accent.

"Cindy never said anything about a cousin," Paula said, eyeing me with a perfectly justified uncertainty.

"Well, who does? I mean, how often do you talk about your cousin?"

She didn't answer. She pivoted to face me straight on. Behind her, the Sphinx was pretending not to listen.

"What's going on?" Paula said.

"I'm looking for Cindy," I said. "Nobody at home has heard from her for a couple of weeks now, and I'm down here on business so I thought I'd look her up. I understand this is one of her spots."

"And you just happened to run into me?"

"The truth is I asked around," I said. "I was told she's living with you."

"Who told you that?"

The Sphinx gave me a bloodless look.

"That's not important," I said. "The thing is the family's worried. I just thought I'd tell her. My aunt and uncle are concerned."

"Who's that? Her parents?"

"Yes."

"I thought her father was dead."

"He is."

"But you said her parents were concerned."

"Her stepfather. I meant her mother and her stepfather were concerned."

"I didn't know Cindy had a stepfather."

"She . . . she doesn't talk about him much. That concerns him as well."

Paula considered this. "So you're in contact with them?"

"With Cindy's parents? Well, sure. That's what I just said."

"Then maybe you can get them to send me some money," Paula said. She tapped a purple claw on the bar. "Cindy owes me close to a thousand bucks. I'm not going to get it out of her, but maybe her parents will pay me."

"Why does she owe you so much money?" I asked.

"Rent. Last month and this month. Plus I loaned her a hundred dollars. She'd been yakking about all this money she was going to be getting and the next thing I know I'm out two months' rent and she's gone."

"Gone?"

"That's what I said."

"Any idea where she went off to?" I asked.

I'd made the question sound as casual as I could manage. Nonetheless, Paula took a pause. She pulled a cigarette from a small purse she was carrying and lit it. She directed the smoke out the side of her mouth. That was nice. Into my face and I would have had to clobber her.

"Cindy's in some sort of trouble," she said.

"Well that's what I was beginning to wonder," I said cautiously. "What kind of trouble is she in?"

Paula held up her hands. "Hey, I don't know. She was just my roommate, she didn't tell me stuff like that. All I know is that she got real freaked out one day and took off." She added, "Without paying me what she owes me."

I asked again, "And do you know where she went?"

Paula frowned. "She told me not to tell anybody."

"So you do know."

"What if I do? She said not to tell."

"But she didn't mean family, did she?"

"I don't know. . . ."

"Look, I just want to talk to her. It's no big deal. Come on, I'm her cousin. We used to take baths together."

Paula pulled on her cigarette. I hoped that the ultrainnocent look I had slapped onto my face didn't look too dopey.

"Let me call her," she said. She reached into the purse and pulled out a cell phone and punched in a number. The phone was about the size of a half-eaten chocolate bar. She held it to her ear and leveled her eyes on me.

"It's ringing," she said. A second later she added, "It's the machine."

"Don't bother to—"

Paula held her hand to her ear so that she could hear better. "Hey. It's me. Paula. It's a message for Cindy. Cin, there's a guy here at the Swan who says he's your cousin from Boston. His name is Hitchcock. At least that's what he says. Like the director. He says he wants to make sure you're okay and everything. If you get this message in the next couple of hours call me on my cell. This guy says your family's worried and all that, so maybe you should call them, you know? And look, I still need that money, okay? And I—"

She lowered the phone.

"It cut me off."

She dropped the phone back into her purse and finished her drink. I bought her another, as promised. She asked me what I did up in Boston and I decided to tell her the same thing I did down in Baltimore. It wasn't that my lying skills needed oiling; it just seemed simpler. Besides, there are certain questions I can guarantee being asked of me when someone hears what I do for a living. Paula asked them. I was able to keep an amiable chat going with Paula while reserving a corner of my brain to think about what to do next. Somewhere along Paula's third cosmopolitan an idea came to me. The plan involved a little jostling and close contact, but that was certainly no problem, given the environs we were in. I ordered another beer. A few minutes after it arrived, a guy was squeezing in behind me to order a drink and I made as if he had accidentally bumped too hard into me. I pitched forward, knocking into Paula, and spilling half the contents of my very full mug very specifically on Paula's skimpy blouse. My jostling Paula caused her to bump into a few people who had been standing in close. Nothing huge. Just a little domino action. It quieted down in no time. I handed Paula a napkin and reached down to fetch her purse, which had fallen to the floor. Just as I'd planned.

"Sorry about that."

Paula dabbed at her soaked front with the napkin then popped off to the ladies' room. And I popped out of the bar and into my car. I waited until I was down the street and around the corner to pull Paula's little cell phone out of my pocket. I hit the redial button. The machine picked up. It was a male voice.

You have reached 410-555-5660. Nobody's here right now so please leave a message after the tone.

I didn't.

I swung by the George Washington Inn and started down the stairs to the Wine Cellar. I stopped halfway. Lee and her combo were working their way though "Miss Otis Regrets." I scanned the crowd but couldn't see Pete anywhere. I watched for a minute. Lee didn't seem especially engaged in the tune; it was a walk-through. I scanned for Pete a second time. No dice. No enchilada. None of it. He wasn't there.

I went back upstairs and peeked through the porthole window of the kitchen door. The scene was a blur of activity and smoke. I went to the bar and wrote a note on a cocktail napkin and asked the bartender to get it to Faith before the end of the night. I knew that he would read it so I didn't make it cute.

Had to run. Will call. H.

And I ran.

I can walk and chew gum at the same time and I can even hum a nonsense tune in the bargain, but trying to punch numbers into Paula's itsy-bitsy cell phone while driving a car at highway speeds nearly showed me my limits as a human being. I managed. I called Julia's number. I was surprised when she answered.

"I didn't really expect to find you in," I said.

Julia crooned, "There's no place like home."

"But on a Saturday night? Don't you want to be where the action is?"

"You're not listening. There's no place like home."

"I see. Say, old Saint Nick wouldn't be there by any chance, would he?" I asked.

"Well, as a matter of fact he is." She giggled. "He seems to be wandering around in a daze. Would you like to speak with him?"

"Is he capable?"

"I'll put him on."

Fallon came on. Rather, a murmur and a groan came on.

"Hey, Nick. It's Hitch. How's it going?"

His voice was low. I thought I detected a slight tremor. "I can't even begin to—"

"Don't worry about it," I said.

"Look, I've got to go."

"Whoa, whoa, whoa, hold on, partner. I need to ask a favor of you."

"Now? Hey, man, I don't think so. You don't understand, this—"

I cut him off again. "I do. Nick, I do understand. Completely. But just get a grip for a minute, okay? This is important."

"I'm hanging up."

"Christ. Give the phone back to Julia."

I realized that I was slowing down too much. A pickup truck was riding me. He leaned on his horn and I sped up. Julia came back on the line.

"Jesus, Jules, don't kill the guy," I said.

"Aw, he's a tough bird."

"That's all fine. But look, Julia. I need Nick to do me a favor and I need him to do it right away. I've got a phone number where Cindy Lehigh is staying. It's a Baltimore number. She's not there right now, but there's a message on the machine that might scare her off when she gets it. I need to get the address of this place pronto."

"What do you want from Nick?"

"I need him to get ahold of some crony of his at the paper or with the police, whatever he can do . . . someone who has a reverse directory. He'll know what that is. I'm going to give you a phone number. I need Nick to get me an address."

"He can do that?"

"I'm sure he can. Honey . . . lock yourself in the bathroom and tell him you're not coming out until he does this. From the sound of things, he'll set a new speed record."

She laughed. "Okay, give me the number."

I gave her the number. I tried to find the number for Paula's phone so that Julia could call me back. I nearly ran into a road sign trying.

"Have you got star 69?" I asked. "You can get the number of the last call that came in?"

"I've got that."

"Use it. Dial it as soon as we hang up. That'll give you this number."

"Okay. I'll get back to you," Julia said, and she hung up.

I hadn't gone much more then ten miles when the cell phone went off. It played a beepy version of "Hall of the Mountain King." It was Fallon. He sounded out of breath. He gave me an address.

"Are you happy?" he growled.

"She'll make it up to you, Nick. Now run along."

I was talking to air. He was already gone.

CHAPTER

24

The sun came peeking through the telephone lines, sending an orange splinter across
the hood of my car and through my closed eyes
to a section in the northwest quadrant of my
brain, where it began to sizzle the goods with a sound not unlike
bacon and eggs on the griddle. At least that's what I thought. The sizzling sound turned out to be a man hosing down his car in the driveway across the street from where I was parked. My right eye popped
open and watched as the man thumbed the hose, training the spray
along the roof of his car. In his other hand he was holding a coffee
mug. He was in his bathrobe. I opened my other eye. . . . He was still
in his bathrobe.

The sun was a shiny bald head now and I was bathed in its glow. I
watched as the man moved to the front of his car—which was parked
in the driveway facing out—and focused the water on the headlights. I
did similarly, rubbing my knuckles into my bleary eyes. I glanced at
my car clock. It had read 3:18 for as long as I'd owned the car. It still
did. My head was tilted back, resting on the top of the seat—my car is

preheadrest—and my neck complained bitterly when I endeavored to lift my head up. I swiveled my head to the left, letting out a soft groan as I did.

I was a stakeout boob. I had fallen asleep on the job. The address that Nick Fallon gave me had directed me to a part of town called Rogers Forge, a middle-income neighborhood of so-called semide-tached brick row houses. After pulling up directly in front of 493 and seeing no lights on in the small two-story house, I had settled in to wait for Cindy Lehigh's return from her Saturday night. I have no idea what time it was when I drifted off (3:18 comes to mind), but regardless, I slept upright in the figure S, which is fine if you're lying on your side on a soft or even semisoft surface, but not fine if you're in a car seat with your head thrown back and your mouth wide open. I had no idea if Cindy Lehigh had come home at all, or if maybe she had listened to the phone messages and already skedaddled. The small brick house was giving me no clues. It simply sat there, small and brick.

The man in the bathrobe moved around to the rear of his car, where I couldn't see him clearly. A woman emerged from the front door of the house. She was also wearing a bathrobe. She was carrying a drip coffeepot and she padded over to the driveway. The man's arm extended and she refilled his coffee cup, then she disappeared back into the house. I guess the remarkable thing is that somewhere in this little scenario there existed—at least for the two of them—a logic.

While I was working the kinks out of my neck and trying to put together a plan of action, a car rounded the corner behind me and pulled to the curb, skidding to a stop just behind my bumper. I watched this in the rearview mirror. The driver's-side door opened and I saw a woman getting out of the car. I switched to the side mirror as the woman swung the door shut. It was her. It was Cindy. Tall and thin, wearing a pair of tight-fitting leather pants and a pink fuzzy sweater. She was barefoot. A pair of spiky high heels dangled from her right hand. I glanced over at the neighbor. He had come around to the side of his car and was standing with the hose at his hip, looking across the street.

Cindy ran her free hand through her long thin hair and started up the walk toward the house. She stepped heavily, like someone who is still getting the lead out. I had to make a snap decision. Do I let her get inside the house or do I get out of the car and confront her here in the front yard? Hitchcock Sewell, Man-Who-Sits-on-His-Ass-for-a-Continued-Unspecified-Amount-of-Time? Or Hitchcock Sewell, Man-of-Action? Oh what the hell. As Cindy was approaching the pair of steps leading up to the front door, I got out of the car.

She didn't see me. And she apparently didn't hear me approach. She had pulled open the storm door and was keeping it open with her hip as she fumbled with her free hand in her shoulder-slung purse. It wasn't until I came up onto the first step that she noticed me. The rising sun was behind me and my shadow crossed over her.

She was quick. Quicker than I.

"Shit!"

Cindy swung at me and a stiletto heel caught me directly in the temple. I saw yellow. And damn her little hide, before I could react she cracked me a second time. Harder. Then, with a nifty balance of power (in my automatic reflex I had leaned away from the flailing shoes), she shoved me in the chest and I fell backward off the step and into a perfectly squared off shrubbery. The bush seemed to open up and take me in like a hungry animal. For an instant all I saw were my own shoes and a pink shred of cloud in a pale blue sky. I batted with my arms but got no immediate purchase; in fact I only seemed to sink that much lower into the bush. Failing in my second attempt to lift myself up, I instead rolled sideways and spilled out onto the grass.

Cindy was halfway down the block, kicking as high as her skintight leather pants would allow. I scrambled to my feet and gave chase. After a night camping out in the car my muscles weren't ready to fire on all burners. Lighter, more lithe, and fueled by adrenaline, Cindy was beating me in the sprint. At the corner she left the sidewalk and cut across somebody's yard onto the next street. I called out.

"*Cindy!*"

It had no effect. Why should it? I followed her course across the yard, and as I did I saw something moving out of the corner of my eye. Glancing quickly over my shoulder I saw that it was Mr. Bathrobe. His arms were moving like pistons and he was coming up fast. *My* adrenaline kicked in and I galloped to the sidewalk. Cindy was some twenty or thirty feet in front of me. Her hair was flying all over the place. She turned and saw that I was gaining on her. I could hear the huff and puff of the guy behind me and I knew that *he* was gaining.

Cindy suddenly veered right and bolted down an alley. I romped after her. She cut to her left, next to a garage, and slammed her hands against a metal gate. It was a gamble. And it paid off, for the gate flew open and she dashed into a backyard. The gate swung back and smacked my knees but it didn't slow me down. I threw an arm, hoping I could catch the gate and swing it closed behind me, but I missed it altogether. Cindy veered onto the grass then hesitated for just a fraction as she scanned for the way out to the front. She cut back toward the garage and that's when I leapt. My leap was compromised by a metal swing set that Cindy's cutback had placed between us. But once I was airborne there was nothing I could do about it. I rattled the chains as I went, but stupid luck was with me. I cleared the swing set and got my arms around Cindy's waist—such as it was—just as I was returning to earth. She came down with me, the both of us *oomph*ing as we hit. A second later Mr. Bathrobe piled on.

"Wait!" I cried out. Cindy was trying to squirm free but I had a good hold on her and I wasn't about to let go. Mr. Bathrobe grunted as he clawed at my arms. "Wait!" I cried again.

Cindy snarled, "Let . . . me . . . fucking . . . *go!*"

Mr. Bathrobe seconded her. "Let her go!"

"Let *me* go!" With the strength of ten Hitchcocks I somehow managed to shrug the man off of me and at the same time clamber to my feet, taking Cindy with me. I still had her around the waist. She was completely off the ground and kicking her legs like a classic damsel in distress. I pivoted so that as the guy in the bathrobe got up off the ground I could use Cindy's flailing legs to keep him at bay. A door opened in the house and a black dog bounded into the yard and ran up to us barking its fool head off. The dog was followed by a teenage boy and his mother, who came out onto the grass and stood with their mouths hanging open. The resemblance between the two was striking.

And there we were.

I wish I had a picture of it.

The untangling took some work.

After her snarling *"Let me down!"* about a dozen times, I had finally lowered Cindy to the ground, maintaining a firm grip around her arm so that she didn't dash off again. Now that I was up close and personal I could see a faraway look in Cindy's eyes, or more specifically in her pupils. The whites of her eyes . . . well, they weren't white, they were nearly as pink as her sweater. She was throwing defiant looks all over the backyard. Her aim seemed distinctly off. Her pretty brown hair smelled of tobacco and stale beer.

The man in the bathrobe demanded to know what was going on.

"He's trying to kill me!" Cindy snapped.

"Slow down," I said. "I'm not trying to kill anybody."

The adrenaline was still running through Mr. Bathrobe. "Do you want me to call the police?"

Cindy's scowl did not seem a particularly fervent endorsement of the idea. The dog had stopped barking now and was standing with an expectant look on its face. Its owners hadn't yet uttered a word.

"It's just a misunderstanding," I said to the assemblage. "I just wanted to have a talk with Miss Lehigh here. I didn't mean to scare her."

The woman finally spoke. "Are you okay, honey?"

"He's going to kill me," Cindy said again, though with a lot less fervor than the first time.

"Josh, go call the police," the woman said to her son. But the boy had pretty much settled down to just staring at the girl in the leather pants. He didn't budge.

"There's no real need for that," I said. I released Cindy and took a step back from her. "But if you want to, go right ahead. I have no problem with the police." I turned to Cindy. "I'm a friend of Libby Gellman's. I'm trying to find out what happened to Sophie Potts. That's all. If you want to bring the police in, just say it."

Cindy was studying my face. Yes, no, yes, no, yes, no, yes, no. . . .

"Why were you sneaking up on me?"

"I wasn't sneaking. You just didn't hear me."

"You scared the hell out of me."

"And you *beat* the hell out of me." I put my finger to my temple. A nice welt was on the rise.

I could see Cindy's gears cranking a few clicks. She muttered something under her breath then marched off toward the alley.

"Rain check," I said to the woman. Her son seemed disappointed to see Cindy leaving. Nothing like a spitfire in leather pants in the backyard to give your morning that extra little pop. I followed after Cindy. The guy in the bathrobe pulled up beside me as I reached the alley.

"What am I missing here?" he asked.

We followed some twenty feet behind Cindy as she marched back up the street. I don't know precisely when it became fashionable for women to forgo shape of any kind, but I'm going on record right here to say that it can cease any old time now. Mr. Bathrobe and I were essentially following a leather-and-pink-clad pipe cleaner.

Cindy didn't even bother to acknowledge her hero as he veered off and returned to his house. She hesitated at the front steps as I came up the walk. Okay, I thought. We've been here before. I eyed the shoe in her hand.

"What exactly do you want?" she asked.

I reached deep into my very being to locate the most honest answer I could find.

"Right now? Truthfully? Breakfast."

Cindy insisted on a public place. I assumed she didn't mean the median strip on 695. We took two cars. I followed her, ready at an instant to go on a wild ride . . . but she played it straight. We went to the Bel-Loc Diner, which is a glass and aluminum place that looks like a Jetsons-era spaceship, perched at the point where Loch Raven Boulevard runs steeply downhill to the Beltway. We took a booth in the rear and our waitress took our order. She was a Baltimore classic. Beehive hairdo, gnomish grandmotherly face, as friendly as pie.

Cindy Lehigh was not as friendly as pie.

"You cleaned out Cap'n Henry's till," I said to her as soon as our waitress had gone off with our order.

"You can't prove that."

"That's not my job to prove," I said. "You also stole from the Gellmans."

"I don't know what you're talking about."

"Spare me, Cindy. You're a little thief. I'd say that much is pretty well documented."

"Why's any of this your business anyway?" she asked.

I ignored the question. There was no question that Cindy's was the voice on Nick Fallon's tape.

"Whose house is that where you're staying?" I asked her. "I know you haven't paid Paula rent for the last two months. I doubt very much that you're ponying up for this place."

She flushed red. "Did Paula tell you how to find me?"

"She didn't. Don't blame her. Blame me. I tricked her. So whose house is it?"

"It's not important," she said.

"In that case just tell me."

"James."

"And who is James?"

"James is Paula's brother."

"I see. Well . . . nice guy letting you stay at his place."

"He *is* a nice guy," she said. "So what?"

"So nothing," I said.

We sat in silence tossing hostile vibes across the table until our food arrived. I looked on my lumberjack breakfast and nearly wept. I was ravenous. So was Cindy. She had ordered the same thing. Yes, sir, just a couple of good old lumberjacks. We dug in. Cindy ate exactly twice as fast as I did. I don't know where she put it. Jittery metabolism, I guess. By the time I was halfway done Cindy had vacuumed her plate clean.

"Would you like a little sirloin steak to follow up?" I asked.

"I was hungry. Jesus Christ. What's your problem?"

I skidded my plate to the side and put my elbows up on the table. My appetite would have to wait.

"Why don't you explain to me why you thought I was going to kill you back there," I said.

"I told you. You scared me."

"Not good enough, Cindy. Why should someone stroll up to you in the middle of Rogers Forge first thing in the morning and try to kill you? That doesn't make a lot of sense to me."

"It can happen."

"Sure it can happen. But it's not what usually happens. You were scared well before I showed up. What gives, Cindy? You dropped right off the screen a couple of weeks ago. Something tells me you've been looking over your shoulder ever since. Why don't you tell me what's going on?"

"I don't have to talk to you."

I picked up my coffee cup and took a bitter sip. "That's a fact. We can go on down to Annapolis together and you can talk to the police if you'd like to do that. If you'd rather not, I can always just give them a call and put them onto you. It makes no real difference to me."

She sat back in the booth and roped her arms. She glared at me. Finally she said, "I'm sorry about your head."

Gingerly I touched the welt on my head. "I'm sorry about it, too."

Cindy had turned her head and was gazing out the window. Her tough act was pretty good, but I could see that it wasn't all that securely in place. She squinted, looking out the window at absolutely nothing of consequence. Her lip was trembling.

"Listen to me. I'm not looking to get you in trouble, Cindy. Believe me, that's not my agenda here."

"Then what is it?"

"I'm going to ask you a question," I said. "You can lie your little heart out if you want to. Whether or not I believe you is a whole different thing, but I'm going to ask it anyway."

"What?"

"Did you have anything to do with the murder of Sophie Potts?"

She continued staring out the window—unflinching—almost as if she hadn't heard me. I waited. Her lip was still trembling and her breath seemed a little short. The tough girl act was crumbling. She stared out at the gray parking lot as if she wanted to melt into it. She looked tired.

I asked her again. Gently. "Come on, Cindy. Did you have anything to do with Sophie's death?"

She tried for one more blast of defiance, but she was out of fuel. Her answer came out in a harsh whisper.

"I think so."

I used Paula's cell phone to call Julia as I headed down to Fell's Point. I was hoping to catch Fallon.

"Is he there?" I asked when Julia picked up.

"Well, it *looks* like him."

"Funny. Don't let him leave."

Twenty minutes later I found a parking spot on Bond Street and came around the corner to Julia's place. Fallon was looking downright sheepish and not a little pale. He was up in Julia's studio, laid out on one of her butterfly chairs. I wasn't sure he could move.

"She's lethal," he murmured.

From the back of the studio I could hear Julia humming happily in her shower.

"Jack Barton," I said. "What's his story? What's his connection with Crawford Larue? You told me once."

"They're old cronies from their horse-breeding days. When Crawford got out of prison it was Jack Barton who got him set up in Washington. Barton had the strings to pull."

"Well, it looks like Big Jack exacted a pretty revolting price for his help."

"What are you talking about?"

"I'm talking about Sugar Jenks. Sugar Larue, actually. Jack Barton's been having his way with the girl since she was sixteen."

"*What?*" Fallon failed in his attempt to get out of the chair, but with a second effort he managed to sit up in it. "What in the world are you talking about? Jack Barton? Are you sure?"

I pulled Nick's cassette tape from my pocket. "That's what your anonymous call was all about."

"You found the girl."

"Cindy. Yes, I did."

"And she told you this?"

"It seems Big Jack had a thing for Crawford's daughter. From the sound of it, Crawford conveniently looked the other way. He let his old crony have carte blanche with the girl."

"Jesus Christ."

"Exactly. Not a terribly ARK way to behave."

"The hell with that," Fallon said. "It's not a terribly human way to behave."

I dropped the tape on his lap. "Those were the abortions."

"Sugar?"

"Sugar."

"What about the sterilizations?" Fallon asked.

"Just one. Sugar."

Fallon clambered out of the chair. The sound of the shower ceased. The metal rings of the shower curtain screeched. Fallon waved the tape at me.

"Jesus Christ, Hitch, tell me you're not kidding with this. This'll definitely blow 'em out of the water."

"It's what Cindy overheard."

Fallon frowned. "From who? Where did she get all this? It's no good if it's just gossip."

"How does Owen Cutler work for you?"

"Cutler?"

"The ARK's very own personal lawyer and inside man. Does that work?"

"Hell, that works just fine. But you're not telling me that Cutler just sat down and told this girl all of this. I don't care how cute she might be, Owen Cutler knows enough to keep a great big lid on something like this."

"No, he didn't sit down and tell her. But she managed to overhear him talking about it."

"No shit?"

"Shit none."

"With who?"

Julia stepped into the room. She was in her silk robe. She was running a towel over her head.

"I thought I heard voices. Good morning, Hitch."

"Hello, sugarbeet."

"What brings you here?"

"Oh, just a sordid tale of sexual treachery."

Julia did her best demure. "Why, Nicky, I thought we weren't going to tell."

CHAPTER

25

Life goes on. I had people to bury.

I dashed home and took a shower. My form wasn't great but I set a new speed record. I hopped into my somber suit and knotted my somber tie around my neck. Then I remembered today's funeral and I switched to a snappier tie. Alcatraz was phoning the S.P.C.A. by the time I was ready to leave so I clipped on his leash and dragged him along with me. Halfway down the block I commanded, "Pee!" in my best Charlton Heston–as-God voice. Damned if the dog didn't oblige. I got to the funeral home just as Sam was loading the casket into the hearse, with the help of Darryl Sandusky.

"What are you doing here?" I asked Darryl.

"Helping out. Where have *you* been?"

"Out game hunting little fellers like you," I said.

"And I guess you think that's funny?"

"In fact . . . not really."

We shoved the casket the rest of the way into the hearse and Sam set about securing it. I reached into my pocket and handed Darryl a twenty.

"Here. Go buy some dope."

"You are so yesterday," Darryl said, and we had to leave it there since Sam and I were about to be running late. Aunt Billie came down onto the front steps and called Alcatraz over to her. Darryl went over, too. Billie nudged Darryl to join her in waving at us as we pulled away. They looked like the closing credits of *The Beverly Hillbillies*, which happens to be Billie's favorite television show in reruns.

We arrived at the church just on time and got the casket inside, front and center. The eulogies were short and for the most part amusing. The dead man sounded like someone I might have enjoyed knowing. Sam and I stood in the rear of the church. I was feeling a little light-headed, the combination of having slept the night in my car, along with the full-body slam of information that Cindy had unloaded on me at the Bel-Loc. Sam asked me at one point if I was okay.

"You look a little like shit," he said, chuckling behind his hand.

The service ended and we got our guest back into the hearse for his final road trip. On the drive to the cemetery Sam told me a long involved joke that hinged on the teller's having a decent Scottish accent. His Scottish accent stank. He sounded more like he was speaking in tongues. The poor joke didn't stand a chance.

As promised, a boom box was produced at the grave site and after a few assertions by the priest that our guest of honor was truly heaven bound, the boom box was switched on and Norman Greenbaum's "Spirit in the Sky" kicked up. Give that song half a chance and you've just got to clap along. Our little crowd did, Sam included. It was the happiest funeral I'd been to all month. I'd have loved to attend the postfuneral party but I had places to go and people to see. Sam took a crack at singing "Spirit in the Sky" on the drive back. I wish he hadn't.

The reason that Cindy Lehigh had thought that I was going to kill her when I had approached her earlier that morning was that ever since hearing that Sophie Potts had been pulled from the Severn River, Cindy had been afraid for her own life. The day that the papers identified Sophie by name, mentioning that the young woman had been employed in the household of Michael Gellman of the Annapolis District Attorney's office, was the day that Cindy grabbed her handful of cash from Henry Aranow's cash register and performed her vanishing act. She told me that she had had no trouble convincing Paula's brother to let her crash at his place. Without elaborating, Cindy told me that James had "been only too happy" to accommodate. I am assuming, of course, that this means Cindy had promised she would serve him some nice home-cooked meals for his troubles. What Cindy insisted to me was that she had never served Mike Gellman any home-cooked meals. I had asked her straight out.

"Were you sleeping with Mike Gellman?"

She told me that she was not. She admitted to there having been a little mild flirting now and then, especially at the beginning.

"That's who he is. He's always after the women. I never knew how his wife put up with it."

Whether I completely believed Cindy's assessment that there had never been a successful pass completed between her and Mike wasn't terribly relevant. More to the point was the fact that the person with whom Cindy had overheard Owen Cutler discussing the sordid facts of Sugar Jenks and Jack Barton was, in fact, Mike Gellman. The discussion had taken place out on Gellman's deck. I knew the logistics. Mike had apparently thought that the coast was clear. Libby and the kids were gone, and a quick check of the house had told Mike that the nanny was also not at home. As it happened, Cindy had been in the basement folding laundry when Mike and Cutler had arrived and she had just stepped outside the basement door for a cigarette when Mike popped downstairs to see if anyone was there. She had still been outside when she heard her employer and Owen Cutler come out onto the deck a minute later. With the words "Okay, there's no one here. We can talk," Cindy had been all ears. By the end of the conversation Cindy had been wracked with fear that she would be found out a mere twenty feet below where the two men were sitting. She hadn't dared budge, not even to scratch a persistent itch in the small of her back. It was a week later that Cindy had approached Mike while he was in his bedroom polishing his shoes and calmly told him that she wanted a thousand dollars from him or else she would tell everything that she had heard him discussing with Owen Cutler, first to Libby and then to whoever else was interested in listening.

"He was real businesslike about it," Cindy had told me at the Bel-Loc. "He gave me the money the very next day. I couldn't believe how easy it was. He just handed it over to me. He even made me shake on it. But before he let go of my hand he said to me that if I ever told anyone, especially Libby, he'd kill me. But you know, I thought he was joking."

Libby answered the door. The expression on her face was oddly blank.

"They indicted Mike," she said. "He called. He's going to be arrested."

I ignored her. "I know about Lily," I said.

"Lily? What are you talking about? What about Lily?"

"She's adopted. You and Mike adopted her."

Libby looked momentarily confused. "We . . . well, yes, we did. We adopted her as a baby. That's not a secret."

"You never mentioned anything."

"Well, why should I?" she asked defensively. "It never even occurred to me. I've raised Lily since practically the day she was born. It's nothing Mike and I even bother talking about anymore. She's our daughter, pure and simple. Every bit as much as Toby is our son."

"Is he—?" I stopped myself. "Did you adopt him, too?"

She snapped, "No! If it's any of your business, Hitch, no. I got pregnant with Toby. I told you that already."

"I know you did."

"Then why the question?" She crossed her arms tightly on her chest and gave me a stormy look.

"I'm just trying to get the picture, Libby, that's all."

"Well, the picture is that it's one of the little ironies of couples who have trouble conceiving. You adopt a child and the next thing you know you can get pregnant after all. Practically overnight. It's a pretty damned bittersweet irony if you want to know."

"I'm sorry."

"Don't be. It's one of those things. And it happened to us. But what's this all about anyway? Who told you that Lily was adopted? Was it Mike? It must have been."

"No," I said. "It was Cindy Lehigh."

"Cindy?"

"Yes."

"How the hell did Cindy know?" Libby's entire body seemed to sag. "Oh, God. Mike told her."

"Not exactly, Libby. She overheard him talking about it with someone."

"Mike? With who?"

"And she told me something else as well, Libby. She told me who Lily's natural mother and father are."

As if on cue, Lily herself appeared just then in the hallway. She was dragging her giraffe. She recognized me standing in the doorway and a huge smile broke out on her face. A look of complete bewilderment had settled onto Libby's face. No. Correct that. Not settled. Placed there with all the delicacy of a shovel being swung into her face.

"Cindy told you who her natural *parents* are?"

I nodded. Tears had come into Libby's eyes and she did nothing—or could do nothing—to stop them from flowing freely down her cheeks. Her entire body began shaking. In the hallway, Lily started toward us.

"Mommy?"

Libby's voice, when she spoke, was a hoarse hollow whisper.

"For God's sake, Hitch, I don't even know who her real parents are."

On the way down to Annapolis to hang Mike Gellman up by his fingernails over a vat of boiling pork fat (Libby devised this plan, along with about a dozen others), I told Libby the details of what Cindy had overheard. She was horrified.

"Oh my God. That poor girl."

I asked Libby to explain to me the circumstances of her and Mike's coming to adopt Lily. It was not something she felt like discussing, focused as she was on skewering her husband twelve different ways the moment she set eyes on him, but I cajoled her into sketching it out for me. Specifically I wanted to know how Owen Cutler fit into the whole picture.

"Right in the goddamn middle," Libby fumed. "It was Owen who set up the whole adoption in the first place. He was the go-between."

Libby explained to me how Mike's uncle, aware that the couple had been trying since the beginning of their marriage to conceive, had announced one day that he knew of a woman who was due to give birth in a matter of weeks and who was going to be unable to keep the baby.

"Did he explain what he meant by that?" I asked.

"No. He just said that she couldn't keep it. He told us that the mother was young and healthy and that she had been under a doctor's care all through her pregnancy. All he would say was that there were 'circumstances' that made it impossible for the woman to keep the child and that arrangements were being sought to . . . well, to get the baby into a family."

"And he didn't say who the mother was?"

"No. He said that was a matter of privacy. The mother wasn't asking for any contact with the child after the adoption, so her identity really wasn't important. It crossed my mind for a minute that maybe it was a woman whom Owen had gotten pregnant. But that was crazy. That's not Owen. Anyway, the real truth is I didn't care. Owen said he had a baby for us and we jumped on it. You have no idea what this meant to us."

"So then along came Lily?"

"We got her when she was two days old. Hitch, I was in love with that child even before I saw her. The moment I was actually holding her it didn't matter to me who her natural parents were. Owen or anybody else. She was mine. She was my daughter."

The cars on Route 2 seemed like pylons to me. Maybe that's because they were going the speed limit. I was spinning the wheel like a drunken sea captain in a gale, dodging in and out between the other cars with a grace and beauty that I'm sure was going completely unappreciated.

I asked Libby if she thought that Mike knew all along the facts behind Lily's parentage.

"It's so morbid," she said. "It's so sick. I can't believe he knew."

"Uncle Owen apparently knew."

"Hitch, that poor girl. It's horrible. How could her father just look the other way and let that bastard do that to his daughter? He deserves to be strung up. Along with that pervert."

She leaned her head back in disbelief and took fistfuls of her hair.

"They *all* deserve to be strung up. Larue, Owen, Mike. . . . God, Hitch, I just want to kill them all."

She folded her arms across her chest and scowled out the windshield.

"Starting with Mike."

Before we got to her house I came clean with Libby on another matter. I told her about my spying on Mike and Ginny Larue sharing the hot tub several nights previous. She took the information with a grim silence, her fingertips pressed against her lips. I seriously doubted that she was in prayer.

"He's nuts," she said at last. "Hitch, he is just . . ." She trailed off and turned to the window.

Twenty minutes later I pulled up in front of Libby and Mike's house.

"That's his car," Libby said. "He's home."

"Are you sure you don't want me to go in with you?" I asked. Libby had asserted on the way down that she would prefer to speak with Mike on her own. I wasn't thrilled with the idea.

"I'll be fine," she said. "If you come in with me it's only bound to enflame him."

"Libby, I have to remind you that we don't know for certain whether Mike had something to do with Sophie's death."

"I'm aware of that." She shoved the door to open it. "But I need to talk this out with him, Hitch. This is our *daughter*. You can't be a part of this. Mike has some very serious explaining to do and I'm going to make him do it. He's threatening our family. I won't have it. If anyone is going to need protecting, it's going to be Mike."

I started to protest, but she stopped me.

"He's not going to hurt me, Hitch. I can take care of myself, believe me."

She scooted along the seat and planted a sharp kiss on my cheek, then she scooted back out of the car.

I sat behind the wheel and waited until she was inside the house. I waited an extra minute. No one came flying through the plate-glass windows. Of course Libby was right. This wasn't my fight. I pushed the R button and backed out of the driveway.

When I reached the main road I pulled over and called my home phone. Neophyte that I am, I wasn't sure how much juice was left on Paula's phone. The connection seemed especially burbly. There was a message from Lee on my machine.

Hitch, this is Lee. Listen, I'm . . . Peter. He wasn't in the . . . shape last night. We had a little fight. He took off from . . . be back before the end of the night, but I never saw him. He told me he was staying at your place. Could you give me a ring when you . . . and let me know he's all right? Thanks.

I drove into town and parked near the George Washington Inn. Faith wasn't in. I was told that she had worked the brunch rush and was off for the rest of the day. Standing at the front door of the inn I spotted a bar across the street. There was nobody there who could tell me if anyone matching Pete's description had been in the night before. I walked over to the Swan. The same bartender from the night before was there, but when I described Pete for him he said he couldn't recall anyone fitting that description. I came back out onto the street, looked left and looked right . . . and went right, back where I'd come from. I continued on past the George Washington Inn and down to the end of Main Street to McGarvey's, where I had talked with Tom Cushman the week before. I had better luck there. The bartender recognized my description of Pete.

"Oh, he was here all right," the bartender said. "Must've been around midnight we threw him out."

"And I'm sure you had good reason?"

"If you want to fight, I say take it outside."

"Who was he fighting?"

"Pretty much anyone who got close to him," the bartender said. "That dude was in one foul mood, let me tell you. He was putting them away. He almost took a piece out of me when I suggested he slow down a little."

"So did he actually take a swing at anybody?" I asked.

"There's a guy named Dave who comes in here," the bartender said. "Dave's a big guy. Close to three hundred pounds and most of it muscle. Your friend got on Dave's case. I don't know what it was about. It's usually about nothing that makes sense if you're sober. Your friend sure wasn't sober. Unfortunately for him, neither was Dave."

"What happened?"

"Your friend took it right in the face. I think Dave probably broke his nose for him. At the very least he rearranged it a little. Luckily there was a bunch here from the fire department and they hustled the both of them out onto the street. I couldn't tell you what happened after that. I'm not too worried about Dave. Dave can take care of himself."

I thanked him for the information and left the bar. At that point I wondered if I should be checking the hospitals but I decided there was no point. Even if Pete had steered himself toward a hospital he certainly wouldn't still be there. I considered checking in at the police station. Maybe Munger had napped in the drunk tank overnight. But it was the same thing. Even if he had, they'd have booted him out by now. I can't say that I exactly relished the idea of crossing his path. This was the second time in a week that I had brought him down to Annapolis and abandoned him. The first time at least he had ended up smooching with Lee in the front seat of her car. But not this time . . . this time he had found a way to get his nose mangled by a minor giant. I've seen Pete when he enters into his ultra-surly phase. It was my guess that wherever he was, he wasn't sitting around thinking kind thoughts about his good buddy Hitch. He probably wanted my head on a platter.

I headed back up the street. It was noticeably colder. A wicked wind had kicked up, coming off the water and shooting directly up

Main Street. I was still in my funeral suit and was wearing my long coat, but the wind didn't really have a whole lot of respect for my thin gabardine. I popped into a gift shop halfway up Main Street and bought a Navy baseball cap and a blue scarf that reached nearly to my toes.

I continued up the street and found my car. Atop the trees a few blocks off, the deep blue dome of the Naval Academy chapel rose up against the lighter blue sky. I thought, If only Sophie had never met midshipman Bradley Hansen. . . . I didn't bother to finish the thought. Ultimately, these are so pointless, these speculations. I used to spend a lot more of my energy than I do now seeking after the elusive starting point of events. The fact is it can't be done. Had everything really started down its inevitable path as a result of Sophie Potts sleeping with Bradley Hansen? To some extent, yes. Without her having gotten pregnant Sophie would not have been steered toward the Larues. But then without Cindy's having quit her job as the Gellmans' nanny in the first place, Sophie would never have even entered the scene. And Cindy told me that she had quit as a result of the tension after she extorted the thousand dollars from Mike Gellman. The unnaturalness that Libby had sensed between the two had nothing whatsoever to do with them sleeping together. Cindy told me that she had not slept with Mike and I was perfectly willing to believe her. The tension came from the knowledge that Cindy had. But then *that* knowledge came from her overhearing Mike's conversation with Owen Cutler. If anyone was responsible for the chain of events that had led to Sophie's death, Owen Cutler was certainly as fine a candidate as anyone else.

I got into my car and drove the mile or so to Faith's little house. Faith met me at the door wearing a blue smock and a pink smile.

"You look like something out of a fairy tale," I told her.

She laughed. "Well, the big bad wolf is here. Come in."

Faith had company. Her company was sitting at the kitchen table when Faith showed me in. Her company had a blue jaw from needing a shave and red eyes from needing a better sleep than the night had apparently provided. Her company also had a nose that looked like an overbaked mushroom. Her company was huddled over a steaming mug of coffee, and when I entered the kitchen he looked up at me with dark bleary eyes.

"Well, if it's not handsome Pete," I said. "What a teeny tiny world we live in."

"Don't start," Pete said in a low growl.

His nose was larger on the left side than it was on the right. Either that or the entire thing had simply shifted a few centimeters off to the side.

"I heard about your encounter with a moose last night."

Pete gingerly touched his nose. "I should pick on someone my own size."

"How did you manage to wash up on these shores?" I asked.

Faith answered for him. "Pete showed up at the inn last night just about when I was getting off. He was asking for you. Loudly. He, um, didn't look real great. Lee was still in the middle of a set. I suggested that maybe he shouldn't go downstairs."

"Sounds like a good call," I said. "Pete, the broken-nose, blood-on-the-shirt look . . . women aren't going for that anymore. It's a whole new era."

"I see you've got a new look yourself, hotshot," Pete said.

I had forgotten about Cindy's well-wrought signature on my head.

"The lady wore heels," I said.

"Looks like she was walking in a funny place. Or was your head on the ground?"

"My head was where it's supposed to be," I said. "She reached."

"You two seem to have trouble getting along with people," Faith noted.

"I didn't used to be this way," I said to her. "I was once such a man of peace."

"You're a man of bullshit is what you are," Pete said.

I asked Faith, "So how did you end up hosting the galoot anyway?"

"Jason and I—he's one of my cooks—we got him out to my car. I was thinking of driving him up to Baltimore but I just decided to come on home."

"He slept here?"

"I wish," Pete said.

"He was passed out in the front seat by the time we got here," Faith said. "I didn't even want to try to wake him. And there was no way I could carry him in."

"Him so heavy. You but a sprite." I turned to Pete. "So you slept in the car? What a coincidence. I did the same thing last night."

I glanced up at Faith's wall clock. It was nearing four o'clock. "For Christ's sake, so when did you finally get up?"

Pete took a slow gulp of coffee. "I got up around noon. Faith left me a note. The door was unlocked. I came in here and went right out on the couch."

"I had to work this morning," Faith said. "I just got back from the inn a few hours ago. Sleeping Beauty had finally stirred."

"I thought he was the big bad wolf," I said.

Faith shrugged. "That too."

Faith made a fresh pot of coffee and I joined the party. I pulled up a seat across from Pete and told him that Lee had left me a message, that she was concerned about him.

"Do you want to tell me what happened between the two of you?" I asked.

Pete wagged his head. "Nope. I don't."

"Fair enough. It's not really any of my business."

Pete managed a chuckle. "Now you say that."

Faith excused herself. "I have to make a call." She left the kitchen. Munger lofted an eyebrow.

"She's a good kid," Pete said. "Does she know that you're nothing but an opportunistic scoundrel?"

"You misjudge me."

Pete smiled. "Well, if you hurt her I might just have to kill you."

"Sounds like she certainly saved your sorry carcass."

"She did. I barely even remember the end of the night, but I'm sure I was making an ass of myself. Good thing Lee didn't have to see it." He took up his coffee mug in both his hands. "So let's hear it. I'm guessing from that knot on the side of your head that you located Cindy."

"I did. She was up in Baltimore, sponging off the brother of her roommate."

"I take it Miss Cindy did not want to be found."

"Miss Cindy did not want to be found." I told him the story. Faith came back into the kitchen about midway through. I told Pete about Jack Barton's history of dalliance with Sugar Larue, about her abortions and then about her apparently carrying a baby to term. I explained how Owen Cutler had arranged for Sugar's baby to go to Mike and Libby.

"Now five years later, good old Owen is at it again. This time it's Larue who wants a kid. And Sophie just happened to be at the wrong place at the wrong time and pregnant to boot. I think Gellman was telling it to me straight in my office yesterday. Except for the part where he said he didn't tell Libby about Sophie for Sophie's sake. I mean maybe she did ask him not to tell her. But it's pretty clear to me that Gellman didn't want his wife knowing that he was working with Cutler a second time in this damn baby-placing routine. Especially since Larue was again involved. Libby hadn't known where her daughter had come from and she assumed Mike didn't either."

"Not to mention that Gellman's climbing into hot tubs with Larue's wife," Pete added.

"Not to mention."

"So we've got Sophie caught up in the middle of something she probably knew nothing about."

I agreed, "That's what it looks like."

"So who killed her?" Faith asked.

Pete and I swapped a look. "Who do you think can answer that question?" I asked.

"I think we both have the same man in mind," Pete said. He set his coffee mug down on the table. "Uncle Owen. Let's go."

I used Faith's phone to call D.C. information and tracked down an address for Owen Cutler. At the door Munger made some very gracious thank-yous to Faith before we left. Faith and I played a pretty serious eye game (to a draw), then I headed out to the car.

"She's a good kid," Pete said to me as I slid in behind the wheel.

"You said that already."

"I'm just trying to drum it into your head."

"Are you starting to become a meddler, Pete?" I asked.

I turned the ignition and *vroom-vroomed* my V-8. Faith, who was still standing in the door, put her hands to her cheeks and made a face like Edvard Munch's *Scream*.

Pete turned from the window and pulled out a cigarette.

"She's young enough to be my daughter. You know how old that makes me feel?"

"Around fifty?"

Munger interrupted the lighting of his cigarette to give me the finger.

I told Pete I wanted to swing by Libby and Mike's house before we headed over to D.C. I tried using Paula's cell phone to call Libby's house but the batteries had finally died. Pete told me he thought I was nuts for leaving Libby off at her home in the first place. He was right. I really hadn't been thinking. I cut a few corners getting over to the house and when I pulled into the driveway I could see that Mike's car was no longer there.

"Mike's car was here before," I said to Pete.

I parked next to the garage and we got out. Pete rapped on the front door and we waited. Nothing. He rapped again.

"There's a doorbell," I pointed out. He looked over at me and then very deliberately rapped his knuckles against the door a third time.

"Nobody's home," I said.

Pete corrected. "Nobody's answering."

He tried the doorknob and it turned in his hand. I nodded to him and we opened the door. We stepped into the mezzanine entrance.

I called out, "Libby? Libby, it's Hitch!"

"Call the other one," Pete said. "Gellman."

I called out, "Mike? Hey, Mike. Is anyone here?"

We stood a few more seconds, then Pete said, "Looks like we can raid the fridge. Come on, let's take a look around." He started down the steps to the living room.

"What are we looking for?" I asked, following after him.

Pete didn't answer. He stepped across the living room, glancing to his left and his right. He stopped at the sliding glass doors to the deck and first looked up at the trees. Then I saw his gaze settle back down to the deck.

"We're looking for this," he said.

"What is it?"

Munger held his arm out as I approached and put his hand on my chest, stopping me. Then he let his arm drop.

"Oh. That's right," he said. "You're used to seeing dead people."

CHAPTER

27

Using his shirttail, Pete slid the glass door open and we stepped out onto the deck. An unseen crow welcomed us outside. The only other sounds were a low humming of the hot-tub generator along with the *blurp, blurp, blurp, blurp* of air bubbles erupting on the surface of the water. The body in the tub wasn't making a peep and damn sure never would again. The left arm was swung back at an almost unnatural angle and fell straight down; it looked almost as if the hand was stretching to pick something up off the deck. The head was rolled partially onto the left shoulder and pitched back, the remaining eye wide open as if mesmerized by something high up in the trees. In the name of accuracy I suppose I need to amend this. *Most* of the head was rolled partially onto the left shoulder and pitched back. There was a piece about the size of a cookie that Pete and I stepped past as we approached the hot tub. Pete was the one who pointed it out to me.

"Skull."

The burbling water was pink. At very first glance I was helpless against the notion that the tub looked like a vat of cosmopolitans. The notion passed quickly as I saw the trail of blood that was running down the meaty gash at the side of the head, along the neck and into the water. Without thinking—which is to say, my automatic reflex—I caught myself making a mental note: *closed casket*.

The water abruptly stopped churning. The suddenness surprised me. My heart did a little jump.

"Timer," Pete muttered. He had moved to the opposite side of the tub from where I had stopped. "There it is."

There it was indeed. The surface foam had sizzled away and we could see clearly into the tub. In the pink water's distortion it looked like any number of things. But credit the human brain for putting the old two and two together. It was a pistol resting on the bottom of the tub.

The crow cawed again. I finally spoke.

"What do you think, Doc?"

Pete stepped closer to the body; he leaned down and put his face almost as if he was trying to sight through the wound, as if looking for daylight out the other side. After a few seconds he straightened.

"It's going to take more than two aspirin."

We left Mike Gellman in the tub. We left the little piece of his skull on the deck where it had skittered. We moved in reverse, closing the sliding door behind us, Pete again using his shirttail.

"Don't touch anything," Pete said. He headed for the front door.

I said, "I want to look around."

"You don't want to do that. You want to leave."

"I'm going to look."

I moved quickly, heeding Pete's warning not to touch anything. His warning was probably unnecessary on several counts. For one thing, I had been in the house before; I could easily explain the presence of my fingerprints if it were ever to come to that. But more to the point, what difference would it make that it could be proved that I had been inside the house. Was anyone going to forward the argument that Mike Gellman had been carried or cajoled fully dressed into his hot tub and then made to remain still while someone put a pistol to his head and pulled the trigger? Aunt Billie has a saying: It doesn't take a nuclear physicist to recognize a mushroom cloud. This was no murder scene. The man had stepped fully clothed into his hot tub and blown away his command central. Period. This was not a what question. It was a why question.

Period.

I moved swiftly through the house. I wasn't really expecting to find anything . . . or more to the point, anyone. But I needed to be sure. Mike's car was gone. In all likelihood, Libby was in it.

Pete was standing outside when I came out of the house.

"Let's get out of here," I said.

Pete tuned the radio to a classical station as I pulled out onto the main road. He kept his head inclined toward the radio and stared right through my dashboard for about ten seconds, listening.

"Bach," he said, straightening. He pulled out a cigarette, lit it and tossed the match out the window. "Susan says Bach is the perfect music for a Sunday."

"I want to find Libby," I said.

Pete nodded. "Sounds fair. What are you thinking?"

"I'm thinking a million things at once." The delayed reaction from having come across a dead man in a hot tub was beginning to kick in. My skin felt clammy; my palms were wet on the steering wheel. Even with the passenger-side window open, Pete's smoke was making me a little queasy.

"Do you suppose Libby found him like that when I dropped her off?" I asked. "Or do you figure he did that after she left?"

"That's a good question."

"I guess we should have called the police?"

Pete shrugged. "Do we really want to be hanging around talking to the police?"

"Technically, I mean. We should."

"If Libby did stumble onto the same scene then it's obvious she didn't call them."

"So maybe he did it after she left."

"Or maybe she just didn't call."

"We're sounding pretty ignorant, Pete. We don't know a damn thing."

"Not completely. I know that the guy was ripped."

"How do you know that?" I had pulled onto 50/301. Pete had to fiddle with my radio to keep his station in tune.

"Along with a few other unpleasant smells, it was all over him like a distillery."

"You smelled booze?"

"There was also a bottle of Johnnie Walker on the kitchen counter. Cap was off. Looked like there was about an inch left."

"I didn't see that."

"You're young and excitable and you don't know what the hell you're doing half the time." Pete grinned. "I'm old and seasoned."

"Well, I'm glad to hear that you're feeling better about yourself."

Pete flicked his cigarette out the window.

"Yeah, I'm still all fucked up though."

"Sounds fair."

We continued on into D.C. I hoped we would find Libby at Owen Cutler's.

We didn't.

A pleasant-faced, somewhat doughy woman of around sixty answered our knock.

"Mrs. Cutler?"

The woman looked back and forth between Pete and me as if we were here to snatch her up by the elbows and whisk her off to the grave.

"Mrs. Cutler?" I repeated. She nodded. "Is your husband in, Mrs. Cutler? We need to speak with him."

"I would like to know what is going on," the woman said. She looked nervously at Pete. "What is this all about?"

"We need to see your husband, Mrs. Cutler."

"Owen is in the den. He's watching the Redskins game."

"Then he won't mind if we pull him away," Pete said.

Mrs. Cutler gave us a dubious look then asked us to wait at the door while she went to fetch her husband. A minute later Owen Cutler appeared. He was wearing a green cardigan, a simple white shirt and a pair of khakis.

"What can I do for you?" Cutler said. His wife was lingering behind him, standing near the stairs.

"We're looking for Libby Gellman," I said. "We were wondering if you'd seen her."

Cutler's wife let out a small gasp. "Owen?"

Cutler turned his head. "Ronnie. Please."

"We were just at the Gellmans' house, Mr. Cutler," Pete said. "I don't know if you're aware of what's happened over there."

Cutler opened the door wider. "Come in."

We came through the door and followed him down the hallway and into the den, a small cozy room that looked out onto a fenced-in backyard. Cutler's wife trailed after us. On the television, one of the Redskins was being chewed out by a coach.

Cutler turned to me. "We've met."

"Yes, we have." I gave him my name. For good measure I tossed in Pete's name as well. "We met in Annapolis," I reminded him. "Last week. The Naval Academy Bridge, to be precise."

"Libby," he said.

Ronnie Cutler reacted. "Owen, I demand to know what is going on with Libby. I wish you'd just tell me why she—"

"Ronnie." This time the man put a little heft into his voice. "I need to speak with these men, Ronnie." He stepped over to the door and shooed his wife out of the room, then gently closed the door.

"Drinks?" We refused. "Then you won't mind if I refresh mine." Cutler picked up a drink glass from a table in front of the television and took it over to the stationary butler. He tossed a couple cubes of ice into the glass and poured himself an inch and a half of Maker's. He gestured us to have a seat on the couch and he returned to his armchair. He picked up the remote and killed the picture.

"How are they doing?" Pete asked.

Cutler answered, "The game? I haven't the foggiest. I'm not watching it."

"You're just sitting in your den with a glass of whiskey and the game on but you're not watching it."

He ignored the question. "So what's this about?"

"We told you. We're looking for Libby."

Cutler looked at me a few seconds before he responded. He was definitely a handsome man. Robust. The platinum hair looked like it had been customized expressly for him.

"She was just here. I suspect you've already guessed that."

Pete gestured toward the glass. "Did she stop and have a drink with you or did you pour that after she left?"

"What's this all about?"

"Did Libby say anything about her husband while she was here?" I asked.

"About Mike? In fact she did. She said quite a lot. And not too much of it was kind."

"He's dead," Pete said. "Did she happen to mention that?"

Cutler showed no reaction for several seconds. He could have been a man of wax. I realized that the color had gone out of his face. Wax was exactly what he looked like.

"My God." Cutler lowered his head. A minor tremble set up in his hand. The ice chattered in his glass. "My God," he said again.

"We know all about Sugar Larue," Pete said. "We know that you arranged for the Gellmans to adopt her child. We know who the father is and how all that came about. That's what Libby came over to talk about, isn't it?"

Cutler was still staring at the floor. I couldn't be sure he was even listening.

Pete went on. "You knew what was going on over there between Jack Barton and Sugar Larue. Hell, it sounds like *everyone* knew what was going on. You've got the look of a gentleman, Mr. Cutler. Aren't gentlemen supposed to intervene when a young girl is getting mistreated like that?"

Cutler looked up. "I didn't—"

"Don't lie to me!" Pete snapped. "I really don't want to hear any crap from you. You passed that baby along to the Gellmans four years ago and now you're at it again. You arranged for the Gellmans' nanny to meet with Larue. You're an awfully goddamn helpful man, Mr. Cutler."

Cutler sat up straight in his chair. He allowed himself a long look at the both of us, slowly twirling his drink glass. Some of the color had returned to his face. "Crawford enlisted my assistance," Cutler said.

"And something went wrong," I said. "What was it? Why did you kill Sophie Potts?"

Cutler's glass froze halfway to his lips. Slowly he set the glass down on the table next to him.

"I didn't kill Miss Potts."

"I think you did," Pete said.

"So do I." I leaned forward in the couch. "Maybe you hired someone to actually get their hands dirty, I don't know. But it keeps coming back to you. Somewhere along the line here something broke and you came in to fix it. That's what you do, isn't it? But it really hasn't worked. You can't just sweep what Jack Barton did to that girl under the carpet. Or what Crawford Larue did, for that matter. Looking the other way. I can't even imagine how Mike Gellman has been able to live with himself all these years. Every time he looked at his daughter . . . It's vile."

"I didn't kill that young woman," Cutler said again.

"Then who did?" I asked. "There's no way in hell you can convince me that you don't know."

"You're wasting your time, Hitch," Pete said. "It's this guy."

Cutler rose abruptly and stepped over to the sliding glass door that looked out onto the backyard. There was a pole planted in the ground with a metal bird feeder affixed to the top. Several small birds were flittering around the feeder. As Cutler watched, a blue jay that had been on the grass flew to the feeder and scattered the other birds. Cutler laced his fingers behind his back and looked out beyond the glass. Pete caught my attention and gave me a knowing wink. When Cutler turned back to us, his face was again set with a morose gravity.

"Mike," he said softly.

I echoed. "Mike?"

"It was Mike." Cutler looked down at tasseled Weejuns.

"Mike Gellman killed Sophie Potts?"

"Yes."

Pete let out a harsh laugh. "Nice try."

Cutler looked up sharply. "What's that supposed to mean?"

"It means nice try. It means how convenient to lay it on the guy who can't defend himself." Pete reached into his pocket and pulled out a pack of cigarettes.

"I'd prefer if you didn't smoke in here," Cutler said.

Pete produced a pack of matches and he lit up a cigarette. "I'd prefer you stop feeding us a load of crap." He put the spent match into the cigarette pack and put the pack back into his pocket.

"Mike had an alibi," I said to Cutler. "It's not one he would have been happy trotting out for all to see, but it's one he has already given the Annapolis police."

Pete got slowly to his feet. "Why would Mike Gellman kill his nanny, Mr. Cutler? Could you explain that to me?"

Cutler stammered, "I-I don't know."

Pete stepped toward him. "You don't know? But suddenly you're very willing to tell us that he's the one who killed her? No good. You want my opinion? I still like you for it. You're the man in the middle."

"I'm telling you, it wasn't me."

"What did Libby have to say when she came over here?" I asked.

"She didn't stay long."

"What did she say?"

"Pretty much what you just did. About Lily. About Sugar. She came in here and she shrieked at me like I've never heard before. And then she slapped me."

I got off the couch and stepped over to him. "I'm going to ask you one more time, Mr. Cutler. Did you kill Sophie Potts?"

He shook his head. "I didn't. I swear to you."

"Where's Libby? Did she say where she was going?"

"No. She was furious. And she was crying. She slapped me and then she screamed, 'I hate you. I hate you all.' Then she took off."

So did we.

Ten minutes later I skidded to a stop behind Mike Gellman's car. Pete and I bounded up to the front door and pounded on it. We heard a noise from inside the house that sounded too damned much like a scream. Pete shoved the door open and we rushed into the house. We raced into the living room. It was the wrong thing to have done. We practically skidded to a stop. My heart came flying up into my throat.

"Oh shit."

Crawford Larue was seated in a wooden rocking chair in slacks and an open-neck shirt, his chubby fingers laced across his belly. Libby was on the white couch to his right. A small scab of dried blood was on her face, beneath her nose. Some of the blood had gotten onto the couch. Her eyes were the size of half-dollars.

Standing behind the couch was Russell Jenks. Jenks had a handful of Libby's hair in one hand and a small black thing in the other. It was a pistol. When Pete and I first burst into the room the barrel of the gun had been resting lightly against Libby's crown. Now it was aiming at us.

"Stop right there," Jenks said coolly.

It should be noted, I am in the death business. I have the greatest respect for things that have the potential to put me on the wrong side of the embalming table. Apparently Pete didn't.

"Forget it, Jenks," Pete said. "It's over."

I looked at him like he was crazy. Where in the world did he get off with a stock line like *that* when we had this guy waving a pistol at us? Jenks didn't seem too impressed with Pete's bluster. He jerked harder on Libby's hair, forcing her head back. She let out a small cry and I started forward. Jenks took dead aim on me. His eyes behind his Buddy Holly glasses appeared almost lifeless.

"I wouldn't."

I didn't. Libby's hands were out to her sides, her fingers splayed against the cushions, gripping like a cat against a wall. She was bone white. She squeaked out a single syllable.

"Hitch."

"Let her go, Jenks," Pete said. His voice was steady, with the faint hint of a growl just below the surface.

Jenks didn't seem inclined to obey. He waved the gun. "Keep your hands where I can see them."

For his part, Crawford Larue seemed oddly detached from the scene. He was pitched forward in his rocking chair as if he were watching something unfolding on television. Without his dapper cream suit he looked much more like what he really was . . . a dumpy little man who needed to lay off the fats and sugars.

My heart was slamming against my rib cage like a prisoner demanding to see the warden. Forcing a note of calm into my voice that had no right to be there, I said, "Look, Jenks, be reasonable. Just put the gun down. This can only make things worse. We know what happened."

"What the hell do you know?" Jenks snapped.

"We know what she knows." I indicated Libby. I threw her what I could in the way of a reassuring smile.

Jenks ran his tongue over his lips. Reptilian. With his gun hand he knocked his glasses back up on his nose. He waved the pistol again at Pete and me.

"Then maybe it's going to be a real mess here, huh?"

"Be reasonable," I said. "All you can do now is make things worse. Just put the gun down. Let her go."

"Fuck you."

I turned to Larue. As I did I spotted something outside the window just slightly behind and to the left of where Jenks was standing. It was in Jenks's blind spot. If Larue had not that instant turned his head in my direction, he might have seen it also. But he didn't. It was a face. It popped up into the window for just a fraction of a second and then was gone. With the glare on the glass I couldn't be certain, but I was pretty sure I recognized it. I put my telepathy to work. *The police . . . Call the police. Quick. Pronto. 911. Chop chop. Any second now we could be dying in here.*

Pete gave me a very restrained look. A glance, really. Nearly imperceptible. But I knew what he was saying. Pete had seen it, too. *Stall. Keep him talking.*

"Tell him to let her go, Mr. Larue," I said. "Come on. This is ridiculous."

Larue's chin was dipped down toward his chest. He cocked an eyebrow at me. "I am not convinced that that would necessarily be efficacious."

Pete snapped, "Screw that!"

Libby pleaded again, "Hitch." Tears had started running down her cheeks. Jenks tightened his grip on her hair. I implored Larue again.

"Tell him, damn it. Don't be an idiot. The ARK is finished no matter what. You know that. You can't keep a lid on this thing any longer. Cindy Lehigh is sitting safe and pretty with the police right now." This was a bald-faced lie, of course, but it seemed like a particularly good time to toss in one of those.

"Or maybe you don't even know who Cindy Lehigh is," I went on. "Cindy is the person who was threatening to air your dirty laundry to the newspapers. It wasn't Sophie."

Jenks blurted, "You're bluffing."

"I'm not," I said. "Cindy knows everything. She overheard Cutler and Mike Gellman talking the whole thing out this summer. It's what she tried to sell to the papers after she quit working for Gellman. It's what got Sophie killed."

"Is that so?" Larue said calmly.

The man seemed outrageously bemused. It was no challenge to my imagination to imagine my shoe pressing ever so firmly against his face.

"It is. Cindy's a little hustler. I have no doubt she'd have come to you directly and tried for a shakedown after *The Cannon* didn't take her bait. Except before she could she heard about Sophie Potts being found dead in the water. She knew damn well what had happened. She knew it was the wrong nanny who had been killed."

I turned back to Jenks. My ears were buzzing. No sirens. Not yet, anyway. I was sending out telepathic 911s to the face in the window.

"You killed the wrong nanny, Jenks. That's what happened. Fallon told me it was you who he took his story to after he received his anonymous call. He told you he'd gotten a call from a woman who was going on about some sort of scandal involving the ARK and sex with minors and all the rest of it. You knew exactly what he was talking about. It was about Sugar Larue being pimped to Jack Barton when she was all of fifteen. The ARK would go down fast with a story like that coming out. If not the entire organization, sure as hell the both of you."

"There is no ARK without me," Larue declared coolly.

I ignored him. I was still locked on to Russell Jenks.

"When Fallon told you that he'd gotten an anonymous call from a woman claiming to have the goods on the ARK I'm sure you wondered just who the hell could know about all that. That must have driven you crazy. That is, until Mike Gellman's nanny came walking in here not a week later and sat down for a little chat with Crawford. Crawford didn't know at the time who she was. But Cutler did. He told you, didn't he? He told you she was Mike Gellman's nanny. That was a huge mistake on his part. It cost Sophie her life."

Jenks was sweating profusely. His eyeglasses were sliding down on his moist nose and again he slammed them back into place. He was scared. But he had the gun. Libby was sobbing, but trying to choke back her tears. I took a step forward. Jenks jerked back again on Libby's hair.

"Don't move!"

I stopped. Damn it. Where were the police? I raised my hands out in front of me as if I were popping my sleeves in slow motion. I attempted to find the most velvety tone possible, under the circumstances.

"I can see how you did it, how you made the mistake. Sugar's baby is being raised by the Gellmans, and not a week after this anonymous threat, who comes in? None other than the Gellman nanny herself. You never even consulted with Larue on this, did you? Or if you did, he told you there was something fishy about the woman and the fellow she was with. Right? Crawford here wasn't completely buying their story. He told me that himself. That's why he wanted to meet with me. He thought I was Tom Cushman. In cahoots with Sophie. He thought Cushman might know what Sophie allegedly knew.

"So then you were the good soldier, weren't you? You thought the Gellmans' nanny was poised to bring everything down around your ears. If the word got out about what Crawford allowed to happen to his daughter, and that he put her through several abortions on top of it all, that would be it for the ARK. So you marched off, didn't you, and saw to it that Sophie would never breathe a word."

Jenks slapped his glasses again. Next to me, I sensed Pete loosening his shoulders. I remembered. Pete carried a pistol. He even carried a license to shoot the thing. I couldn't imagine his being able to get to it without Jenks doing something terribly rash and terribly stupid and terribly fatal. It occurred to me that if I could get myself between Jenks and Pete . . . if I could block Jenks's view of Munger for just a few seconds . . . My heart issued a swift *no thanks* as it also occurred to me just who would then be in the middle of two guys with guns.

Sweat had broken out on me as well. I could feel it traveling south along my spine like I was being washed down with a sponge.

"I handed Tom Cushman over to the two of you without even knowing it," I continued. "I told Crawford and Crawford told you. You knew where to find him. You stole those plates, didn't you? You stole those plates and ran him down, you son of a bitch. Then you—"

"Shut up!"

"You're a coward, Jenks."

"Shut up!" Jenks raised his arm and pointed the pistol directly at my head. "Just shut the hell up."

I did. Locked my lips and threw away the key. There was something well worth hearing besides my own damn voice anyway. Even through the buzzing in my ears, I think I heard them first, before the others. Of course I had been straining the whole time to hear them. Sirens. The cavalry was on the way. An instant later it appeared that Russell Jenks heard them. Libby as well. At least that's what I thought initially. Except that the look on Libby's face was anything but relieved. Just the opposite, in fact. Her eyes opened wide with terror.

A split second later I heard a sound behind me. Simultaneously, Libby jerked free of Jenks and lunged forward. She was screaming. So was Jenks. I only had time to half turn before a terrific explosion sounded in the room. It seemed to come from directly behind my left ear. Behind the couch, Jenks lifted completely off the ground. Remarkable. He looked like a marionette being jerked suddenly by its manipulator. A starburst of red exploded on his chest and he flew backward a good six or seven feet, where he slammed violently into the wall. If the wall had not been there he certainly would have continued on twice as far, maybe even more. His head hit against a framed painting of a windmill. Jenks and the painting fell to the floor. I was suddenly aware of something grabbing hold of my feet. It was Libby. She had pitched off the couch and continued entirely across the floor on her hands and knees. She was wrapping her arms around my ankles.

My ear was ringing. I wondered for a moment if I had maybe mistaken the ringing for the sirens. But then I remembered that I had heard the sirens before the explosion. Next to me, Pete Munger muttered, "Jesus Christ."

I turned around.

Standing several feet inside the living room entrance was Sugar Jenks. She was holding on to a shotgun that looked to be damn near as long as she was tall. She was expressionless, even though she had just blown her husband off his feet with a blast from the gun. I remembered the gun case in Crawford Larue's study. Sugar snapped a look at me.

"Move."

I obeyed. I jerked one foot free of Libby's grip and I dragged her with me as I took an Igor-like step sideways, bumping into Pete. Pete's pistol was out. Crawford Larue was now rising out of his rocking chair. My moving had given Sugar the shot she wanted. She said no more. Crawford did. He extended his hands, palms up, and with the most syrupy voice he could bring up, he said his daughter's name.

"Sugar."

His head was slightly cocked and he had a great big smile on his face when he said it. Sugar hefted the rifle up to her hip and fired. No hesitation. Another explosion. Crawford took a trip similar to his deputy's, only in his case he ended up sprawled half on and half off the couch. The smile was gone. Half the face was gone. I looked over at Sugar Jenks. Like a conjurer's trick, Crawford Larue's smile was now on his daughter's face. Not as seasoned. Not as large. Not as smarmy. But it was still the same smile. Her daddy's smile.

At my feet, Libby let out a huge sob.

The sirens grew louder.

CHAPTER

28

I had two long talks the day before we buried Mike Gellman. The first was with Eva Potts. She phoned me at home. She spent most of the conversation talking about her daughter, telling me random stories of Sophie's twenty-three years. I listened. The undertaker's ear is accustomed to this exercise; I've always considered it one of the more important parts of my job. Eva Potts thanked me for my part in helping flush out what had really happened to her daughter. It was painful to see Sophie's name in all of the newspaper articles, but she was gratified that the truth—ugly as it was—had been uncovered.

The other talk was with Lee Cromwell. Lee drove over to Fell's Point and I took her out for a snazzy breakfast at Jimmy's. Pete was going back to Susan. He had decided the night before; he was giving his marriage another shot. Pete was still in the shower when I popped out to meet with Lee. Lee wanted to talk with Pete, but she wanted to talk with me first. Her eyes were dark, with a mood to match. She looked tired. Lee had performed two shows at the Wine Cellar the night before. By my calculations she was working on five hours' sleep at best. Probably less. I had to be at the funeral home soon to get things rolling for Mike's service. Lee was in jeans, cowboy boots and a loose-fitting pale green sweater. She took exactly two bites of her scrambled eggs and left the rest, pushing the plate to the side.

"Will they let me smoke in this damn place?" she asked me, her eyes casting about for an ashtray. The cigarette was already in her mouth. She sounded so much like Pete just then it broke my heart.

Our talk ended out on the pier, across the harbor from the ubiquitous Domino Sugar sign. Lee had her fingers jammed into her rear pockets and was gazing across the water.

"I was so miserable when I left Ben. I was drinking too much. Ben was two-timing me with a younger woman. I hated the corner I had gotten myself into. I hated Ben, too. Our love was gone. It was an autopilot marriage and even the autopilot was breaking down."

She looked out over the water. "Peter doesn't hate his wife," she went on. "He's very angry and a lot of it is aimed at her. Susan has been a convenient place for him to dump all the blame for his unhappiness. And he knows it. And he doesn't like himself for it."

"He's not happy with Susan," I said. "You make him happy."

"I'm easy, Hitch. I'm a girl singing in a nightclub. I love my independence. I don't make demands on Peter. He's not responsible for me. A marriage is a lot harder."

"I think he's making a mistake. He adores you."

"He told me that he loves me," Lee said.

"He loves you but he is going back to his wife. That is so Munger. He just wants to make *everyone* miserable."

Lee tilted her chin as if she were sniffing a new scent in the air. An inquisitive look came onto her face.

"No. I think Peter wants to make everyone happy but he can't do it. I think he's overlooking the fact that unless *he* is happy it's not going to work at all."

"I guess," I said. "And you make him happy."

"So does being loyal to his marriage."

"You don't believe that," I said.

The toe of one of Lee's boots had found a large splinter chip on the pier and she looked down at it as she worked it loose. She kicked it into the water.

"I guess I don't." She looked over at me and gave a thin smile. "It's all your fault, Hitch. You introduced us."

"Pete said the same thing."

She looked past me. I turned. Munger was standing at the bottom of the pier, next to the Oyster. He seemed uncommonly interested in his shoes. I looked back at Lee. I was struck with the urge to tell her what Pete had done the day before at Crawford Larue's house. But I didn't. Pete had sworn me to secrecy. He had acted incredibly swiftly. It couldn't have been less than ten seconds before the police came bursting into the house and Pete had stepped over to where Crawford Larue lay sprawled half on and half off the couch. Pete was still holding his own pistol, and taking hold of Larue's right hand he pressed the dead man's hand around the grip. Then he let the pistol drop to the floor. He stepped back over to where he had been standing and addressed Sugar Jenks. "Your father relieved me of my gun. When you burst in here just now, he was holding my gun on Hitchcock and me. That's why you shot him. That is the only story you know. That is what happened." Sugar had looked perplexed and then Munger had given her one of his great big crooked smiles. "Thank you for saving our lives, ma'am. Hitchcock and I appreciate it."

Lee pulled her hands from her pockets and crossed her arms. She was still looking past me at Pete.

"I've got to go bury someone," I said to her.

Lee took a beat. Then she smiled. "Oh, right. *That* old excuse."

The media was having a veritable field day. Kids in the candy shop. *The Daily Cannon* in particular was so rife with purple prose that its readers practically had to wear gloves in order to keep their fingers from getting stained. Fallon swore to me that even he had protested—to no avail—over *The Cannon*'s banner headline that ran the day after the shootings.

SUGAR POPS POP

"We have to sell papers, Hitch," he said to me over the phone. "It's a screaming match out there."

Most of the news accounts had little to go on beyond the bare-bones facts of Sugar Larue Jenks having gunned down the executive director and the CEO of the ARK, one of whom happened to have been her father, the other her husband. Speculative pistols were being shot off in all directions. It wasn't until two days after the killings that Nick Fallon bylined *The Daily Cannon*'s scoop, setting out the reasons and rhymes for Sugar Jenks's bloody actions. Nick was greatly assisted in his efforts by a detailing from none other than Sugar herself. Owen Cutler had moved swiftly to secure Sugar's release on bail, exerting his considerable influence as well as digging deep into his own pockets to come up with the sum set by the judge. The prosecutor protested, but Owen Cutler's personal promise that he would keep a short leash on Sugar had carried the day. Nick Fallon had been tipped off that Cutler was planning to intervene on Sugar's behalf, and when Cutler and Sugar arrived back at Cutler's house after the hearing, Nick was camped out on the doorstep. So was I. Nick had urged me to be on hand. He wanted someone there who Sugar Jenks would recognize—and possibly trust—as he made his pitch for an exclusive interview. Cutler balked of course and attempted to get Sugar swiftly into the house, but with a tall undertaker blocking the door he failed.

It was something of a long shot on Fallon's part, though in truth he had little to lose. It paid off. I put the matter to Sugar, who took no time shaking free of Cutler's grip and inviting us inside.

"I do not agree to this," Cutler protested.

Sugar told him that was fine. We could go off to a coffee shop and talk.

"You can't keep me from talking," she said. "Maybe you think you can, but not anymore you can't."

"It's the devil you know," Fallon said to Cutler. "You might as well listen in. It's tomorrow's news."

Cutler conceded. He held open the door and we filed in.

It was not a happy chronicle.

Sugar Larue Jenks sat at the Cutlers' kitchen table and in her soft, nearly whispering voice detailed a lonely childhood in Kentucky. Her father, she said, had little time for her, consumed as he was with raising and training his champion racehorses. He was cold to her, she said, and he also had little time for his wife, who shared none of her husband's passion for the caballos. Honey Larue—that's right, you can't make this stuff up—Honey Larue had a pair of outlets for her own loneliness. One of them was Kentucky mash. The other was her daughter. Sugar Larue grew up on a steady diet of bitter invective directed against her father.

"I never knew someone could hate another person so much," Sugar whispered into Fallon's tape recorder. "I felt sorry for Daddy."

When she was thirteen, Sugar got involved with one of the horse trainers under her father's employment. Ten years her senior, the trainer seduced the boss's daughter in a horse trailer next to one of the ranch's several riding rings. The affair was brief, ending the day Sugar Larue looked beyond the jolting shoulders of the trainer to see her father standing at the door of the trailer, arms crossed on his oval chest, a look of casual disdain on his elfin face. Crawford Larue never mentioned the incident, either to Sugar or to his wife. Nor did he fire the trainer. On the contrary, he promoted him, putting him in charge of one of Larue's personal favorites of the stable. Larue had recently made his decision to run for the statehouse. Sugar fell into a heavy depression and remained in it throughout the campaign and after she and her parents had moved into the governor's mansion. A year later, Crawford Larue was in federal prison and—the ranch sold—Sugar and her mother were living in a modest house in a Louisville suburb. The day that her husband was released from prison, Honey Larue drove her car into a lake. When divers reached it there was no indication that Honey had made any attempts to escape. Her seat and shoulder belts were still affixed and her hands were gripped tightly on the steering wheel.

Sugar had paused at this point in her story to get herself a glass of water. Cutler, who was standing off by the refrigerator the entire time, had not budged. When Sugar sat back down, she had again whispered, "I felt so sorry for Daddy."

Crawford and Sugar moved to Washington, where Jack Barton had arranged for his old friend to take the reins of the Alliance for Reason and Kindness. By that point Sugar's depression was chronic and she sought refuge in a variety of medications, few of which did little else but dull her already insensate senses. It was in such a state that she let out her very small whimper of protest the first evening that Jack Barton excused himself from cordials in Crawford's den and made his way upstairs to Sugar's bedroom.

Sugar would not—or could not—detail the number of encounters she had with Jack Barton over the next several years. Fallon had pressed gently, but Sugar frowned him off. "A lot," she whispered. That her father was fully aware of what was going on was evident not only in Barton's boldness, but in the abortions—three in all, she said—that Crawford Larue quietly arranged for his daughter.

Here, Sugar corrected herself. She had told most of her story to the kitchen table, her eyes fixed on Nick Fallon's tape recorder. But now she looked up. She looked across the room at Owen Cutler. The poor girl was incapable of getting off a withering stare. There was too much pain in her eyes to pull it off. But she tried.

"They tried one more time," she said hoarsely. "I ran away. I . . . I couldn't do it again. I was killing too many babies. I couldn't do it anymore."

Sugar had been scheduled for another appointment with her doctor. Instead she went to the bus station and took the first bus out. The bus took her to Florida, where she stayed a while before moving on to California. She had withdrawn some money from her savings account and as that ran out she took a series of jobs waiting tables.

Tears appeared in Sugar's large black eyes and they flowed unimpeded down her cheeks.

"But I . . . I was no good. I was scared. And I was sick all the time. I've never taken care of myself before. I didn't have anyone to protect me. It was . . . I was lonely." Her voice dropped to a whisper and she closed her eyes.

"I couldn't live out there."

Crawford Larue had the resources—and he used them—to locate his daughter and to bring her back home. Sugar was too far along at that point to safely abort the child, so she carried the baby to term, never once leaving the house until it was time for the baby to be born. Sugar told us that she has almost no memory of that stretch of time. The child was delivered by cesarean. A baby girl. Sugar never saw her.

"You stole my baby," Sugar said, pointing a trembling finger at Owen Cutler. "You told me she was dead." She turned to Fallon and sniffed back her tears.

"They made it so I would never have a baby again. They never asked me, they just did it." She took a deep breath and held it. The tears welled up again in her eyes.

"And that's when I died."

———

Crawford and Virginia Larue had never intended to adopt a baby. Leastwise, not for themselves. Fallon had been right about that. Neither of them was interested in raising a child. The baby was intended for Sugar. For Mr. and Mrs. Jenks. A little bambino all their own. Ginny Larue swore she knew nothing of her stepdaughter's wretched past. I was inclined to believe her. She told the authorities that she was in fact aware that Crawford was on the lookout for a child to "present" to his daughter and her husband. Ginny knew that Sugar was unable to conceive a child on her own, although she insisted she was in the dark as to the reasons. Owen Cutler admitted that Larue had initially told him that he wanted the lawyer to "fetch Sugar's baby back." This was what Cutler had told Mike during their conversation on Gellman's deck. Cindy Lehigh had not heard this part, or if she had, had not understood what Cutler was saying. Of course Cutler steered Larue away from such a ludicrous notion. There were, he assured him, plenty of babies out there.

And, of course, he was right.

The day of Mike Gellman's wake, state senator Mickey Talbot was indicted for influence peddling in the matter of the half-finished sports arena on Route 50. Senator Talbot pleaded not guilty, even though the evidence against him—as spelled out in the indictment—looked pretty damning. Another indictment in the case—that of Michael P. Gellman—never saw the light of day.

Pete got me on the phone.

"Mickey Talbot," he said.

"Yes."

"Talbot. Ring any bells?"

It did. A large gong. "Bud Talbot. Annapolis police."

"First cousins."

"Acting police chief Talbot," I said. "This is the fellow not too terribly interested in making waves for Mike Gellman?"

"It's called vested interest."

"I'm not the lawyer here, Pete. But isn't that also called obstruction of justice?"

"Hey, you know what? I think you're right, Hitch."

"We don't want him getting away with that, do we?" I asked.

There was a pause on the other end of the line. "Hey, you know what? I think you're right, Hitch."

Pete said he had to go. He said he had a call to make.

At Mike's wake that night, Libby told me that she was trying very hard not to blame herself for her husband's suicide. Mike had been well into his bottle of Johnnie Walker by the time I had dropped Libby off at the house and was already in a deep misery when she came through the front door. He knew his arrest was coming. And he knew what that meant to his career.

"But I made it deeper," Libby acknowledged to me at the wake. "I know it. I hammered away at him. As far as I was concerned Mike was as responsible as anyone else for Sophie's death. Not that he wasn't already feeling that himself. He definitely was."

We were standing in front of Mike's casket. A framed photograph of Mike sat atop it. Libby picked up the photo and looked at it.

"I didn't do it, Hitch," she said to me. "I didn't forgive him. I know it's what you're supposed to do, but I just couldn't do it." She set the photo back down. She placed a hand on the casket. Tears were forming in her eyes. "I still can't."

The service for Mike Gellman was held the next day at St. Luke's Church on Charles Street. Sam and I got the casket to the church before anyone had shown up. We set it in place and distributed the flower arrangements. Sam was trying to sort out where to put one of the larger ones when the first guest arrived. He came slowly down the aisle and went directly up to the casket and placed his hand on it. He stood a long moment, his head bowed, his shoulders shaking nearly imperceptibly as he quietly wept. Our eyes met when he finally turned away. Owen Cutler began to say something, then apparently changed his mind. He stepped over to the front pew and parked himself all the way down at the end. He dropped his hands into his lap, his chin to his chest. He did not look up as the others began to arrive.

I was standing off near a side exit in the front of the church when Mike's parents and Libby entered the church and made their way down the aisle. The parents both looked as if their entire understanding of how our lovely world ticks had been completely obliterated. Their son had been destined for big things. Coming to grips with the squalid facts surrounding his taking of his own life . . . that adjustment would take a while. The three went up to the casket and stood staring at it. I could tell them from years of experience . . . caskets give off no answers. They are smooth and blunt and silent. Stare a hundred holes through them if you like; they give back nothing.

As they turned from the casket to take their seats, Libby saw me standing off to the side. She said something to her in-laws, then crossed over to me. Instinctively I held both of her hands within mine. It always surprises me when I do this. I hate appearing unctuous, but unless you're on guard for it it's one of those automatic things that you do as an undertaker. Libby's eyes were free of tears. Her skin was pink. She seemed the picture of health.

"We're leaving this evening," she said. "As soon as I can get away from all of this I'm picking up the kids and we're getting out of here."

"Where are you going?"

"Back to California. It's as far away as I can get. I know I can't escape all this, but it'll at least give us a little space. I'm going back to my maiden name. The children will take it, too. If we stay here we're just a freak show. Especially Lily. I couldn't bear that."

"I understand," I said. "I think it makes sense."

Libby looked up at me. "So do I say good-bye to you here or at the cemetery? It seems kind of gruesome either way."

"Say it now."

She did. She squeezed my hands and then released them. She held my gaze for just a fraction, then she turned without another word and walked past the casket and into the pew where Mike's parents were sitting. Mike's father had slid partway down the pew and was talking quietly with Owen Cutler. Libby sat a moment with her eyes closed, her head bowed in prayer, then she straightened and leaned over slowly, resting her head against her mother-in-law's shoulder.

Several minutes later the priest stood up and began the show. I know it by heart. I stepped outside into the sun.

The stoop outside the funeral home was getting crowded. Along with Aunt Billie and Darryl Sandusky there was a newcomer. As I approached, the newcomer chased some wispy blonde hair from her face.

"Hey, stranger."

"Praise be," I said. "I could sure use a little faith right about now."

"Hey, man," Darryl said. "You think that's funny or something?"

"What's in that mug?" I asked the kid.

Darryl poked his nose into the mug he was holding. He sneered up at me.

"Coffee."

I turned to my aunt. "Billie? You're caffeinating this monster? If you don't stop soon someone is going to bring you up on charges."

You pretty much expect a kid like Darryl Sandusky to stick his tongue out at you. It's slightly disconcerting when he is joined by your dear old auntie.

"Let's get out of here," I said to Faith. "This is bad company you're keeping."

Faith accompanied me back to my place, where I changed out of my funeral duds and into something a little more comfortable. My timing was off, for no sooner had I changed into something more comfortable than I stepped into the front room to see that Faith had changed as well . . . only she had nothing comfortable to change into so she had changed into nothing at all. It's all very complicated. *I* then swiftly changed *out* of something more comfortable and into the same nothing that my guest had achieved, all of which paved the way for making the next hour and ten minutes extraordinarily *more* comfortable than . . . well, it was a nice way to shake off the gloom of the day, let's just leave it at that. Faith was a wonderful panacea. A restorative. A credit to her name.

Alcatraz was bundling his belongings into a bandanna, which he was ready to attach to a bamboo pole, so Faith and I returned ourselves to the "something comfortable" state and took the neglected canus out for his stroll. The first crisp taste of autumn was in the air. In another few weeks we'd be getting whatever version of leaf changing this year was going to bring. Faith and I walked on air down to the harbor. The cat that Alcatraz never catches came flying out from behind the Oyster and took off down the street. Alcatraz bounded hopelessly after it, woofing outrageously. I explained to Faith that the dog never catches the cat.

"He seems to enjoy the chase," Faith remarked.

I agreed. "Yes. He seems to."

We could still hear Alcatraz's baying off in the distance. Out in the harbor a tug sounded. It was difficult making out where the dog faded out and the tug took over. In a few seconds, both had stopped. Faith looped her arm around my elbow.

"It's a beautiful day," she said.

It was. No question. Diamonds were dancing all along the water. The sky was a rich blue. The air was clear.

Faith abruptly withdrew her arm. "Race you to the end of the pier!" And she took off. I hesitated, watching her run. She was all loose limbs, her hair kicking left and right. Very pretty girl, I thought. Which of course I already knew. With no warning, my chest contracted—it was almost painful—and a deep sigh, nearly audible, ran through me. A seagull off to my left let out a pair of cries, swooping into the wake of Faith's laughter. I sent the signals down to my legs and I took off running.